Return to Barcelona Harbor

A Mac Morrison Murder Mystery, with Buddy-dog

"Where Mac goes, Mayhem follows"

A Novel by Philip Laurien

Copyright December 14, 2023

ISBN: 979-8-89324-362-8

This book is a work of fiction. Any names of characters in the book bear no relationship to anyone real, living or dead. Geographical location names are used for the purpose of scene setting and depicting a realistic tone and readability. None of the geographical locations or individual names mentioned in any part of this book are based on actual occurrences. The story line developed in this book is a work of fiction and should not be taken literally.

Acknowledgements

It takes a good team to produce a novel. I'd like to thank my Amazon Project Managers Hasan Azizi, Erik Peterson, and David Selcer for their help on Return to Barcelona Harbor, the second in the Mac Morrison mystery series.

Thanks to Karen Ackerman, for advice and encouragement on elements of style and punctuation.

To Becky Hernandez Michaels, thank you so much for editing the Spanish dialogue.

Thank you to Melissa Bartok, Chautauqua County's Mayville Librarian. She quickly realized that the Mac Morrison series describes familiar places that local residents could identify and enjoy. Readers can follow the action with the familiar backdrop of scenic Chautauqua County.

Special thanks to Nancy Nixon Ensign, Librarian at the gorgeous and historic Patterson Library in Westfield, New York. She also took an early interest in these novels, perhaps because I was an unknown first-time author who was writing about her home community. She organized a delightful author's night with her local mystery readers, which was fun for all.

Phil Laurien
July, 2024

Table of Contents

Part One
Sunapee Bloody Beginnings

Chapter One	1
Chapter Two	5
Chapter Three	8
Chapter Four	10
Chapter Five	23
Chapter Six	33
Chapter Seven	44
Chapter Eight	52
Chapter Nine	64
Chapter Ten	81
Chapter Eleven	105
Chapter Twelve	149
Chapter Thirteen	153
Chapter Fourteen	168

Part Two:
Return to Barcelona Harbor

Chapter Fifteen	179
Chapter Sixteen	182
Chapter Seventeen	202
Chapter Eighteen	212

Chapter Nineteen	225
Chapter Twenty	237
Chapter Twenty One	257
Chapter Twenty Two	279
Chapter Twenty Three	291
Chapter Twenty Four	304
Chapter Twenty Five	319
Appendix	330
Author Profile	334

Part One
Sunapee Bloody Beginnings

Chapter One

Sunday, October 1, 2023
Newbury NH, south shore of Lake Sunapee
6:00 p.m.

All eyes were on the big excavator and the birthday cake. No one was watching the black Suburban as it slowed, paused, and passed the construction site.

Mac Morrison should have noticed. But he missed it because a huge excavator snuffing the candles on a birthday cake was more interesting than the strange vehicle cruising his rural country road. Besides, this was tourist season for leaf peepers in Northern New Hampshire. Strange vehicles were expected.

So, the black SUV registered no threat to the hunter-gatherer portion of his brain. It took a picture but did not notify his frontal lobe, which was watching the cake like everyone else.

The cake was one foot in diameter and weighed five pounds. The John Deere digger was 29 feet long and weighed 45,000 pounds. Its fifteen hundred-pound steel bucket had dagger teeth that could rip a 23-foot-deep hole with 25,000 pounds of tear-out force.

In the hands of an unskilled operator, the JD 200-G was a lumbering yellow elephant. But in the hands of Ramon Rodriguez, it was a ballerina on her toes, wielding a giant iron-toothed comb that could split a man's beard and never touch his cheek.

It was Ramon's 21st birthday, so to show off, he lowered the bucket into the tuck position and snuffed the candles, then dipped the shiny-clean steel teeth into the cake and deftly cut the first piece. Mac Morrison and his friends clapped and shouted their approval.

Ramon leaped down from the bright yellow monster, landing next to brothers Paco and Tomas. The three young Mexicans were helping Mac build a home for his friend Roger Lemonier.

"Mac," said Roger, taking cake from Maria, Ramon's mother, "I always thought I was a good operator, but Ramon's hands on the levers are like a surgeon's."

"Well, you'll need bigger jobs to pay for this machine, Rog. You got something lined up?"

Mac studied Roger's face while waiting for an answer. It was a face weathered by ten years of Special Forces' covert missions fighting America's enemies and twenty years since digging the rocky soil of the Granite State. Roger ran his own excavation business in New Hampshire's North Country; he and Mac had been best friends since fifth grade. They were both outdoorsmen who still looked ready to wrestle alligators.

"Mac," said Roger, "I won a DOT contract to replace fifty manholes and lay two miles of drain pipe in the grass median on I-89. That job will take months, and make big payments on this digger. So I need Ramon on my excavation crew, not here working on my house."

"Just one more day Rog, and then you can have him back. Tomorrow, we deck your roof, so I need Ramon on the Lull to lift the plywood up top."

Three hundred feet away, the black Suburban slowed as it passed again. The driver lowered his window, paused, and peered at the gathering.

Sun glinting off the windshield caught Mac's eye. This time, the Cro-Magnon sliver of Mac's brain alerted his frontal lobe: this time, he noticed.

It was the kind of fall day when "flatlanders" flock to New Hampshire's mountains to enjoy the brilliant crimson and yellow leaves. But tourists rarely found their way to Mac's rural road.

Paco shoved a bite of cake in his mouth. "Mister Mac," he said, "when we saw your '57 Chevy in New York, we never dreamed that we would work for you."

"Paco," said Mac, "It's been a good summer. I just hope your young cousins are good carpenters like you. Then we can quickly finish Roger's house."

"You will see them Wednesday, Mister Mac. They will work hard. After Roger's, we will finish your cabin."

"This winter, Paco, we'll finish the cabin this winter. So, how is the mobile home I got for your family? Big enough?"

"We love it, Mister Mac! Compared to farm housing, it's a palace."

The black Suburban returned. This time, it pulled into the long gravel driveway. Red and gold leaves were falling like snow, but Mac could see a large man get out, set a camera with a zoom lens on the hood, and take pictures.

"Paco," said Mac, "we have a visitor."

Mac slipped out his cellphone and snapped a picture of the truck. A white blur raced up beside him and whapped his leg with its tail. It was his Malamute-Shepherd, Buddy.

"Hey, Buddy, is that cake on your face?"

'Rowrf!' Happy dog.

"C'mon Bud. Let's see who's taking our picture." Mac ran down the long, curving driveway with Buddy at his side.

The cameraman saw Mac. He saw the big dog. He jumped back in the truck, and the driver reversed and sped off. Mac was too far away to read the plate, but it was white with black letters. There was some kind of symbol in the corner. He snapped more pictures. As he walked back to the house, his phone buzzed. (*Marybeth Murphy calling.*)

"Hi, Marybeth," he said. "We just set the roof trusses on Roger's house. Ramon showed off by snuffing his birthday candles with the excavator. What's new in Barcelona Harbor?"

"It's the fall wine festival, so my B & B is fully booked. But Mac, something just happened, and I wanted you to know."

"That sounds ominous, what's up, M?"

"Hubcap Harry fell downstairs and broke his hip, Mac. Bella-dog ran next door and barked. The neighbors came and called the squad. They took him to the hospital, where they put a pin in his hip. He is OK, but he can't go home because there is only one bathroom in his old house and it's on the second level. He's 85 Mac; it will take him a long time to heal. He needs a caretaker and a place with no stairs."

"You're right, M."

"Mac, I want Harry and Bella to live with me until he's well. I'll take care of him. The B & B is going into off-season, so I have the time, and my cottage would be perfect. What do you think?"

"He should jump at that chance, M. But Harry is proud; he won't take charity. And he'll be worried about his hubcap collection. They could get stolen if he's not home."

"Mac, we have to help him."

"Course we do, Marybeth. Look, can I call you back? I gotta check something right now."

"Uh-oh, I know that tone of voice, Mac. What just happened?"

"Probably nothing M, but, as you would say, my Spidey Sense[1] is tingling."

"Promise me you'll be careful, Mac, and call me back soon, OK?"

"I will. Give the Labradoodles a smooch."

"Hey! What about a smooch for me?" Marybeth said.

"I'll do that when I collect Harry from the hospital."

---

1 Spidey Sense: Peter Parker's (Spider Man) sense of impending danger

Chapter Two

Sunday, October 1
Newbury, NH
7:00 p.m.

Mac looked at the Suburban picture on his phone. The plate was blurry, but it seemed like a pattern of *two letters, a number, a letter, and three numbers, black on white.*

Mac had lived to be 50 by recognizing threats. His penchant for helping "sympathetic people" out of "sticky situations" had made him enemies. Even though most of those enemies were now dead, it still paid to be on guard.

He found a website with all the USA license plates. Texas looked like the one. He walked out of his new shop across to his new shed and looked at Paco's pickup truck. It had a 2023 Texas plate. It had a white background and black letters: same pattern.

He knocked on the mobile home door. Maria answered.

"Mister Mac, please come in." That was about the extent of Maria's English. She was learning, but Paco usually translated for her.

"Thank you, Maria," Mac said. "Maria, do you know someone who drives a black Chevy Suburban with a Texas license plate?"

She waved her hands. "*No comprendo, Meester Mac.*"

Mac pulled out his cellphone and showed her the picture of the black truck. Her eyebrows shot up, and she turned pale.

"Paco!" she shouted, scurrying away and throwing her hands up in the air, wailing, "*ay yi yi!*"

Paco appeared in the doorway.

"Yes, Mister Mac?"

"Paco, did you see the black Suburban that stopped in the driveway an hour ago?"

"Uhhh, yesss…"

"Did you recognize that truck, Paco?"

"Mister Mac, there are a lot of black Chevy Suburbans."

"Not on this road, Paco. And if there were, they would not have a Texas license plate."

"Mister Mac, you said people come from all over the world to see the leaves change colors, so that truck, it could be a rental, right?"

"It could be, Paco. I'll ask you again. Did you recognize this particular truck?" He showed him the picture on his phone.

"I couldn't say."

"Paco, I like you and your brothers. If you are in trouble, tell me. I will help you."

"Mister Mac, I think we are OK."

Mac paused and looked Paco in the eye. Paco looked down at the floor.

"All right, Paco. Look, tomorrow we deck the roof. The weather will be good. With Ramon on the Lull, we can work fast. We have to get it dried-in tomorrow because I leave Tuesday for New York. Norman Pelletier will shingle the roof while I'm gone. You and Tomas will install the windows and start the siding. You can do it. And Paco..."

"Yes, Mister Mac?"

"If you are in trouble, tell Roger. You can trust him the same as me."

"I think we are OK, Mister Mac."

**

Sunday, October 1
7:30 p.m.

Roger Lemonier was greasing the tracks on his D3 CAT bulldozer inside Mac's new shop that replaced his ancient timber barn destroyed by lightning five months prior.

"So that's it, Rog," Mac said. "Someone in a black Suburban was taking pictures. Were they taking pictures of your house, or Ramon snuffing his birthday cake, or us? Who knows? Maybe I'm making too much of it, but I'm pretty sure Paco knows who was in that truck. Could mean trouble."

"Feds drive black Suburbans, Mac. You think it was Immigration cops?"

"No, I do not. These boys have visas and work permits. They are paid legally."

"Now they are, Mac, but what about before they came here?"

"Rog, if there was a tax problem, IRS would not be cruising this road on a Sunday, nor would they high tail it out of here when I approached them. Doesn't pass the smell test."

"So, what are you saying, Mac?"

"I'm saying maybe this could be a situation, and I don't like it because I have to go back to New York and help Marybeth. Hubcap Harry is in the hospital with a broken hip. Marybeth wants him to rehab in her cottage, but that means I also gotta secure his cars while he is in Barcelona Harbor."

"I'll keep an eye on the boys, Mac. Is Paco qualified to keep going on my house?"

"Yes. And his two seventeen-year-old cousins should arrive while I'm gone. They are supposed to be trained carpenters."

"Good. I need to get started on the I-89 project."

"OK, let's just be extra aware, Rog."

"I will, Mac."

**

Chapter Three

Monday October 2
Newbury, NH
Mac Morrison's Cabin
7:00 a.m.

Buddy and Emma, the Labradoodle, were leading Mac around the back beaver pond. The temperature was already 65 degrees. It would be a great day to deck the roof, but the weather can change fast in the mountains, so Mac would push the crew to take advantage of the warm conditions.

The new cabin looked empty in the pale morning sun, and it was. Its peeled log exterior had the rustic appearance Mac liked, but he knew there was a ton of work inside to finish it. That was OK because that would be winter work. Since Marybeth was going to be caring for Hubcap Harry in Barcelona Harbor, she would not be coming to visit soon, so he did not have to hurry. Life was all about sequence. It always is.

**

7:30 a.m.

With Ramon on the Lull, the plywood got set on top of the trusses. Two brothers positioned the panels while Mac nailed them with the gun. Beneath them, the drywall crew was screwing up the second-floor ceiling to the bottom of the trusses.

By lunch, the simple A-roof was decked, and the ceiling below it was done, creating an attic floor. After the crew ate pizza at the picnic table, they were back on the roof, laying self-stick ice and water shield around the edges and placing heavy felt on the rest. They overlapped the felt on the peak in case of rain. Norman Pelletier would cut the slot for the ridge vent when he shingled it.

By three o'clock, the roof deck was watertight, so Ramon used the Lull to lift 80-pound bales of stone wool insulation up to the attic. With an eight-pitch roof, there was plenty of headroom to walk around inside. Mac and Paco installed soffit baffles between the trusses while Tomas began laying batts on top of the ceiling. Then, a second layer of batts was placed crossways to make an R-60 attic blanket.

By six p.m., the roof was ready for shingles, the attic was insulated, and there had been no sighting of a black Chevy Suburban. Maybe he *was* being a worry wart, Mac thought.

Buddy and Emma had spent the day splashing in the beaver pond behind Roger's new house, chewing on sticks, chasing each other, and sleeping in the sun. As Mac grilled burgers on his new cabin deck, the sun went low over the back pond. He could hear the slap of beaver tails as they approached their den. It was his daughter Gabriella's favorite sound, which was why she had named this Gabby's Pond.

He sipped a cold Canadian Pilsener beer from a long-necked brown glass bottle, held Emma in his lap, and scratched Buddy's outstretched head. Buddy purred his pleasure. The only thing that would make this day better, Mac thought, would be if Marybeth had shared it with him and the dogs. They needed to spend more time together, but for now, they were still four hundred miles apart.

They needed to work on that.

Mac was sad that Hubcap Harry had broken his hip but also glad because it gave him an excuse to see Marybeth for the first time since August. And, of course, Buddy and Emma would be coming with him. The weather report for the week looked promising, so they would be driving his baby blue 1957 Chevy Bel Air convertible with the hot rod engine and modern chassis.

Yes, it had been a very good day.

Chapter Four

Tuesday October 3
Newbury, NH
6:00 a.m.

Mac Morrison was ten years old when his parents were killed. He was raised by his Uncle Abe and Aunt Madelaine from age ten to his enlistment in the Army at age eighteen.

Abe was a large man who had lived a large life. As a WWII B-17 pilot, his bomber was shot down over Belgium. The Nazis hunted him as he trekked 1,000 miles to freedom at Gibraltar. During the Cold War, he flew atomic bombs in 24-hour-round-the-world shifts, ready to strike Russia if they started WWIII.

So, it was fitting that the hot-shot B-52 pilot bought a hot-rod 1957 Bel Air for his 34th birthday. Forty-two years later, he gave it to Mac for his 16th. Over the years, Mac had upgraded the Chevy but kept its stock looks. Staying true to its heritage, he replaced the 283 cubic inch V-8 with a 383 Chevy crate engine with fuel injection. He added a modern six-speed automatic transmission, four-wheel disc brakes, and modern coil-over suspension with rack and pinion steering. It now could keep up with all but the newest Corvettes.

The Bel Air made a throaty burble as it backed out of the new steel shop. Mac drove to his cabin, loaded both dogs, their beds, bowls, and tools into the big trunk, and headed for Eleanor's Café.

His contractor buddies were already there. While Mac ate, Roger Lemonier huddled with Mac's electrician, Remy Montague. The house was ready for rough wiring. While Remy's crew worked inside, the roofers would start shingling and Paco and his brothers would install windows and siding.

Mac did not want to leave, but Marybeth needed help. He knew he should quit worrying about the Rodriguez family and start thinking about the other people in his life.

He drove the same route he took to New York five months prior, reminiscing as the miles flashed by. That trip had turned his world upside down when he discovered his parents had not died in a car crash 40 years ago but had been murdered. He doggedly pried apart the mystery until he determined who their murderer was.

Their murderer, Joey Minetti, had tried to kill Mac and Marybeth inside her B & B, but Mac instead snapped his neck, killing him. Justifiable homicide by reason of self-defense, the police said.

The violence of that trip was overshadowed by the joy of meeting the lovely widow Marybeth Murphy. She was the owner of the Captain Murphy B & B in sleepy Barcelona Harbor and a woman unlike any he had met before.

Marybeth bore a striking resemblance to the green-eyed actress Ella Raines,[2] Mac's film noir favorite. She was five foot six, with auburn hair and a slender athletic build. She was six years younger than Mac, an early riser, dog lover, hard worker, and a classic car junkie. In addition, she sang like an angel and was a gourmet cook. And - she liked Mac! He still had no clue how it happened.

In unearthing his parents' 40-year-old mysterious deaths, Mac believed he had also solved the murders of Marybeth's husband and parents *by the same killer*. While the New York legal system had yet to *officially* agree with him, their cases were working their way through the courts.

People often wondered why "stuff" always happened to Mac. Being taken from his family vineyard in western New York at age ten and raised by an elderly uncle in the New Hampshire north woods was a rude awakening to the randomness of life. His diminutive size and different accent made him the object of bullies. He fought them every day. From those battles, he developed hardened fists, an inner toughness, and a clear picture of good and evil in the world.

As he hit his teen growth spurt, he also became a keen observer of human behavior. Later, using his military training and deadly combat experience, he naturally began helping "sympathetic people" resolve their "sticky situations," which sometimes led to more "justifiable homicides."

And that is why "stuff" always happened to Mac Morrison.

**

---

[2] <u>Ella Raines</u> (1920-1988): Film noir actress of the 1940's and 50's.

Westbound I-90, the New York State Thruway
1:00 p.m.

Mac shook his head to end his daydream. That woke Emma, who was sleeping on his lap, and Buddy, who had his nose against his leg. He was hungry, so they exited at mile marker 173.5 for Amsterdam. He found an old gas station with a deli counter, ordered takeout, and enjoyed a brief picnic with the dogs by the lazy Mohawk River. Then it was back onto I-90 and hammer down until he reached mile marker 485 and the Westfield exit.

**

Barcelona Harbor, New York
Captain Murphy B &B
4:00 p.m.

"Gronk!" went the rusty spring. "Whap!" The ancient screen door slapped Mac's backside.

"Mac? Is that you?" called a dulcet voice. The sweet smell of pie in the oven wafted from the kitchen. Marybeth Murphy poked her head through the pass-through window to the porch and shrieked.

"Mac! Buddy! Emma!"

She had a pale blue scarf wrapped around her auburn hair. She threw off her apron and ran into Mac's arms, hugging him with all her might.

'Rowrf! Rarf!' protested Buddy and little Emma. Marybeth scooped up Emma as her gang of Labradoodles came out to see what all the fuss was about. Buddy jumped up and slurped Marybeth's laughing face.

"Mac! How goes the cabin? How is Gabby? Is Roger happy with his house? Have you restored the '71 Chevy? Tell me all! But first, gimme a smooch!"

So he did.

They sat on the back porch, just as they had the day they first met five months before. Two mugs of steaming coffee floated tendrils to the ceiling as the dogs lay at their feet while all the news of the past two months was recited. It didn't matter that most of it had already been given in numerous phone calls. He was back. He was here. They were together. That's all Marybeth cared about.

"So M, where is Pops?" asked Mac, referring to Pops Rodgers, the retired Navy owner of the 1966 Bertram that rescued Mac last May. Tim Riley had knocked him overboard into forty-degree waters and left him clinging to a log in darkness, pounded by three-foot waves three miles offshore.

"He had *Miss Bertie* hauled last week and put in winter storage. Then he left for his cabin on the Little Tennessee River, Mac."

"Does he know his pal Harry is in the hospital?"

"Of course. I called him right after I called you. He offered to drive up here, but I told him you were coming and we would get Harry settled, then let him know how things were."

"Smart, M. We can't have too many octogenarians running the roads with their dogs. Gotta think about their safety."

"Right. So, Mac, you look great."

"I feel good, M."

Mac was six foot three and two hundred twenty pounds, not an ounce of it fat. Building docks and houses will do that. His sandy hair contrasted with his sun-tanned face, burned from years of working outdoors. Against his darkened skin his crystal blue eyes were spooky.

"How are the brothers working out, Mac? Will you keep them after Roger's house is built?"

"If I can. Roger wants Ramon to stay on his excavation crew because that kid can make a twenty-ton excavator dance like a ballerina. He is phenomenal. Roger bought a new digger and took on a huge pipe job for the state just because he had Ramon."

"What was worrying you, Mac? I heard it in your voice on the phone."

"I saw a black Chevy Suburban make three passes by Roger's house within fifteen minutes. The truck had a Texas license plate, and the passenger stopped and took pictures of us. They sped off before I could talk to them. Ramon was dancing the excavator on its toes, snuffing the candles on his birthday cake with the bucket, which could have stopped any tourist for a picture.

"But, being wary, I took a long-distance photo of the truck, too far away to make out the license plate number but clear enough to see the pattern and color. When I showed the photo to Maria, the boys' mother, she turned pale and scurried away, wailing. Paco said he could not be sure it was anyone he knows and assured me they were OK."

"Are they in trouble, Mac?"

"Not that they will admit, but eyes never lie. They have work permits and visas, so it can't be that. So, maybe this is family or someone they worked for in Texas. Maybe they owe money. Who knows? Anyway, Paco said they were OK, and even if they aren't, Roger is on Level One alert, and he can handle it until I get back. Now, let's talk about Harry."

"Mac, Harry is still in Conneaut Community Hospital. I called the duty nurse, told her I was a relative, and asked about his status. They will only release him to a safe care facility like a nursing home."

"No way, Marybeth. People go to nursing homes to die. And they bleed them of their money."

"They can't all be like that, Mac."

"Look, M, you set the ball in motion when you told them you were a relative. So you are going to play the part of his doting niece, Marybeth, who operates an elder cottage behind her B & B. We'll take pictures of your cottage with grab rails and no steps, and we'll update your website. When we show up at the hospital Harry can sign himself out into your care."

"Sounds like a plan. But Mac, the cottage does not have grab rails."

"I know, M, but it will by tonight. I'm going to leave Buddy and Emma with you and go to the hardware store. Meanwhile, get started changing your website, and put a rental rate in for the elder care guests."

"I have no idea what to charge, Mac."

"What did I pay for the cottage last May? $1,000 per week, right? And the meal plan added $50 per day, so, $1,350/week, but less on a monthly basis. Look, I'm doing a web search on my phone for senior housing in Buffalo suburbs. Here is a 720-square-foot apartment, the same size as your cottage, includes three meals per day in a three-story, forty-year-old building. There is one outside wall in each unit, which means dark tunnel interiors. Ugh."

"How much, Mac?"

$2,600 per month; the tenant pays their own electric, gas, internet, cable TV, and phone. So add $400 for those. Call it $3,000 per month for senior independent living, crammed into a building with 100 others, all interior access, shared laundry, and three pages of rules, for God's sake.

"Marybeth, let's advertise the Elder Cottage for $3,750 per month. And that includes three quality daily meals, all utilities, Wi-Fi, cable TV, Internet, call button, weekly cleaning, free laundry, and unlimited towels. We won't charge Harry that. That's just for the website to pry him outta the hospital if they check on you. OK, I gotta go. Buddy, you take care of Marybeth, OK?"

'Rowrf!' Buddy whapped his leg with his tail, then went and sat by Marybeth.

"Good boy, Buddy. And Emma, you have fun with your sisters."

'Rarf!'

"Welcome home, Mac. Did I tell you I love you?"

"I think you just did, M. Now, gimme a smooch."

**

4:30 p.m.

The hardware store had everything the *cottage* needed but not the stuff *Harry* needed. The clerk suggested a store on the edge of Westfield.

It was cavernous. In a small town like Westfield, it doubled as a one-stop convenience store with prescription and over-the-counter drugs, cosmetics, groceries, casual clothes, toys, essential hardware, office supplies, beer, and wine. The array was dizzying. He bought crutches, a walker, a cane, a grabber-reach tool, and a dog bed for Bella. He rented a folding wheelchair, just in case.

Back at the cottage, Mac used his power screw gun and stud finder to quickly install grab bars by the bed, the toilet, the shower, in the shower, the kitchen table, and even the front door. He installed a call button that would ring Marybeth's phone.

With the equipment installed, he took pictures with his cell phone and downloaded them to Marybeth's laptop. While she got busy updating her website to show the elder care cottage, Mac went outside with Buddy and did his last chore of the day. He used self-stick script letters that matched the font of the Captain Murphy B & B sign to say '*& Elder Care Cottage*.'

Satisfied, he took a picture and went back inside to download that final bit of proof that they were ready for Harry. Marybeth added it to her B & B website and proclaimed a good job done by all.

"Now, how about some dinner, guys?" she said. "I have no guests, so it's just us and the dogs tonight."

"Surprise me, M," said Mac. "I'm gonna take Emma and Buddy down to the pier and walk the beach. When I come back, I'm hoping there might be a Canadian Pilsener in your fridge."

"I think there just might be a whole case," she said with a wink and gave his butt a playful slap. "Go walk the dogs. I'll have appetizers ready by the time you get back and then you can grill some Lake Erie walleye fresh caught by Tim Riley. I told him you were coming back. He wants to see you."

"Great. How is Tim? And how is Anna's cancer?"

"They are doing great. She has been in remission for six months now; looks like she beat it."

"Fabulous. OK, see you shortly. C'mon Buddy, c'mon Emma."

**

6:00 p.m.

The Harbor boat ramp was busy. With a mild afternoon winding down, there were plenty of fishermen still on the lake and more hauling out with a full catch in their lockers. Mac sauntered into Todd's Gas N Go and looked around. Buddy and Emma sat outside, watching through the glass door.

"Mac Morrison!" shouted Todd. He was making one of his famous submarine sandwiches.

"Hello, Todd."

"You're not gonna make more mayhem, are you, Mac?"

"Nothing like that, Todd. I'm here to help Marybeth with an old friend. Heard from Pops?"

"He called me from his cabin. He wasn't too happy."

"Oh?"

"Tenants trashed it. You know he lists it with an internet vacation rental service. He said it was gonna cost thousands to repair, and it's not livable. He's staying in a neighbor's spare bedroom at the moment, but that's dicey because they are not dog people, and you know he loves his Ginger. He can only stay a week, and then he'll have to go."

"That's funny, Todd. He didn't mention that to Marybeth, and she just spoke to him."

"I've known Pops twenty years, Mac. He's proud. You saw how beautiful he keeps his Bertram. He won't talk about the damage until it's repaired, and that will be next spring."

"Todd, Pops built that cabin when he was 38 and just out of the Navy. Now he's 85. If the place is unlivable, then he can't repair it himself. And he's got Ginger-dog to care for."

"Right, Mac. He's got contractors lined up but nowhere to live."

"Huh!" said Mac. "We'll have to see about that. I'm glad to be back in the Harbor, Todd. We'll be in to buy subs before I head back to New Hampshire."

"Sounds good, Mac. Say hi to Marybeth for me."

**

"Well, Buddy, what do you think of that? First Harry and now Pops. Things happen in threes. That's an old human myth; do you believe that, Budso?"

Buddy cocked his head.

"HA! No, I don't believe it either, Buddy. Let's go down to the beach."

With little Emma trotting double-time to keep up, Buddy and Mac walked past the stone lighthouse. As they neared the boat ramp, a booming voice shouted.

"MAC MORRISON!"

Mac turned to see an open fishing boat motoring up to the ramp. It had a familiar look, and even more familiar was the vehicle attached to its boat trailer. He also knew the large man gunning the outboard engine and slipping the boat into its cradle.

"Hello, Tim. Shall I pull you out?"

Tim Riley smiled. "Sure Mac, keys are in the ignition."

Mac slid behind the wheel of the former State Trooper Police Interceptor. It was the same car that, in the hands of Joey Minetti, had pushed Marybeth's parents down a ravine to their deaths two years prior. That was the same man who had killed Mac's parents in 1983 and who, in his final act, tried and failed to kill Mac and Marybeth last May.

Mac clipped the winch cable to the bow cleat, pulled the boat trailer into the parking lot, shut off the engine, and hopped out. Tim jumped out of the boat with athletic grace for a giant 62-year-old former State trooper. He shook Mac's hand with his huge bear paw and grinned.

"Marybeth said you were coming to town. I wanted to talk to you. Did she grill the walleye?"

"That's for dinner, Tim. How are you doing? I understand Anna is much better."

"Anna is great. We had a bit of a scare. They thought her cancer was coming back, so she got referred to the Cleveland Clinic. I drove her down there. Fortunately, it turned out to be a false positive on a test. But the stress caused me to blackout in the waiting room. They rushed me into their hospital and found I had pressure on my brain from fluid buildup. It had probably been building for years, ever since the wreck that retired me from street duty. One of the screws used to implant the plate in my head worked loose. That's the way I would describe it. They did emergency surgery and removed the screw. I have not had any headaches since, and no anger issues either."

"Tim," said Mac, "I always felt like there was a physical reason for your behavior because Marybeth said how good you and Anna were to her growing up. So, it was the car wreck and the skull implant all along. Huh! Well, glad that is resolved. Say, this looks a lot like Jim Murphy's boat."

"It is. Marybeth lets me borrow it since she's not using it. Did you want to go fishing?"

"No, Tim. I'm just here for a few days to help Marybeth and then I'm heading back to New Hampshire. I've got two buildings going up and a crew to supervise, so I can't stay long."

"Mac, you know I turned state's witness in their case against Joey Minetti for the death of Marybeth's parents. You also know I had nothing to do with that. They were our friends, me and Anna. Joey used my car to kill them, and I will never get over that, but I had no idea he did that, Mac."

"I know that, Tim, I knew it last May."

"But Mac, you might not know that a Coroner's Jury concluded Minetti was responsible for the Murphy's deaths. The County Prosecutor took the Coroner's jury conclusion to the Grand Jury and they just indicted him posthumously. The Prosecutor will go to court and seek a directed verdict against him for first-degree murder."

"Tim, when did all this happen?"

"The Grand Jury indictment came down yesterday, Mac. I figured Marybeth's attorney would have told her by now."

"He will have been notified. Thanks for letting me know."

"Well, there may be a press release in the local papers, so you might want to prepare her."

"Right. OK, Tim, I'll talk to her attorney, Morgan Hillman. Thanks for the heads-up. Glad I ran into you.

"Mac, there's one more thing."

"Yes, Tim?"

"I've been using this boat for the past month, but I just noticed something today. The sun had to hit the side at just the right angle or I never would have spotted it. And then when Joey's old boat came into Harbor with that fat guy Mace..."

"Wilkins?"

"That's it, Mace Wilkins. He owns a scrap yard in Ashtabula."

"I know. I met him last May when we were tracking Joey."

"Oh, yeah, OK. So he came up here for a day cruise from Erie. His boat, *Mace's Mistress*, used to be Joey's boat, *Deadly Serious*. Mace tied up at a slip and went into Todd's for a sandwich. Look at this Mac."

They walked around to the bow of the Tracker 175. There was still black gel coat residue on the port side gunwale from the collision that had knocked Jim Murphy overboard. Mac had felt certain it was the *Deadly Serious*, with Joey Minetti piloting it, that had struck the Tracker and that the impact had killed Murphy when his head hit the hull of the bigger, heavier boat. The Coroner's report two years ago concluded Murphy drowned, but Mac found evidence that suggested otherwise. Attorney Hillman had been trying for the past five months to get the coroner to open an inquest, but so far, he had not prevailed.

"Mac, see this dent in the aluminum hull on the Murphy boat?"

"OK Tim, yes, I do. Something bumped this hull at some time."

"Mac, the Tracker 175 is a flat-sided boat, very popular in these Lake Erie waters, so popular that Jim Murphy had his wrapped to make it stand out."

"So these graphics are not factory, Tim?"

"No. Jim had this wrapped in a red panel. Custom, never seen another one like it."

"OK..."

"So Mac, when Mace Wilkins tied up, I was just coming in with my catch. There were a lot of boats going out at the launch ramp, so I tied up next to Wilkins. I noticed that his bow cleat was bent. It's chrome-plated steel, so it would never get bent unless you hit something hard. But this one had some color on it. Red color, Mac. Red like Murphy's wrap on this boat.

"So I looked real close at Murphy's boat and found this dent. I motored up beside Wilkins' boat, and the bent cleat matched this dent. And, there is some sticky red material stuck to the underside of the cleat, which is why I never saw it before. But sitting below it on the water, I spotted it. I took a picture, Mac."

Now Mac was focusing on the dent in the Murphy boat because there was a scrape a foot long behind that dent where the red wrap and its graphics had been peeled off a half-inch wide. This could be the smoking gun in Jim Murphy's murder.

"Tim, who else knows about this?"

"Nobody, Mac. That's why I wanted to talk to you."

"Tim, we knew that the black gel coat from the *Deadly Serious* was the same material on this gunwale rub rail," he said, pointing to the faded black residue that remained after two years. "But that did not prove that Minetti's boat was the boat that struck this Murphy boat, only that a black boat with this same gel coat had struck it. There was a faint line on the *Deadly Serious* where a professional repair had been done, but it was impossible to get any kind of metal sample beneath that repair to tie that boat to this one. But now, just maybe...Tim, did you touch that red material in any way?"

"No."

"Good. What is your cell number, Tim?"

He gave it to him.

"I'm sending you a text requesting that picture you took of the bent bow cleat and the date and time you took it, plus your statement that it came from Mace Wilkins' boat *Mace's Mistress*, formerly Minetti's *Deadly Serious*. Please text me the photo right now."

Mac waited until he got Tim's response.

"Tim, man, you may have just cracked a murder case. Talking about cases, were you ever charged in any of Minetti's cases?"

"Mac, I was charged with impersonating an officer of the New York State Police for using my old Trooper badge to try to get information for Joey. I took a plea deal to cooperate and turn state's evidence, and I resigned from my vehicle inspector job with the BMV. My deposition helped indict Joey for Marybeth's parents' murders. Since you dropped your charges against me for our episode on the lake, my other charges were dismissed. Mac, now that my brain is back to normal, I have a new life. Minetti would have no power over me now, Mac. He did once, but not now."

"Good Tim. Was your pension affected?"

"No, that was part of my resignation and plea deal."

"Were you involved in Minetti's modifying stolen vehicles and issuing new salvage titles?"

"Mac, I never knowingly passed a salvage vehicle that was stolen and modified with legit VIN tags. Minetti did pay me a one-time consultant fee to show them what I looked for in reviewing salvage vehicles as a BMV inspector. I know that was a conflict of interest. I know that now, but then my brain wasn't working right, and we had Anna's cancer expenses, so we needed the money.

"So I took the consultant fee, but I never was paid to pass a car. Besides, Joey's work was so flawless, no one, not even an expert, could have determined the cars' identification tags and frame markings were altered."

"Ok, glad to know that, Tim. Now, I *do* need you to tow this boat back to Marybeth's barn. I am going to lock it up for testing by the state police lab. Sorry Tim, but no more fishing for a while."

"I understand, Mac. I'll help Marybeth if I can."

**

Murphy B & B
7:00 p.m.

"You were gone a long time, Mac. Everything OK?" asked Marybeth as she took a bowl of iced shrimp cocktail from the fridge and laid out skewers with walleye and veggies.

"Yes. I saw Tim. He had some news. Did Morgan call you?"

"No, why?"

"Come sit next to me, M. We are going to conference-call BCI Investigator Jonetta Pope and Morgan Hillman. I am going to text them some photos Tim Riley took today."

Mac made the call connection and put it on speaker so Marybeth could listen. He meticulously repeated what Tim Riley had told him. Marybeth started shaking with emotion, but Mac had a firm arm around her, and the dogs all lay at her feet like her protecting army.

Jonetta assured them that BCI would get a warrant to seize the *Mace's Mistress* and tow it to Fredonia for testing. She also would have Jim Murphy's Tracker 175 towed there, too. Chain of evidence would always be an issue two years after the death of Jim Murphy, but hard physical evidence could easily have been preserved during that time. Mac fired up the big outdoor grill and put on the skewers. While they cooked, he thought of two more things that needed doing tomorrow. He could sleep on those overnight. That is, if Marybeth let him sleep.

**

Chapter Five

Wednesday, October 4
Murphy B & B
6:00 a.m.

"You've gotten lax in your rules, lady," said Mac as he lay with Marybeth in his arms. Buddy was sprawled across his legs, and Emma was tucked next to him. Marybeth's three Labradoodles were, as usual, nestled around her head, making her look like some strangely beautiful creature with one human and three dog heads, all combined.

"Well, I can't have you sleeping in the cottage since it's all ready for Harry, so yes, the dogs get house privileges for night sleeping. Daytime, they stay on the back porch. Did you get any sleep, my love?"

"Finally, and thank you for asking, as Piglet[3] would say."

"Many happy returns of the day to you," Marybeth chuckled. "What would you like for breakfast, Mr. Builder?"

"I'll feed the dogs while you fill your big thermos and grab a picnic basket. We'll stop at Todd's for three breakfast subs."

"Yum. Who is the third sandwich for, and where are we having our picnic breakfast, Mr. Mystery?"

"In Sol Weinstein's scrap yard."

**

En route to Erie, PA.
7:00 a.m.

They drove the '57 Bel Air because it would be easier for Harry to slide into the front bench seat than to squeeze into a bucket in Marybeth's Outback.

---

[3] Piglet and Eeyore the donkey are characters in the Winnie the Pooh series of children's books written by British author and poet A.A. Milne, illustrated by E. H. Shepard and published in 1926 by Methuen Press, London and Dutton Press, USA. Young boy Christopher Robin fantasizes about a life with his friends Winnie the Pooh (Pooh-bear), Eeyore the donkey, Piglet, Kanga, Roo, Owl and Rabbit in the hundred acre woods behind his home. Pooh Bear speaking to Eeyore, the depressed donkey in Chapter VI- Eeyore Gets a Birthday Present.

With the crutches and folding wheelchair in the trunk, they were off.

It was a 35-mile drive from Barcelona Harbor southwest on I-90 to Erie's Bayfront Connector. Marybeth called Pops in Tennessee. She knew the old mariner would be awake and out of the house, looking for coffee and yesterday's free newspaper at a local gas station.

And he was.

Mac laid out his idea, and Pops jumped at the chance. It would all depend on Hubcap Harry.

With that piece of the puzzle in place, it was time for breakfast. They exited the Bayfront Connector and drove East Street directly to the old lakeside industrial docks. Mac pulled up to the tall chain link fence with coils of razor wire on top and pressed the call button. A familiar voice answered.

"Vee closed! Come back at eight o'clock. Sorry!"

"Your breakfast will be cold by eight o'clock, Mr. Weinstein. I think you should let us in." Mac chuckled as he said it.

"Vaaa? Dat voice! I tink I know dat voice!"

"It's Mackenzie Morrison, Mr. Weinstein. I've come to visit you. I brought a pretty lady, and coffee, and breakfast sandwiches."

"Mackenzie Morrison! You vait! I come down und unlock da gate. Pretty lady und breakfast sandviches! Oh boy!"

In a minute, the back door of a shabby old house creaked open, and a short fireplug of a man in his 80s came shuffling out with his arms open to welcome Mac and Marybeth. He unlocked the gate with a giant ring of keys and gestured with a sweep of his hand.

"Come in, come in, I lock behind you! Velcome Mackenzie Morrison! Velcome Mrs. Morrison!"

"Did we get married on the drive down here?" Marybeth giggled.

"Marybeth, this is my friend Sol Weinstein. Sol, this is my good friend Marybeth Murphy, owner of the Captain Murphy Bed and Breakfast Inn at Barcelona Harbor, New York."

"Barcelona Harbor! I vass there vun time, maybe 30 years ago. Nice place. Qviet. Anything changed?"

"Not much, Mr. Weinstein," said Marybeth. "Grapes and fishing. We brought you Todd's famous breakfast sandwiches. Do you have an oven?"

"In my blue buildink. Come, I show you. Velcome, velcome!"

Surrounded by neat piles of shredded metal, steel I beams, and stacks of aluminum siding, one building stood out. It was a steel pole building with a marine blue finish and white trim. Mac commented on how clean it was.

"Dis spot here gets no dust from da crusher and da grinder. I pay a man to come and pressure vash it. It is my special buildink. Come, come, I show you. Velcome, my friends, velcome."

Sol Weinstein used his stubby fingers to enter a code on a keypad and open a heavy door. He flicked a switch, and the two-story building lit up like a museum. Soft lights were directed downward. The exhibits were not paintings or sculptures, but they were definitely works of art. The building was lined with two-story racks loaded with classic cars.

Mac did a quick count: ten racks per side and five racks on the end: fifty cars total. Most were from the 1950s, perhaps a dozen from the 60s. These were special cars, the cream of their era. 1957-69 Cadillac Eldorado, every year represented. 1957 Buick Special. 1958 Buick Invicta convertible. 1953-1957 Oldsmobile 98. 1955-1957 Chevrolet Bel Airs. 1963 Pontiac Catalina. 1964 Pontiac GTO. 1967 Camaro RS.

Mac's eyes glazed over at the beauty and quality of the cars because, he could tell, they were all original. None were restored, but none were perfect either.

"Sol, this is an amazing collection!"

"Mackenzie, you drive a 1957 Chevy Bel Air. Pretty car. Looks original, but I can tell you lowered it and repainted it. It has a new interior. You updated it so you can drive it, right?"

"That's right, Sol."

"So, Mackenzie, I love da General Motors cars from da 50s to da 60s. Dose vere da golden years for me. I come to America after da vor as a baby, like I told you. Born in Poland, 1938. I vas in prison camp by da Nazis after dey kill my parents at Auschwitz."

He pronounced it 'Auschvitz.'

"After da vor, I got sent here, to Erie, age ten. I vas adopted by a Jewish family, tank God for dem. I don't know English, I am scared, but I am tough. Small, but strong like a bull. I leave school age sixteen and go to vork in da train plant. You know, da General, he makes da trains here in Erie."

"General Electric," Mac said.

"Yah, da General. Diesel-electric locomotives. Dere is a lot of viring in tight spaces. I vass small, could fit, and strong, could pull da vire. So dey teach me electric, and how to vire da engines. And I do dat vork 60 hours a veek, alvays. Take all da overtime I can get. I vork hard, make good money. Lived at home still. Vee had a barn, my parents did behind da house. I vould see a good car, maybe five, six years old, I could buy it for $300, $500 dollars in da 50s, maybe a tousand in da 60s. So, ven I see one, I buy it and put it in da barn.

"Ven my parents died dey left me a little money, a house, and many good memories. I had saved. Never married, no woman interested in tough little man like me. But I had my dog and my cars in da barn. I vould alvays come here on Sunday to see Mr. Banks, he owned da scadap yard. I vould look at da cars going to da crusher. He alvays gave me choice of da good vuns. Some cars I buy for $20! So, dat is how I collect all dese cars. Dis is my family. I come here and look at my babies, I call dem. Dey talk to me sometimes: a little creak, a little groan. Dey telling me dey old, but dey warm and dry, and happy.

"I sit here in my kitchen, have good coffee and kuchen, or streusel, vatever da old baker makes down da block. Fifty years I go to da baker! Now he is gone, bakery gone. No more kuchen, no more streusel."

"How did you come to own the Banks business, Sol?" asked Mac.

"All dose years I come here every Sunday. Vun day I come in 1972, and da gate is locked, Mr. Banks don't answer da bell. Someting is wrong, I tink. I call police. Vee find him in his chair, vere he alvays sat, holding a picture of hiss vife. Broke his heart ven she die. I tink he died of broken heart, too. Vee find a note to me. He vas not feeling good. I tink he knew it vas da end, so he wrote me. Dere vas a vill. His attorney tells me Mr. Banks left da scadap yard to me. He had no children. I vas his only friend. Sad."

A tear fell from Sol's eye.

"So, I take it over. I vas young, only 34. I leave da General, no more trains; now I kink of da scadap vorld!" He chuckled.

"What about your dog, Mr. Weinstein? Do you still have a dog?" Marybeth asked.

A great look of sadness fell over the old man's eyes, and he wiped another tear as it fell.

"No. I had many dogs, dey vould come strays. Sometimes, I had two, tree at a time. I vould feed dem, let dem sleep in my house, and dey guard my yard. But dey all get old like me, and now, no strays like da old days. People fence dere yards. Dis area by da lake going upscale, dey call it. Neighbors don't like my scadap yard no more. Too dirty, too noisy. Dey making a park along da lake. OK, looks nice, but vere is industry? Got to have industry to pay for parks, I tink.

"Dey say dey going to take my land. Vat is dis? Germany 1935? Russia? Take my land? Dis is America, how can dey do it?"

"Sol," said Mac, "the city can't take your land. But they can buy it for public purpose, like a road or a park. They have to pay you for it. Have they made you an offer for your land, Sol?"

"Offer? Nobody come talk to me about my land. I read in a newspaper, how I know. Nobody come see me."

"Did they send you a letter, Sol?"

"I don't know. If I don't know who send a letter it I trow it in da trash."

"They might have sent you something you had to sign for. Did the mailman ask you to sign for a letter, Sol?"

The old man rubbed his chin. "I tink...hey, our breakfast getting cold! Marybeth!"

"Yes, Sol?"

"Marybeth, dis is an air fryer oven. You can toast da sandviches, OK? Mackenzie, you come. I tink maybe I did get sometink. Had a green card stuck to it."

Mac and Sol walked into an office behind the kitchen. Unlike the old house that Sol lived in, this office was spotless and organized. On the desk was a stack of mail. And sticking out of the bottom of the stack was a letter with a USPS return receipt requested green card. By its date, it had been sitting on the desk for three weeks.

"Sol, you can see it's from the city of Erie. You should always open official mail. Let me see what it is."

Mac read it quickly and reread it twice to be sure.

"Sol, it seems like the city wants to buy your land. Actually, it does not appear to be the city itself. It seems like this is a partnership that wants to expand the waterfront greenbelt next to you. Your property is part of a comprehensive plan for waterfront redevelopment as parks, marinas and housing."

"Vat if I don't vant to sell? Vere would I go? Vat vould I do? I be here 51 years now, I'm gonna die here too."

"Sol, like I told you, the government can buy private property like your land, even if you don't want to sell it, but they have to use it for a public purpose. They can't force you to sell in order for them to give it to a developer, but they can force you to sell for a fair market value, based upon appraisals, for redevelopment as a public park. Do you understand what I am telling you?"

"I understand I am hungry and vee haff breakfast in da kitchen. Let's eat and look at my cars."

"Great idea," said Mac.

So they ate Todd's delicious breakfast sub sandwiches, drank brewed coffee from the big thermos, and gazed at Sol's fabulous collection of old cars.

"Sol, how many of these cars run?"

"Maybe half, but vould take some verk. I pickle dem before dey go in storage."

"They are beautiful, Sol," said Mac, "but I want to talk about this letter. It says they want to negotiate a price with you so they do not have to use eminent domain. That is when they take your land over your objection but pay you a fair market price based on appraisals. So you need to contact them and see what they will offer you. It's in your best interest to do that, Sol. You don't want to fight them because they will win, and you are going to get paid either way. But you might get more money if you negotiate, and you also might get something of value in addition."

"Vat ting of value?"

Mac said, "We could get them to name your land Sol Weinstein Park and make a historical monument to you and your history with the city. You are a WWII survivor, holocaust survivor, orphan, adopted by a local family, worked hard at the train factory, inherited this scrap yard, and worked it for 51 years. It's time for you to retire, Sol. Aren't you ready to do something else?"

"Sol," said Marybeth sweetly, "what kind of dogs were they?"

Sol brightened up and said, "All kinds, any kind. I loved dem all."

"And they all loved you, Sol," said Marybeth. "You know, this offer from the city is a lot to think about. You have been the caretaker of this scrap yard for 51 years. It has been your baby, and your special cars have been your family. I have an idea. Mac, can this building be moved?"

"Yes, very easily. It's steel posts and beams, steel skin with insulation and wiring. It can be unbolted and taken apart off the concrete slab and re-erected. What are you thinking, M?"

"We'll talk about it in the car. Sol, we have to go to Conneaut to pick up a friend of ours at the hospital. He fell and broke his hip, so I am bringing him back to Barcelona Harbor. He is going to live in my cottage while he gets well. He collects hubcaps from the 1940s through the early 1970s, but only for General Motors cars. He has a barn with thousands of hubcaps. Would you like to meet him?"

"Hubcaps for General Motors cars? Maybe he has some for mine. I have cars vit no hubcaps or wrong hubcaps! Yes, I vant to meet him. Vat is his name?"

"Hubcap Harry. Sol, I want you to come to Barcelona Harbor later this week, have dinner with us, and stay overnight. Will you do that for me?" Marybeth asked.

"OK, but I don't see so good to drive at night now."

"You won't be driving, Sol. We will arrange for a friend to drive you. And you will enjoy meeting him too. You will be staying overnight as my guest. What night would be good for you?"

"Friday sundown to Saturday sundown is Shabbat, so I don't vork and da scadap yard is closed."

"Good, let's plan on Friday night. Can you close a little early this Friday, Sol?"

"OK, I can close at 4 instead of 5."

"So be ready at 5:00 p.m. Friday, alright?"

"All right, my new friend Marybeth. I come have dinner vit you, Mackenzie, and Hubcap Harry."

**

Conneaut, OH
9:00 a.m.

Conneaut Community Hospital was a modest-looking affair. The staff was efficient and polite, but the nurse was not going to let Harry go without proof he was going where he would be cared for.

Marybeth showed her the website with photos of the cottage and all the handicap equipment. Then she swept into Harry's room, rushed over, and gave him a big hug while chattering away.

"Uncle Harry, you are looking good. I was so worried. Have they been treating you well? Have you been eating? Are you ready to come home with me? You are going to be staying in the cottage, you know, the one behind my B & B. All one floor, no steps, handicap shower, grab rails everywhere, and I will be rolling you into the dining room for all your meals. We'll pick up sweet Bella on our way. Mac will collect your clothes and anything else you might need. And you don't need to worry about your house or your cars because Pops Rodgers is going to house-sit for you and keep an eye on all your property. Isn't that great?"

Harry was momentarily taken aback by Marybeth's niece's act, but he could see she was playing to the stern look of the discharge nurse. By the time Marybeth caught her breath, he was ready.

"Let's go home, Marybeth!" he said. "Nurse Kincaid, I am leaving. Send the bill to Medicare or wherever because I know I am covered."

"Well, I need your signature on this paper, Harry," she snapped. "Are you sure you feel ready to go? You are not going to be very mobile, you know. Can you get physical therapy?"

"All taken care of, Nurse Kincaid," said Marybeth firmly. "Are there any medications or prescriptions I need to have filled?"

"He can take these pain pills, but as soon as he does not need them, please stop taking them. He can take over-the-counter pain meds. There was a pin inserted in his hip. The stitches will absorb, and there should be no infection, but watch for redness, swelling, or fever. Come right back if there is. The main thing is to use the wheelchair to be safe and keep him upright on crutches when he is out of the wheelchair. Later, he can use a walker. You said your cottage is one story. Is it thick carpet?"

"No, it's hardwood," said Marybeth. "The wheelchair can roll easily. There are grab rails everywhere, plus there is a call button that prompts my phone 24/7."

"Well, it sounds like you are well prepared. Harry, thank you for coming here. I know you could have had the squad take you to Ashtabula, but we appreciate your business and hope you will come back anytime you need us."

"Marybeth, let's get outta here!" cackled Harry. "Hee, hee!"

Nurse Kincaid said, "I have to take you to the front door, Harry. That is to make sure you can get in their car."

She was surprised to see a 1957 Chevy Bel Air.

"Oh, that's a pretty car, but it's old. Is it reliable? We don't want you to break down on the way home."

Harry snorted.

"Kincaid, you may know nursing, but you don't know squat about cars! Mac, load me up!"

Nurse Kincaid helped Mac stand Harry up on his one good leg, pivot, and sit on the broad front seat. Marybeth had slid in the back. With a wave to Nurse Kincaid, they were off.

"Boy, that was slick, you two!" cackled Harry. "Now, what's this about Pops house sitting for me? Is that for real?"

"For real, Harry," said Mac. "Is it OK with you?"

"That's great, and I'll get to see him! Where is he now?"

"On his way here from Tennessee. He can't move back into his cabin because his tenants trashed it, so this helps him, too. He'll be at the B & B tonight."

"Good deal, Mac. Did you dream that up?'

"I most certainly did. And we have another surprise for you too, but I think we'll wait until later. We are going to have a very special guest for dinner Friday night, and you two will absolutely hit it off."

"Good! I like meeting new people! But right now, I can't wait to get my sweet Bella-girl in my arms. I have been so worried about her!"

"Well, you will be home in two minutes, so get ready, Harry!" Marybeth said.

**

Hubcap Harry's House
Conneaut, Ohio
US Route 20
9:15 a.m.

"Bella, come to Daddy, baby!"

'WUFWUFWUFWUFWUFWUFWUF!'

The eight-year-old Pit mix scrambled out the door and rushed up to the

Bel Air, jumping up onto the front seat next to Harry and excitedly licking his ear as he laughed.

"Bella baby, I missed you, you big nut!"

'Wuf!'

"We are going to stay at Marybeth's, Bella, in a new home with your old friends. Won't that be great?"

'Wuf!' Bella was leaning against Harry like she was afraid he would leave her again. She had spent months at a rescue shelter after her owner died. She was 8 and one half years old, and Harry was her human, and she was never going to let him out of her sight again!

The house had been closed up for several days. It smelled musty, like old houses do, especially when their owners are in their 80s and have a dog. But it was tidy and clean, except for where Harry fell and the muss created when the squad carried him out to the hospital.

While Mac cleaned that up, Marybeth went through the fridge. She tossed expired foods and took the trash out to the refuse cans. From Harry's closet, she selected clothes and shoes and packed them in a battered pasteboard suitcase that looked as old as the pre-WWI house.

Mac installed a motion activated doorbell camera on the front porch with a clear view of the front yard and the two dozen 1950s vintage classic cars on blocks that were the stuff of Harry's classic car parts business. Then he made sure the barn was locked with its thousands of hubcaps.

With that done, they piled back into the Bel Air and drove fifty minutes to Barcelona Harbor with Harry telling tales of his 85 years in the old three-story house and the great hubcaps he had collected.

**

Chapter Six

Wednesday, October 4
Barcelona Harbor, NY
Captain Murphy Bed and Breakfast Inn
3:00 p.m.

Mac's phone buzzed. (*Attorney Morgan Hillman calling.*) While Marybeth got Hubcap Harry settled, Mac walked into the back porch with Buddy behind him.

"Morgan, what's up?"

"Four things, Mac."

"First, Jonetta Pope got a court order to seize Joey Minetti's former boat. It is being towed from Ashtabula to Troop A Substation in Fredonia. A State Police vehicle will also come to pick up Jim Murphy's boat. If tests prove the Minetti boat *Deadly Serious* caused the damage to Murphy's boat, that, plus depositions from Pops Rodgers and Tim Riley, which put Minetti behind the wheel of the *Deadly Serious* at the time of Jim Murphy's death, should be enough to get our inquest granted. Jim Murphy's body would be disinterred and reexamined by a neutral coroner to determine the cause of death. And the Coroner's Jury would reopen the case. I want Marybeth to be emotionally prepared."

"Got it," said Mac.

"Second. The Coroner's Jury concluded that Minetti was responsible for Marybeth's parents' deaths, and the Grand Jury has indicted Minetti posthumously for first-degree murder. The Attorney for the Minetti family, Joe Delmonico, has declared that the family will not intervene. There will be no defense presented. Minetti will be found guilty in absentia, posthumously. That allows me to sue his estate for wrongful death. Joey Minetti Jr. inherited posthumously from Joseph Senior, but he predeceased his father. So, I will have to sue the Minetti Family Enterprise.

"The Minetti Family Enterprise is cash, investments, property, and businesses owned by Joseph Senior, with the exception of Gino's salvage auto parts business and Gina's wine importing business. That could be a complicated financial empire to unwind and liquidate.

"Third, you sent me a text about Sol Weinstein and an eminent domain letter. I am not licensed in Pennsylvania, but I know a good guy who is: Joe Delmonico."

"Minetti's lawyer?"

"Yes. He has a young partner who does real estate work and is a real ballbuster. Name's Sarah Lieberman."

"I'm sure Sol will like her! Text me her contacts, and I'll set up a meeting with her and Sol."

"Mac, I'm asking this next question as your lawyer. Be careful how you answer. Were the Rodriguez brothers with you all last Monday?"

"Yes. We were putting the roof on Roger's house from sunup to sundown. Why?"

"A farmer was murdered near Ascutney, Vermont, last Monday. He was shot with a large bore gun, possibly a .44 Magnum revolver, because no shell casing was found. The slug went right through the farmer's skull and wound up in a hay bale."

"Jeezuz, that's a fuckin' cannon."

"Mac, his wife was in a gun battle with his killers, but they got away. The cops are on a two-state lookout for four men in a black Mercedes van. The Vermont Police found the Rodriguez boys' pay stubs in the farmer's file cabinet, and also your address as a future contact for them.

"New Hampshire State Police came to your house two hours ago. You weren't home, but they saw activity next door at Roger's house, and they found the three young Rodriguez men there with Roger. He alibied their time for Monday, but the police still want to interview the boys separately. Roger would not let them be interviewed without a lawyer, so he called me. I insisted on an interpreter because Ramon and Tomas are not fluent in English. The interview is scheduled for tomorrow morning at the State Police Headquarters in Concord. They want to talk to you too, Mac."

"Wow. Well, I'm sure they'll call me. The boys have an iron-clad alibi. What's the fourth thing, Morgan?"

"Roger tells me you were spooked by a black Chevy Suburban that stopped in your driveway. Mac, this time of year, the out-of-towners close up their summer cottages, so criminals are always scouting opportunities for break-ins. That could be all that was."

"Maybe, Morgan, but local criminals don't have Texas license plates."

**

3:30 p.m.

Mac called the Delmonico law firm, got connected with Sarah Lieberman, and was immediately impressed. He gave the quick rundown on Sol's situation and the address of the scrap yard in Erie. She would make a hole in her Thursday schedule to meet with Mac and Sol. And yes, she knew a baker who would make her a kuchen. They would meet at ten a.m. She would be coming from Buffalo. Mac completed the loop with a call to Sol, and that chore was done.

**

3:45 p.m.

No sooner than Mac had hung up, his phone buzzed again. The screen had a New Hampshire 603 area code.

"Hello," said Mac. "This is Mackenzie Morrison."

"Mr. Morrison, this is Colonel Trammel Bradford, Field Superintendent of the New Hampshire State Police. I believe we have a mutual friend in attorney Morgan Hillman."

"Colonel Bradford, yes, Sir, we do. And thank you very much for your assistance last May in pursuit of my parents' killer."

"Well, I didn't do much, Mr. Morrison. As I recall, all I did was make a phone call to my counterpart, Colonel Justice of the New York State Police, asking for their assistance in the matter."

"And that made all the difference, Sir. What can I do for you?"

"Has Morgan called to advise you of the murder in Ascutney?"

"Yes, Sir, he has."

"Did he tell you New Hampshire State Police are interested in speaking with the three young men you have working for you?"

"He did, yes, Sir."

"Well, since Attorney Hillman is representing them, our investigators are waiting until tomorrow to question them individually. I have here in my office Investigator Jaqueline Beaulieu of the Major Crime Unit of the Investigative Services Bureau. She is heading up our state's effort to find the killers of Rupert Bisbee, the man murdered Monday. Since you are out of state, I would like to have Investigator Beaulieu ask you some questions over the phone. You are not a suspect, of course, but you do have the right to be represented by an attorney if you insist."

"Please, go ahead, Investigator Beaulieu, and call me Mac; everyone does."

"Thank you, Mister Morrison, that is, Mac. When did you first hear of the murder of Mr. Bisbee?"

"Ten minutes ago when Attorney Hillman phoned me. He did not tell me the name of the victim."

"You mean you did not know the name of the man killed until Colonel Bradford just informed you?'

"Correct."

"Did you know Mr. Bisbee personally, Mac?"

"No, I did not. Never met him; never heard of him."

"We found your contact information in his file cabinet together with a file he had for his farm laborers, specifically the Rodriguez brothers Paco, Ramon, and Tomas. How do you explain that, Mac?"

"I can't explain it. I met the Rodriguez family while traveling to New York in May and struck up a conversation with them. They seemed like nice young men. I was looking for carpenters and equipment operators to assist me in building houses, which is my profession. They said they had experience, and after they completed a three-week job at an Ascutney orchard, they would be interested in working with me.

"They were traveling from one seasonal job to the next in response to a jobber who found them work. Since the jobber had not lined up their next job, I offered to give them two weeks of trial work. I gave them my business card. Two weeks later, they arrived at my house in Newbury, and I put them to work."

"When did you meet them in New York?"

"What date? Well, let me think. I left for Dewittville, New York, where my parents are buried, on my 50th birthday, so that was May 19th. And I stayed in a motel that night in LeRoy, New York. The Rodriguez family was also staying at that same motel. Technically, I met them the morning of May 20th because they woke up early to look at my car. It's a 1957 Chevrolet

Bel Air, and it grabs a lot of attention. They were admiring it, so I offered to show it to them. That was the first time I met them."

"The first time?" asked Investigator Beaulieu. "Was that when you contracted with them, Mac?"

"No, I met them again, by chance, on my return trip from New York to Sunapee. I stopped for lunch in LeRoy and saw them playing soccer at the motel where I had stayed. So I spoke to them. That is when I discovered they had no new job lined up. I offered them a chance to tryout with me. I did not *contract* with them. I simply invited them to come to New Hampshire and work with me for two weeks as a test."

"And when was this second chance meeting, Mac?"

"Oh, let me think. OK, Joey Minetti died on a Sunday, May 28th. That is a day seared in my mind. You can check that date with Attorney Hillman. I had driven him, his secretary Angie, and Roger Lemonier to the airport in Jamestown for their charter flight back to New Hampshire early that morning. Upon my return to the B & B in Barcelona Harbor, Joey Minetti entered the back door and tried to kill Marybeth Murphy and me. He got off six shots, but my dog bit his arm and diverted his aim. I struggled with him to get his gun. During the struggle, his neck got broken, and he died. That's why I will always remember that date, May 28th.

"I stayed one additional day at the Murphy B & B after that and then left the following Tuesday. So, I believe I met the Rodriguez boys in LeRoy on May 30th after lunch."

"That is a very precise recall, Mister Morrison. Did Attorney Hillman prepare you in any way for this interrogation?"

"Have you ever killed a man with your bare hands, Investigator Beaulieu?" Mac asked.

"No, I have not."

"It is not something you forget. That is why I have a precise recollection of the time and date. And no, Attorney Hillman did not, as you put it, 'prepare me for this interrogation.' Since I am not a suspect, I thought this phone call was just friendly questions to assist you in your investigation."

"Ahem," said Colonel Bradford. "Thank you Mac, now just a few more questions. And I think I'll ask these myself. You may stand down, Investigator Beaulieu."

"Please go ahead, Colonel Bradford," said Mac.

"Mac, you did not personally know farmer Bisbee?"

"No Sir, never met him, never heard of him. I did not know it was his farm that the Rodriguez brothers worked at."

"And both you and Roger Lemonier can attest to the Rodriguez family being with you all day this past Monday."

"Yes Sir. We were decking the roof of Roger Lemonier's new house, which I am building for him. We worked sun-up to sundown and the boys, I should call them young men, were with me at all times."

"Did the Rodriguez brothers mention any trouble they had at their job in Ascutney last spring?"

"No Sir. I presumed the Ascutney job ended early because I expected them to arrive three weeks after I met them on May 30th, but they actually showed up early, two weeks after that meeting."

"Did they give you any reason why they left the Ascutney job a week early?"

"No, they did not."

"Did the farmer Bisbee communicate with them after they left his job one week early?"

"If he did, I am not aware of it."

"Would you generally vouch for the Rodriguez boys' good character?"

"I would, Colonel. They are hard workers, have been no trouble working with me now for four months. They are an integral part of my future business plans and Roger Lemonier's business plans. Roger bought a new excavator and obtained a large drainage contract with NHDOT because he has Ramon as an operator."

"Would you have any other helpful thoughts regarding our investigation, Mac?"

"Well, maybe there is one thing, Colonel, probably unrelated, but it happened just last Sunday, and it has bothered me a bit. While we were celebrating topping off Roger's house, Maria Rodriguez brought a cake over for Ramon's 21st birthday. He made the excavator do a trick by using the bucket to snuff the candles and cut the cake. While he did that, a black Chevy Suburban with tinted windows stopped in the driveway 300 feet from the birthday party. A man got out, set a camera with a long telephoto lens on the hood, and took pictures of us. That got my attention, so I ran down the driveway to see who they were, but they immediately sped off.

I snapped a picture of their truck with my phone, but they were too far away for me to read their license plate. It had a white background with black letters and numbers. I am fairly certain it was a Texas plate. When I asked Paco and Maria Rodriguez if they recognized the truck in the picture, they clammed up, and Maria was scared."

"Mac, did you save that picture?"

"Yes, I did."

"Can you text it to me? We may be able to use our technology to enhance the resolution and read the plate. It's a lead we don't have yet."

"I'll do it right now, Colonel. I'd like to know more about the guys in that truck myself."

"Mac, Morgan is tight-lipped about some of your 'adventures,' shall we say, but I know that you have been involved in solving some dangerous situations for people, and I know that you can handle yourself. But these are killers, Mac. If the Rodriguez boys are linked in any way to them, and if they ask you to help them, please let us take care of it. That is our job."

"Colonel, I have two houses to finish before winter, and I am helping good friends in New York. I am not looking for trouble with killers armed with big guns. I promise I will keep you informed."

"Thank you, Mac. Investigator Beaulieu will text you her contact info, so please coordinate anything you have with her."

"I certainly will, sir. Goodbye."

**

4:00 p.m.

"Hello!" Mac called out, knocking at the cottage door. 'Rowrf!' replied Buddy.

"Come in, Mac, come in!" called Harry.

Marybeth was sitting at the kitchen table playing cards with Harry. Her three labradoodles were lying on the floor surrounding Bella.

"Well, this looks cozy! What do you think Harry? Will this work for you?"

"Man, this is 'puttin' on the Ritz,' as we used to say in my youth! I'll be spoiled! And I told Marybeth, I am paying for all of this hospitality."

"Harry," Marybeth said, "I told you not to worry about it. We can discuss it later."

"No, we are going to clear this up right now. Nurse Kincaid went to your website, and we saw your elder care cottage, which is fabulous, and the $3,750 per month rate with all meals and utilities and everything included. That is ridiculously low, Marybeth. I did some internet searching while I was in the hospital because they said they were going to send me to a nursing home to recuperate. Do you know the average monthly cost for a nursing home is $12,000 in Buffalo?"

"Harry," said Marybeth, "first of all, this is not a nursing home, and second, you're a friend. I'm not trying to make a profit on you. I just want you to be comfortable and get well. And I am not charging you $3,750 per month, either. We'll discuss that later."

"Marybeth, I have two kinds of insurance. Medicare, which can cover this cost, I am sure, but also private insurance for long-term care. Never used it, been paying for it for 20 years! So you just give me the bills, and I will get you paid. It will give me something to do, and I always pay my way. If you don't agree then I'm goin' home and make Pops take care of me! Hah!"

"No, you are not, you scoundrel!" Marybeth said with a twinkle in her eye. "OK, we'll do it your way. But Mac and I just wanted you to be here, safe and comfortable with me."

"I just wanted to see Bella," said Mac. "If you leave her here, you can go live with Pops in your drafty old house in Conneaut."

"HA HA HA! Mac, you are shrewd, you are. And you too, Marybeth. Thank you both, from the bottom of my old heart, for taking me in and for getting me away from that old bat, Nurse Kincaid!"

"OK, guys," Marybeth said, "Pops called a little while ago and said he was going to be arriving between 7 and 8 p.m., so I will be holding supper until he gets here. That means you might like a snack on the back porch in half an hour, correct?"

"Man, I figured it would take him 12 hours. How can he be here by 8 p.m.?" said Mac.

"Easy, he left at 7:30 a.m., as soon as I called him. He wasn't gonna wait for the come-ahead sign from Harry. He was gonna come no matter what."

"Great," said Harry. "I'll have someone to play double solitaire."

Marybeth said, "And Ginger will be so glad to see her buddy Bella. It's going to be just like Thanksgiving with all the family coming home."

Suddenly, she burst into tears, turned, and ran out of the cottage.

"Did I say something to make her cry, Mac?" said Harry.

"No, Harry, Marybeth is very sensitive. Two years ago, she lost both her parents and her husband to a killer. She has been running the B & B to keep from thinking about it. Then, we all came into her life and turned everything upside down. Now, we are her family. Everyone who sat on that back porch in August, they are now her family."

"And she has always wanted that. She never had children, but now she has a new family, and she is crying because they are all coming home to her. You broke your hip, Harry, that's bad, but you coming to stay with Marybeth while I am working in New Hampshire is the best thing that could happen to her. C'mon Harry, I'll play you double solitaire and wait for Pops to arrive."

**

7:30 p.m.

Pops walked in the back porch, and it was Old Home Day, and Thanksgiving rolled into one. Marybeth gave him a big hug, Mac shook his hand, Buddy danced, and Bella and Ginger chased each other in circles. Harry was the happiest of all to have his pal here. He could not stop smiling.

Over dinner, Pops regaled them with the story of the night he plucked Mac off a log in freezing waters after Tim Riley knocked him overboard and left him three miles off shore. And then he told them of the mess he found at his log cabin.

"It seems amazing," said Pops. "It's been 47 years since I built that cabin. I was 38 and just out of the Navy. I didn't know anyone in that little mountain town. I just saw the sign 'lots for sale,' and talked to this old feller who was selling cabins like his, so I bought one and built it with his son. It's been good, but I ain't ever lived there year-round. This summer rental has been good income, but the cabin is about ready for a new roof, the kitchen could stand an update, and my housekeeper wants to retire. Retire? I tell her, you're only 65, and I'm 85! Hah! Problem is, if she retires, I have to find another housekeeper, and folks don't seem to want to do that anymore."

"Pops," said Mac, "what would you like to do if you had your 'druthers'?"

"You know Mac, the two weeks you were here last summer were the happiest I have been in many years. I know, I know, you stirred up a hornet's nest, nearly got yourself and Marybeth killed, caught a murderer, and generally caused a lotta mayhem. But it was fun bein' a part of it! And Marybeth's cooking! It was like family, Mac. I don't know exactly what I want to do, but I know I don't have many summers left, and I sure enjoyed this last one with you guys."

"Pops, do you think it's time to sell your cabin?" asked Marybeth.

"Marybeth, I been thinkin' about that too. I got summer renters who want to buy it, so I wouldn't have trouble selling. And if I did, I wouldn't have to fix the roof and kitchen and a dozen little things. And I wouldn't have the worry of bein' a landlord. But, other than my boat here in summer, and my old RV at Daytona Beach, I got no place to call home if I sell. It's too damn hot to live in Daytona, and the Bertram is good, but you can't live on a boat here in winter. I don't know what I'd do. I'll say this: if I had a nice little cottage here like yours, then I could see my pal, Harry, see you and mooch your cooking now and then, maybe visit old friends in Westfield. I think that would be great.

"And Bella and Ginger could see each other as often as they like. Yes sir, Mac, I think I just answered your question. And by golly, Marybeth, that was the best meal I've had since I left Barcelona Harbor. Danged if you aren't half the reason I came back, that and to house sit for Harry. When you called, my heart just leaped at the chance to come home."

Marybeth leaned over and gave Pops a big hug and kiss.

"We are family now, guys. We are the survivors of Mac Morrison's summer crusade against evil here in Barcelona Harbor, and it has made us a family. We have to think about how to keep the family together. And, on that note, guys, I am going to leave you old pals to talk while Mac and I clear the table."

**

**10:30 p.m.
Captain Murphy B & B
Master Bedroom**

"Mac, I'm thinking about closing the B & B."

"Really! When did this all come about, M?"

"The day you left in August. But after today, with Harry and Pops and all of you here, I have an idea, and I know we could do it together."

"OK, I'm listening."

"The cottage is the key. Everyone loves the cottage. It's the perfect size. One story, no steps, everything a retired person would need and nothing he or she wouldn't. Mac, I'm tired of being at the beck and call of fifteen hundred guests a year. With an average length of stay of 1.6 days, I am cleaning five suites, stripping beds, making beds, and doing laundry on a daily basis. I'm a hotel with gourmet food. But at the rates I charge, I barely break even.

"I don't even pay myself a salary. I've been living off Jim's pension for the past two years. The B & B income pays housing expenses and my costs of operation. I can't raise my rates because of competition from on-line vacation rentals, many of which are illegal. They are not zoned commercial, so they don't pay commercial property taxes like I do. And they don't pay sales or bed taxes because they are flying under the radar until they get caught. It's unfair competition, and worse, those temporary rentals are taking housing out of the market for young people who are trying to buy.

"And then I met you, Mac. I just want us to be together. So here's my idea. You are a builder. I have five acres. I want you to build me an elder village of four more cottages on a half-acre behind the B & B. That would leave four acres behind my fence line in grapes. I rent that. My land is zoned commercial, so the rental units are permitted.

"My cottage is my model for the village. If we made it a one-bedroom instead of two, added a front porch and an attached garage it would be perfect senior housing. There is nothing like it anywhere near here, Mac. We could invite Harry, Pops, and maybe even old Sol to come and be part of our extended family. I would look after them like kin and cook for them, and not have to worry about when my next guest will arrive. So, I want you to build me four more cottages, Mac."

"How much income would you need to run that kind of business with five tenants, Marybeth?"

"I don't know yet. I will need to hire a full time staff person, but I could offer free housing and meals, so that person should not be too expensive. You run the numbers to see what you would charge me to build four cottages. Tomorrow, we will do a budget. OK? Now, I want your full attention, my love, and then I will let you sleep tonight."

"Yes, *Ma'am*!"

Chapter Seven

Thursday October 5
Murphy B & B
5:00 a.m.

With cottage plans and budget swirling in his head, Mac dressed quickly. He took Buddy and Emma for a walk and fed them.

His prototype cottage would be his *Morrison's Cabin Number 2*, a 672 square foot woods cabin that he had built a dozen times for hunters in New Hampshire. He had recently built one, so he knew his costs. He could add a one-car garage for $15,000 and a porch for $5,000. He would have to investigate the availability of public water and sewer at Marybeth's land.

Since he would not charge Marybeth *any profit* or for his *personal* labor, he figured he could build four cottages with utilities for $500,000. Paving and site work would add at least $50,000.

If she could make a $70,000 down payment and borrow $480,000, her mortgage costs would be $3,034/month for 30 years at 6.5%. Interest rates were high at the moment, but maybe they would go down before she committed to a loan. She had told him her mortgage on the B & B was $2,000 a month. So, she would need to cover $60,000 in combined annual mortgage costs.

Mac figured $90k salary for her and a staff person. If food cost her $100 per day, that would be $37k. He figured $25k for utilities and property taxes, plus $5k in supplies for cleaning and linens, and $5k for landscape and yard maintenance. The total annual costs to run the elder village and pay the mortgages would be $222,000.

Five cottages at $3,750 per month would yield $225,000 income. It was too tight, but with a larger down payment or lower finance costs, it could be doable.

He called up the online County Auditor's topographic base map, overlaid it with aerial photos, and printed it on Marybeth's printer. He drew in the location of the four new cottages around a quadrangle with connecting sidewalks and looped a driveway to feed all the garages from the rear, leaving a lovely green common in the middle for a peaceful view from each front porch.

And that would leave the cavernous house as a home for Marybeth and Mac.

**

6:00 a.m.

With that task handled, Mac prepared for his meeting with Sol and Sarah Lieberman. He went to Marybeth's laptop and began searching for a website that would describe the waterfront improvement plan for east Erie. Interestingly enough, it was not found under either the city, the county or metro park websites. He found it posted under "City County Basin Urban Transformation Triad," an unfortunate title that would make the ironic acronym of "CCBUTT." But if he added the word "and" after city and county, it would be CaCa BUTT, which any third grader knows means "poop."

"*What idiot put this plan together?*" Mac wondered.

As someone who had spent three years in the Army and built houses, Mac was naturally skeptical of anything that smacked of a "master plan," and with good reason.

Military plans were not made by the men who fired the first shot, and everything always changed after that first shot.

And, community master plans were rarely well enough parsed to result in a beautiful, well-functioning, and environmentally sensitive city or town. No, they were usually the work of bright-eyed young people with minimal training and good intentions advising older volunteer citizen boards who might or might not have good intentions.

And as Mac well knew, the Road to Hell was paved with good intentions.

Mac was a student of history, so after bumping heads with such young, inadequately trained, and sometimes foolishly arrogant planners, he had studied the history of the planning profession. King Philip of Spain's 1565 Spanish Law of the Indies yielded some of the most beautiful early American cities like Savannah, Georgia, and St. Augustine, Florida. But Robert Moses' "master plans" for New York had the collateral effect of destroying minority neighborhoods and cultural heritage. And yet, one hundred years later, similar "master plans" still made the same mistakes.

So yes, Mac was very skeptical as he read the "poopy butt" plan for redevelopment of the eastern shore of Erie's lakefront. This looked like another case of "doing good" by taking from one and giving to another because, as he quickly surmised, the "poopy butt" plan would be doing just that.

Oh, he had no doubt that the park aspect of it was a very desirable public purpose, and for the residents of the immediate environs, it would be a cleaner, quieter use than a metals scrap yard. But what about the parts of the plan that were not park land? The maps were vaguely drawn on purpose, since they did not want to identify property lines and proposed uses because that would reveal whose ox was being gored and whose was being fattened. And in so doing could reveal an illegal "taking" without just compensation.

Mac knew his limitations in looking at all this. He was not an attorney, and certainly not a land use attorney. But he smelled a rat because someone was trying to screw his friend Sol Weinstein.

So, he mused, who were the members of the CCBUTT? He paged through the colorful website. There was a picture of CCBUTT's first *invitational meeting.* There were titles and names under the faces in the group photo of County Commissioners, Metro Parks Staff, and ...who dat?

Here was a familiar face! Was that... yes, the caption said it was...Mace Wilkins! The very same guy who had bought murderous Joey Minetti's boat, the *Deadly Serious*!

How the Hell, Mac wondered, was Mace Wilkins from Ashtabula, Ohio, a member of CCBUTT in Erie, Pennsylvania, 40 miles up the coast? Maybe it had to do with his boat and the fact that he had friends at the yacht club? That was where Pops and Mac and Roger had trailed him last May. He had been showing off the *Deadly Serious* to his friends in Erie. OK, there was the answer. It said that Mace Wilkins was a representative of the Greater Area Sailing & Boating Affiliates Group (GASBAG).

Mac was laughing, and then frowning, because the thumb of the peninsula that included Sol Weinstein's scrap yard was not colored green for public parkland. No, Sol's five acres seemed to be proposed for one acre of parkland, one acre of marina, and three acres of waterfront luxury condominiums.

Dark blue on the plan designated future marina, docks, and storage buildings for concierge boat racks. Mac knew that on the Boston waterfront, some people paid $50,000 to buy a hole in the air where their boat would be racked and stored until they called to have it placed in the water. A 200' long steel building with two levels of racks could easily accommodate 80 boats, and one acre of land could accommodate two such buildings. Not including dock value, 160 racks alone could be worth $8 million.

It would be hard to argue *that* was a public purpose.

Moving on to the dark brown color, the waterfront condominiums were designated as luxury housing at twenty units per acre. That would be 60 units on three acres. If the condos fetched at least $400,000, that was a $24,000,000 project.

And that was *certainly not* a public purpose.

Yes, Mac smelled a big fuckin' rat. He kept reading until he found a credit that said the plan was paid for by a grant from B & W Futures, LLC. The internet did not list any such organization. Maybe Sarah Lieberman could track it down, but for the moment, he figured there had to be another way.

It was eight a.m., and Marybeth was calling him to breakfast. He made a phone call to Mars and Hollister, Planning Associates, who had compiled the master plan. In a two-minute conversation with a bubbly staff intern, he got the answer. B & W were well known in Erie as Billy Barnes, the 'Condo King' and Mace Wilkins.

Interesting. He sent all of this information to Marybeth's printer, grabbed the copies, and said good morning to Pops, Harry, and Marybeth. He gave her the site plan for her senior cottages, kissed her on the cheek, and excused himself to get on the road, taking Buddy and Emma with him.

While driving, he called Jonetta Pope to ask where Wilkins' boat, *Mace's Mistress,* had been picked up. She said it had been at the B &W Boat Club in Ashtabula, and she gave him the location. He logged the address into his phone and then asked it for directions.

**

B & W Boat Club
Ashtabula, Ohio
35 miles southwest of Erie, PA
9:00 a.m.

The B & W Boat Club was located on the back side of Wilkins Scrap Yard. Mac could see trucks being unloaded with wooden bins. He did not see a shredder or magnetic sorter like Sol had at the Banks yard. There was a car crusher. Crushed cars were being placed on rail cars for a short haul to the end of a private pier for shipment by freighter.

The gate was locked, but there was a bell, so Mac rang it. While he waited for someone to respond, he whipped out his cellphone and snapped some pictures from the street.

A big guard in an ill-fitting uniform came out of a shack. He unfolded his 4x frame as he ducked under the doorway. Stooped over, he was well over six feet. When he stood straight up, he added six inches. He was a bit paunchy, like a beer drinker with a layer of hard fat over harder muscle. He moved like a fighter, and his nose implied it. He was late thirties with a nasty expression and a bad haircut sticking out from under his shiny-billed cap.

"Hey!" he yelled, "No pictures!" His shirt patch read 'Herman'.

"Are you talking to me, Herman?" Mac said.

"Management don't allow pictures. You should know to ask." Then he snorted "Ah-eeee" like a donkey. It sounded like he had a nasal obstruction. His deformed nose pretty much confirmed it. Someone had punched him hard; it never got straightened, and now his deviated septum meant he had a breathing problem.

"Sorry," said Mac, "I'm standing on a public street, so I didn't think to ask. But I'll put the camera away, OK?"

"Well, OK. I'm just doin' my job. Whattaya want?"

"I just stopped to say Hi to Mace. He bought a boat from a guy I knew. Met him at the boat club. I was in the area, so I thought maybe he'd be around."

"Nah, his boat got towed away by the cops, and they didn't say why. It's getting late in the season, so he may put it up for winter whenever they bring it back."

"Business must be good. That was a nice boat."

"I'd say he does OK, but he's gonna do better when they close down his competition."

"Oh? I hadn't heard," said Mac.

"No? The city's gonna buy up a lotta land on the east end of the Erie waterfront. The Banks scrap yard will be a park, marina, and condos. Big fuckin' deal. B & W Boat Club can move outta this mud hole and go over there. Wilkins and Barnes should do all right. They're sharp, those two."

"Sounds like it. Well, thanks, guess I'll shove off."

"Should I tell Mace you stopped by?"

"No, I'd like to surprise him. See ya."

**

Erie, PA
Banks Breakers and Scrap,
10:00 a.m.

The first rule of business is: be on time.

And Sarah Lieberman was.

When Mac drove through the gate, the crusher was crushing, the grinder was grinding and the giant drag line with the huge magnet was moving scrap from finished piles to rail cars. It was organized cacophonic chaos.

But not inside Sol's blue building. Sarah and Sol looked like granddaughter and grandad, laughing and clinking their coffee cups as Mac walked in with Buddy and Emma. Sol smiled his one good tooth and jumped up to embrace Mac. Buddy offered Sol his paw, and Sol shook it. Emma jumped up into his arms to say hello, and Sol almost melted, his face just beaming.

Buddy offered Sarah his paw, and she shook it. Mac introduced the dogs. Both Sol and Sarah had passed the Buddy test, so it was time to get down to business.

"Mackenzie," said Sol, "vee just having kuchen. Sarah is telling me lies how smart she is, und how she kick ass in court."

"Sarah, I am pleased to meet you", said Mac. "After what I've learned this morning, I think we will need to kick ass, but I think you will do it before we ever get into a courtroom."

"Oh? Do tell!" she said with a wink.

As Mac munched a chunk of kuchen and gulped steaming coffee, Sarah read over the printouts, frowning as she listened to the gossip Mac gathered from the B & W Boat Club cop.

"So," she said, "Condo King Billy Barnes and Scrap King Mace Wilkins have a plan to close down the Banks scrap yard via a pseudo-public improvement project, which is a Trojan horse for commercial marine storage and high-end waterfront condos. They would be hard pressed to say in court that they should be allowed to take Mr. Weinstein's land by eminent domain proceedings for that kind of re-use. This CCBUTT plan does not pass the smell test. It's not a public body with the power to use eminent domain. I would doubt their attorneys would ever attempt it.

"No, Mac, I think what we have here is an 'aspirational' plan, drawn up and funded by a dummy corporation hiding Barnes and Wilkins, who would finance the private portion of the redevelopment and keep it for themselves - if they can get Sol's land. That letter Sol got from the city of Erie was not from the City Council or the Mayor. It was from Mars and Hollister, Planning Consultants, on their letterhead. Somehow, they got a city envelope to send it. Not illegal, but slimy. And, the letter does not threaten the use of eminent domain, but it hints that private property like Sol's can be obtained by eminent domain for a public purpose. That is clever wording.

"They are fishing, Sol. If we respond, they'll make a lowball offer. If they can get your land under contract, then they can go to the city and county to partner up, and the parkland can be acquired either by private sale or eminent domain. And it would all be legal.

"Yes," Sarah concluded, "what we have here, in this letter, is an offer to negotiate. They want to buy you out, Sol, but they are bluffing that they can use eminent domain if you won't sell at the price they offer."

"Sol," said Mac. "This boils down to one question. What do you want to do? Don't think about a price if you sell. Leave that up to Sarah. You are 85 years old. Life has been hard. What do you want to do with the time you have left?"

The tough old man hugged little Emma in his lap and bobbed his head left and right like he was ducking punches in a prize fight, weighing options in his mind.

"OK, Mac, I remember Barcelona Harbor 30 years ago. Marybeth says it has not changed. Good, because it vas qviet, so qviet. Here, so noisy all day long, vit da crusher and da grinder. I vould like some peace and qviet by da lake. I vould like to see you, Mackenzie, and Marybeth. You gonna be like my family if you let me. Mac, talk to your pretty lady Marybeth and see vould she like me to be a neighbor. Dat is vat I vould like. I gotta bring my cars. Dey are my family too."

"I am sure Marybeth will say yes, Sol, but we can discuss it over dinner tomorrow night in Barcelona Harbor. Pops Rodgers will pick you up at 5:00 p.m. and drive you to Marybeth's house. You will be staying overnight."

"Meanwhile," said Sarah, "I'm going to follow up on this letter and do some checking with the city of Erie."

"OK, tank you both, my friends Sarah and Mackenzie. And Emma, I love you, Emma, baby."

**

Chapter Eight

Thursday October 5
Barcelona Harbor
Captain Murphy B & B
12:00 noon

Hubcap Harry and Pops were on the back porch reading yesterday's newspaper, purloined from Todd's Gas N Go, when Mac pulled back the wooden screen door with a "gronk" of the rusty spring.

"Mac," said Harry, "me and Pops have been talking."

"Uh-oh," said Mac, rubbing Buddy's head, picking up Emma and placing her in his lap. The three of them sat on the couches farthest from the kitchen.

"Marybeth says she is serious about building four more cottages," said Harry.

"She is," said Mac.

"Same layout as the one I'm in?"

"Better. Yours is 720 square feet and has two bedrooms. These would be 672 square feet with one bedroom, a larger living, eating, and kitchen area facing front, overlooking a full-width, Chalet-style covered front porch. With the attached garage, you would have a total of 1064 square feet under roof.

"There would be no steps, a fully equipped galley kitchen, and a stackable washer dryer in the bathroom with a walk-in shower. Lots of windows. Super-insulated with hydronic radiators and mini-split AC. A sidewalk would connect each cottage to the Murphy house, where you would take all your meals. Guys, I've built this cottage a dozen times. Look at these pictures on my phone."

They did, and they liked what they saw.

"Mac, is there enough room for four more cottages on this lot?" Harry asked.

"Yes. Marybeth owns five acres. They would be placed in the vineyard behind the B & B. There will be a private yard around each cottage, with a place for your own garden. A looped driveway will circle a quadrangle with two cabins on each side facing inward and the existing cottage being at the head of the table, so to speak."

"Do you think she can provide the cottage, all utilities, cable, Wi-Fi, internet, meals, cleaning and linens, plus a garage for $3,750 a month?"

"I think she can. The only cost we don't know is mortgage rates but I figured 6.5% for 30 years, which is the current rate. And the Auditor can tell us her taxes while we work out a real budget."

"Mac," said Pops, "my cabin and Harry's house are paid for. They both need a new roof, which is gonna cost $15-20,000. We figure our current costs for maintenance, lawn care, property tax, food, insurance, utilities, and cable are about $2,700 a month. So, $3,750 is a lot of money. If we were younger, it would not be affordable. But how much longer will we live? We can both sell our houses and invest the money and with our pensions and Social Security, we could probably live like kings here until we die."

"And have a pal next door," Harry chimed in. "If we lived here, we could walk across the street to Todd's Gas N Go, stroll the beach, and fish at the pier. You walk outside your own little house and smell the flowers in Marybeth's garden. And it's quiet here, not like the busy road in front of my house. Sounds like a good deal, Mac."

"It is a good deal, guys. I've done some research on senior apartments." He showed them a picture on his phone of a three-story complex in the Buffalo suburbs.

"Look at this. Rent with meals starts at $2,600. You know the food quality wouldn't be as good as Marybeth's. Tenants pay their own utilities, cable, and internet, so add $400 per month, and you are at $3,000 for 720 square feet in a three-story building with people living on all sides of you.

"Only ground floor units, which cost extra, have a tiny porch. There are no garages, so cars sit outside in the snow. Shared laundry facilities serve a building with 100 people. All units are accessed by interior hallways. Exterior doors are always locked. Units only have windows on one wall. Small pets are allowed, but there is an extra charge. And, there are rules: lots and lots of rules, three pages of rules on their website."

"Jeezuz," said Pops, "that sounds like a fuckin' prison, Mac."

"Mac," said Harry, "me and Pops would be interested in two cottages."

"Well, I have another gent your age, a classic car guy who Pops is going to pick up tomorrow night and bring here for dinner. I have not told him about Marybeth's cottage idea, but he is thinking of selling his business in Erie and moving to Barcelona Harbor. Maybe he would consider joining us. He has a fabulous collection of 1950s and 60's GM cars that he wants to move with him."

"What's that you said, Mac?" Marybeth shouted from the kitchen. "Sol wants to move to Barcelona Harbor? And he wants to bring his cars?"

"That's what he said. Everybody loves you, Marybeth, and once Sol tastes your cooking, you'll never get him to leave."

"Mac, remember I asked you if his blue building could be moved?"

"Yes, I knew you were scheming, M. You are starting to think like me," said Mac.

"I know. Scary, isn't it? But what do you think? Could it work?"

"Sure, it could work, but you are not paying to move Sol's building and his cars, M."

"No, but if he sells his business he would have plenty of money to pay for that himself. He could buy a piece of my vineyard for his building."

"Let's discuss it over dinner tomorrow night. He asked me to ask you if you would like him as a neighbor."

"He did? Mac, that's fabulous! Pops, Harry, I think you might have another car guy pal in the future!"

'Rowrf', said Buddy. 'Rarf', said Emma.

∗∗

12:15 p.m.

Mac's phone buzzed. He walked outside to take the call. (*Morgan Hillman*.)

"Yah, Morg, what's up?"

"State Police crime lab confirms that Wilkins' boat, formerly Minetti's boat *Deadly Serious,* is a match for the dent and the vinyl wrap on Jim Murphy's fishing boat. They dissolved the glue on the red vinyl stuck to the underside of Minetti's bow cleat, removed it, and laid it flat. When it dried, it fit perfectly into the tear on the Murphy boat's red wrap. Even the partial graphics lined up. It's a total match. And when the boats were floated in the water, the bow cleat matches the dent on the side of Murphy's boat.

"Minetti's boat hit Murphy's boat, for sure. Can't say when, but with Pops and Tim Riley's deposition, we know that Joey Minetti was out on the lake in his boat *Deadly Serious* at the time of Jim Murphy's death, and Pops witnessed the long scrape on its hull when it came back into port. The repaired scrape line on Minetti's boat lines up with the gunwale metal rail on Murphy's boat, and we already knew the black gel coat on Murphy's gunwale was the same gel coat as on Minetti's boat. We got him, Mac. We got him."

"Wow, Morgan. What happens next?"

"A State Assistant Attorney General has already notified me that the Coroner's Jury will reconvene. Murphy's body will be dug up, and a new autopsy will be performed. It really doesn't matter if he drowned or suffocated or died of head trauma, Mac. Dead is dead, and Jim Murphy died as a result of Minetti's boat striking him. Pending the outcome of the Coroner's Jury, I will seek a posthumous indictment from the Grand Jury for murder one against Joey Minetti for Jim Murphy's death, just like we did for Marybeth's parents. Once we have that directed verdict, I will sue the estate of Joey Minetti for ten million dollars in compensatory and punitive damages in Jim's death."

"Great work, Morgan."

"Mac, it was your work and persistence that paid off."

"It was the team, as usual, Morgan, always the team. OK, I'm gonna break this news to Marybeth as 'if-come' findings because this is still speculation until the court rules, and then you still have to get a court order on damages, correct?"

"Correct. But we will win on both cases now, Mac."

"Lunch!" called Marybeth.

"In a minute, M," Mac called out. "Morgan, did the State Police interview Paco and the boys this morning?"

"Yes, and I don't like it, Mac. They have a perfect alibi for the time of death in the Ascutney murder, but they know something and are not being forthcoming. They're scared. Investigator Jaqueline Beaulieu may be young, but she is sharp, and she sensed it too."

"Did the State Police read the license plate in my picture of the black Suburban?"

"Mac, they got a partial, but the sun glare was too harsh to read it all.

Investigator Beaulieu questioned Paco and his brothers about that truck, and they claim they don't know. They only said it could be their jobber, but they could not say for sure."

"Their jobber?"

"Yes. They had been using a jobber named the Diaz Boyz, spelled with a 'Z,' who finds them work."

"Are the Diaz Boyz from Texas?"

"Yes. El Paso. And the Rodriguez family is from Juarez, just across the Rio Grande from El Paso. The Diaz Boyz are actually two brothers who are part of a group that finds farm jobs in the U.S. for migrant workers. Then they help Mexicans get work permits through a Texas human resources and payroll firm to work those jobs. It sounds legitimate, but Bisbee kept good records, and there was one thing that did not jibe."

"What's that, Morgan?'

"According to farmer Bisbee's records, he paid the Diaz Boyz a 15% finder's fee upfront *in cash*. No legitimate business transaction is done in cash. And he contracted for *three weeks of work* by the Rodriguez brothers. But farmer Bisbee only paid the jobber's Texas HR firm for *two weeks wages*. The HR firm did the withholdings and paid the workers electronically."

"Wait a minute, Morgan. So, are you saying that the employer, like Bisbee, would be a sponsor for migrant labor and pay them their wages through an HR firm and also pay a finder's fee to their jobber?"

"Correct."

"So Paco and his brothers did not get paid directly by Bisbee."

"Correct. They got paid electronically by the Texas HR firm."

"Morgan, do you remember I told you the boys showed up one week early to work for me?"

"I do."

"Well, if they left after only two weeks, but their jobber contracted with them for three, that black Suburban could be their jobber looking for them."

"Then why are they scared to identify the truck?"

"Think about it, Morgan. If they left one week early, maybe Bisbee demanded a refund on his upfront cash referral. Maybe he threatened to never use the jobber's services again unless he got that refund. Maybe the Diaz Boyz are looking for the Rodriguez brothers to get paid back for that refunded cash."

"Mac, are you suggesting the Diaz brothers murdered Bisbee over a cut of one week's pay for three farm workers? That would not be a lot of money. It doesn't seem like a good motive."

"I don't know, but if I were Investigator Beaulieu, I would want to find the Diaz Boyz and question them because they obviously had an encounter with Bisbee."

"It's a thought, Mac. I'll pass it along. I gather you did *not* make a good first impression on the young lady State Police Investigator."

Mac snorted. "You know how I am with chippy authority figures, Morgan."

"I do. When will you be back in Sunapee?"

"Saturday night."

"I'll see you then, Mac."

**

Thursday October 5
Dewittville, NY
Morrison cemetery, eastern shore of Chautauqua Lake
3:00 p.m.

"Mac," said Marybeth, as she helped him clean his parent's headstone, "when you walk past his gravestone, do you think about the hardships your great, great, great Grandfather Mackenzie Morrison must have suffered when he came to America in 1847?"

"No, M, I think about what an adventure it must have been. Can you imagine how wild and pristine this landscape must have been? And how huge the open spaces must have seemed to a young man from the Scottish Low Country, where thousand-year-old villages were spaced a half day's donkey cart ride apart? To look out over Lake Erie from the top of the escarpment would have been like gazing from the bluffs of Kirkcudbright over the Irish Sea. I would have loved to be with him then."

"The adventurer still rustles in your soul, Mac. You're a builder, a minstrel, a kind helper, and a dangerous avenger when your heart is stirred. Your grandfather Mackenzie would recognize it in your eyes in an instant, my love. I just hope I can keep your feet under my quilts and not lose you to the adventures that always find you."

"M, I would be happy if I could be the builder, the minstrel, the mate to you, and father to Gabriella for the rest of my life. That would be enough."

"Ah, you are a terrible liar, Mackenzie Morrison, for I have seen how alive you are when you and Roger were on the hunt."

"And why are you telling me this, M?"

"Because it's happening again, I can see it in your eyes and your movements. You're fidgety. Something is stirring within you. You are ready to spring like a lion upon your next prey. Buddy senses it, too. Look at him lying next to you with his head on a swivel. He is scanning the horizon for your next threat. Tell me what is happening, Mac."

"I feel there is trouble brewing in New Hampshire with my three Mexican workers, M. Not for something they did, but for something they didn't do. And it could lead back to the murder of the farmer they worked for in Vermont. They didn't kill him. I know that because they were with me the day it happened. But they worked for him last May before they came to work for me. Morgan is sure there is something they are not telling the State Police. Or him."

"Morgan is involved? Have they been arrested and charged? Are they suspects, Mac?"

"No, but they know something. Roger hired Morgan to represent them when they were questioned by a State Police Investigator. I met her. She is young but smart, and she knows they have information that could help her, but they are holding back. I might have a lead, and I passed it on to Morgan to give to the Investigator. The head of the New Hampshire State Police, Colonel Trammel Bradford, asked me personally to stay out of this and let them handle it, and I as much as told him I would. But I have to get back there and make sure they are not in danger, so I'll be leaving first thing Saturday morning, M."

"Well, I get two more nights with you, and while you are gone, I will plan my beautiful elder village that you drew up for me."

"M, don't get your hopes up yet, but you may be getting a large damage award from the estate of Joey Minetti. And if you do, you will be able to build your elder village and not borrow a dime. Let me tell you what has happened."

**

Return to Barcelona Harbor

Thursday October 5
4:00 p.m.

Of course, Marybeth was right. Mac *was* antsy. His Spidey sense *was* tingling. He needed to be back in New Hampshire. He should go now, today, this minute. His work here was done. Hubcap Harry was safely out of the hospital and in Marybeth's cottage. Pops Rodgers had safely arrived from Tennessee and would be house-sitting Harry's place in Conneaut.

But now he had to help Sol. Having exposed a conspiracy to screw him out of his land and business, Mac had been fortunate to hire competent Sarah Lieberman and her high-powered law firm to castrate the bastards. And, maybe she could get a good price for Sol's land so he could retire in peace to Barcelona Harbor.

He couldn't leave before their Friday night dinner, but there was something he could do while he was still here.

He pulled out his cellphone and punched the speed dial. Colonel Trammel Bradford himself answered.

"Mac Morrison, what can I do for you?"

"Colonel Bradford, Sir, I expected this line would be answered by a secretary or perhaps a Lieutenant. Sorry to call you directly."

"Mac, nothing is more important to me right now than catching the Bisbee killers. Did you have some information for us?"

"Maybe a lead, Sir."

"I'm all ears. Go ahead, Mac."

Max explained the link between the Diaz Boyz, their cash finder's fee, and the victim Bisbee's murder.

"Colonel, maybe the Diaz Boyz went back to see Bisbee, and he wound up dead. But would that have occurred four months later? I don't know, but we know Diaz had a relationship with Bisbee.

"It's October, apple harvesting season. What about having your investigators check with all the apple orchards in Vermont and New Hampshire to see if any of them use the Diaz brothers? Farm Bureau could give you a list of the growers. If growers have pickers in the orchards now, Diaz will be visiting the growers to get their cash finder's fee. You could grab them when they show up to get paid."

"Mac, we should have thought of that. I could find a spot for you as a special investigator if you get tired of building cabins and helping unfortunate widows. Morgan told me something about your last adventure in New York."

"Then maybe you know that I not only helped the pretty widow Murphy but she's got me on a short leash. No Sir, I like my life just fine at the moment, but I am privileged to have you on speed dial, Sir, and if you don't mind, I will call you again if I feel I can help you.

"Anytime, Mac, and thank you for the tip."

**

Dewittville, NY
Betty Wilson's Bar B Ranch
5:00 p.m.

"Mrs. Wilson," said Mac, "I think I remember how to saddle a horse, but I'm sure I've forgotten how to ride. It's been 32 years since I last rode a horse here as a Bar B counselor, so take it slow at first, please."

She laughed and pointed to his cinch.

"Mac, if you don't tighten that, you'll be on the ground before we get out of the corral. Marybeth knows how to saddle a horse."

"M, have you been holding out on me?" said Mac.

"HA! Of course! I've been riding here since I was a kid. We picked Baby for you, Mac."

"Why Baby?"

"She knows you are nervous, so she will baby you until you gain confidence. When she does, you better hang on because she'll run when we come out of the trees into the meadow."

"I remember that cantering is easy," said Mac, "but I might be a chicken and hang onto the saddle horn if she gallops."

"No, don't do that, Mac," said Betty. "Grip her flanks with your knees and put your weight on your stirrups. Get your fanny an inch off the saddle, crouch over her neck, and Baby will run for you."

"You're not worried she might stumble and toss me on my head?"

"Not a bit. Baby is a descendant of the rare Camarillo white horse. Her sire was a Morgan. She is so sure-footed she leads our night rides. She won't *pitch* you off, Mac, but if you're rough with her, she'll head for the nearest tree and *scrape* you off!"

"So, be nice to Baby," Marybeth laughed. "C'mon Mac mount up."

"Betty, is it OK if my dog Buddy runs with us?"

"Of course! The horses are used to the ranch dogs, so long as he stays clear of their hooves."

"Don't worry about Buddy. He can take care of himself."

The Bar B consisted of 50 acres of woods, meadows, and corrals. Betty Wilson took the lead, walking the horses thru the narrow woods path. She trotted as the path widened, then cantered as they entered a large corral. She cantered three times around the corral, watching Mac to make sure he was up off the saddle and working with the horse.

He was.

She led the ride out of the corral back into the woods. Marybeth passed her at a canter and took the lead through a winding trail with overhanging branches showing splashes of fall color. Mac was concentrating on not getting whacked in the face, so he crouched low over Baby's neck.

As soon as they came out of the woods into the big meadow, Baby broke into a full gallop and raced to the front of the pack. Buddy was barking happily and running by her side. Mac got his ass an inch off the saddle, put his weight on his feet in the stirrups, and let her have her head. He was doing well until his sneakers slipped out of the stirrups, and his ass bounced up and down on the saddle. He had to grab the horn and slow down. Marybeth was looking back and laughing at him. He was, for once, not in control, and she was enjoying it. Baby let him get his rhythm back, and she cantered for him, but he knew she was in charge.

They ran for half a mile, and then Betty led them back into the home corral. Soon, they were back in the barn with the sweet smells of leather, hay, and oats.

Buddy ran to a water bowl and took a long drink, then came and sat by Mac as he unsaddled Baby. Marybeth showed him how to brush her down and let her drink from the trough before she was turned out to pasture with the other two horses.

"Well, Mac, did it all come back to you?" Marybeth asked.

"No. Well, some of it did, M. Having been a camper for six summers, I think I knew how to ride way back when. But I'm not gonna lie: today I was terrible! But it was fun!"

"Great. Now, let's head back home. I've got three men to cook for!"

**

Captain Murphy B & B
10:00 p.m.

Pops wheeled Hubcap Harry out to the cottage and helped him into bed, then returned to the main house. He bid Mac and Marybeth goodnight before retiring to the downstairs suite. Mac and Marybeth locked up the big Victorian ship Captain's house and went upstairs to their third-floor master suite. The five dogs followed them and found their places in their five beds that Marybeth laid out for them. They would start the night on the floor, but by morning, Marybeth's three Labradoodles, Buddy, and Emma, would be cuddled around them on the big king-sized bed with a view of Barcelona Harbor.

"Mac," she said, tracing her fingernail across his jaw where a scar was hidden on the underside, "is this starting to feel like home to you?"

"Hmm, trick question, M. So, I'm gonna say this. Being with you in your big Victorian house in Barcelona Harbor feels like home. Being with you in my New Hampshire cabin, even though it is still not finished, feels like home. In both cases, 'home is where the heart is,' isn't it?"

"Mac, every time I think I have you lassoed and tied up in my barn, you slip the halter and run away."

"No, I do not. You know you've had my heart since our dance at the shake shack last May. You got me, but if you're trying to make me choose between here versus there, meaning my home in New Hampshire, I choose not to choose. I simply choose to be with you as often as I can, but I will always have one foot in two worlds. I would like you to move between those worlds with me so we can go together as much as we can. It would be perfect if we could include Gabriella in that world, but she is 25 and in Colorado. I know that young people go to Colorado and never come back. So, I have to realize that she will make her own life out there, and I will see her when I can. But there is a hole in my heart whenever I leave her. Can you understand that?"

"Mac, having met Gabriella, I can absolutely understand. You have been her only parent for ten years. Her own mother turned her back on her, so you are her everything, at least until she finds a perfect partner."

"Marybeth, let's just choose to make a life for ourselves, both here and in New Hampshire."

"Agreed. Will you build my elder village next spring, Mac?"

"Yes, I will."

"Good, now guess what?"

"You want my undivided attention?"

"Correct. Turn out the light."

**

Chapter Nine

Friday October 6
Newbury Harbor, Lake Sunapee, NH
6:41 a.m.

The black Chevy Suburban drove slowly into Fisher's General Store. It backed into a parking space under a low-hanging hemlock tree, shut off its lights, but left its motor running. It was ten minutes before sunrise and already there was a golden glow on the southwest shore of Lake Sunapee.

The General Store was named after John Fisher, brother-in-law of then-Colonial-Governor John Wentworth, who in 1772 granted a plat for a settlement, the third such plat, the first two having been rescinded for failure to settle the land. The store was a quintessential New Hampshire relic, meaning it had been constructed entirely of locally sourced wood, with the typical narrow wood clapboard siding encrusted with layers of peeling white paint. The historic signpost out front said it was built in 1824, forty-eight years before the Concord and Claremont Railroad began bringing tourists to the clear waters of Lake Sunapee and the construction of summer houses and Inns began dotting the lake shore.

The square stately building had housed many uses over the years, including a tavern, a boarding house, and, some said, a bawdy house. Its boards and beams had sagged comfortably onto its stone foundation, much like the bottoms of the "comfort ladies" had once sagged comfortably on the barstools of the former ale house.

There was history in Newbury, lots of it, but none of it was of interest to the two brothers in the black suburban, Manuel "Manny" Diaz and his dim younger brother Raoul, or "Roofy" as Manny called him. Why Roofy? Because when he was very little, he could not say Raoul, but when the family dog barked, he would respond, "Roof-roof!" And so "Roofy" it was, especially when they all realized that Roofy was a bit goofy, not to say addle-brained, but not quite bright either.

Manny realized this first, and so his whole life, all twenty-five years of it, he had looked out for his younger brother. Roofy was now twenty-two. While Manuel was five foot six inches and skinny with a mean face like a rat, Roofy was six foot three inches and almost two hundred and twenty pounds with a pleasant, if vacant, look on his face. Roofy obeyed all commands from Manny, so they got along just fine.

The Diaz Boyz, as they called themselves, were actually an adjunct part to Los Locos, Louis Lopez' ragtag gang of three friends who had a penchant for violence on the streets of Juarez, Mexico. After some scrapes with the Juarez law, Los Locos had relocated to El Paso and begun looking for an economic niche to fill.

And they stumbled on it almost by accident.

Louis Lopez had been filling the gas tank on his beater Ford pickup one morning when he observed local ranchers driving up to the parking lot and shouting out a number. That was how many workers the rancher needed that day. There would always be a crowd of young men hanging around, so a mad scramble would ensue to jump into the back of the rancher's pickup truck for a day's cash.

To Louis, this seemed like a very primitive way for the ranchers to hire help. How did they know they were getting strong men who would work hard? How did the workers know how much they would be paid? And, of course, to be legal, they needed to have a paycheck with taxes withheld.

So Louis, who had done well in school, went to the library and studied. It seemed complicated, this working system. But then he saw a TV ad for a company called Hard Work and Payroll. Like their name implied, they handled Human Resources and payroll for small employers.

With the money he got from robbing a fat man at an ATM, Louis paid the company to show him how to set up his own contract labor business. He would go to the ranchers and ask them what kind of labor they needed, and then he would go to the gas station parking lot and choose the men best suited for the job.

He would use HWP, as he called them, to get work permits for the laborers. The ranchers would pay HWP; they would take a cut, pay Louis a cut, and then pay the laborers, all legal. They even got Social Security numbers for them.

The system worked well until thousands, and then millions of migrants started spilling over the US-Mexico Border. Suddenly, there were illegals willing to work under the table for next to nothing. Louis's legal laborers were not in demand. With too much competition, Louis knew the answer was to move his business north to new markets.

So he and his band of Locos fanned out over the fertile Midwest and into New England, constantly seeking labor-intensive farms like vineyards and orchards where the pay was better.

They also learned about a more lucrative business: human trafficking. The closer they got to the Canadian border, the more they started running into illegals coming across. These migrants came from many countries, and they had money to pay an agent who could smuggle them in and get them started.

So Los Locos turned their attention to this new business and turned over their established farm labor business to the Diaz brothers. It was a simple business. Stay between the lines, and everything was legal. Los Locos gave their farmer contacts to Manny Diaz, and he worked the system, paying HWP for every contract that he took. But Louis 'Loco' Lopez kept a close eye on the Diaz Boyz because he knew that Roofy was goofy and Manny was shifty.

So, when HWP called Louis Lopez to say the finder's fee was now being paid to them by the Diaz Boyz and not the farmers, Louis decided it was time to check things out. HWP also hadn't gotten paid by a farmer named Bisbee in Ascutney, Vermont for the third week contracted last May, despite several requests for late payment and no reply from Bisbee. Louis did not know that the Rodriguez brothers had left after only two weeks, which was why farmer Bisbee refused to pay HWP for work not done.

Louis Lopez told Manny Diaz to collect the money in person, but Bisbee still refused to pay. When Roofy roughed him up, Mrs. Bisbee heard the commotion and came running and put a load of birdshot in Roofy's pants, whereupon the Diaz boys hightailed it out of Ascutney.

But that was not the end of it. Louis 'Loco' Lopez could not have a failure to pay go unpunished, especially since Roofy Diaz had to have his ass mended, and there were medical costs now entering into this debacle. It was all Manny's fault, as far as Louis was concerned, so he gave Manny an ultimatum: pay the lost wages out of his own pocket or find another job.

Manny had paid Louis Lopez his money but swore he would get it back. While he worked the labor business over the summer months he searched for the Rodriguez boys, to no avail.

When apple picking season came, Manny and Roofy Diaz herded their laborers to New England, and it was there that they got a tip from a waitress at a Mexican restaurant in Concord, New Hampshire. She reported serving three brothers named Rodriguez who came in for dinner on a Saturday night. They had said they were working construction up near Sunapee.

But where near Sunapee? The waitress did not know. That area had a lot of rural roads with dense woods. It would be hard to find them by chance. So they started hanging out at gas stations early in the morning, hoping to see Paco gassing his truck.

But no luck, that is, until one Sunday, they passed a house being built way back off the road in the trees. There were young men helping an older man put up a roof. Manny cruised by, but they were too far away to see if it was Paco and his brothers. So they drove past again, stopped, and used a telephoto lens to take a picture. But a big man and his big dog came running at them and they did not get a clear picture before they had to jump in their Suburban and drive away.

So Manny called Louis Lopez and told him he might have a lead on the Rodriguez boys, and that they might be building a house near Sunapee, New Hampshire.

Building a house, Louis thought. That would be very good pay, much better than farm labor. And if they had been putting on the roof, they could have been working this good job for many weeks, perhaps all summer. That would be a lot of money they should have paid to Los Locos through HWP. But HWP had no record of any such payments, and Louis trusted HWP.

Louis did not trust Manny Diaz. He was barely competent, and Roofy was just goofy, that one. So Louis used his brain to think backwards and follow the money trail. He took his Locos and their driver Andrés down to Ascutney, Vermont, the next day, Monday October 2, to visit with this farmer Bisbee. They would reason with him and get him to tell them his contact information for Paco Rodriguez.

But farmer Bisbee surprised them with a locked gate and an intercom button. They had to fool him into thinking they were a package delivery service, so he would open the gate and let them drive up to his barn. When they got out of the van, farmer Bisbee could see this was trouble, so he grabbed his shotgun. Louis had no choice but to put a hole in his head with his magnum .44. He did not want to do that, but he had no choice. He did not feel bad about killing the farmer, but he was sad that they did not learn the address or phone number of Paco and his brothers.

The gunshot alerted the farmer's wife, and she opened fire from her kitchen door, blasting their truck with birdshot from a pump-action shotgun. She put five rounds into the side of the van, then dropped the shotgun and opened fire with an AR-15. Los Locos was clearly outgunned, so they jumped in their van and sped off. The farmer's wife could not read their mud-smeared license plate, but she gave a description of the van to the police, who found it abandoned in a shopping center parking lot in Newport, New Hampshire, six hours later. It had been reported stolen in Methuen, Massachusetts, three months prior, but it was wearing a New Hampshire license plate when found. There was nothing found in the van, not a fingerprint, a cigarette butt, or a scrap of paper that would identify Los Locos. They had been very careful.

But now Louis and Los Locos had to lay low. He had no van to transport illegals, and he had no transfer partner. He needed a new hideout, but one not far from Sunapee, because Paco had caused him a lot of trouble, and he wanted to get paid for his lost wages. He figured the Rodriguez brothers owed him ten thousand dollars. He did not dare to contact farmers himself, so he grudgingly hired the Diaz boys to get back to work scheduling jobs for his migrant labor.

And that was why, on this particular morning, Manny and Roofy were sipping coffee in their truck under a hemlock tree, watching the sparse traffic filter past; sparse because Newbury was a very small town in a very rural area. While they were waiting, Manny Diaz was doing a little research on Newbury. And now he found the information on history. It was old in American history, but not old by Mexican history. It had a population of a little over 2,000 people, and they were wealthy. So this was a good place to watch for Paco if he was building houses near there.

The hemlock branches covered the entire windshield of the Suburban, but Manny and Roofy could see through gaps in the needles. Manny had tossed the Texas license plate and stolen a New Hampshire plate from a wreck behind a gas station, so when Paco's eyes gazed up from the gas pump, he did not compute that this could be the Diaz Boyz truck because New Hampshire was full of black Chevy Suburbans.

Manny and Roofy watched Paco fill up, go inside to pay, and come out with a bag of groceries. He got in his truck and drove off. Manny followed, staying way back. He could have been easily spotted on these empty rural roads, but Paco did not seem to notice him.

Yes, thought rat-faced Manny Diaz, he is heading for that house under construction, so that must have been him we saw working that day. But no, Paco passed the tree-lined driveway to the new house and drove a half-mile down the road and around the corner onto another, even smaller two-lane road. Now Manny had to stop, for this road was completely without cover. He could certainly be spotted if Paco looked in his rearview mirror. So he waited while Paco rounded a bend and went out of sight.

After two minutes, Manny drove the black Suburban cautiously down the narrow road all the way to its end. There were a few expensive-looking houses on this street but no sign of Paco's truck. He turned around and drove slowly back the way he had come. There was a driveway with a crooked mailbox with hand-painted letters that said 'Morrison.' The gravel driveway sloped down a long hill through the trees and swept around a bend past a rock bigger than a house. The driveway bore fresh tire marks and looked like it was used by heavy trucks. It was recently graded. So, whoever uses this driveway must have heavy equipment, like a contractor, he thought.

Satisfied that he had found where Paco had gone and where the Rodriguez boys were working, he drove back to Fisher's General store, bought a fresh coffee, and called Louis "Loco" Lopez.

"Yeah?" answered Louis (*speaking in Spanish*).

"*I found them,*" said Manny. "*They are building a house in Newbury, New Hampshire, and they are staying around the corner at a house named Morrison on the mailbox. I got Paco's phone number from a lady at the gas station. I told her we were old friends and we wanted to surprise him.*"

"*That is good, Manny. What have you done about it?*"

"*Nothing, you told me do nothing without your orders.*"

"*OK, I want you to find a spot where you can park your truck so it can't be seen by the house they are building. They will be working today. Have Roofy take pictures with the long lens. Make sure you are positive it is them, and then bring me your truck and the camera. I will make a plan.*"

**

Friday October 6
Barcelona Harbor, NY
Captain Murphy B & B
6:41 a.m.

Mac had not slept well. He kept thinking about what might be happening in New Hampshire.

At 5:00 a.m. he had quietly crept downstairs with Buddy at his heels and gotten on Marybeth's laptop. He closed the door to her office and worked a hunch.

The jobbers were the key, he felt. It was almost certain that Paco knew how to communicate with them or had at one time. Perhaps his leaving the Ascutney orchard a week early had been his way of cutting ties with them, so maybe he had erased their contact from his phone. Since they would know his phone number, he had probably changed numbers to avoid them. That would make sense because clearly, he was hiding something and was scared of them.

Mac had met Paco and his brothers in LeRoy, New York. It was a small village surrounded by fertile farmland. The Rodriguez boys had been doing seasonal farm work near there.

So, Mac reasoned, there could be other farmers in the area who had used the Rodriguez brothers as seasonal farm labor, and if they had, they might have the contact information for their jobber.

Starting with Google™, Mac did a search for orchards near LeRoy. It was apple picking season and that was labor intensive. He was surprised to find there was a directory of New York orchards, which made his search easier. He printed out a list of orchards within 20 miles of LeRoy and set it aside.

Next, he did the same with vineyards within 20 miles of LeRoy and again found a dozen candidates. He now had two lists. They had phone numbers. That would be the best way to inquire. This was going to take some time.

Mac looked at his watch. It was now 6:41 a.m. Marybeth would be in the kitchen by seven a.m., and that meant coffee would be ready soon. He wanted a large mug before he started calling. Farmers are early risers, but he didn't want to call so early they would be annoyed and hang up on him.

He hit speed dial for New York State BCI Investigator Jonetta Pope. He hoped she was awake. She was. The phone only rang twice.

"Mac Morrison! You are the early bird today. What's up?"

"Jonetta, sorry to disturb you. I am working with the New Hampshire State Police on a murder case that happened this week in Vermont. They have reason to believe the killers are in New Hampshire, and I may be able to provide them a lead with your help."

"Mac, are you referring to the apple farmer murdered in Ascutney? New York State Police have a BOLO for any four men matching the loose description given by the farmer's wife. Since we share a long border with Vermont, we got notified the same as New Hampshire State Police. How did you get involved?"

Mac quickly gave her the background and his idea about tracking the jobbers.

"Makes sense, Mac. You always were a creative thinker, and I bet no one has thought to do that here in New York. "

"Well, I provided that lead to Colonel Trammel Bradford of the New Hampshire State Police. We have a mutual friend in criminal Attorney Morgan Hillman."

"I'll just bet you do, chuckled Jonetta. Sorry, go ahead. This is getting juicy."

"Jonetta, I was thinking that maybe we could contact the area apple orchards and vineyards in Genesee County where the Rodriguez boys worked last spring. If we could find the farmers they worked for, they should have contact information for their jobbers, and we think the jobbers could be the killers. If we could get their phone number, you could ping it and determine the location, couldn't you?"

"Yes, and that is a great idea, Mac. So how can I help?"

"I've got a list of two dozen farms, Jonetta, too many for me to quickly run down. I was thinking that some kind of call from the New York State Police to the Farm Bureau in Genesee County might get them mobilized with a phone bank of staff to contact them. If I call, they won't know me and might just hang up. But if they get a call from the Farm Bureau at the request of the State Police, I am sure they would quickly tell what they know, if anything. I am hoping that we might get a lead."

"Mac, I will call Colonel Justice, who I think you know, and ask for his help. Genesee County is within Troop A, and I am assigned to Troop A, so technically, he could assign me to this case and to make this contact to the

Farm Bureau. Can I call you back?"

"Perfect, Jonetta."

"Where are you now, Mac?"

"I'm at Marybeth's B & B in Barcelona Harbor until tomorrow morning and then I drive back to New Hampshire."

"OK, I'll try to call you back within the hour, but I WILL call you."

**

7:00 a.m.

Marybeth was humming as she turned the cheese and mushroom omelets over in her huge cast iron skillet, the one Mac bought her last May to replace the one Joey Minetti dented with bullets meant to kill her. That sturdy pan had saved her life. She did not want a new age, non-stick, thin stamped aluminum, chemical coated replacement pan, no sir.

As Mac walked in, she turned and threw her arms around him for a "hello, soldier" kiss.

"You left me with the dogs last night, Mac. I missed you."

"My mind would not let me sleep. I had a hunch and got up to start my research. By 6 a.m. I had a list, so I called Jonetta Pope and got her on the case. Even though she is New York State Police, they are coordinating with Vermont and New Hampshire to find the killers of farmer Bisbee in Ascutney last Monday."

"You're in Lone Ranger[4] mode, Mac. I better feed you well because you never know when you'll eat again."

"Well, I know I'm not missing a great homecoming dinner with you and our SOS club."

"SOS?"

"Single old souls, I call them."

"But in the meantime, you have that faraway look, Mac. I need you to come down to earth for me and Gabriella today. Sounds like you can

---

4   The Lone Ranger: TV western drama series that ran from 1949-1957 on ABC network, starring Clayton Moore. The Lone Ranger was a masked former Texas Ranger (believed to be dead), who roams the west administering his own brand of justice for people victimized by outlaws. His sidekick Tonto was played by actor Jay Silver Heels.

make time if Jonetta is running down your lead in New York and the New Hampshire State Police are doing it up there."

"Marybeth, did Gabriella call you?"

"She did, while you were on the phone just now. Sounds pretty important. Maybe even urgent. Not dangerous urgent, but important urgent."

"Did she tell you anything more than that?"

"No, but she wants us both on speakerphone for an extended conversation after breakfast."

"Is she still in Colorado, M?"

"Yes."

"Must be urgent if she called you at 5 a.m. her time."

"Well, she knows her Dad is an early riser, and then he goes off on his missions and is out of touch with the rest of the world."

"Not true. I am always available to you and Gabby, M."

"Maybe most of the time, but not when you go Lone Ranger, and I know it's happening, Mac. You just have not left me yet. So let's enjoy breakfast with the SOS club and then call her."

**

8:30 a.m.

"Hi, Dad, thanks for calling me back. Is Marybeth on the call with you?"

"I'm here, Honey, and we are totally devoted to you, so go ahead. We are interested in what you have to say."

"Thanks, Marybeth. Dad, you set up a $200,000 trust for me in May, payable at $25,000 per year for 8 years, with the codicil that if I needed more in any year, you could override the annual draw and notify Morgan Hillman to release an additional amount."

"Correct."

"Well, I have an idea for an investment that could potentially become a business, but I wanted to run it by you and Marybeth. I need both of your opinions."

"OK."

"Have I ever mentioned J.P. to you, Dad? Did I ever include him in my letters from France while I was on the ski tour?"

"Not that I recall."

"Jean-Paul Bernard is his full name, but everyone calls him J.P. He's 25, like me, and he is a great skier, better than me. But like me, he found that being the best skier on your home mountain is no guarantee you can compete at the top of the sport on an international basis. He's won some GS and downhill races, but he isn't earning enough money to make a living at it, so, like me, he has been thinking about what to do next with his life.

"His family owns a small vineyard in the Bordeaux region of France. Dad, have you read about the oversupply of French wine? It's been on the Net news. The growers are going to destroy 80 million gallons of wine this year because of reduced French demand. If they don't destroy the wine, they further erode the price of the wine they can sell. Had you heard that?"

"No, I had not, Gabby. Marybeth?"

"No, I had not either, but it has been a very busy summer for both of us, as you know, Gabby. We don't spend much time reading internet news."

"Well, it is a disaster for the Bernard Winery. Now, this is not the famous Bernard winery in the Rhone Valley. No, the Appellation Bordeaux, René Bérnard is J.P.'s family label. It harvests about 50 acres of grapes annually, which yields 250,000 bottles in a good year. Prices for their Bordeaux wines in France typically start at 35 Euros, about $39.

"Historically, large established vineyards make a 50% profit, depending on conditions. For smaller operations with higher production costs due to the scale of their operation, they might make as little as 20%. If René Bérnard made a 20% profit, that would be $2,000,000. That's very good for a small winery.

"But there is trouble in the French wine industry. Overproduction is one. Less consumption is another. Forty years ago, 50% percent of the French drank wine. Today it's 20%. The pandemic closed many bars and cafés. Many never reopened. The war in Ukraine disrupted the bottle supply. Finally, climate change is shifting the types of wines that thrive in regions from south to north, as the south gets too hot and dry, and the north is warmer.

"So it's adapt or die. And part of the adaptation is the government's order to destroy 80 million gallons of great French wine, which cannot be dumped. It must be rendered down to alcohol for reuse, which costs more than the value of the alcohol."

"I sense an opportunity," said Mac.

"Let her finish," said Marybeth, firmly but sweetly. "Continue, Gabriella."

"Five years ago, J.P.'s father bought five hectares, which is about ten acres, in an established vineyard in Northern France. It's near a small village called Puttelange-les-Thionville across the French border with Luxembourg at Mondorf-les-Bains. Mondorf was occupied by the Romans around 65 B.C. Its thermal spas date to the 1840's."

"You've done your homework, Gabby."

"It interests me, Dad. Before I returned from France last spring, I went with J.P. to Mondorf and we visited his vines in Puttelange. What struck me was how similar the landscape is to Barcelona Harbor, Dad. I mentioned that Chautauqua County is a big wine growing region to J.P. He did some research on climate and wineries and got very interested.

"American wine consumption is up 31%, and America is the largest wine-consuming nation by far. So J.P.'s father wants to graft his Bordeaux-Puttelange grapes to American established rootstock and develop a new strain of fine French-American wines to save his business and expand it.

"J.P. got a research scholarship at the Ag extension. They started a trial vineyard there just 16 miles from Marybeth's B & B. He brought over a hundred grafts last spring. If the vines survive this winter, then his father will send more grafts, and they will expand in Chautauqua County. Isn't that exciting?"

"Very. So, drop the other shoe, Gabby."

"Mac, don't pressure her," said Marybeth, "let her get to it on her own."

"Dad, three things. First, because of the overproduction, Rene Bernard has to destroy a large quantity of wine. I can buy a 40-foot shipping container for just the cost of bottling and shipping. That's 18,600 bottles of wine. Shipping will be about $2,000 to the East Coast and another $1,000 to Barcelona Harbor. For $25,000, we could have our own unique French wine to sell here in the US. This wine would sell for $35 per bottle in France. I would market it on-line at $19 per bottle.

"And yes, Dad, I did the math, that would be $353,400 gross sales. So I could afford to pay shipping and make it an even better deal. And I could pay Gina Minetti for shelf display and sales in her store, too."

"That would be an incredibly good deal, Gabby!" said Mac.

"Second, if it sells well, I can buy more from J.P.'s vineyard, but my hope would be that the new strain grown in Chautauqua County could produce local wine with an international pedigree.

"Third, the Ag Extension campus would like a dedicated plot to do a partnership project, and they need established vines. A few acres would be perfect, near the lake with the longer growing season. The hope is that the Puttelange vines could survive in Barcelona Harbor…behind the Murphy B & B on Marybeth's back vineyard. Marybeth, would you let me do that?"

"Honey, of course I would! I think this is a terrific idea!"

"What do you think of this as a business venture, Dad?"

"Is J.P. pressuring you to invest in his plan, Gabby?"

"No, I want to buy the shipping container; that is my investment, but I don't see a lot of risk. The wine will sell if it's marketed right. As far as the new wine venture, if Marybeth will lease us her acreage, me and J.P. will work it, and whatever wines we can sell, the profit will be divided between J.P, me, and Marybeth.

"If the wine seems like it can succeed, we will want more acreage in established vines. J.P. and I would have to negotiate a business plan for any such expansion. What do you think?"

"Gabby," said Mac, "I say go for the shipping container. But how will you market it with all the competition already out there? How will you get noticed?"

"Marybeth will be my secret weapon. I'm gonna ask her to talk to Gina Minetti and see if she will let me put my wine on her website and in her store: for a cut of the profit, of course."

"I would be glad to," said Marybeth, "and I already know Gina will say yes, especially if you offer to help her with her booming business. Remember, she lost a father and a grandfather. She had to take over the vineyard business that Joe Senior ran, and she told me it's too much, she needs help. So there you go, Gabriella."

"Wow. Now, only one favor left to ask of you, Marybeth. I will need a place to live in Barcelona Harbor."

"Gabby, you can have your choice of suites on the second floor. Breakfast starts at 7:00 a.m., and I'll expect you to help me out with the B & B. Just tell me what day you'll be coming home, and I'll leave the light on, and the back door unlocked."

"Marybeth, I love you."

"Of course you do, Sweetie. We are going to be one big happy family. See you soon, and drive safe."

**

Barcelona Harbor Beach
9:30 a.m.

Mac was tossing balls to Buddy and Emma when his phone rang. *(Trooper Andy Gregor calling)*

"Andy Gregor! Or, is it Trooper Andy this morning?"

"It's Trooper Andy, Mac. How the heck are you? Please don't turn over any bodies this visit."

"Who says it's a visit? Marybeth is trying to chain me to her bedpost."

"Mac, I had a call from Jonetta Pope. She briefed me on the Ascutney murder case and assigned me to coordinate the Farm Bureau contact with the growers around LeRoy. We have eight off-duty Troopers sitting around a phone bank calling that list."

"Great. Andy, if you get a hit I will be driving through LeRoy tomorrow on my way back to New Hampshire. I would like to meet any farmer that could give us a lead on the Mexican jobbers. Would that be stepping on toes?"

"Mac, if we get a lead, I will escort you personally. I'll let you know, OK?"

"OK, thanks, Andy!"

**

10:00 a.m.

While walking the dogs back to the B & B, Mac found a shingle on the front lawn. He stepped back and took a good look at the roof. There were more shingles missing. He put the dogs in the house and went out to the barn. He found a pack of shingles on a shelf. He grabbed three, got a hammer and some roofing nails from Jim's mayonnaise jars, and headed back inside.

"Uh oh," said Marybeth, "where are you going with those, Mr. Builder?"

"Up on your roof. This won't take long. You have some shingles missing. The attic hatch leads out to the roof, doesn't it?"

"Yes, but be careful. Some of those old attic floorboards are weak."

The roof was worn out. The shingles were dried and cracked. There were a dozen missing. Marybeth needed a new roof, and she needed it before winter. He stripped the bad shingles out, laid his three new ones, went back to the barn, and got a dozen more. Doing the tear-offs and replacing them took him all the way up to lunch. He could hear Marybeth calling from the back door. It reminded him of his Mom doing the same on their Ripley farm at age 9.

**

Friday October 6
Barcelona Harbor
Captain Murphy B & B,
 6:00 p.m.

Mac wheeled Harry into the back porch just as Pops and Sol Weinstein arrived. Mac opened the wooden screen door with a 'gronk' of its rusty spring and welcomed them.

They sat on the three sofas at the far end of the porch, away from the kitchen. Marybeth was cooking. The delicious smells immediately grabbed Sol Weinstein's attention.

"Mackenzie, vat is dat I smell? Home-baked bread?"

"Apple strudel, Sol, baked in a wood-fired brick oven. Harry, Sol has owned the Banks' Breakers and Scrap Yard at the Erie docks for 50 years. He is Polish by birth but a naturalized American and proud of it. He came here as a child after World War II, having survived the Holocaust. His parents were killed at Auschwitz. You three men were all born in 1938, so you already have that in common."

"Welcome, Sol," said Marybeth. "This is the dining area for the B & B, and it would be the dining area for my elder cottages. I will be closing the Bed and Breakfast Inn to serve my elder guests. Now, thank you all for coming, and let's enjoy our dinner and get to know each other better."

Marybeth brought in baskets of hot dinner rolls baked in her bread oven, standing rib roast, baked walleye, and mashed potatoes. There was a choice of Canadian Pilsner beer, white and red wines from Sardinia, courtesy of Gina Minetti, and goblets of locally bottled water.

"So, Marybeth," Sol Weinstein said as he chewed with his one good tooth, "you are serious, you are gonna haff Mackenzie to build dis little village for old men he tell me about?"

"Yes, I am, Sol, next year. Mac, could we have the first two cottages built by May 5?"

"July 1 was my planned move-in date if I framed them," Mac said. But if I hire local Amish to prefab the walls in their shop and erect them with a crew, they could put up two cottages in two days. I would have to get some underground utilities done this fall, but it might be possible to have the first two done by May 5. This is a rectangle footprint with a simple A roof. It is a model I have built a dozen times, so I know what my costs should be and how long it takes to build."

"Marybeth," said Harry, do you still think rents will be $3,750 all-inclusive?"

"I do, pending Mac's final budget."

"Marybeth," asked Pops, "aren't you worried about high interest rates for financing?"

"First of all," said Mac, "we may not have to finance the project if Marybeth gets a settlement from the Minetti estate. But if we have to finance, we will get the best rate we can and it will not prevent the project."

"Vee not gonna vorry about da money," said Sol, wiping a crumb from his chin. "Because if you haff to finance da project, I gonna lend Marybeth da money at 4%. Und I am telling you right now, tonight, I gonna rent one of da first two cottages, and I hope dat Harry and Pops gonna join me."

"Oh, Sol!" exclaimed Marybeth, "Are you serious? That would be so generous!"

**

8:45 p.m.

Mac's phone buzzed as Marybeth was clearing away the dessert dishes. (*Trooper Andy calling.*) With the SOS club telling tales, Mac excused himself and walked outside with Buddy.

"Mac, one of our Troopers working the phone bank got a hit. He is talking to the farmer now. I want to go up early in the morning to talk to him. Jonetta authorized me to be your escort. From the Westfield toll booth to the LeRoy exit is 107 miles by Thruway mile markers. If we drove the speed limit, it would take two hours, but with me leading the way, lights on, and clear roads we can drive 100 miles per hour. Are you game for an early start?

"Andy, tell the farmer to meet us at the LeRoy Diner at 4:00 a.m. I'll meet you at the Westfield Toll Booth at 2:45 a.m. You better have a good engine because my Bel Air will smoke you!"

**

10:00 p.m.

"M," said Mac, "another great dinner, and you got your first three elder village tenants. It couldn't have gone better. I'll be gone when you wake up, so I'm gonna say goodbye tonight, Sweetheart."

"Mac, you're not leaving me without a kiss in the morning!"

"Gotta meet Trooper Andy at 2:45 a.m. at the Westfield Toll booth."

"Then I am setting my alarm for 2:15 a.m. While you get dressed and walk the dogs, I'll make your thermos and walk you to your baby blue Bel Air."

**

Chapter Ten

Saturday, October 7
Westfield NY Thruway toll booth
2:45 a.m.

Trooper Andy Gregor arrived in his Ford Explorer Interceptor, flipped on his lights, and they were off. With its high center of gravity, the Interceptor would have been no match for Mac's hot rod on curvy roads, but it was good on the highway. There was a full moon, no traffic, and the roads were clear and dry. Andy put the hammer down, and they boogied at 100 miles per hour.

Time is of the essence in a murder investigation. Every minute lost to delay allows the trail to get cold, which was why Jonetta authorized the Trooper escort to the early meeting with the farmer. Little Emma slept curled up in Mac's lap. Buddy-dog sprawled across the front bench seat and tucked his nose behind Mac's back.

One hundred and seven miles later, they exited for Leroy at 3:50 a.m. Mac led the way to the diner. A Ford F 250 pickup with 'Reasoner's Orchards' on the door was idling. When the driver saw the police flashing lights, he shut off his engine and stepped out wearing a Vietnam Veterans ball cap. He looked to be late sixties, tall and sturdy. He extended his hand to Trooper Andy and introduced himself.

"I'm Matthew Reasoner, Officer. I appreciate people who are on time."

"Thank you. I'm Trooper Andy Gregor, and this is Mac Morrison. Mac is a friend, and he is already involved in the search for these killers in New Hampshire. He has helped out Troop A on another case, and we know he has an inventive mind when it comes to murder investigations. It was his idea to canvas the farmers in this area. Let's go inside and order breakfast. We'd like to hear what you have to say, Mr. Reasoner."

They all ordered the giant Farmer's Breakfast, took their first sip of steaming hot coffee, and got down to business.

"So, Mr. Reasoner, you have the background on this murder case, correct?" Andy said.

"Yes, and I was surprised to hear the Rodriguez boys were involved. I would vouch for them as good hard workers, never in trouble."

"They are not involved at all, Mr. Reasoner," Mac said. "We can assure you of that. But we think that the jobber they used may be. We don't have a way to locate them, so we are backtracking from the farms where the Rodriguez boys worked. When did Paco and his brothers work for you?"

"Last May. They were here for three weeks last spring. May 29 was their last work day." He pulled a time card from his pocket. It had the time and date stamped and the names of the workers.

"Did you contact them and offer the job?" Mac asked.

"No, the way it works is their jobber contacts me in advance and asks how many workers I need, what skills, how many days, and how much I am paying. They match my needs to the right workers and they arrive here in their own transportation."

"How do you pay them?"

"I pay the jobber a finder's fee upfront, and then I pay the wages to a company called Hard Work and Payroll in Texas. They do the payroll and withholdings. I presume they have some kind of kickback to the jobber, and then the paychecks are downloaded to the workers electronically. Saves me a lot of time not doing payroll, and it's all legal. My accountant and attorney checked it out."

"When did you first use them?" said Mac.

"Four years ago. And I have been very satisfied until this past year when the new guys took over."

"New guys?" said Trooper Andy.

"I was initially contacted by Louis Lopez four years ago. He was working his way up from the southern farms to develop new clients in the Midwest and New England. Too much competition from illegal workers in the south, what with the border situation."

"Louis Lopez, spelled like it sounds?" said Mac.

"Yes. For three years, I dealt with him or one of his partners. I think there were three others. Very efficient. A little bit brusque, I could say, but maybe that's just a cultural thing."

"Brusque?" said Andy.

"Not so polite, all business." He referred to Paco's time card. "Lopez got a ten percent finder's fee up front from me. I paid him by check in person here at the farm. In the past three years I had been paying the Rodriguez brothers $14 per hour. They worked 40 hours of regular pay and 16 hours of overtime, which was $895 for seven days. For three weeks, that was $2,685 dollars per brother. That meant I paid $269 per brother up front to book their time. Total upfront finder's fee was $807 to Lopez as the jobber."

"And you paid that upfront, in addition to their wages you paid to Hard Work and Payroll?"

"Correct," said Matt Reasoner. "Hard Work and Payroll set up a PayPal account and I would deposit to it. I got an electronic copy of the worker's pay stub for my files. Good system."

"So, what happened this year?" said Mac.

"I got a call from a different guy. Diaz. Manuel Diaz. He said he had taken over the farm labor accounts from Lopez, like a subcontract. I would pay him upfront, like I did them, and pay HWP like before."

"Why were you dissatisfied with Diaz?" asked Andy.

"He told me the finder's fee had gone up to 20%, payable in cash to him. I had always paid by check to Lopez. I told him 20% was too much, I wouldn't pay that. So he told me OK, he would settle for 15% this year, and we would go to 20% next year. That meant he wanted $1,200 in cash in advance. I couldn't back out of the deal because it was spring trimming season, and I needed the workers. The Rodriguez boys, young men I should call them, are excellent workers, and unlike some others, they want the overtime, so they will work seven-day weeks."

"So, what did you do?" asked Mac.

"Well, I paid it, in cash. The Rodriguez boys showed up on time and worked extra hard, so I was grateful for that. But when they left, I called Louis Lopez and complained about his new subcontractor and the new deal with 15% cash advance. He was very angry. I was overcharged, he said, and I should not have had to pay in cash. He offered me a refund or a credit for next year's contract. He was nice about it, but like I say, brusque. I got the feeling that Diaz would not be working for him after that."

"He was obviously skimming the 5% in cash," said Mac.

"That's what I figured. I accepted the credit, but later, I decided I wanted the refund. So, I tried to call Lopez but I got a message that said that number had been disconnected."

"Do you still have that phone number?" asked Trooper Andy.

"Yes, it's here on my phone, and I wrote it on this pay card."

Trooper Andy wrote it down. So did Mac.

"What is even weirder is that Diaz showed up just last week asking if I needed workers for the fall harvest. I figured he had been fired, but no, he said he is still running the farm labor contracts."

"So, do you have his contact information, Diaz, that is? And, when did he call you?"

"He actually came to see me in person last week. Here is his phone number. Do you want to see pictures?"

"Pictures?" asked Mac.

"Yeah. I have a camera system. You know, one of those doorbell cameras. So, the first contact with Lopez was when he came here four years ago. It was a word-of-mouth lead from other farmers. I got a picture of Lopez when he came to the farm and rang the bell at the farm store. I have my office out back. Diaz did the same, so I got his picture too: his and the big goofy guy with him."

"He had a big guy with him?" said Trooper Andy.

"Yeah, they have a familial resemblance. Manuel, the short one, was skinny with a rat face. The big one was about Mac's size, with a pleasant but vacant look on his face. Like a big gorilla just waiting for the word from the little one to tear my head off."

Matthew Reasoner pulled back his jacket and revealed a Glock 21 pistol in a shoulder holster.

"I keep this at the farm store because we've had a few break-ins, so when I got a bad vibe from the Diaz boys after their first visit I had my Glock on the desk in easy reach the second time we were talking. Good thing, too, because the big ape looked like he wanted to tear me apart when I told them I wasn't doing business and to get the hell off my land before I called the cops."

"Is that their vehicle in this picture?" Mac asked. It was a dark-colored Chevy Suburban.

"Yeah, that's it. It's the same one Lopez drove four years ago, same license plate."

"You have the plate number?"

"Sure. My doorbell camera grabbed it. It's a Texas plate."

"This is terrific, Mr. Reasoner," said Trooper Andy Gregor. "Can you text me those photos?"

"I'd like them too," said Mac.

"Sure, give me your numbers, and I'll do it now while we get Wendy to top off our coffees. Funny you picked the diner to meet at Mac because I have 4:00 a.m. breakfast here several times a week, so they all know me."

"I stayed at the old motel across the street on my way thru town last spring," Mac said. "Had several good meals here. Well, if that's all you can tell us, Mr. Reasoner," said Mac, "I think I'll walk my dogs and head for New Hampshire. You have been very helpful."

"Glad to be of assistance. If any of these jobbers are responsible for that farmer's murder in Vermont, I count myself lucky it wasn't me."

"You showed them the Glock," said Mac. "Could be the reason you are still alive."

**

5:00 a.m.

Mac woke the dogs and let them out of the car for a pee break.

"Andy, that was worth an early trip, wouldn't you say?"

"Absolutely. I'm a street cop, Mac, so I'll be reporting this information back to Jonetta Pope as the lead investigator for the BCI Major Crimes unit. What will you do?"

"I am going to wake up the Field Superintendent of the New Hampshire State Police and download these pictures and phone number to him. I hope that Diaz' cell phone can be located by pinging it. If he is in New Hampshire then they should be able to pick him up or at least pinpoint their last known location. And we have a license plate to look for. I would almost swear that is the same Chevy suburban that stopped in my driveway last Monday and took pictures of me, Roger, and the Rodriguez boys. They sped off before I could talk to them."

"Huh. Well, I'll hope to see you back in Barcelona Harbor soon, Mac."

"With the plans Marybeth has for me, I am sure you will, Andy. Thanks for the escort. Now, let's get this info on the wires as fast as we can. Time is critical."

**

Trooper Andy called Jonetta Pope from his cruiser to relay the information from farmer Reasoner, while Mac called Colonel Trammel Bradford. It was early, but Mac knew that the Colonel would want to know ASAP.

And he did.

"Mac, this is terrific. So now we have pictures of persons of interest and at least two names, Manuel Diaz and Louis Lopez. But Mrs. Bisbee shot at a van with four men, so there are at least two more persons of interest out there. We don't know if Diaz and Lopez were part of the four she shot at, but it's a good bet at least one of them was. Farmer Reasoner's picture of the Suburban with the Texas license plate will let us run down the owner. Mac, if they are smart, the killers will be out of New England by now, which means New York may have a shot at picking them up. I will call Colonel Justice and coordinate."

Mac said, "Investigator Jonetta Pope of the New York State Police BCI is running down the other farmers. She will be reporting to Colonel Justice. Anything else I can do for you right now, Colonel?"

"Well, I am serious about making a spot for you as a consultant on special cases, Mac. You seem to have a gift for creative thinking."

"You mean I think like a criminal? Ha! Well, I'm flattered, but right now, I have so much on my plate I don't even think I'll have time to sleep. Let's just say I'll consider it."

"Sounds good, Mac. I will keep you posted on this case."

"Colonel, did the stolen Mercedes van abandoned in Newport last Monday have a New Hampshire license plate?"

"Yes. The van had been stolen in Methuen, Massachusetts, several months ago. The New Hampshire plate had been taken off a wrecked vehicle being stored outside a body shop in Concord, New Hampshire. Why do you ask?

"If the Chevy Suburban that stopped in Roger Lemonier's driveway was one of the jobbers we are looking for, then it stands to reason they may have gotten rid of that license plate. If the jobbers are legal owners of that truck and registered it in Texas, where we believe they are from, they will not want to attract attention after the murder in Vermont."

"But that Suburban was not the vehicle used in the murder."

"You said the van was abandoned at a Newport shopping center on October 2, the day of the murder, correct?"

"Correct."

"Then how did they disappear into thin air? Four Mexican men walking around Newport would be conspicuous. Was there another car reported stolen in Newport on October 2?"

"We checked that. No there wasn't, Mac."

"So an accomplice picked them up. Was there a security camera at the center, Colonel?"

"Yes, but the camera angle did not include the corner where the van was left."

"What if the black Suburban picked them up? They would not want the Texas plate on it. So, if they did it once, they might have done it again."

"Done what, Mac?"

"Find a body shop with wrecked cars stored outside. One of them is missing its New Hampshire license plate. I would start in Newport and work outwards from there."

"You just did it again, Mac: provided us a lead that was so simple we should have thought of it ourselves."

"Well, first, let's see if it pans out. I'm on my way back to New Hampshire now and should arrive in Sunapee late afternoon, but you can call me on my cell anytime. Good luck, Colonel."

"Thank you, Mac."

**

Saturday, October 7
Enfield, N.H.
One Half Mile from Mascoma Lake
10:00 a.m.

Louis Lopez and his band of three Locos were huddled around the kitchen table in a small cabin tucked back in the dense woods. The cabin was 1,000 yards off NH Route 4A near the old Shaker Village. Louis had scouted this cabin when the rich 'flatlanders' were closing down their summer camps. As a successful burglar on his climb up the criminal ladder, Louis was observant. That was a trait he did not share with the other Locos or with the dumb Diaz boys. And it was one of the reasons they followed his lead. Louis saw things in a way they did not.

Even though there were a number of ski resorts nearby, Louis decided this was not a ski cottage because he did not see a ski locker anywhere. There were no silly chairs made of old skis or ancient wooden skis mounted to the wall under the front porch. And, it was not a hunting camp because there were no trophy heads on the interior walls. And it was not a weekly rental. He had checked all the on-line listings before choosing this one. This cabin belonged to a wealthy owner who did not share it.

This was definitely a summer camp. There was a water skiing boat under a three sided open shed, well secured with locks on the boat and the trailer. Bicycles hung on the back wall. Mascoma Lake was four miles long but only three-quarters of a mile wide at its widest point. Louis had seen many people water skiing on it in summer when he scouted farms in the area.

Even though the mornings were chilly, Louis forbade any use of the wood stove. He did not want to attract attention. The cabin had electricity so they had turned on the electric baseboards to make it cozy. The thoughtful owners had left canned goods and freeze-dried coffee in the pantry. Although the water was shut off, there was a spring-fed stream that ran down the ridge they sat on, and they could gather water and boil it on the electric stove.

But the best advantage about this cabin, other than its remote location, was the bicycles in the shed, and a grocery store and gas station in Enfield just the other side of the lake. Since they did not have their van, and the Diaz boys had their Suburban, they could ride the bicycles down the gravel drive, across the bridge at Shakoma Beach and get groceries and beer at Gallagher's. They made sure that only one Loco made the shopping trip, and always at the busy time of the day when he would be less noticed.

Gallagher's store had very good hot submarine sandwiches. Louis did not allow the purchase of more than one super-sized sub by the Loco he sent to the store. It was always Andrés, the smallest. He had the lightest skin and no facial hair. He looked clean-cut. And he spoke good English with no accent, like many of the border people from Juarez-El Paso.

Andrés was told to be polite if spoken to, pretend to be shy, and say little. If he were casually asked, like those crazy Americans often did, where he was from and where he worked, he was simply to respond that he was doing maintenance work near the Shaker Village and would be leaving as soon as cold weather came. That was believable but vague. Americans were too inquisitive, but they also were polite and knew not to pry. At least the

Americans in New Hampshire were like that. New Yorkers were more aggressive.

So they had been in the cabin for five days, with five bicycle trips to the grocery store. Louis was still thinking of the best next move. The Diaz boys were staying at a motel in Lebanon, six miles away, using fake ID and paying cash. It was an old motor court run by an Indian family who didn't ask questions like Americans, and it had an auto body shop behind it with a graveyard of several dozen wrecked cars, all but one of which had New Hampshire license plates. That missing plate was, of course, on the back bumper of Louis' Chevy Suburban, which the Diaz boys kept parked inside a storage locker next door to their motel when not in use.

Louis had been waiting for confirmation that Manny Diaz had found Paco, and now he had! He was sure there was a dragnet in Vermont looking for four Mexican men for the murder of the farmer in Ascutney. He figured the police would be looking for them in New Hampshire, too. He had hoped he could get back to Indiana or Missouri or some safe Midwest state where there would be lots of Mexicans, and they could just blend and then start over.

He didn't dare rent a vehicle using his credit cards and driver's license. He had plenty of cash, but rental agencies would want a credit card as security. Even with a stolen license plate he wasn't sure the Suburban hadn't been traced back to him, so he didn't want to use that. He needed wheels.

But Paco had wheels, and an American CDL license, and credit cards.

If he could get Paco to rent a self-move truck, Andrés could drive it to central New York with the three other Locos hiding in the back. Louis had a crew working at a vineyard in LeRoy. He could buy their old beater van for double what it was worth and pay one of them to drive the rental truck back to New Hampshire and take a bus back to Leroy. Once they had the old van, Andrés could drive his Locos far away from trouble.

And Louis had a plan to decoy the police. He would give them the Diaz Boyz for the murder in Vermont.

It was a half-day job for Paco. Drive 45 minutes from Newbury to Enfield and pick up Andrés at the gas station. They would drive six miles to Lebanon. Paco would rent the truck using his credit card as security but prepay it with Louis' cash. He would drive the moving truck to Shakoma Beach by Mascoma Lake, just a quarter mile from the cabin. Andrés would drive Paco's truck and follow him. Louis would ride the bicycle from the cabin down to the parking lot and pay Paco $300 for three hour's work. Since the truck rental would be paid in cash, there would be no charge to Paco's credit card. This was just going to be a favor for an old friend.

So, Louis had a plan. Now, it was time to put it in motion. He hit the speed dial on his burner phone. It was the third phone he had activated this week. After every call he stomped the old phone and had Andrés toss it in the trash at the gas station in Enfield.

Paco answered.

"Hello? (Speaking in Spanish)

"Hello, Paco. How are you, my old friend?"

Paco looked at his phone. He did not recognize the number, but he thought he recognized the voice.

"This is Paco. Who is this?"

"Paco, you don't recognize my voice? Three years we work together, man. I am disappointed in you. It's your old boss, Louis, man. Don't you know my voice?"

Paco froze. He didn't answer.

"Paco, why did you skip out on your job in Vermont, man? And you changed your phone, man, but we found you anyway. We have eyes and ears everywhere, Paco. You cannot hide for long from Los Locos. We wanted to make sure you were OK, man. Is everything good with you, man?"

"We're good, Louis. We have a permanent job. We don't need your service anymore."

"But I did not get paid for that week you did not work Paco. I promised the farmer you would work three weeks, but you skipped out, and he did not pay me. And we have a contract, Paco. I get a cut of your work. If you have a good job, I am happy for you, but I still have a contract, man. You will owe me a cut for what you got paid over the summer."

"No, Louis, we don't have a contract with you. I talked to a lawyer, and he said that is not legal what you did. I never got a paper, I never signed anything, so it was all just a good faith bargain, he called it, and the bargain is over, Louis. Just leave us alone. Ok? Just leave us alone."

"You hurt me, Paco; all that work I give you for three years and now you do me like this? Really, you would do me like this? You know, Paco, I have many friends in Juarez. If I was angry with you, I could call my friends, and they *could pay a visit to your little niece when she is walking home from school. You wouldn't want anything bad to happen to your little niece, would you?"*

Paco was scared and unsure of what to say, so he said nothing. But Louis was a master manipulator. He knew what to say, so he kept talking.

"So Paco, I don't want to be angry with you, man. I want to remember all the good times we had working together these past three years. So I am gonna forget about our agreement, Paco. I am gonna let you and your brothers go. Is that good?"

"Yes, that would be good, Louis."

"OK, then let's part friends, OK, Paco? If you would just do me one favor first, then I will let you go, and Los Locos will never bother you again, OK? And I will pay you $300 for your time. Just 3 hours tomorrow is all it will take. Can you do that, Paco?"

"What do you want me to do?"

"I would like you to drive 30 miles up to Enfield and go to the gas station by the lake. Andrés will meet you there. You both drive six miles to Lebanon and rent a moving truck, a small one, for a two-day rental. You use your driver's license and credit card to rent it. I will give Andrés cash to prepay for the rental, so there will be no charge to your card when the truck is returned. You drive the moving truck to the parking lot at Shakoma Beach by Enfield while Andrés follows in your truck. You park behind the trees. Andrés will call me when you get to the parking lot and I will come and pay you $300. That's it, nothing illegal, just this one favor, and after that, you are free. Will you do that for your old friend Louis?"

Paco didn't like it at all, but now that Louis knew where he was working, he could make trouble, and he did not want to make trouble for Mr. Mac. He would do this one thing, and then they would be free.

"Yes, I can do it, Louis. What time tomorrow do I meet Andrés at the gas station?"

"8:00 a.m., Paco. You will be back at Morrison's house by noon. All done forever, and we part as friends. Agreed?"

"I'll be there at 8:00 Louis."

Paco hung up, put his phone in his pocket, and went back to hanging siding on Roger Lemonier's house.

"Who was that Paco?" said Tomas (speaking in Spanish).

"Loco Louis."

"Lopez? No! How did he find us?"

"Manny Diaz found us. Remember when his truck pulled in the driveway? He must have seen us. He knows where we are working. He even knows we are living at Mr. Mac's."

"That is bad. How did he get your phone, man?"

"I don't know. Louis said they have eyes and ears everywhere, man. Maybe they do. It's scary."

"What did he want? Money?"

"I told him we don't pay him anymore. He said he would give us our freedom if I do him a favor. It will only take three hours and then we are free."

"Did he kill that farmer in Vermont, Paco?'

"Do you think I asked him that, Tomas? That would be stupid and put us in danger. As far as he knows, we know nothing about that farmer."

"Are you going to tell Mr. Mac?"

"No, I want to keep him out of this. Los Locos can be very dangerous, and I don't want Mr. Mac to get hurt for our trouble."

"I think he would want to help us, Paco."

"Yes, he would, but it could get him killed. If Los Locos killed that farmer, they might kill Mr. Mac, too. It is a small favor, a very small favor he asks, and not illegal. I will do it and then we are free. Do not tell Ramon, and do not tell Mr. Mac. Now hurry up and get back to work. I want to show Mr. Mac that we will be finished with this siding today. He will be very surprised and pleased."

**

Saturday October 7
Newbury, New Hampshire
4:30 p.m.

Mac turned into his gravel driveway, stopped to check the crooked mailbox, then drove down the long sloping drive, around the rock bigger than a house, over the small creek, past the second of thirteen beaver ponds on his land, and pulled up to his new steel barn.

Roger Lemonier's truck was parked outside an open bay. Roger was inside cleaning the tracks on his John Deere excavator. It looked huge sitting in the barn, but with the extra tall door, it could tuck itself low enough to fit. Roger had laid thick wooden planks on the concrete to prevent the heavy machine from damaging it.

"Good trip, Mac?" asked Roger.

"Mission accomplished. Marybeth and I got Hubcap Harry safely moved into her cottage, and Pops drove up from Tennessee to house-sit Harry's place while he recuperates. Harry was worried about parts theft off his yard cars and his hubcap collection in his barn. Having Pops there is good for both of them because Pops' cabin got trashed by a tenant, and he could not move in until it's repaired."

"Sounds like a good solution."

"Yeah, but now I have to go back with my crew and put a roof on Marybeth's house before winter. The shingles are blowing off by the dozen. And she wants me to build her four new cottages in the spring, which will be rented to single seniors.

"Marybeth is closing down the B & B to make room in the big house for me and Gabby, who will be moving in to go into the wine business with a French guy friend. His father owns a vineyard in Bordeaux and is sending over grape grafts to see if they can thrive in Barcelona Harbor."

"Holy crap, Mac! You stirred up all that in five days?"

"Actually I left out the part about Mace Wilkins trying to force Sol Weinstein out of the scrap business using public money to buy him out. It's a scam. I got Sol a ball-buster young woman lawyer who just happens to be in the Delmonico law firm, which represented Rosemary Minetti."

"Mac, you are a menace to a quiet life, you know that?"

"Speaking of that, Rog, has it been quiet around here with the Rodriguez boys?"

"We have had no more sightings of a black Suburban. And I have not heard anything about the killers of that farmer."

"Well, Rog, there is more news on that subject, but for the moment, I am out of it, and Colonel Bradford of the New Hampshire State Police and Colonel Justice of the New York State Police both have me on their speed dial as an unpaid consultant."

"Holy shit, Mac! Will you just nail your ass to Newbury and finish my house?"

"Roger, I would love to. Let's go see what the boys have done while I was gone. Slide over, Buddy, Roger is coming with us in the Bel Air."

'Rowrf!'

**

Mac was surprised, as Paco predicted, and very pleased. All of the windows and doors were installed correctly. The pre-painted siding was on and looked fabulous in very colonial dark red with cream-white trim. The siding was made for hidden nail installation, so no paint touch-up was needed. The exterior was finished.

Roger had wasted no time in pouring a concrete sidewalk to the front door. He had also graded the loam, tilled it, and seeded a cover crop of winter rye, which must have gotten rain because it was already beginning to sprout.

They went inside. Rough wiring was done and inspected.

"Did you double-check the outlets and appliances?" Mac asked.

"Yep. Remy came in with a crew of three helpers, and they knocked this out in two days. He reconnected your alarm board for the cottages."

"I'll have to ask him if the motherboard fried when the transformer blew in the barn fire."

"That's what he thought because the board is lit up like a Christmas tree, Mac."

"Great, that's one more thing to figure out. Well, it's good to be home and see progress. I'll call Infantini tonight. Maybe he can get in here and insulate the walls early next week. I want to be hanging drywall by next weekend and then get painters in here. Did Paco's cousins get here OK?"

"Yes. Lupe and Miguel jumped right on the siding, which is why it's done. Now that you're back I'd really like to keep Ramon on my drainage project. Can you spare him?"

"I think so, Rog. Hey, do you want to do the underground work for Marybeth's elder village next spring?"

"Mac, you're talking big money to move equipment 400 miles for a fairly small job."

"Rog, I've got a local contractor with a big dozer and small excavator, but he would like to partner with your small dozer and big excavator. Two weeks max. I can pay you to move the equipment. There are five bedrooms in the house, so we can all squeeze in since the B & B will be closed. You get to eat Marybeth's cooking."

"Hey, I'll go just for that, Mac."

"All right. Let's go home. Buddy and Emma are hungry, and so am I. I think I'll feed them, then run down to Fishers and buy some steaks. Do you and Ursula want to join me?"

"Sure. She'll whip up a salad and bake some potatoes."

"Come over around 6:15. I'll have the grill going, and we can have a beer on the deck and watch the sun set."

**

Newbury, New Hampshire
Near Lake Sunapee
Mac Morrison's log cabin on Gabby's Pond
5:00 p.m.

Buddy and Emma spilled out of the Bel Air and barked with delight to be home again. Mac wasn't sure if they knew if this was their home or Marybeth's was home. He wasn't sure he knew either. He walked around and checked to make sure everything was OK and fed the dogs. Then he jumped in the Bel Air and headed for Fisher's Grocery and Gas.

Fisher's was at the south end of the lake, opposite Newbury Harbor. It always had a great view of the sunset over the lake. Technically, the sun sets behind Fisher's, but a red sunset would light up the water like blood, which is why the locals called it a Sunapee Bloody Sunset. It looked like there would be one tonight.

Mac gassed up the Bel Air and strolled inside.

"Mac Morrison!" shouted Jodie Moreno, the store's raven-haired co-owner. "When did you get back?"

"Just now, didn't I?" said Mac with a smirk.

"Don't be a wise ass, you scoundrel. Come gimme a smooch. Mickey is in the back cutting your steaks."

Mickey suddenly appeared with three gorgeous thick sirloins. He was a descendant of the original builder.

"Bone in for the dogs," Mickey said, grinning as Mac kissed his wife on the cheek.

"How did you know?" said Mac.

"Ursula called," he said. "And I'm not jealous 'cause I heard you got yourself a lady in New York."

"Hmph! I won't ask who told you. Anything happen while I was gone?"

"Well," said Mickey, "I guess you know a farmer got murdered in Ascutney. State police have an alert out for four Mexicans. Pretty vague descriptions: medium height, possibly early 30s, one with long hair. They had a van at the murder scene, but that was found abandoned. I don't figure they would ever show up in this burg, but I keep my eye out."

Jodie said "We had a couple Mexicans buying coffee in the morning, but there are just two of them, and they don't seem to be hiding. They gassed up, bought cake and coffee almost every morning this week until today. Didn't see them today."

"Driving a black Chevy Suburban?" asked Mac.

"Matter of fact, they were," said Jodie.

"Did you get their name?

"No."

"License plate?"

"Oh, I have it," said Jodie. "It's a New Hampshire plate, Mac."

Mac pulled out his phone and compared the plate number to the one given by Farmer Reasoner. They didn't match. Reasoner's photo showed a black Suburban with a Texas plate.

"Anything else, Jodie?" asked Mac.

"Well, I could hear them talking. We have a sign outside that says Spanish spoken here, so you'd think they might know I could understand."

"What did they say?"

"They were excited because they thought they had found their friend Paco."

The hair stood up on the back of Mac's neck.

"And?"

"So, I asked them in Spanish if they were looking for Paco Rodriguez. He comes here in the mornings, sometimes with Maria. They said yes, they wanted to say hello. They were looking for work here and heard Paco had found some. Paco phones me to see if we have certain foods, so I have his cell, and I gave it to them."

Mac's face hardened.

"Mac, did I do something wrong?"

"You were being helpful like a good American, Jodie, but maybe it would have been better not to be so helpful this time."

"Are they the killers, Mac?"

"I don't know, maybe. Or, they might be looking for Paco to collect some money. Anyway, the damage is done. It's not your fault, but do me a favor, OK?"

"Sure, Mac."

"If they come in here again, call me immediately."

"OK. Gosh, Mac, I hope I didn't put them in danger."

"I'll be on the lookout. Thanks for the steaks, Mickey. Remember, call me."

**

5:30 p.m.

Back at the cabin, Mac grabbed a little disc the size of a key fob from a desk drawer. He put the steaks out to warm to room temperature, then called Buddy and Emma for a walk. They danced to the door with Buddy spinning in circles.

Mac walked the dogs 1,000 feet from the cabin to the mobile home behind the steel equipment shed. He could smell Maria's cooking through the open window. When he knocked, Ramon answered the door.

"Mr. Mac, come in!" Ramon's English was getting better.

"Thank you, Ramon. Is Paco here?"

"Paco got a phone call. He went out for a while." Ramon seemed nervous.

"That's too bad. I wanted to talk to him."

"I will tell him you came over, Mr. Mac."

"Thank you, Ramon." Mac noticed Paco's jacket hanging on the chair next to him. Using his left arm to rest on the chair back and block his right hand from view, he slipped his right hand into his sweater side pocket, grabbed a little disc, and dropped it in Paco's jacket pocket like a magician.

Maria called out from the kitchen.

"*Mister Mac, tacos en dos minutos. Esperas, si?*"

Ramon translated. "Momma will bring you tacos in two minutes. You can wait, yes?"

"Yes," said Mac. "I have the dogs, so I will wait outside."

"OK," said Ramon.

Two minutes later, a worried-looking Maria came outside with a covered platter of steaming tacos. She handed them to Mac, and motioned him to sit at the picnic table. She began speaking in a very worried tone, gesturing with her hands and reaching up to the heavens in fear, clasping her hands in prayer and hoping Mac understood. It seemed very important, but he did not understand. But he knew who would. He gestured to Maria to wait, pointed at his phone, and called Jodie Moreno.

"Yes, Mac, did you forget something? We are closing, but I can run it over."

"Jodie, something is very wrong. Maria Rodriguez is trying to tell me something, but I can't understand. Please talk to her."

Mac put the phone on speaker and held it under Maria's chin. Jodie began speaking to her. Maria looked relieved. They held a rapid-fire conversation, finally ending with "*si, si si, muchas gracias, Jodie.*"

Mac took the phone back.

"OK, what's up, Jodie?"

"Mac, Paco got a phone call from his old jobber, a man named Louis Lopez. He said Paco and his brothers owe him money for the work they did the last four months. Paco told him they don't work for him anymore, to leave them alone. Lopez got mad and threatened to have his people in El Paso take his little niece, who is only ten years old. Something bad could happen to her if they don't get paid. But then he told Paco he was willing to let them go, tear up their contract, and part as friends if Paco would do one favor for him.

"Paco told Tomas not to tell Ramon or you, Mac. But he did not tell Tomas he could not tell Maria. So he told her, and she is scared. She is afraid these are the men who killed the farmer in Vermont. She does not want Paco to go, but she cannot stop him, so she is afraid."

"OK, Jodie, can you ask her what is the favor?"

"Maria," Jodie asked, *"Que es el favor, Maria?"*

"No se, no se," said Maria, shaking her head.

"She doesn't know, Mac."

"OK, tell her I will do what I can to help them. I will help them."

"Mac te ayudará, Maria."

Maria nodded her head and looked up at Mac, who towered a foot over her. She reached up and pulled his face down and hugged him as if she would never let go.

"Muchas gracias Meester Mac, muchas gracias! Te amo! Te amo!

"I think I understood that, Jodie. Now look, like I said, call me as soon as you see those Mexican boys in the black Suburban, all right?"

"I know you, Mac. Don't go all Lone Ranger on us again. Get some help. Please, Mac."

"I'll be careful, Jodie."

**

Mac took the tacos and walked around the mobile home. The 50-year-old red and white Chevy pickup was gone, so Paco was gone.

Emma and Buddy had been patiently waiting, but now they wanted tacos. Mac lifted the towel and gave one to each of them as they walked back to the cabin.

**

6:15 p.m.

Ursula Lemonier walked thru the door and gave Mac a big hug. She was a handsome brunette and almost as tall as Roger. Tonight, she was wearing tailored jeans and a fuzzy pink Angora sweater with new Adidas sneakers. She was North Woods hot.

"Welcome back, Mac. Now tell us: what mayhem is tracking you tonight?"

"Well, I think we are safe for dinner. How do you want your steak? Maria made us tacos for appetizers. Do you want wine, beer, or something harder?"

Roger said, "I'm sticking to beer until you explain the lines on your forehead. I know that look. Is this still Level One with the boys?"

"I don't know, Rog, but something is about to happen. Two young Mexicans in a black Suburban have been hanging around Fisher's store asking about Paco. They claim they are friends looking for work. They conned Jodie into giving them Paco's cell number."

"Uh-oh. Is it the same Suburban that came into my driveway at the birthday party?"

"Could be, but I don't know that either. This one had a New Hampshire plate, and the other was Texas. A jobber named Louis Lopez called Paco this afternoon and shook him up pretty bad. Lopez claims the boys owe him a cut of their wages from you and me, and he threatened their 10-year-old niece in Texas if they did not pay. But then he said he would forgive the money if Paco would do him one favor. Maria does not know what the favor is."

"I don't like the sound of that, Mac. Are you going to notify Colonel Bradford?"

"What would I tell him, Rog? We don't know if Lopez is one of the four who killed farmer Bisbee. We don't know if the two at Fisher's store are part of the four, we don't know what the favor is, we don't know when or where Paco is going to perform this favor, and we don't know where Lopez is. And if Ramon and Maria don't know and Paco won't tell me, he surely won't tell the police."

"Well," said Roger, "tomorrow is Sunday, our day off. Easier to respond to a threat."

"True, but it also means the boys are on their day off. They have three trucks. We can't follow them all, and it's hard to run a tail on these rural roads. I dropped an Apple Air Tag™ into Paco's jacket, so maybe I could follow him. My Bel Air is too conspicuous, and the F 450 is too slow, which only leaves the '71 Impala."

"What's wrong with the Impala, Mac?"

"Other than new tires, a battery, brakes, and a tune-up, I have not really given it a shake-down since I bought it, so any of its 50-year-old parts might be ready to fail."

"When was the last time you drove it, Mac?"

"I took it to Concord to buy a new bow at that big sporting goods store. Hey, let's get these steaks on the grill."

**

It was a cool clear night, with a hint of frost in the air, good for grilling out. Definitely flannel shirt and sweater weather in northern New Hampshire. The food was hearty and well enjoyed. After dinner, the three friends sat around the wood stove while they caught up on current events.

Mac's phone buzzed. (*Paco calling*.) He put it on speaker.

Maria Rodriguez screamed: "*MEESTER MAC! VEN RÁPIDO! VEN RÁPIDO!*"

Ursula Lemonier was a nurse. She had been learning Spanish to converse with the influx of Latinos coming into her hospital's emergency room. She shouted:

"MARIA SAYS COME QUICK! GO GUYS, GO!"

Mac and Roger bolted. As the door slammed behind them, Buddy howled because they did not take him!

"My truck!" shouted Roger. The tires spit gravel as they raced up the driveway. The trailer was 1,000 feet away. They covered it in twenty seconds. It was dark, but the security lamp was shining by the trailer's front door. Roger slammed on the brakes and slewed to a stop.

A big man was slugging Paco while a little man was holding Maria. He was pointing a gun at Ramon and Tomas. Paco was getting the worst of it. The big man clubbed him down to the ground.

Mac threw open the passenger door and launched himself at the big ape. He turned and threw a roundhouse right that sailed over Mac's head. Mac ducked and came with an uppercut that slammed the ape's jaw shut, staggering him.

"Kill him, Roofy!" the little man cackled as he raised a Magnum .44 at Roger. "Stay back, dude!" said the little man.

But Roger did not stay back. He walked toward the little man, who held Maria in front of him like a shield. Roger bobbed his head back and forth like a mongoose stalking a Cobra, waving his hands in a sign of submission. Suddenly, his foot lashed out with a sideways kick that snaked around Maria and collapsed the little man's knee.

"A-yeeeeee!" yelled the little man as he pulled the trigger. The .44 exploded with a 'BOOM' that shattered the night air. The slug flew harmlessly into the sky as Roger grabbed Maria's arm and yanked her away with his left hand, then threw a hard right-hand punch to the sternum. He put all his weight behind it and drove it until his fist slammed into the little man's backbone.

The air whooshed out of the little man, and he went down in convulsions, crabbing in circles and fighting to breathe.

Mac saw the flash of a knife in the spotlight and jumped back just as it slashed his shirt. He followed the blade arm, grabbing its elbow and pushing it up and out, driving the big ape backward and stabbing the knife into a tree, where it stuck.

But the big man was quick and lashed back with his elbow. It caught Mac on the top of his head, stunning him. A thousand fight memories kicked in as he spun backward and took a punch to his face. He used its momentum to whirl around and kick the big man's knee with a CRACK! He grunted and doubled over.

Mac needed to end it. He hit him with a left hook to the neck hard enough to fell an ox. The big man went down on his hands, gagging. Mac swung his right knee up and kicked him under the jaw, clacking his teeth so hard you could hear them shatter.

Now, there was silence. Neither of the two goons moved. The little one was having trouble breathing. Blood was pouring from the big man's mouth.

"You good, Rog?" Mac said.

"All good Mac, you?"

Maria knelt and picked up Paco's head. His eyes were closed. His tongue hung out.

"Padre celestial, salva a mi hijo!" she shouted with her eyes to the sky. (Heavenly father, save my son!)

Mac's '57 Bel Air screeched to a halt as Ursula and Buddy spilled out. Buddy raced over and clamped his jaws on the neck of the big man sprawled at Mac's feet. He growled. The big man grunted, *"no mas, no mas!"*

"Ursula, check Paco!" Roger said. She gently took Paco's head, raised his lids, and felt his pulse.

"He's unconscious, but he has a pulse. Roger, call Sunapee Squad. We are transporting to Newport Hospital. Tell them the person is unconscious from head trauma. Mac, can you get him in your car?"

Mac scooped up Paco like a rag doll. Ursula supported his head and neck.

"Ramon!" shouted Ursula, "get in the back seat! Hold his head! Roger, you clean up this trash!" she said, pointing to the two men on the ground.

"Buddy! Aus!" Mac ordered. Buddy released his jaws from the big man's neck. "Watch'em, Buddy!" Buddy growled and stood over the big man, who turned to look up. Roger was holding the .44 Magnum on him.

"Just one second, Ursula," said Mac. He hit his cell phone's speed dial for Colonel Bradford. While it rang, Ramon touched his arm.

"These are Manny and Raoul Diaz, our jobbers, Mister Mac."

"I figured. Hang on, Ramon...COLONEL BRADFORD! Mac Morrison, here. Have to hurry, Sir. We have a badly injured man, and I have to get him to Newport Hospital. We've had a scuffle with shots fired at my house. It's the two Diaz boys you have been looking for. One of my workers is unconscious. Both Diaz boys are down. My friend Roger is holding their gun on them now, Colonel. They are both injured, so they are not a threat at the moment. Their gun is a .44 Magnum revolver, Colonel, possibly the same one used to kill farmer Bisbee. I would appreciate an escort to Newport Hospital and a Trooper response to my house on Morrison Lane. It's off Old Post Road off of Route 103, one mile south of Newbury center. Roger will text you coordinates. Got it?"

"Got it, Mac! Good work! I'll call for an escort."

"Colonel, we'll be driving fast on Route 103. I'll have a flashing strobe light on the hood of my blue '57 Chevy Bel Air convertible with a white top."

"Copy that. Go!"

Mac tossed Roger his phone. "Text him the coordinates, Rog. Ursula, you have your phone?"

"Yes."

"OK. Ramon, you have his head?" He nodded. "Buddy! Watch'em!"

'Rowrf!'

**

8:00 p.m.
NH Route 103
En route to Newport Hospital

Mac stuck the magnetic strobe light to the Bel Air's hood and raced off as fast as he dared. The 450 Horsepower Chevy was plenty willing, and so was his modern chassis, but the lumpy, narrow roads weren't made for high speeds.

Mac pushed it to 70 and no more. He had to slow for corners and thickly-settled hamlets. Ten miles to Newport. Halfway there, a New Hampshire State Police cruiser saw him coming and turned on his lights and siren. Mac slowed and let him pull out in front and lead them to the Emergency Room door.

The hospital staff had been alerted by Sunapee EMS. Paco was semi-conscious but not speaking. This was Ursula's Emergency Room. She had the full respect of the staff as she told them what had happened. She barked out orders as they hooked Paco to machines.

Once he was stable, they turned their attention to the lump on his head. It was swollen and hot. They began gently applying cold compresses and regularly calling out his breathing and heart rate.

"Mamá, salvese!" Paco said incoherently, rolling his head back and forth. (Mama, save yourself!)

"Collar!" ordered Ursula.

"Paco," she cooed gently in his ear, *"María está sin peligro."* ("Maria is safe.)

"Mister Mac...." he said, fluttering his eyelids.

"Mac is here, Paco, he is OK. We are all OK. Maria, Ramon, Tomas, all OK. You must be quiet and rest. Does your head hurt?"

"Si".

"Is it bad, Paco? Does it hurt bad?"

"Bad. Maria is OK?"

"Maria is OK. Paco, the doctors are here now. I will not leave you, Paco. This is Ursula, Roger's wife. You remember?"

"Ursula. Thank you. Ursula."

"OK, Mac," she said, "Take my phone. Call Roger. I think Paco has a pretty severe concussion, but if that is all, hopefully, he is OK. Maria will want to know. And make sure those two dudes did not suddenly wake up and get away."

"Don't worry, Ursula. Roger had their gun, and Buddy would tear their throat out."

"Oh, I almost forgot Buddy! He went crazy when you raced off without him. He grabbed my pants and dragged me out to your car. Thank goodness the keys were in it. Mac, why is there always trouble when you are around?"

Mac had no answer to her question.

"Ursula, go scrub. I'll call Roger and be in the waiting room."

**

Chapter Eleven

Sunday, October 8
Newbury, NH
Mac's cabin
12:15 a.m.

Mac rolled into the cabin's gravel parking area to be greeted by a dancing Buddy dog and Roger. Roger was not dancing.

"How is he?" Roger asked.

"He's stable. Ramon is in with him. If he starts to fall asleep, Ramon's job is to press the nurse button and wake him. Once they are sure he is out of danger, they'll let him sleep. He got hit in the head pretty hard trying to protect Maria."

"That guy was an ape, Mac. He was as big as you."

"Yeah, and he could punch, let me tell you. He got me a couple good ones before I put him down. Almost gutted me with that knife."

"State Police took the gun, Mac. It was a .44 Magnum. They pried the knife out of the tree."

"Rog, Vermont State Police recovered a slug from the Bisbee murder. When they test fire this gun maybe ballistics can match it."

"Yeah. The Troopers were pretty excited they might have Bisbee's killer in custody. Here's your phone. Colonel Bradford called an hour ago. He'll call you in the morning."

"Lucky Ursula was here. She was the cool head, Rog. Hey, I caught a glimpse of you doing the mongoose dance for the little guy with the big gun."

"I read his eyes, Mac. He was watching Raoul beat the shit out of you, so I went in fast."

"What the hell were they doing here, Rog? Paco was supposed to do some favor for Louis Lopez, and then these Diaz guys show up with guns and knives. Why?"

"Mac, Tomas said they were trying to collect money. Paco told them to fuck off. The big ape, Raoul, nicknamed Roofy, went nuts. The little one pulled the gun and grabbed Maria. They were going to take her hostage until they got money owed them."

"The boys don't owe them anything, Rog. This jobber Diaz probably got stiffed for a cut of their pay when they left the farm early in Ascutney. That was five months ago. Can you imagine coming here with the cops looking for them? Must be fuckin' crazy. Anyway, we are out of it, at least for now."

"Mac, you got any of that good bourbon left?"

"Hell, yes, I do."

"Let's have a nightcap, and then we both need a scalding hot shower and a few hours of sheet time."

'Rowrf!'

"No bourbon for you, Emma and Buddy."

'Row-Row-Rowrf!'

**

Sunday October 8
Sunapee, New Hampshire
Eleanor's Café
8:00 a.m.

Firemen Doc and Johnny were seated with Mac, Morgan Hillman, and Roger. Doc and John had responded to the EMS call, but they never rolled on it because Mac transported Paco.

"Jeez Mac," Doc said in his New Hampshire drawl, "you ain't been back in town one day, and already we got attempted murdah, assault, shots fyad, concussion, transpawt to hospital and State Police all ova the gawd-dang place. What the hell, man! Jawney he-ah says, and he's right, that trouble swawms to you like worka bees to the queen!"

"Ahh, you two," said Mac, chuckling, "where do you come up with these quasi-sexual weirdo analogies?"

"Well, Mac" said Johnny, "you must admit, if the glove don't fit, you take a shit."

Morgan Hillman howled with laughter and doubled over, gasping for air.

"Johnny, you idiot! The famous quote from O.J.'s lawyer was 'if the glove won't fit, you must acquit."

"Wal, up he-ah in New Hampsha, we reserve the right to say 'if the glove don't fit, we don't give a shit! HAHAHAHA!"

"You clowns," Mac said. "Rog, any word on Paco?"

"Ursula is on shift this morning, so she texted me. Paco is awake and talking, but has memory loss. He remembers trying to protect Maria, and then the lights went out."

"But he is stable?"

"Yes, his vitals are good, but clearly, there is some brain damage. He has residual swelling around the temporal lobe. But he can talk. Mac, what the hell is with these friggin' jobbers? Is this the end of them?"

"Well, I'm waiting to hear from..."

Just then, Mac's phone buzzed. (*Colonel Bradford calling.*)

"Good morning, Mac. How are you and Roger this morning?"

"We're fine. Maybe a few aches and pains, but no serious damage. If Roger doesn't have a scuffle now and then, his special forces training gets rusty, so he is feeling feisty today, Sir."

"Good, glad you weren't hurt. From the accounts we got from Ramon, Maria, and Roger, that was quite a fight."

"Good fights don't last ten seconds, Colonel. This was not my best outing, but I'll take it."

"Mac, we I.D.'d the attackers as Manuel and Raoul Diaz of El Paso, Texas. Neither one is talking. Actually, Raoul can't talk. His jaw is wired shut. They lawyered up with the public defender. Manuel has three broken ribs and a collapsed lung. Roger must have hit him with something pretty hard."

"He did. His fist."

"He must have rocks for fists. Anyway, Raoul has a broken jaw, busted teeth, and a cracked femur. Neither one of them will be out of the hospital for a while. We have them under guard in a secure room in Claremont. They will transfer to Concord's lockup when they are able.

"Mac, we test-fired the revolver taken from Manuel Diaz. It is the same gun used to kill farmer Bisbee. Vermont is charging Manuel and Raoul Diaz with first-degree murder for Bisbee. And we are charging them with assault, attempted murder, and kidnapping in conjunction with their attack on the Rodriguez family, you and Roger. We will send an Investigator to take your statements today, if that is convenient."

"Colonel, I'm going back to the Newport Hospital to check on Paco, but this afternoon I will either be at my house or around the corner at Roger's place. It's the red house at the corner of Old Post and Morrison Lane. Colonel, there were four men reported at Bisbee's. How does that fit with the Diaz brothers?"

"We believe that they were two of the four. The other two are still out there. We have a BOLO for Louis Lopez, but we don't know the name of the other guy. We ran the Texas plate you gave me from the picture taken at the Reasoner farm in New York. The Suburban belongs to Louis Lopez, so the Diaz brothers are part of the Lopez gang, for sure. "

"Can Bisbee's wife confirm Diaz killed her husband?"

"Too soon to know. We will be taking her photos of them today, but after you and Roger beat them, their faces may be unrecognizable to her. Anyway, great job. I am beholden to you and Roger, and I'm starting to see why Morgan Hillman says you are Velcro™ to trouble, Mac."

"Talk to you soon, Colonel."

**

Sunday October 8
Sunapee, New Hampshire
Eleanor's Café
8:15 a.m.

"Hey Eleanor!" yelled Mac, "What's this bug on the floor? Is that a cockroach?"

A stocky lady with a tangle of gray hair came stomping out of the kitchen with a dimpled pot that looked like it had been dropped ten times and shot twice. She waved it menacingly around her head and slammed it upside down on Mac's plate. A pile of steaming raisin oatmeal sent tendrils up in his face.

'Rowrf!' Buddy jumped up and put both his paws on Eleanor's shoulders and slobbered her face.

"Mistah Mac, you ze killer of rats," she said in her thick German accent. "You got another rat last night, eh? Und now, you come in my café and make trouble? I give you plenty. I bonk you onna head with zis pot und giff you a German kick inna pants! HA, HA, HA!"

"I'd like a bowl for my oatmeal, Eleanor."

"HA, HA! When you go away, I think you don't love Eleanor, but always you come back!"

"Eleanor, Marybeth wants your strudel recipe."

"I give it if you promise to bring her to come see me. Zis old lady likes company."

"I promise. Now, can I have a bowl and milk?"

"Of course. You not hurt last night? You cannot stay out uff trouble, you two!"

"Not hurt, just hungry."

"OK, one bowl coming up!"

**

Sunday October 8
Enfield, NH
Gallagher's Grocery and Gas station
8:00 a.m.

Andrés had arisen at 6:00 a.m. before the other Locos. He had warmed some water in a pot on the stove, washed his hair, and shaved. He had put on the new pair of pants and shirt he bought at the nice gas station by the lake. He opened Louis' leather 'clutch' bag and took the envelope with a thousand dollars for the truck rental. The other money in the bag was very tempting, but he did not dare steal any. Nobody dared cross Louis, so he only took the envelope, as instructed. He wanted to leave early, get some breakfast, and wait for Paco.

Andrés had worried about Louis ever since he killed that farmer. It's not like Louis hadn't killed before. He had killed the Russian who tried to hijack the van. The price was $15,000 per man to get into the U.S. and Louis sold seven every trip, so the Russian knew he would have a lot of cash. It was a setup all the way.

The Russian was a Canadian 'Dryback,' a guy who came across the border of northern New Hampshire by walking down forest roads above Saint Venant de Paquette in Quebec, fording a narrow stream and meeting the van at the chosen location in the middle of the night.

Andrés would drive lights-out using night vison goggles. The border was a dense forest. No one lived within miles of the pickup spots. They changed the locations every run. There were thirty five miles of wooded border above Stewartstown to the Maine state line, with plenty of opportunities to walk across.

The Border Patrol was spread thin up there. Andrés had seen their white and green Chevy trucks in the daytime near Berlin but seldom on the woods roads at night. Still, he was always nervous. He did not like this business. Louis had told him they would do legal work when he started with him. That was back when they were jobbers for seasonal workers. Andrés liked doing that. He had made some friends.

After the pickup, Andrés always drove the back roads to Berlin, where Louis would be waiting behind an abandoned building. The Drybacks would pay Louis and get into the back of a transfer truck, usually a rental moving van with no windows.

And that's where the rip-off happened. The Russian's plan was to take the cash and steal the van. But Louis had a bad feeling about this trip because he had never transported a Russian before, and he did not trust them. So Louis had his .44 Magnum in his coat. Santo and Luca had their Glock 17s hiding behind a dumpster.

When the van stopped in Berlin, Louis emerged from the shadows to get paid as the passengers disembarked from the front door. Santo and Luca snuck up behind the van with the key to the back door. They silently unlocked it and cracked it open, guns drawn. When the back door squeaked, the overhead light came on. The Russian spun around, saw their Glocks, and fired his Sig Sauer pistol. But Luca quickly slammed the door while Louis pumped four bullets into the Russian's back.

The .44 made a lot of noise at 3 a.m. The transfer truck took off at the sound of gunfire, so Andrés had to drive forty miles south to a state forest north of Tamworth. They dumped the body and then drove all the way to Lowell, Massachusetts, and left the other six Drybacks at the bus terminal with some extra cash for their trouble. Louis knew they wouldn't talk. Killing the Russian was bad, but he brought it on himself.

But killing farmer Bisbee was different. Andrés didn't like that. The farmer had been good to them. They liked doing business with him. Louis hoped to get Paco's current contact info from him and also "persuade" Bisbee to pay for the Rodriguez' third week last May that HWP reported was unpaid. But HWP did not know that the Rodriguez boys left a week early to get away from Manny Diaz and his crazy brother Roofy.

When Los Locos arrived at Rupert Bisbee's farm on October 2, Bisbee was still angry about the Diaz brothers, so when the black package delivery van turned out to be a surprise visit from Los Locos, he reached for his shotgun. Andrés felt like they could have worked it out had he not gone for the gun, but suddenly, he was aiming it at them, so Louis killed him with one shot through the head.

And then came all the shooting from the house. That farmer's wife was tough, and she was a good shot! They had to scramble to get into the van as she blasted it with her shotgun and then her AR 15! Los Locos were outgunned, so Andrés scrammed the black van out of there.

That was bad, killing farmer Bisbee. And it had been bad since then. Louis seemed unable to think right. This plan for Andrés to meet Paco at the gas station, rent a truck, then come back and pick up the other three Locos was not a good plan to Andrés. With the police looking for them, a Mexican like Paco renting a moving truck in Lebanon, New Hampshire, seemed stupid. It would attract attention, he thought.

But Andrés did not have a better plan. They needed wheels, and they needed to get far away from there. Louis had told him to take the Ruger Pistol in case Paco needed convincing. It was in the gun bag. But the Magnum .44 was not in the bag. That was odd. Was Louis sleeping with it? They always put all the guns back in the gun bag when not using them. Did Louis loan his favorite gun to Manny when they went over to the Diaz's motel to take showers? He did not know.

He liked the Ruger. It was lightweight and fit into the pocket of his new jacket. Everyone in northern New Hampshire wore the tan canvas jackets they sold at the gas station, and he had bought one, too. It made him look like a local, and it was very warm. It had big pockets that swallowed the Ruger, no problem.

So, Andrés had ridden the bicycle from the cabin down to the lake and crossed the bridge at Shakoma Beach. That was a funny name for a beach, he thought, probably some kind of Indian name. Enfield was kind of a funny community, too, he thought. He read about the Shakers, how they would get so excited at a revival they would shake. Weird. But the Shakers were all dead now. Just their village and their simple furniture survived. The Catholic Church had bought the Shaker Village and made it a tourist trap.

Weird. Mexican Catholics would never do such a thing.

It was only a two-mile ride from the cabin to the gas station in Enfield, and even though the morning was cold, his canvas jacket was warm. But his hands were cold on the handlebars. He was going to buy gloves at the gas station. He had his burner phone and money for the truck rental, tolls, and food. Now, he just needed Paco to show up.

And that was starting to worry him because Paco was always on time. But at 8:10, there was no sign of Paco, and none at 8:20. By 8:30, Andrés knew something was wrong. He wanted to call Louis on his burner phone, but by Louis' rules, he could not use it again, and he might need it later.

So, he bought a second round of packaged cakes and a second coffee and sat at a table inside the gas station. There was a newspaper laying there with crumbs and coffee stains on it. It was today's paper from Lebanon. The morning news had a big headline:

Vermont Killers Caught!

Andrés had gone to school in Juarez, but had also lived in El Paso. He spoke good English and could read very well. He put down his coffee and read the article. It said that Manuel and Raoul Diaz had gotten into a gunfight with Paco Rodriguez and his boss, Mackenzie Morrison, in Newbury, New Hampshire!

Andrés got up, walked across the store, and took a thick book of maps off the display rack. He sat back down and looked up New Hampshire. He found Newbury. It was not too far away, maybe 30 miles from Enfield.

The article said Raoul nearly killed Paco, but he survived and was in a hospital in Newport. Manny and Raoul were injured and were in another hospital in Claremont.

Andrés looked up Newport and Claremont and found them on the map.

The article also said the State Police matched the ballistics from a Magnum .44 revolver taken from Manuel Diaz to the bullet that killed Rupert Bisbee in Vermont! They were charging Manuel and Raoul Diaz with the murder of farmer Bisbee. Police were still looking for two other Mexicans because there were four present when Bisbee was killed. Police were looking for Louis Lopez. No name of the other fourth Mexican was given.

There was a picture of Louis Lopez with their black Suburban in the background and part of a sign that said 'Reasoner Orchards'. Below the picture, in bold letters, it read:

'Have you seen this man? Call NH State Police!'

Andrés recognized that photo. It was taken at the Reasoner Orchards in LeRoy, New York. He had been driving. When he parked, Louis went inside to speak to farmer Reasoner. Andrés had stepped down to say hello to his friend Ruiz, who worked there. Otherwise, he might have been in the photo sitting behind the steering wheel. How lucky!

So, Andrés figured Manuel had taken Louis' Magnum .44, or maybe Louis lent it to him. But the good news was the police had captured Bisbee's killer. At least, they thought they had the killer and one accomplice! And now they were looking for Louis Lopez and one other Mexican!

Andrés, with his light skin, his clean-cut appearance, his American gas station clothes, and his tan canvas jacket could pass for an American. But Louis, Santo, and Luca could not. They had the dark skin and the wispy mustaches they refused to shave.

Andrés now knew he could get free! He did not have to go back to Los Locos. The police were not looking for him. He had money, a full belly, good clothes, good English, and a bicycle. He only needed a plan.

He walked up to the counter and paid for the map book. It was called an Atlas, like the superman who held up the world. A funny name for a map book, Andrés thought. But it was a good map book. It had all of the United States, Mexico, and Canada. With this Atlas, he could go anywhere! He asked to use the phone book. They gave him a battered copy from under the counter. It was small, not like the big books in El Paso. That was because the towns were small way up north.

He read through the Yellow pages and found what he was looking for. There was a bus stop in Lebanon, only six miles from Enfield. He looked at his map. He would buy a ticket to Concord, New Hampshire, and go south from there. He did not want to cross back into Vermont. He had a bad feeling about ever going to that state again.

From Concord he could connect to Lowell, Massachusetts. He had been to Lowell after they killed the Russian. He could see Interstate 495 curled around Boston and connected to I-90. He could see that I-90 would take him to LeRoy, New York, where Ruiz was working at the Reasoner vineyard. He could get work there and start over.

Yes, now he had a good plan, so he needed to get going! He bought a sandwich to go into his big pocket before he began his ride to Lebanon and a new life.

But in his excitement, he almost forgot about Louis' burner phone and the gun. He liked the gun, but he didn't need it now. If he got stopped and searched by the police, that would be bad. He knew there were rules for owning a gun and more rules for hiding it in your clothes, and he did not have a permit. So he would get rid of the gun.

And Louis' burner phone, he had to get rid of that too. It was the phone he had used to call Paco. Louis was careful; he knew he could not trust Paco, so he stomped the phone and gave it to Andrés to take it away and get rid of it. He had told Andrés to throw it out of the moving truck.

But Andrés was not going to be driving a moving truck. Not with Paco in the hospital. No, he was going to get on a bus and get away from Los Locos for good. So, before he got on his borrowed bike and rode to Lebanon, he walked outside and put some air in the bicycle tires. When he was done, he took the gun and the phone and dropped them into the trash can on the side of the gas station by the air pump, making sure his back was turned, and no one could see him do it. All the cameras were up high on the wall and they faced the front of the parking lot.

Then he got some blue paper towels and wet them from the windshield squeegee bucket, washed down his bicycle, and wiped it off. He covered the gun and the phone with the wet towels so no one would ever see them. Then he got on his clean bicycle and happily began pedaling to Lebanon, following the roads on his Atlas, which was tucked neatly inside his warm canvas jacket.

Yes, this was a good plan, Andrés thought.

**

Sunday October 8
Near Enfield, NH
Los Locos' cabin
 9:30 a.m.

Louis Lopez was worried. He figured a half-hour for Paco to drive to Lebanon, a half-hour to rent the moving truck, and a half-hour to return.

Either Paco or Andrés would call when they got back with the truck. But they had not called. They should have been at the parking lot at Shakoma Beach by now. Something was wrong. Maybe they were delayed at the truck rental. Maybe they got a flat tire. Or, maybe Paco had pulled a fast one and never picked up Andrés. But if that had happened, Andrés would have called him. He was worried.

So, he called Andrés' clean cell phone. It was a burner, of course. Louis was down to his own last clean burner, so he did not dare use it to call the rental company to see if they had rented Paco a truck. But he could call Andrés. That was a safe call.

But Andrés did not answer. "How could this be?" Louis asked himself. "Was there no cell service out here in these woods?" But he had called Paco from this cabin, and his phone had worked. Something was definitely wrong.

So Louis had taken the other bike off the shed wall. Its tires were soft, and he could find no air pump, so he walked the bike down the gravel driveway and only rode it on the smooth asphalt to the Shakoma Beach parking lot.

But they were not there. The gravel did not look like a heavy moving truck had come in, turned around, and left. So Louis rode across the bridge over Mascoma Lake to Gallagher's Grocery and Gas. That was not far, maybe a mile. He needed to find out what happened to Andrés. Maybe he was still waiting there, but if he was, why did he not call him? Louis did not want to use his last clean burner to call Paco and find out where he was, because then he would have to throw it away in case Paco told the police about Louis. They could trace his phone location.

But when Louis arrived at the gas station, there was no sign of Andrés. He did not want to go inside. He wore a floppy hat he found in the cabin that made him look like a local. It covered his face when he walked in front of the cameras. He was also wearing an old coat he found in the cabin, so he looked like an American, he thought. Nothing to do now but ride back. But first, he would put some air in these tires. So he pumped up the tires and got his hands dirty. He walked over to the squeegee bucket, soaked a blue paper towel in the windshield washer fluid, and cleaned his hands. Then he threw the towels in the trash can by the air pump.

Two layers of trash below was the Ruger Max pistol. And the smashed burner phone, the one he had used to call Paco. The glass was smashed on the phone; yes, it was, but inside, its little electronic heart was still beating, and its battery still had a full charge. It was just resting, ready to come to life.

**

**Sunday October 8
Newport, NH
City Hospital
10:00 a.m.**

Emergency room nurse Ursula Lemonier had pulled a double shift by coming in at eleven p.m. with Paco. Her regular shift began at seven a.m., so she stayed over. She was tired but keeping a close watch on Paco because brain injuries are bad. Even if the patient is stable and talking, there could be a brain bleed. That was why she was wheeling him into the room with the CAT scan machine.

For Paco, being shoved into the big metal tube was scary. He could not move his head because it was strapped securely. It was cold in that tube. He shivered. But he was alive, and he could see, although there were double edges around everything. And he could hear. But he could not remember what happened or why he was here. The nurse had explained it to him, but his mind was fuzzy and the words made his head hurt. So she stopped talking to him and said he should rest and let them take pictures inside his head.

Why did they need pictures inside his head, he wondered? But thinking about it made his head hurt, so he just rested while the machine whirred and purred, and pretty soon, they slid back the tray that he was laying on, and he was out of the tube.

"OK, Paco, we are going to take you back to your room now," the nice nurse Ursula said. Ursula looked familiar, like someone Paco should know. He seemed to remember seeing her before, but he could not remember where.

"Do I know you?" Paco asked.

"Yes, Paco. I am Ursula Lemonier, Roger's wife. You are building us a new house with your brothers, your two twin cousins, and your boss, Mac Morrison."

"Mister Mac," Paco said uncertainly. That name made sense, but he did not know why he said it.

"Yes, Mister Mac. Do you remember Mister Mac, Paco?"

"57 Chevy. He showed us his '57 Chevy. New York, LeRoy, New York, at the motel. Mister Mac has a big white dog and a '57 Chevy."

"Yes, that's right, Paco. Do you remember what you did after leaving LeRoy, New York?"

"Mister Mac said he had work for us. In New Hampshire."

"Yes, that's right, Paco. Do you remember where you worked after Leroy and before Mister Mac?"

There was a long pause. Paco was trying to think, but he couldn't think, and he couldn't remember.

"My head hurts," he said.

"OK, Paco, we'll talk later. We're going to put you back in bed. I want you to close your eyes and rest. Would you like some soft music?"

"Music? Yes."

"Tell me if you like this, Paco."

She pushed the button, and Spanish flamenco guitar music floated through the room. Very nice, this music, Paco thought. It reminded him of Juarez, his home.

"That is nice, Ursula, thank you."

"Sleep now, Paco, Maria will come to see you."

**

Newport City Hospital
11:00 a.m.

The neurologist and radiologist concurred with their reading of the CAT scan.

"There is no bleeding in the brain, and I do not see structural damage," said Dr. Bender, "but clearly there has been some internal damage as manifested by his severe headaches, blurred vision, and loss of memory. But I think we can send him home with strict orders to rest, sleep, and stay in a dark room. It will be good for him to be back in familiar settings and have his mother's cooking."

The translator repeated into the phone to Maria, who had asked Tomas to call the hospital. She sobbed into her handkerchief and nodded her head.

"*Dios mío, gracias*" she said, over and over.

Ursula told the translator to tell Maria she would come and check on

Paco once he was back home at Morrison's compound.

**

Newport City Hospital
11:10 a.m.

NH State Police Investigator Jaqueline Beaulieu had hoped she could question Paco, but the doctors would not permit it. He was not ready, they told her. He could not remember much after leaving LeRoy, New York, and that was last May, according to Ramon, who had stayed by his side ever since the beating.

So she questioned Ramon, using an interpreter, but he offered little information. He said Paco had gotten a call from a jobber, Louis Lopez, and he agreed to do him a favor, but he did not say when or what. Then, these other jobbers, Manny and Raoul Diaz, showed up and demanded money. When Paco told them to get out, they grabbed Maria. Paco tried to pull her away, but then Raoul started beating him over and over in the head. Raoul would have killed Paco if not for Mr. Mac and Roger. They came and saved them.

Investigator Beaulieu was starting to get a different picture of Mac Morrison. Her first impression was that he was rude, uncooperative, and did not respect her authority. And the stories she had heard about him, Roger Lemonier and Morgan Hillman as some kind of swashbuckling Three Musketeers fighting for the little guy were obviously just barstool tales from the north woods.

But, in front of a half-dozen witnesses, the two of them had run directly into a fight with a guy armed with a cannon and a giant who was clubbing poor Paco down to his knees. And all the people that saw it said the same thing. Roger walked directly at the gun, kicked the shit out of Manny, who had been holding it, then caved in his ribs and collapsed his lung - with one punch!

And Mac had jumped in and taken on an ape half his age, broke his jaw, busted his teeth, and cracked his thigh bone, all in less than ten seconds. Mac and Roger took care of business.

So, Investigator Beaulieu had to reset her opinion of those two. She knew that Colonel Bradford thought highly of Morrison, and now she began to see why.

"Ramon," she said, "Paco got a phone call yesterday, and then the Diaz brothers showed up. Do you think those events were related?"

She waited for the translator to repeat and the get Ramon's response. He shrugged his shoulders. He didn't know.

"Ramon, where is Paco's phone?"

He understood that.

"At home," he said, "Maria has it. She used it to call Mr. Mac. He saved us."

So Investigator Beaulieu got in her State Police Explorer and headed for Newbury. It would take her half an hour to get there, and on the way, she could call in and report her findings, which were nothing so far.

**

Sunday October 8
Enfield NH
Gallagher's Grocery and Gas
11:15 a.m.

Jaime, which means 'I love you' in French if you put an apostrophe after the 'J,' was a drunk. Yes, he was, and always had been. Jaime preferred to be called Jamie, but nobody did. Jaime Charbonneau was a drunk because his father had been a drunk, and he learned from the best, as he used to say.

The Charbonneaus owned a sawmill because, after all, in New Hampshire's north woods, there were few things to do that did not involve cutting down trees and sawing them up. Oh, there was fishing and hunting, but you couldn't make a living doing that unless you were a guide for the rich and stupid flatlanders who inhabited the cabins sprinkled around the territory in the summer time. But as soon as cold weather arrived and the good fishing and hunting began, they all scattered back to Boston or Chelmsford or Revere, where they made money pulling teeth or selling advertising or some other pedestrian nonsense that would never support them in the north woods.

No, Jaime was a drunk by DNA, as he used to say, and people were astonished he knew what DNA was. But in truth, Jaime was a very intelligent man. He just did not choose to use his brain for creative purposes. And, of course, he was continually depressed by the death of his father Marcel, who, in a drunken stupor, had tripped while sawing a log and fallen into the 60-inch spinning circular blade that chopped him in half, thereby ending his drinking days for good.

Had young Jaime reported to work that day, as he was supposed to, he was sure that if anyone had fallen into the saw, it would have been him. However, he had tied one on the night before, and he was so proudly drunk by morning that he did not even open his eyes before eleven a.m., and his father had closed his at ten.

Jaime had had to live with that guilt now for twenty years. He was forty, but he looked sixty. Hard drinking will do that to a person. But Jaime had another, better habit, and that was he never spent more than he had, and after the sale of the mill and 100 acres of fine forest land, Jaime was left with a tidy sum with which to spend his life pursuing meaningless ventures that cost little and allowed him time to drink and consider his circumstances, which were rather pathetic.

And so it was Jaime's habit, every day, regardless of the weather, to ride his decrepit bike to Gallagher's Grocery and Gas station, buy a coffee and some packaged cakes, and read yesterday's leftover newspaper, which was always thrown in the trash can on the side of the station by the air pump.

Today, though, there was no yesterday's paper on the top of the trash in the can by the air pump. Someone had used a lot of blue paper towels for the windshields and tossed them in the barrel by the side of the store, far from the gas pumps and squeegee bucket. That was odd.

But Jaime knew that whoever the reliable person was that always tossed his paper in that can, it would be there. And so he reached down and rummaged through the thick wads of wet blue towels, feeling for the familiar texture of a folded-over newspaper. But instead, his hand hit something smooth and hard.

"Huh!" he said, now feeling much more sober, having had his coffee and cakes, and being on the edge of a mystery that would brighten his otherwise pathetic day. He now started tossing blue towels on the ground and making quite a mess until he discovered the hard, smooth something and grabbed it.

"Huh!" He said again as he sat on the curb and tapped the cracked screen of the obviously damaged cell phone. It looked damaged, but the phone came to life and offered him a dozen icons to play with. Jaime did not have a cell phone of his own, that being an unnecessary expense to his lifestyle. But he knew how they worked because whenever he needed to make a call, he borrowed someone's, usually his neighbor's. Now that there was a delivery service app, he could order a fifth of good Kentucky Bourbon anytime he wanted, and he did not even have to go out in cold weather. They would deliver to his cabin door.

He knew the delivery number by heart, so he punched it in and immediately was connected to his favorite order robot. He placed his order, put it on his credit card with tip, and knew it would be on his front porch soon. Wonderful! He knew that this phone would eventually lose power, and if it had been thrown out, whoever owned it was not going to keep paying for it, so this would be a short-lived luxury. But he would love having the convenience of his own phone for however long it had to live.

Now intrigued, he dove back into the trash can, because if someone threw out a working cell phone, maybe they threw out other good stuff, too. Those rich flatlanders were incredibly wasteful people. They would often come up for a week's vacation, buy a new set of skis, boots, and poles, and then just leave them by the dumpster at Gallagher's when they left town because they would buy new ones next year. So, the locals made a habit of dumpster diving when cabins were closed up.

Jaime jammed his hand back into the barrel, pushed aside more blue towels, and felt something like a tool. He gently grabbed it and pulled his hand out, holding a Ruger Max pocket pistol. It had a magazine in it and was fully loaded.

Now fully sober, Jaime considered these two objects. If the phone was a throw-away and the screen got damaged, he could see someone tossing it in the trash when they stopped to fill their gas tank. But a gun like this? This had to be worth some money.

Let's find out, he asked himself, and spoke to the phone, asking for the cost of a Ruger LCP Max pistol.

The robotic voice answered quickly.

"The manufacturer's suggested retail price for a Ruger LCP Max pistol is $479.00."

"Wow," said Jaime out loud. Those rich flatlanders sure were wasteful and careless. If they wanted to throw out the gun, they should know enough not to throw out the ammunition with it. A pistol like this was for personal protection; he knew that. You couldn't hunt with it. But he might be able to sell it on the internet. So, Jaime popped the ammo clip out, stuck it in the left pocket of his warm canvas jacket, and put the pistol in his right pocket. Then he reached down into the trash barrel and grabbed yesterday's newspaper, tucked it inside his jacket, and rode home on his bike.

Upon arriving at his cabin, he noticed that the bourbon had not yet been delivered, so he decided to have some fun with his new pistol. He walked out back and set some empty bourbon bottles on a log, then measured off 15 paces to a stump. Since Jaime lived on 50 acres tucked back in the woods, no one would likely hear pistol shots, and even if they did, he was target shooting on his own property. It was too early for firearm deer season, so he was not worried about gun hunters being in his woods. It was archery season, but not many archers hunted here in the pines because you could not see more than 20 yards in any direction.

Jaime knelt and took a firing position with the pistol sitting on the stump. Then he squeezed off eleven shots: 'pop, pop, pop, pop, pop, pop, pop, pop, pop, pop, pop!' After each 'pop' there was a 'ping' as the brass shell casing ejected from the pistol. He hit four bottles. The other seven bullets went into a pile of dirt behind the log. The brass shell casings lay on the ground next to the stump. He would clean them up later. There was one more thing to do while he was sober. He took out his new phone and took pictures of this pistol for the internet ad.

As he walked around to the front of his cabin, his delivery service was pulling up his gravel driveway. It was Ted Downing, his usual driver. Ted was surprised to see Jaime walking around, and he looked steady like he was sober. Usually, he would be sitting on the battered porch sofa, half-potted, with an empty bottle at his feet.

Then he saw the gun.

"Whoa, Jaime, it's me Ted, Mr. Bourbon, dude! Don't shoot the delivery man!"

Jaime laughed.

Ted had never heard him laugh before. He *was* sober.

"Oh, this?" Jaime said, laying the Ruger down on the porch. "Naw, Ted, I was just doing a little target practice out back. Shot 4 bottles out of 11; first time I ever fired this thing. Shoots pretty straight at short range. Helps if you're sober, too. It's empty, and the safety is on. Wanna see it?"

"You bet, Jaime. You just get this?"

"Yeah, found it this morning. I'm gonna put it on the Net and see if I can get a couple bucks for it."

"Looks almost new," said Ted.

"Does, don't it? "Well, it can't be new, 'cause its got a few scratches on it, but if it were new, it would be $500."

"Shoots straight? Can I try it, Jaime?"

"Sorry, I used the clip, and I don't have any ammo. Why, you interested?"

"Jaime, with those killers still out there and me doing deliveries up north where the illegals are coming in, I would feel better having some protection. Little gun like that could go in my pocket, and I would always be armed. How much you asking?"

"Ted, I don't have paperwork for it. What is it worth to you?"

"Would you take fifty bucks cash, Jaime?"

"No, but I would take two bottles of bourbon, Ted. And no paperwork, no receipt. You take your chances. I can tell you, it does work and shoots straight."

"Jaime, you got a deal. Let me get you three bottles, the one you paid for, and two more. Is that good?"

"Ted, the way I feel now, I don't even think I'm gonna drink today. Maybe a little sip before bed, but I want to see how it feels being sober for a change."

"So, we both got a good deal, eh Jaime?"

"Yes, we did, Ted. Now, be careful with that pistol. Get the right ammo for it, no cheap stuff. And take some practice before you put it in your pocket."

"Good advice, Jaime. I gotta make a delivery down in Newbury. Think I'll stop in at Pierre's Bait and Guns. He knows everything, and he's got a practice range. He'll sell me the right ammo. Thanks for the advice, Jaime."

"You're welcome, Ted."

"Jaime," said Ted, "I'm cutting my own pay by saying this, but I hope you start drinking less. I think you are an interesting person, but drinking is killing you, man. I hope to come see you out in your yard or riding your bike and not asleep on that sofa. OK?"

"I think I'll give it a whirl, Ted, just because you asked me to. Thank you."

"Good deal. See ya, Jaime!"

**

Philip C. Laurien

Sunday October 8
Newbury, NH
Mac Morrison's barn workshop
12:00 p.m.

Gravel crunched under the tires of the State Police Explorer as Investigator Jaqueline Beaulieu turned down the long sloping lane with the crooked mailbox that said "Morrison." She had called ahead. Mac said he would meet her at his steel barn-shop, and then they would walk to the mobile home where Maria Rodriguez and her boys were staying.

Buddy heard the tires on the gravel, got up off the floor, and alerted by sitting down in front of Mac. Someone was coming.

"Good boy, Buddy, that's probably Inspector Beaulieu."

Buddy was sticking extra close to Mac after last night's fight. Mac was different after he came back from the hospital, not his usual self. He rubbed Buddy's ears this morning and gave him a pat. Usually, he would engage Buddy in all of his thoughts by conversation. Buddy did not understand most of the words, of course, but he understood tone, facial expression, and body language. And today, his Master Mac, who had rescued him from that abusive police dog breeder, and who had been so good to him and made him part of his home, was sad.

Yes, Buddy could tell that Mac was sad by the tune he was whistling. Mac did not go to bed after Roger left. He had picked up his 12-string Martin guitar that he bought to replace the one lost in the barn fire last May. Every physical thing that Mac had built or cherished in his 50 years was burned in that fire: everything except his baby blue '57 Chevy.

Mac had sat on a stool by the wood stove and played that one tune all night until it finally started to sound like the tune that came out of the black box with the silver discs.

"Buddy, I might as well admit it," Mac had finally said, "I can play the chords and a bit of the fingering, but Feliciano, I am not. Do you know what that tune is, Buddy-boy?"

Buddy had cocked his head sideways as if to say, "No, tell me Mac."

"That's Feliciano's instrumental version of *And I Love Her*[5]. I cannot

---

5   "And I Love Her", song by recorded by the Beatles, written mainly by Paul McCartney(credited to Lennon-McCartney). The fifth track on their third album, A Hard Day›s Night. Covered as an instrumental by Jose Feliciano on his 1967 album "Feliciano."

make my guitar sing like he can. I don't have his hands or his soul, Buddy. I feel Gabriella and Marybeth in my heart today, Buddy. They are over there, 400 miles from you and me and Emma, Budso. We should be together. Not busting up fights with thugs like the Diaz boys. We should be with them. We gotta do something about that, Bud."

So Buddy knew that Mac was sad. And now someone was coming.

'Rowrf!'

"Yeah, let's go see Ms. Beaulieu, Buds."

She got out of her Explorer, brushed off her dark green uniform shirt, placed her flat brim gray hat on her head, and looked in her side view mirror to check her appearance.

"While you were primping, I could have snuffed you," said Mac.

She whirled around. Her hand was on her Smith and Wesson M&P 45 pistol, but she kept it holstered.

"Morrison, just when I think maybe I'm going to like you, you piss me off again."

"Well, since we are on a last-name basis, Beaulieu, I was just trying to save your life. You don't arrive at the scene, any scene, checking your appearance. You scan for danger; you assess. Your life may depend on it someday, even in rural New Hampshire."

"You're giving me advice? I know you can build houses, Morrison, and I guess you can fight, but I've been to the State Police training academy. I can handle myself. And by the way, how the hell did you and your excavator friend manage to defeat those two gun-wielding thugs and do so much damage to them? They are both going to be in the hospital a while and then they will be in jail pending their trial for the murder of Farmer Bisbee."

"You know Jaqueline," Mac said, changing to a first name basis to lower the temperature of the conversation, "that's another thing. Never judge a book by its cover. How old are you, 26?"

"Oh, now you're going to say I'm inexperienced? I'm twenty-seven."

"Military service?"

"No."

"So, no hand-to-hand combat experience?"

"Of course not."

"Get in fights as a kid?"

"No. I was the peacemaker type."

"Why did you want to be a cop?"

"To help people."

"OK, Good answer. But you better get some cop instincts, and quick, or you could get dead. Just sayin'. I got my fighting experience starting at age ten, dealing with bullies bigger than me. Fighting was a daily thing for me until age 18 when I enlisted in the U.S. Army and learned techniques that served me well in Desert Storm. Did three years in Kuwait and Iraq. Combat, search and destroy. First Lieutenant of my platoon. Later, I did two years of security for U.S. Forces, meaning hired gun, in Afghanistan."

"And Lemonier?"

"Ten years Special Forces. Morgan Hillman, too. We don't strut our stuff. We have lives to lead, but we can handle ourselves when we need to. Now can we knock off the chippy 'I'm smarter than you' bullshit and get down to business?"

"OK. Sorry."

"Let's go see Maria."

**

Maria stood in front of the mobile home with Tomas and the twin seventeen-year-old apprentice carpenters, Lupe and Miguel. She handed Paco's phone to Investigator Beaulieu. Beaulieu looked at the call history.

"What day and time did Paco get a call from Louis Lopez?" she asked.

The twins translated.

"She thinks it was mid-morning yesterday," they said.

Beaulieu scanned the call history. There was a call at ten a.m. Saturday October 7. She was about to press the button to reverse the call when Mac snatched the phone from her hand.

"What are you doing, Morrison? That is evidence!"

"Trying to keep you from making another mistake, Jackie." Now, he was using the more familiar name, one he had not been given permission to use. It softened her expression, however.

"What?"

"OK, first of all, what were you going to say? Were you going to identify yourself as a New Hampshire State Police Investigator?"

"Yes, of course."

"No, no, no. First of all, you don't know if that is Louis Lopez' number. Maria might have gotten the time wrong. Second if it is Lopez, you just told him you were a cop, so he'll hang up the phone and trash it and take off from wherever he's at. So now you can't trace his location because he will be gone, and the phone will be at the bottom of a lake or under a bridge or sitting on a railroad track waiting to be crushed by the next freight train.

"You need to first have your techs determine if they can trace ownership of that number. If they can't, it's a burner. But even so, they can trace its last known location. Then, you can organize an approach to that location. Remember, if these guys are part of the foursome that killed Bisbee, they are armed, and they are not going to surrender without a fight. Yes, the phone is a tool, and it might be evidence, but look before you leap."

Mac could see the anger and embarrassment on Investigator Beaulieu's face. He was right; she could see that. She was not using good judgment.

"OK, you're right, thanks for stopping me. May I please have the phone back?"

"Of course, Jackie. Look, if it was an emergency, we might make the call now, but it's not. You have the Diaz boys and the gun that killed Bisbee. Lopez and his sidekick, or sidekicks, are persons of interest. It's better to take the time to work up the situation."

"OK, Mac, I'm going to run this phone down to Concord and have our techs check it out. I like the idea of tracing its location, and then we'll converge on that spot and hopefully get our hands on the other two accomplices in Bisbee's murder."

"Now you're talking, Jackie."

"Mac. I'm gonna call Colonel Bradford and update him. Unless I miss my guess, he'll call you."

"Glad to help. I'll be at the Newport City Hospital. If they release Paco, I'll be bringing him back here. I won't get much work done on Roger's house today, but the twins will. That's where I'll be later."

"Copy that. Thanks, Mac".

**

Philip C. Laurien

**Sunday October 8
Lowell, Massachusetts
Greyhound Bus Station
12:30 p.m.**

Andrés finished his sandwich and tossed the last of his Coke in the trash. They had just called his bus. It would be stopping at Worcester and Springfield, then no stops until Albany, New York, where he would have to change buses and wait for two hours to transfer to Syracuse.

He was having fun studying his new Atlas. With this book, he could see America, and Canada, and Mexico, his home! It was very exciting. And even more exciting to be free of Los Locos! He had wanted to get away from Louis, Santo, and Luca ever since they killed that Russian. Andrés had been hired to pass for an American and be the driver, not to kill people.

And now, with Manny and Raoul arrested for the murder of that farmer and the police looking for Louis and one other Mexican, Andrés had a chance to start his life over. He was eighteen when Louis had plucked him from the barrio and told him he had a good job for him, nothing illegal. Well, mostly nothing illegal. That was before Louis branched out into smuggling migrants across the Canadian border. That bothered Andrés, but when you are twenty-two, and far from your pitiful home in the barrio, it is hard to go your own way.

But now he had almost one thousand dollars in his pocket and a bus ticket to a new life! And he was going to do it right. He would be in LeRoy by nightfall. He would call his friend Ruiz to come and pick him up. Ruiz had an old Chevy van with a good engine that ran and ran and never quit. Andrés would get up in the morning and start his new life working for Mr. Reasoner, he hoped. He would do anything, any kind of honest work. He would go to church and confess.

And on their days off, Andrés and Ruiz could go camping and explore this region called the Finger Lakes on his Atlas. New York had many beautiful areas, and the pictures of the Finger Lakes entranced him. It was so green, and the lake waters looked so clear and beautiful. It looked peaceful, not like the violent barrio he had come from. Yes, it was a good plan; he had a chance now for a new future.

**

Sunday October 8
Newport NH
City Hospital
1:30 p.m.

After his release, Paco sat on the broad front bench seat of Mac's 1971 Chevy Impala while Maria and Ramon rode in the cavernous back. The doctor said Paco had a severe concussion. He had been unconscious for the better part of twenty minutes. There was memory loss, but it would likely return in time.

Mac had had a dozen concussions in his life, and a couple of them were just as severe, so he knew that it takes time and quiet rest. For a while, one cannot think. The little electrical circuits in the brain are broken and have to mend themselves. It is no good to strain them. Just let the brain heal. But it would be good to test and see how Paco was progressing.

"Mister Mac," Paco said, "this is another nice Chevy. Do you still have the '57?"

"Sure, Paco, don't you remember? I drove you to the hospital in it."

"I don't remember driving to the hospital."

"What's my dog's name, Paco?"

"Buddy."

"Correct. Whose house are we building?"

"Roger's."

"Correct. Who is Louis Lopez?"

Paco paused as if he was not going to answer. "He was our first jobber, Mister Mac. Before Manuel Diaz."

"Did Diaz work for Lopez?"

"Yes."

"Why did you switch to Diaz for your job leads?"

"We didn't switch, Mister Mac. They did."

"Do you know why?"

"No."

"When did that happen?"

"Maybe sometime last year. I tell dates by where we were when things happened. But I don't remember when that was."

"What is the last thing you can remember, Paco?"

"I remember putting siding on Roger's house."

"That is a big improvement since this morning, Paco. Ursula said you couldn't remember past the motel in LeRoy last May."

"Yes, with your '57 Chevy, the blue one. It is so beautiful. I remember that you bought this car in LeRoy on your way back to New Hampshire. We were kicking the football at the motel and you drove up with this car on a trailer."

"Your memory is coming back, Paco. Louis Lopez called you Saturday morning and asked you for a favor. Do you remember that?"

Paco tilted his head to the side and rubbed his temple.

"Does it make your head hurt to try to remember Saturday, Paco?"

"Yes, I'm sorry, Mr. Mac."

"Then don't think about it now. Let's think about the dinner Maria is going to cook for you and the boys tonight."

Paco smiled.

"I would like steak enchiladas, guacamole and beans, and a cold, cold Coca-Cola."

"Paco, tell Maria your menu for supper, please." Paco spoke to her. She smiled and nodded her head, then spoke quickly in Spanish.

"What did she say, Paco?"

"She says she will need some things from the store."

"Have her make a list. I will get them for her. Here we are, home again, Paco. Does it look like home to you?"

"Mister Mac, it looks like heaven. Ramon says you saved my life. I don't remember. But I say thank you, and I will pay you back. I am in your debt."

"Paco, you don't have to pay me back. I am happy you are doing well. You are making great progress. Soon, you will be back helping us build Roger's house. That is all the thanks I need."

**

Sunday October 8
Near Enfield NH
At the Los Locos' Cabin
2:00 p.m.

Louis was thinking: what to do now? No Paco, no Andrés, no phone call from either one. He and his two Locos still had no car to get away, and they had eaten all the canned food in the cabin.

(Speaking Spanish)

"Luca," he said, "we cannot think on an empty stomach. Wash your face and shave your mustache. Tuck your hair up inside this hunter's cap hanging on the peg, and wear this old canvas jacket. You will look more like an American. Ride the bike down to the gas station and order a submarine sandwich, the biggest one they can make. Buy a liter of cola and some packaged cakes. Buy a pair of sunglasses, too. Not too dark, just enough to hide your eyes. Try them on while they are making the sandwich. Tear the tag off and give it to the cashier. Wear the sunglasses when you pay. They will put the food in a bag that you can hang on the handlebars. Be careful, keep the hat down low, and only speak softly, try to sound like an American. I am giving you $200. That is much more than you need, but if you see a shirt that looks like an American would wear, you can buy it."

So Luca washed his face, shaved his mustache, and tucked his hair under the hunter's hat, then rode two miles to Gallagher's Grocery and Gas station. He parked the bike to the side and went in, ordered the submarine sandwich, and began trying on sunglasses. He found a pair he liked, then tore off the tag and put them on. The cashier was looking at him, so he walked over and handed him the price tag, then pointed to the T-shirt rack. The clerk nodded.

He picked out a T-shirt that said *New England Patriots* and walked back to the cashier. The packaged cakes were on a rack to the left of the counter below the newspapers. As he made his cake selection, he caught a glimpse of something familiar. He glanced at the newspaper and saw a picture of Louis Lopez! There were bold words below the picture:

Have you seen this man? Call NH State Police!

Luca felt the hair stand up on his neck as he stared at the picture. He put the cakes on the counter.

"One, two-foot-long super-sized submarine sandwich, extra toppings, sunglasses, T-shirt, and four cakes. Is that all?" the cashier asked.

Luca stammered. "Uh, one liter of Coca-Cola, a pack of Marlboros, and a newspaper." He grabbed the Coke from the cooler and put the newspaper on the counter face down.

"Thirty-two dollars, please," the cashier said. He was an older man with a beard. He sounded bored. He did not look at Luca as he scanned the items and he was not looking at him now. He was looking at the wad of money Luca was pulling from his pocket. Maybe he had not read today's paper.

Luca did not look at him. The man put everything in a big shopping bag with handles. Luca gave him two twenty dollar bills and the man gave him back his change. Luca turned around and quickly walked outside to the bike. He looped the bag over the handlebar and rode as fast as he could back to the cabin.

He went inside and put the submarine sandwich on the counter. Santo poured three glasses of Coca-Cola while Louis cut the sub into three even sections and put them on plates. They put the cakes on the table for dessert. Luca turned the newspaper upside down on the counter with the cigarettes and sat with the others. The sub was very good. The cakes were very good, and the Coca-Cola was cold and refreshing.

Luca passed out cigarettes, and they all lit up. They were feeling better. Now they could talk. Now was the time to show Louis the newspaper. He went to the counter and got the paper, brought it to the table, and laid it down without fanfare. Louis took a big drag on his cigarette and inhaled, enjoying the sting of the smoke in his lungs. As he blew it out, he glanced down at the front page of the paper and saw his face staring up at him.

He choked on the cigarette smoke, waved it away from his eyes, picked up the paper, and read it. **Vermont Killers Caught**! Then he read about Manny and Raoul and their fight with Paco Rodriguez. What the fuck? Why were Manny and Raoul fighting with Paco? Shots were fired, and a guy named Morrison had injured Raoul. Manny and Raoul were in a hospital in Claremont, and Paco was in a hospital in Newport!

So, that is why Paco never showed up with the rental truck! He was in the hospital! But what the fuck were Manny and Raoul doing fighting with Paco? He had given no orders for them to do anything! He had put them in that motel, with the Chevrolet Suburban in the storage garage next door, to keep them away from him! If they were caught in the black Suburban with the stolen plate, he did not want to be with them!

But he had done one thing right. He gave Manny his .44 Magnum so that if he were stopped and questioned and they found that gun, maybe the police could match it to the bullet that killed Bisbee. Then Louis would never be blamed. And now, it had happened! He was thrilled! Manny was being charged with Bisbee's murder! Wonderful!

But then he snapped back to reality. He glanced at the newspaper and saw the picture of himself! There were bold words below the picture:

Have you seen this man? Call NH State Police!

This picture of him was bad. Very bad. Everywhere he went people would be looking for him. And he did not look like an American. Ahhh! So that is why Andrés did not come back! Andrés always bought packaged cakes when he sent him to the store. When Paco did not show up, he must have sat there waiting, eating packaged cakes. He must have seen this newspaper story and realized the police were not looking for him, and he had $1,000 to get away! Andrés had bought American clothes at the gas station, and with his light skin, he could pass for an American.

This did not make Louis angry. In fact, he admired Andrés. Good thinking, Andrés! That showed ingenuity and courage! He wished him luck. He hoped he made it.

But now, the three Locos needed a new plan. And they needed to get out of this cabin and out of this state because Enfield was near Newbury. The police arrested The Diaz Boyz in Newbury. The police would be looking for him in this area. They would do a house-to-house search. They would eventually come to this cabin. Louis needed wheels.

They couldn't walk the roads. They only had one bike. They certainly could not hitchhike. They could not take a bus, all three of them together. Everyone would be looking for him. But not Santo and Luca, because the police must not have their pictures or their names. Yet. But Paco would tell. He knows Santo and Luca, and now that Manny and Raoul are in jail, they can't threaten him. And with Louis' picture in the paper he could not go see Paco. There will be people guarding him.

He thought about carjacking. They had guns. They could jump out in front of a car and make them stop. But the road by the cabin was a fast road. People drove 60 miles an hour. If you jumped out in front of them, they would just drive around you or run you over. He could have Santo steal a car while people were inside the gas station if they left their keys in the car. But that was not good. They would be seen right away and be on camera. Besides, so many of these people up north carried guns. They could just kill you.

Louis was turning the pages to see if there were any other stories about him and his gang, but there weren't. When he got to the back of the newspaper, he was in the classified ads. People were selling washing machines, baby clothes, TVs and...old cars!

There were not many cars for sale, perhaps a dozen. Louis knew that most people bought cars on the internet these days. But in small towns, many people still used the local paper. They would be the cheap cars. And the sellers would probably be old people, people who didn't use the internet. He read the ads. Louis liked GM cars, but any car would do. As long as it worked and was reliable, it didn't matter. But a plain color would be good.

An ad for an old Cadillac said the car could be seen at the boat rental on Mascoma Lake. This cabin was on Mascoma Lake. He thought back to when he was scouting this cabin. He had driven this side of the lake and seen a boat rental sign. Yes, he remembered, it was perhaps two miles north of the bridge.

Now he read more about this car. It was a white 2002 Cadillac Deville, 140,000 miles, new battery, good tires, reliable. For sale by owner. $3,995. There was a phone number listed, but he did not want to use his clean burner phone to call. He would go see it in person.

But first, he would shave his mustache and cut his hair short. And then he would ride the bike two miles to see if the car was still there.

**

Mascoma Lake Boat Rentalz
4:00 p.m.

And it was. The "For Sale" sign was old and dirty.

Louis casually parked the bike by some picnic tables overlooking the lake. He strolled over to look at the car. He walked around it and checked it out.

The tires looked very good, almost new. There was no rust, but the paint was dull from sitting outside. There were leaves in the cowl, and the windshield was bird-splattered. This car had been sitting here a long time. That was good. The owner was going to take any offer just to get it out of here before winter.

A man opened the door to the little house with the boat rental sign and said, "Would you like to start it up?"

"Yes," said Louis, in his best American accent. He was wearing the hunter's cap and tan canvas jacket he took from the cottage, and he had found some tan leather boots in the cottage closet that fit him. He looked as much like a local as he could.

"It's a good car," the man said. "Belonged to a trailer owner up in the campground. It was his summer car. He died this year. I bought it from his estate. I drove it for a while because I like to trade cars, you know."

Louis let him keep talking. He was one of those chatty Americans, and the less Louis said, the better.

"Anyway," the chatty man said, "I enjoyed it, but then I found a newer Cadillac a couple months ago, so I parked this one and put a sign on it. I want to get it out of here before winter because that spot is where I push the snow. I bought new tires and a battery for her. She is reliable, I can tell you that."

Louis opened the door with a squeak, sat in the comfortable leather seat, and turned the key in the ignition. It fired right up and ran smoothly. He let it run until it warmed enough to come down off high idle, then revved it up a few times. The heater, AC, and radio worked, and so did the windshield wipers. He pressed the windshield washer, and it squirted. The wiper sluiced the bird shit off the glass. The power seat worked, so Louis adjusted it. This was a good car if it drove.

"Can I go forward and back in the parking lot?" he asked the man.

"Sure, we can take it for a drive if you like. Do you have a driver's license?"

"Yes, of course," said Louis, "but if the transmission shifts clean in the parking lot, I don't need to drive it. I know about cars, and I can already tell this is a good car."

So Louis drove it 100 feet forward, shifted to reverse and backed it, then turned a tight circle to the right and left. There were no noises and no puddles under the car. It shifted without a clunk, and all the controls worked. He shut the engine off and got out.

"I can tell you are honest," Louis said, using positive reinforcement psychology. "I read your ad in the paper, and the car is what you said it was. You are asking $3,995. Would you take a cash offer?"

"Mister, if you want this car and you have cash I can let you have it for $3,500. Now, that's a good deal for a good car. And it's got three-quarters of a tank of gas. Do we have a deal?"

"Yes, sir," said Louis. "I think we do. Do you have the title?"

"I do. Do you have the cash?" the man said.

"I do," said Louis. He counted out 35 one hundred dollar bills into the man's hand.

"I'll be right back with the title," the man said. He returned with it, signed it over, and handed the keys to Louis.

"The license plate is expired, so you'll have to get a new one. Did you bring a plate with you?"

"No," said Louis, "but I have one. If you don't mind, I'll leave this one on the car until I get home. It's not far."

"OK with me, but if you get stopped for an expired tag, it's your problem."

"I'll drive slow. Thank you very much."

Louis waved, got into the car, and started it up. The man went back inside, whistling. Louis backed the car up to the bicycle and put it in the big trunk. The back wheel hung out, so Louis unscrewed the thumb screws that held the front wheel and removed it, then the bike fit inside.

**

Sunday October 8
Near Enfield, NH
At the Los Locos' Cabin
5:00 p.m.

Louis drove directly back to the cabin, feeling very good about this deal. The man had not recognized him with his best American accent, his clean-shaven face, and his short hair tucked under his hunter's cap in his tan canvas jacket. He drove up the long gravel driveway and parked behind the cabin by the boat shed. Luca pulled back the curtain, saw it was Louis, and came out to greet him.

(Speaking Spanish)
"Where did you get the wheels, Louis?"
"From a man up the road. I need a knife. Let's go look in the kitchen."

There was a smooth-bladed butter knife that was exactly what Louis needed. He brought it and a towel back outside, walked around behind the boat trailer, and sat on the ground by the license plate. He used the knife to very gently slide under the stick-on tag that showed the expiration date. This tag was still good for another six months. He left it on the knife blade while he walked over to the Cadillac and wiped off the dirty license plate with the towel. Then he carefully placed the little sticky tag on top of the old one on the Cadillac, and presto, he had a valid license plate for the car it belonged to, with a current tag.

He had the title and the car. If, for any reason, he were stopped, the registration was in the glove box, and he would say he just bought it and had not yet registered it. He knew that was sketchy but true, but he was not planning on being stopped. Because, for one thing, he would obey all traffic laws. Since the police were looking for him, he did not want to show his driver's license. But with his hunter's clothes and hat, his clean-shaven face, and a white Cadillac, he would not be suspicious. Besides, the police were looking for him and an accomplice. So he was going to be traveling alone.

There was a wooden garden shed behind the cabin. Louis had not bothered to get into it because there were no windows, so he did not know what was inside. But now, as he walked the dirt path over to the shed, he noticed two sets of tire marks in the soil. Something heavy had rolled into the shed after a rain, and the mud had hardened. The tires were wide enough to be wheelbarrow tires, but they had a different tread. They looked like a small motorcycle tire.

The cabin owner was a very organized man, Louis could tell that from the first minute he broke the glass on the back window and climbed in. And Louis was a very considerate burglar. He had replaced the small pane of glass with one Andrés had made at a hardware store in Enfield. He even re-glazed it and swept up any glass shards on the floor. Louis had made a very thorough search of the cabin as soon as they had moved in six days ago. He found the big key ring in the kitchen drawer right away. So he was able to unlock the bicycles off the shed wall and lock the cabin behind him each time they left. He even was considerate and turned off the alarm while they were in the cabin and turned it on when they left. The alarm code was helpfully typed in bold letters on a card by the door.

Louis went into the cabin, got the big key ring, and brought it out to the shed. He fiddled with the keys until he found the one for the hasp lock and opened the double doors. There was a riding lawnmower, a leaf blower, shovels and rakes, water skis, flotation vests, and fishing poles.

And two Vespa Scooters!

But not just any Vespas. The red one was a GTS 278cc Super, and the green one was a GTS 300 cc Super Sport. Growing up poor in the barrios of Juarez, there were lots of scooters because many people could not afford cars. Louis had a Vespa 50 as his first when he was 14. It was old, but it was durable, and it got him around with a great sense of freedom. That was a two-stroke engine that required a gas and oil mixture.

These two scooters were top-of-the-line, four-stroke modern Vespas. Louis had taken a vacation in Italy after one of his Dryback hauls when he was flush with cash. He had rented one of these. They were fast! He got it on the Autostrada doing 130 km/hour! Louis had read stories on the internet of an Italian man who had been riding the world for six years on a 50 year old Vespa. He had already clocked over 180,000 km, traveling 97 countries in Asia, Africa, and Europe. Louis knew that if you wanted a vehicle to travel the world on a simple budget, the Vespa was the one.

Yes, he was very excited to find these scooters because now he could take care of the Martine brothers. But first, he had to make sure they would start. He saw a pigtail electrical wire sticking out of the side of both scooters connected to battery tenders. The tender lights were green. Louis knew that meant the batteries were fully charged. He disconnected the pigtail, tucked it inside the engine compartment, and turned the key. The engine fired up and ran smooth, as expected with fuel injection. He started the second one, and it too, ran perfectly. Both scooters had less than 500 miles on the odometers. These were run-around toys to ride to town, the beach, and the boat. He checked the fuel gauges. They were low, very low.

Louis knew from renting that these models only carried eight liters of gas, which would be about two gallons. They had less than a gallon of gas in each tank. So Luca and Santo would need to buy gas soon, within 40 miles or so. But he would not recommend they buy it near the cabin because these scooters were very eye-catching and probably the only ones around here. If they rode into town to buy gas, that could arouse suspicion because people would know they did not belong to them.

Louis returned to the cabin with two plans in his head: his and theirs.

"Luca, Santo, we have been a good team for four years. We have done well. We have built our business, but now we have to split up."

"Why Louis? You are our leader, our boss. You have all the connections, man."

"Those businesses are done," Louis said. "After I killed the Russian, I lost my transfer team. They would not work with me anymore.

"And after I killed the farmer in Vermont, we can't go back to our farms because the police are looking for us, especially me. So that business is done too. The main thing is the police think Manny and Raoul killed the farmer. They are looking for me and one other, but so far they don't know your names. But they may find out from Paco.

"So we have to get out of here right now, today, this afternoon. But we cannot all go together. No one can come with me. If I get caught, then you would be assumed to be guilty with me. If you go by yourselves, they are not looking for you. You could make it on your own."

"How, Louis? Where would we go? What would we do? We don't have money, we don't have a car. We've never been on our own. You always took care of us, Louis."

"And I am going to take care of you again, Santo. Come with me."

They followed Louis out to the wooden shed. The doors were open.

"Luca, Santo, have you ever ridden scooters?"

"Years ago in the barrio, our friends had one."

"They are simple. No clutch, just twist the throttle and go. Hand brakes. Right for the front wheel. Left for the rear. You push the right-hand grip to lean the bike over on its tire to turn right at speed, push left to lean, and turn left at speed. Simple. Take your time getting used to the feel of it before you go fast. They can go on the Interstate, and they will go 70, but don't do that right away, 50 max until you get used to it.

"OK. Now, I am going to give you each $5,000. You earned it. It's a lot of money, more than I have ever paid you at one time. But it may have to last you a while. Stick to the back roads at first until you are far away from here. The Border Patrol always covers the Interstates. State Police will, too.

"Stay on numbered roads and get a map. There are maps in the cabin for

New Hampshire, but you will be out of New Hampshire in a few hours. I am going to drive the Cadillac east on Route 4 and follow it to U.S. Route 3, and take that directly south to Massachusetts. I want to get on the Mass Pike and get out of New England and back to New York as quick as possible. There are lots of murders and big news stories in New York, so they won't be looking hard for me there.

"It would be best if you split up, but I know you won't do that. Don't go back into Vermont. That is trouble. They will be looking hard for us. You have to stay on back roads until you are confident in your riding skills at higher speeds. Obey the speed limits. You do not want to get stopped. Riding at night on the Interstate is OK, but not on little state numbered roads because local police may have speed traps, or they may stop you because you are riding bright-colored scooters that attract attention. But you can get away from here and start over if you think and are careful."

"What about guns, Louis?"

"Guns are a bad idea. If you get stopped the worst that can happen is you are caught with stolen motorcycles. If you have guns, then you have big troubles. I will move the guns to the leather cash bag. Pack what you can in the other leather duffle bag and strap it to the scooter. I saw bungee nets in the shed. Anything you cannot carry, I will put in the trunk of the Cadillac. We must clean this place and wipe it down for fingerprints. You will need warm jackets, gloves, and helmets. There are several helmets in the shed. See if they fit. Some states require them, but I don't know which. Now, let's get ready and get out of here in the next half hour."

**

**Sunday October 8
Newbury, NH
Roger Lemonier's House - Job Site
5:00 p.m.**

Rocco Infantini had brought his crew of four insulators into the 3,024-square-foot house at first light. Now, all the walls were stuffed with stone wool batts and covered by a hi-tech membrane. Mac was pleased. Drywall could start tomorrow. A crew of four could hang all the walls in three days. The finishers would need another three days to mud and tape, which meant he needed heat.

The furnace and condenser units were set. Duct work was going in tomorrow. By Tuesday afternoon, he would have heat. The propane tank was in the back yard and the pipe was already run into the basement.

Just then, his phone buzzed. (*Investigator Jackie Beaulieu calling.*)

"Yes, Jackie, what's up?"

"Mac, that number on Paco's phone is a burner. But we did triangulate it. The phone is in Enfield. We are going to send a SWAT team there now. I'll be joining them. I'll keep you posted on what we find."

"OK, good work, Jackie. Be safe."

Mac's phone buzzed again. (*Remy Montague calling.*)

"Yes, Remy."

"Mac, the circuit board in your alarm panel got blown in your barn fire. Now that the new barn is up and working I rewired the panel. All the lights are out except for one."

"Which one, Remy?"

"Doc Lawson's cabin at Mascoma Lake, near Enfield."

"OK, thanks, Remy. I'll have to get up there and see if it's a problem with the alarm or if there was an attempted break-in. I never got a call from the Doc, and he put a doorbell camera on the front door."

"Mac, the Doc retired, didn't you know that? He bought a camper van and hit the road with his wife two weeks ago. Heading southwest to New Mexico, and then driving down to Costa Rica. Won't be back until spring."

"Huh. So if the alarm was tripped it was in the past two weeks. Yeah, I better get up there. OK, thanks, Remy, and thanks for working on Sunday."

"Electricians never get a day off. Didn't you know that, Mac?"

"Electricians and crime fighters. Thanks, Remy."

**

Sunday October 8
Enfield, NH
Doc Lawson's Mascoma Lake Cabin
5:30 p.m.

Louis made one last sweep through the cabin. It was all clean and wiped down. He piled the trash in a trash bag and tossed it in the Cadillac's trunk.

Luca came out last after setting the alarm and brought all the stuff he and Santo could not fit on the Vespa's little tail racks. While Louis was shaking hands with Santo, Luca reached into the leather bag and grabbed two Glock 17s and extra clips. He slipped one in each deep pocket of the tan canvas coat he was taking from the cabin. Santo had a matching one, only black.

With a wave, Louis jumped in the white Caddy, turned, and rolled down the gravel driveway into his future. Only one thing was certain. He had not been captured, and he would not be captured. If cornered, he would fight. He had plenty of weapons and ammo. He had his Glock 17 under the front seat, a machine pistol, two revolvers, and two Glocks in the trunk.

While Louis took Route 4 through rural New Hampshire, the Martine brothers immediately ignored Louis' suggestion and jumped onto I-89. They gunned their scooters up to 70 miles per hour. The evening chill was descending. They slowed down to stay warm and save gas because they remembered what Louis said. 40 miles, buy gas within 40 miles. They also realized that Louis was right about riding skills. Neither one of them felt comfortable over 50 miles per hour, and slower was better.

They exited I-89 at Georges Mills and took SR 11 south towards Sunapee, continued south on SR 103B until they arrived at SR 103 by Mount Sunapee Ski Resort and State Park. It was beginning to get dark, so they pushed on along the western shore of Lake Sunapee and arrived at Newbury Harbor. There was a red sun setting behind them in the west that was making the lake look blood red. It was a very peaceful, scenic spot. There was a gas station in an old white wood building across the street. The sign said: *Fisher's Groceries and Gas, Aqui Se Habla Español.*

**

Sunday October 8
Newbury Harbor, NH
Fisher's Groceries and Gas
6:00 p.m.

The Martine brothers rolled their scooters to the gas pumps and filled up. They were chilled from their ride even though they had come less than 40 miles. A big thermometer on the side of the store read 49 degrees. They went inside and called out, *"Hola!"*

Jodie Moreno called out *"Hola!"* from a back room, pushed opened the door, and emerged with a tray of real Spanish sheet cake with vanilla icing cut into gigantic squares, just like one would find in Juarez.

Luca and Santo smacked their lips and asked, in their best American English:

"Mrs., did you did you make the cake for a party?"

"No, we sell it by the square. Would you like to try it?"

"Oh yes!" they replied. "We also bought gas, and we are looking for gloves. Do you sell them?"

"Yes, on the rack by the door."

"Do you have coffee?"

"Yes, in the back. Help yourself."

They found warm leather gloves, bought two large coffees and four squares of cake. Then, they sat at a table by the window and watched the sun going down. They could not see it, but they could see its blood-red reflection on the lake. When they finished, they paid with cash and went outside with warm hands and full bellies.

(Speaking Spanish)

"Now we can ride for at least one hundred miles, Santo," said Luca. We will be in Massachusetts, where they will not be looking for us. We will find a cheap motel where we can roll our scooters into our rooms, buy some beer, and watch TV. In the morning, we will dress in layers with all the warm clothes and keep going south. The farther south we go, the warmer it will be."

"Where are we going, Luca?" said Santo. Luca was two years older and now twenty-five. He was wiser. He had looked out for Santo ever since they left the barrio.

"I think we should go to New Mexico, it will be warm. There will be many Mexicans. We can blend in with the crowd and find work."

"How far is New Mexico, Luca?"

"Oh, I would say 1,000 miles, maybe 2,000, I don't know. We need to buy a big map. But we can make it on these scooters. We will ride 300 miles per day. That will be enough. It will be an adventure."

"But what if these scooters are reported stolen?"

"That will be a long time. The cabin was closed for the winter."

"But what about the alarm and the camera?

"Louis taped over the camera, and we set the alarm, so no one will even

know we have been there until spring. There were no snow skis, so it is a summer cabin. But to be sure, we should look for a place with a motorcycle shop with wrecked bikes in the back. We could steal some license plates for each state. Hey, the sun is setting. Let's take a picture with the red water and us, OK?"

They rode across to the Harbor parking lot, set their bikes on their center stands, and took pictures of each other with their helmets off in front of the blood-red sun on the water.

Across the road, Mac Morrison and Ramon drove up to the front door of Fisher's Grocery in the green 1971 Chevy Impala. Ramon had Maria's list of supplies for their celebration supper. Mac was buying the big sheet cake Jodie made for them. He backed the Impala to the front door and popped the trunk.

"Hello, Mac! Hello Ramon!" shouted Jodie. "The cake just came out of the oven. I thought those two Mexican boys were going to eat it all, but I saved half for you."

"Two boys?" said Mac.

"Yes, they were on scooters. They stopped for gas and bought gloves and coffee. Mexican boys wearing tan canvas coats like the locals. Oh, there they are, parked across the road. See?"

Mac looked outside. The setting sun was directly in the boys' faces as they posed for pictures.

"LUCA! SANTO!" Ramon shouted.

"Do you know these boys, Ramon?" asked Mac.

"They are part of Los Locos, Mister Mac. They are Louis Lopez's gang!"

Mac's brain processed fast. He remembered the alarm at the Lawson cabin in Enfield. He saw the red and green Vespas. Doc Lawson owned the only red and green Vespas in the North Country. Louis Lopez's burner phone was in Enfield. Los Locos could have been staying at Doc Lawson's cabin and stolen his Vespas!

He whipped out his cell phone and hit speed dial for Jackie Beaulieu.

"Yes, Mac?"

"Jackie, where are you?"

"On Route 4A nearing the Shakoma bridge to Enfield."

"Jackie, Ramon and I are at Fisher's Store in Newbury. We are looking across the road at two of Louis Lopez's gang."

"In Newbury?"

"Yes, right now. They are riding scooters that I believe were stolen from a cabin in Enfield. Where is your SWAT team?"

"Across the bridge on the east side of Enfield, that's where the phone is taking us. Mac, Can you detain them? I can turn around, but it will take me 30 minutes to get there. I can call for backup."

"They are putting their helmets on, Jackie. They are leaving!"

"Mac, they may be armed. Be careful. Wait for law enforcement, I'll call in!"

But Mac was on the move.

"Mickey!" he shouted to the back room. "Get your rifle, Mickey! Hurry!"

Ramon was already outside, trotting across the parking lot. It was only 40 yards between him and the Martine brothers.

"RAMON! STOP!" yelled Mac. "STOP, RAMON!"

Luca turned and saw Ramon. He saw a man coming out of the store with a rifle. He saw a big man reach into the trunk of an old green Chevy and grab something. Too late to get on the bikes and go. Fight!

Luca yanked off the bungee net, unzipped the leather duffle, and grabbed two Glocks and two clips. He tossed one to Santo, and they both ran behind a low stone wall. The man with the rifle had it up to his shoulder. Luca fired three shots, "POW POWPOW." The Glock 17 made a loud noise; it echoed off the hard surface of the parking lot.

The man with the rifle ducked behind the green Chevy with Mac and Ramon. The sun dropped lower in the sky.

"Mickey, you hit?" shouted Mac.

"I'm good, Mac. What the hell?"

"Those two killed the Vermont farmer."

"Oh, shit!"

"Mickey, what have you got there?"

"It's a squirrel gun. Shoots .22 longs."

"Jeez, it would be nice to have something bigger, Mick!"

"Well dang, Mac, I hadn't planned on taking on Al Capone in Newbury, New Hampshire!"

"Is that a pump?"

"Yep."

"How many shells?"

"Twenty. What have you got there, Mac?"

"My new 58" Super Recurve bow. If you can plunk some shots into that wall just below their heads, I'll work my way around to the left. First, I gotta call Roger for reinforcements."

Mac hit the cell's speed dial for Roger.

"ROGER! LEVEL FOUR AT FISHER'S STORE! SHOTS FIRED!"

"Copy Mac. What's your situation?"

"Two guys with pistols behind the stone wall at the Harbor parking lot. Mickey and I are outgunned. I've got my bow, and he has a .22 pump squirrel gun."

"2 minutes with my AR-15, Mac. Hang on!"

"Come in the south driveway and park in front of my Impala. Use your truck to block their line of fire."

"Copy that, Mac!"

Santo made a dash for his scooter and started the engine.

"He's taking off," said Mickey. He put two shots into the bushes in front of Santo to drive him back behind the wall.

Mac slung his quiver over his shoulder and ran with his bow in his right hand. He got to the big hemlock and up on the slope behind it. He was 30 yards from the scooters. He could not see the Martine brothers, but he had a clear shot at the bikes. He strung the bow, set his arrow on the rest, drew back, and fired!

"Thwip!" went the arrow, and "clunk" as it hit a park bench behind the bike.

Mac was counting seconds in his head. One minute forty till Roger arrives. If he could hit their tires, they would be stranded and should give up. Or, they could rush Mickey and overwhelm him. They probably had more than 20 shells in their pistols combined. They could rapid fire while Mickey had to pump.

Mac laid another arrow on its rest, drew back, and fired. "Thwip" and "clink." He needed more arch; he was shooting low. He shot a third and fourth, and now he was getting closer. And the Martines could see what he was doing. He was trying to kill their escape. Luca Martine used the overhanging tree to conceal his movement as he jumped over the stone wall and rushed, firing, at Mac's position.

'POWPOWPOWPOWPOW!.'

He kept coming! Mac was counting his shots as he drew back another arrow.

'POWPOWPOW!' That made eleven shots. He was fifteen yards away behind a tree. Mac heard the sound of a new clip being jammed into the pistol. He had eleven more shots, and he was coming!

Three shots came from came from behind the stone wall as Santo laid down cover for Luca.

'POWPOWPOW!'

Luca was coming! Ten yards. 20 seconds until Roger should get there! Luca was shooting as he ran towards Mac!

'POW POW POW!'

Mac drew back, aimed for the center of the body, and let the arrow fly! "Thwip!"

"CHUCK!" was the sound of the arrow hitting meat.

"AEEEEEE!" Luca screamed as he fell to the ground.

Rogers's truck roared into the parking lot. He jumped out and leveled his AR 15 over the hood. Santo jumped up and began shooting at Roger!

'POWPOWPOW!'

'TATATAT!'

Roger stitched him with three shots. Luca stopped, turned, and staggered towards the lake. He paused at the water's edge and toppled in, face down. Blood pooled on the surface, blending with the red sun's reflection.

It was a Bloody Sunapee Sunset.

"Mickey," said Mac. "Call 911 for a squad. Tell them two down. No active threat."

Mac whipped out his phone and called Jackie Beaulieu. She answered immediately.

"Go, Mac!"

"Active shooters down, all clear. Two shooters down, Jackie."

"You OK, Mac?"

"We're OK. Squad called. Assessing damage."

"Copy that. I'm coming, I'm coming!"

Mac approached the body with an arrow in it. He was just a kid, maybe 25. Blood oozed onto the blacktop. The arrow was near the left shoulder. Mac felt his neck for a pulse. It was there. He put his head to his chest and listened for blood gurgling. He heard none.

"Roger, what have you got?" Mac yelled.

Roger ran across the street, laid his rifle down, and hauled the body out of the water. There was blood everywhere. He turned him over. He was breathing, but just barely. He rolled him on his side to drain his mouth, then propped him against a tree and put pressure on his wounds. He had two in his side. One must have missed.

"Two hits in his side!" shouted Roger. "Call Ursula, tell her to bring her kit!"

"Got it!" Mac shouted back.

Jodie ran out from the store with towels and began applying compresses on Santo.

Mac made the decision: better to get the arrow out. He put his foot on Luca, grabbed the smooth-tipped target arrow, and easily yanked it out. Blood spurted for a second and then oozed. That was a good sign: no artery was hit. Jodie ran over and gave him towels. He began compression.

"Santo..." Luca said, *"Santo..."*

"He's OK. Help is coming," Mac said. "Hang on, Hang on. You're going to be OK."

Sirens blared in the distance, coming closer. The squad pulled up just as Ursula arrived with her emergency kit. She worked on Luca while Doc and Johnny worked on Santo. Volunteer paramedics and firemen began streaming into the parking lot. Soon, the two young men were loaded onto gurneys, and they roared off in ambulances with sirens blaring.

"Shit!" said Mac. "I did not want to shoot that kid."

"Mac, he gave you no choice," said Mickey. "It was you or him."

"I know, Mickey, but damn it man, it never gets easier. And the body count just keeps growing. Roger, you OK?"

"I'm good, Mac."

"Ramon, you good?"

"All good, Mister Mac."

"Ramon, call Maria. She must be wondering where we are. Tell her two hours. We have to talk to the police. Don't worry, Ramon, you are not in trouble. I will take care of it."

"Mickey," said Roger, "you got any bourbon in your back room?"

"I do."

"Break it out," said Mac. "Let's go inside and wait for State Police Investigator Jackie Beaulieu. She will be barreling in here any minute."

**

Chapter Twelve

Sunday October 8
Fisher's Gas and Grocery
Newbury Harbor
6:30 p.m.

Investigator Jaqueline Beaulieu was the first police officer to arrive. Soon, the parking lot was swarming. State Police Colonel Trammel Bradford himself came storming up the road with his driver. It was a short story told over and over as the participants were separated and asked to give their version of what happened. Ramon, Mac, and Jodie told how it began. Mickey chimed in about how he got involved. They all discussed the firefight and who started it. Roger added the ending.

It took two hours. By 8:30 p.m. all the reports were written, and police went back on patrol. The crime scene technicians scoured the parking lots at Fisher's Store and the Harbor. They retrieved thirty .45 caliber shell casings and two Glock 17 pistols. Roger's AR-15 shot three times; they recovered his casings using spotlights in the dark. Mac gave them the arrow he pulled from Luca's chest. He was mentally drained. Ramon had called Maria and assured her that everyone was OK. Everyone, that is, except Luca and Santo Martine.

10:00 p.m.

Mac, Roger, and Ursula returned home, took hot showers, and gathered for a late supper with Maria, Paco, Ramon, and Tomas. No one spoke of Louis Lopez, the Martine brothers, or Manny and Raoul Diaz. The steak enchiladas were superb, and Maria reveled in the praise for her cooking.

"Mama loves to cook, and she loves to please a big family," said Paco. You are our family, too."

Mac's phone buzzed. (*Investigator Jackie Beaulieu calling.*)

"Yes, Jackie?"

"Mac, just thought you would like an update. Luca and Santo Martine are out of surgery. Luca, who you shot with the target arrow, is doing well. He took most of the hit in his shoulder, and no internal organs or arteries were damaged. Might have gotten a concussion when his head hit the pavement."

"It was a lucky shot with a new bow. I did not want to kill him."

"Well, it stopped him, and that was good. Mac, he will recover. The two brothers will be charged with aggravated assault on you and Mickey. We will interview Luca tomorrow and find out what he knows about the Bisbee murder. Ramon said the two brothers had been jobbers for Louis Lopez. So they may have been at the scene when Bisbee was killed."

"That could be why they opened fire on us. If they were part of the Bisbee killing, they may not have wanted to be taken alive."

"Santo has a punctured lung and spleen, but he will survive, Mac. He is in critical condition."

"Roger and I did not want those kids to die, Jackie."

"They aren't kids, Mac, they are 23 and 25, and they knew what they were doing."

"Still, I am grateful they are going to be OK. Anything else?"

"Yes, the SWAT team located Louis Lopez's burner phone that he used to call Paco. A guy self-described as the local drunk, Jaime Charbonneau, found it in a trash can at a gas station in Enfield. Its glass face had been smashed, as if Lopez stomped it, but it was still working. We know Lopez called the Diaz boys on it."

"Were the Diaz boys part of the gang that killed Bisbee?"

"In the presence of their lawyer, Manny Diaz swears they had nothing to do with killing Bisbee."

"Bisbee's wife said there were four Mexicans, but she cannot identify them, right Jackie?"

"Right."

"Huh. If the Diaz boys are telling the truth, that could leave one more of the Lopez gang out there. How did Manny Diaz explain having the .44 Magnum that killed Bisbee?"

"Lopez gave it to him, he says, and that was after Bisbee was killed. He is pointing the finger at Lopez for killing Bisbee."

"Huh."

"I know. It gets deeper and deeper. Hey, about those two scooters,

Mac. You were right. They are registered to a Doctor Maxwell Lawson of Brookline, Mass."

"Jackie, I built his cabin and have a security system that lights a board in my barn if it is tripped. But after my barn burned last May, it hasn't been working. So when my electrician fixed it, Lawson's light was lit. I figured I would go up tomorrow and check it out."

"Well, the Martine boys are not talking yet, but I think they must have been staying in the cabin with Lopez all week and stole the scooters to make their getaway."

"And they would have made it if they hadn't stopped to take selfies at the Harbor, Jackie. If they had gotten back on their scooters and rode off, Ramon never would have seen them. They could have escaped. So, it looks like Lopez is in the wind, eh? Hey, I have a key to Lawson's cabin, Jackie. How about we meet there tomorrow morning and search it. Are you done with the scooters, or do you need them as evidence?"

"We can release the scooters. The techs have finished with them and they had nothing in their compartments anyway. We got a leather duffle that had their clothes. We left the scooters at Fisher's store. Mr. Fisher put them in a locked shed in back."

"OK, I'll bring a trailer and tow them back up to the cabin. Want to meet me there at 10:00 a.m.?"

"Sounds good, Mac. You all OK?"

"Yeah. Roger and I have been through this before, but Ramon is still shaking. He'll be fine. See you at Lawson's cabin at ten."

**

Sunday October 8
Near Enfield, NH
Mascoma Lake Boat Rentalz
10:30 p.m.

Sanford Daltry lit his pipe, removed his shoes, and slid his feet into his old leather slippers. He brought his hot cocoa and today's newspaper to his favorite recliner chair, turned on his 1940s standup wood cabinet, tube-type radio with the big enamel knobs, and sat down to read the news.

The bold headline said: **Vermont Killers Caught!**

After reading the story, he looked down at a picture with the bold header beneath:

Have you seen this man? Call NH State Police!

Sanford dragged on his pipe and enjoyed the aroma of the Prince Albert tobacco from the red can. He was a New Hampshire traditionalist. "If it ain't broke, don't fix it" was his motto. So he was reading the paper, smoking his pipe, and sipping his hot cocoa before going to bed, just as he always did.

It had been a very good day. With a sunny start and mild temperatures, he had moved the last of his rental boats into winter storage. The day's big win was selling the Cadillac. Now, he had a place to push the snow this winter. The buyer was kind of a weird guy, he was thinking. Who doesn't take a test drive? He never did get the guy's name. Odd, this picture in the paper kind of reminded him of that guy somehow. But he had short hair and was clean-shaven, and this guy in the picture had long hair, a fancy shirt with foreign-looking scrollwork, and a wispy mustache. It made him look like the Mexican bad guys in the old 1960s cowboy movies.

That was it! The long hair, the funny shirt, and the mustache! Now, if this guy in the picture wore a tan canvas jacket with a hunter's cap and was clean-shaven, boy! This could be him! Huh! Did he sell his Caddy to a killer? Well, the story said if you've seen this man, call NH State Police!

Sanford Daltry got up out of his recliner, walked over, and sat on an antique plank chair probably made in the 1820s by a New Hampshire farmer. It had a faded red seat pad that once upon a time matched the faded red and brown hooked rug on the floor that his late wife had loved so much. He lifted the heavy old yellow receiver and dialed the 1970s vintage rotary telephone. When an officer answered, he said: "I think I sold my car to the killer Louis Lopez."

**

Chapter Thirteen

Monday October 9
Near Enfield, NH
Doc Lawson's cabin
10:00 a.m.

Mac backed his trailer up to the wooden shed. He used his key to enter the cabin. They must have set the alarm when they left because it was activated. But with passwords written on a card by the door, it was simple for them to do. It was odd that the thieves would go to that trouble, but then again, if the alarm was reset it was not sending a signal to the owner.

He turned off the alarm and retrieved the key ring from the drawer. While the Crime Scene techs began their work, Mac unlocked the shed, rolled the scooters inside, and relocked it. He left Buddy in the car. Buddy barked his disapproval.

Mac looked around outside. There were recent tire tracks from a large, heavy car. He pointed them out to Jackie Beaulieu. He found a small pane that had been re-glazed on a back window, so that was how they gained entry. Since his alarm board had been out of service, he did not get a signal when it happened.

Mac pulled out his phone and called Doc Lawson on his satellite cell. When he had phoned him last night to tell him of the break-in, the Doc had asked him to take care of things and let him know if there was damage. So far, Mac did not see any.

"Good morning, Doc. It's Mac Morrison. I'm at the cabin with the State Police. The techs are sweeping the inside for fingerprints or any other evidence, but everything looks clean, no sign of damage, and they even removed the trash. If you had any canned goods in the cupboard, they ate them, but other than that, I didn't see anything missing. The two boys were caught wearing old tan canvas jackets, and I seem to remember you had some hanging on a peg by the door, but they are gone. The scooters are fine, no damage at all. Did you check your doorbell camera history? You did? But the screen was blank? Huh. OK, I'll check the camera before I leave. Guess that's it, Doc."

Mac walked around to the front door. It was never an ideal angle for a doorbell camera because it did not face the driveway, and everyone used the side door. The Doc had installed it himself. Mac walked up and found a piece of black tape over the camera. That explained the blank screen. He did not touch it, but rather found Jackie Beaulieu and reported it.

"It's black electrical tape, Jackie, ideal for fingerprints."

"Excellent, Mac, I'll tell the techs. Then I'm going to talk to a guy who says he might have sold a car to Louis Lopez yesterday. He's just up the road on the lake."

"Oh? I know many of the cabins on this lake. I've either remodeled them or built their docks. What's his name?"

"Sanford Daltry."

"Sanford! Sure, I built his docks. He rents boats. Mind if I go with you? Sanford had a stroke, and his mind is not as sharp as it was."

"Be glad to have you. You ready?"

"Let's go."

Investigator Jackie Beaulieu let Mac lead the way in his '57 Chevy convertible. It was a mild fall day, so Mac dropped the top. Buddy hung his head out the windows and sniffed all the smells, barking whenever they passed another dog.

Mac pulled into the narrow parking area by the Boat Rentalz cabin. Route 4A runs tight along the lake, and the land slopes down quickly to the water, so parking was limited to the frontage of the cabin. Mac let Buddy out of the car. He romped over to the front door. Buddy always checked out strangers to protect Poppa Mac.

Mac knocked, and Sanford Daltry came to the door. He was stooped, and he shuffled more than walked because he had arthritis and was approaching 80. Hs eyes brightened as he recognized Mac.

"Mac Morrison! Did you get a new dog?"

"I did, Sanford. This is Buddy, and pulling up behind me is State Police Investigator Jackie Beaulieu."

"Come in, come in, glad to have some company! Since Sally died, I get lonely after boating season, Mac. Don't know why I stay in this summer cottage all winter. The floors are cold, and it's drafty, but this was our home the past twenty years. It just never seemed so cold when Sally was in it."

Jackie Beaulieu introduced herself as Buddy was shaking hands with Sanford.

"Sit down, sit down! So are you here about the man in the paper?" he asked.

"Yes, Mr. Daltry," said Jackie, "and thank you for calling us. What can you tell us?"

"Well, he rode a bicycle to come see the car. That was not so odd because many of the cabins and trailers around here have bikes. He was nice, seemed to know a lot about cars. I thought it was funny he did not want to test drive it, just drove it back and forth and turned it around, but he gave it a good looking over. It was a good car."

"What kind of car was it?"

"It's a 2002 Cadillac Deville, cream white. I printed out my ad for you. It has pictures and the VIN and everything."

"I see the license plate on the car in these pictures. Was that your plate?" asked Jackie.

"Yes."

"Did the buyer bring his own plate?"

"No, I let him take this one. I know I should have removed it, but it's hard for me to bend down and use a screwdriver with my arthritis. Anyway, the plate was expired. He said he would risk it to drive a short way home. He said he had his own plate at home."

"Did he give you his name?"

"No. I always read the newspaper before I go to bed. I smoke a pipe, drink my hot cocoa and read the paper, then go to bed. So it was last night, after I sold the car, that I saw the picture. At first, the face seemed familiar. Then I realized if the guy in the picture cut his hair, changed his shirt, and shaved, this could be him!"

"Did he say where he was going, anything that could help us?"

"No, nothing like that, but after he left, I remembered, you know, my memory is not good, had a stroke. I had another set of keys I should have given him. And maybe that could help you."

"Oh?"

"Yes, now where did I put them? Wait, let me get my phone. I have a new iPhone. I don't use it for local calls, but I like to go on the internet. I keep it by my chair."

Sanford Daltry picked up his phone, tapped it, and an arrow popped up. He turned and followed the arrows and said, "Here they are!"

He picked up a set of car keys sitting on the kitchen counter.

"What did you just do with your phone, Mr. Daltry?" asked Jackie.

"I push this button, and it points to the keys. You have to be close, like within 30 feet. But you can find its location anywhere using the app as long as the AirTag™ is near someone with an iPhone that is part of the network."

"Cool!" said Jackie. "And did you have an AirTag on your other set of keys that you gave him?"

"Of course, I lose my keys if I don't have the AirTag. But I never lose my phone because I always leave it right by my chair!"

"Mr. Daltry, would you use your phone to search for that AirTag?" asked Jackie.

"Of course," he said. He knew how to do it and quickly found a location and an address. It even had a label.

"The AirTag is at Boulanger's Café in Hamburg, New York."

"Boulangers!" Mac exclaimed.

"Do you know the place, Mac?" Jackie asked.

"Sure, it's one of my favorite breakfast spots. Let me call. I know the owner."

He pulled out his iPhone and hit speed dial for Boulangers. He was on a first-name basis with Sheila, the owner.

"Sheila, hi, it's Mac Morrison. Hey, great, thanks. Are you on your cell phone? You are? This is very important, and you need to act calm but do exactly as I say, OK? Look around and see if you have a Mexican man. He may be wearing a tan canvas coat and hunter's hat. Early 30s clean shaven, short dark hair."

"Mac," she said, "I see a Mexican-looking man, but he is wearing a green New York Jets jacket."

"Sheila, can you walk outside and look for a white 2002 Cadillac with a New Hampshire plate? I'll wait until you get outside."

"Mac," she said, "I see the car." She read off the plate number. It was Sanford Daltry's car.

"Sheila, did he just order or is he just getting ready to leave? He just ordered? Are there other people seated next to him? The place is full?

"Sheila. The man is a suspected killer, probably armed and dangerous. I want you to keep him occupied. Maybe give him a piece of pie while he is waiting. Just keep him occupied. I am going to call the New York State Police. They will send an unmarked car and plain clothes officer to assess the situation. They will not try to arrest him in the restaurant.

"The officer will come in and ask for you. You point the man out, but be discreet. If he's their guy, then you pull the fire alarm Sheila, got that? They will have officers outside. When everyone leaves, they will grab him. Got it? OK repeat back to me. OK, yes, OK, that's right. OK, now act natural until they get there, and do not tell your staff; they might panic. All right, you can do it, Sheila. Bye."

"Now, Jackie," said Mac, "we are going to do a conference call with Colonel Samuel Justice and Investigator Jonetta Pope of the New York State Police. I will introduce you and then let me talk, OK?"

"It's your show, Mac. Please, go ahead."

Mac selected the two cell numbers and put it on speaker.

"Colonel Justice, this is Mac Morrison, with Investigator Jackie Beaulieu of the New Hampshire State Police. Is Jonetta Pope on the call?"

"I'm here, Mac," said Jonetta.

"Colonel, I believe Louis Lopez, the suspected killer of Vermont farmer Bisbee, is sitting in Boulanger's Café in Hamburg, New York. I just spoke with Sheila, the owner. I told her you would dispatch a plain clothes officer to enter the restaurant. Sheila will point out the man. I believe it is too dangerous to make an arrest inside because the place is packed. Once you confirm it is Lopez, and you have additional officers outside, Sheila will pull the fire alarm. You should be able to grab him as he leaves. He will be heading for his car, which is a 2002 white Cadillac Deville with a New Hampshire plate."

"Mac," said Jonetta Pope, "I am ten minutes from Hamburg, in plain clothes. Colonel Justice, I would like to be the one to enter the restaurant. Can you arrange backup while I drive there?"

"Yes, Jonetta."

"Colonel," Mac said, "we had a shootout with two of his gang last night in New Hampshire. They were desperate not to be captured. I don't believe he will allow himself to be taken alive, Sir."

"I agree, but this sounds like it could work. Jonetta, if it looks like he makes you before the other officers are in place, do not jeopardize the patrons. Let him leave. We will take him on the road. OK, are we agreed?"

"Agreed."

"OK, Jonetta, good luck. Mac, I'll keep you informed."

**

Monday October 9
Hamburg, NY
Boulanger's Café
11:00 a.m.

Louis Lopez had stuck to his plan. He had driven all night to get out of New England and into New York. He slept in the car at a Thruway rest stop sandwiched between rows of tractor-trailers. He did not believe the police knew he was driving this car, but he was not taking any chances. He had the title. He was heading for New Mexico, where he would look like everyone else. He could buy a fake ID, sell the Caddy, and get a red Vespa scooter. He could be like the guy on the internet!

He had pushed hard, and now he was southwest of Buffalo. There was no news of him on the radio and none in the paper he bought at the Thruway truck stop. No picture in the paper was very good. He bought all new clothes at the truck stop, too. He was now wearing a New York Jets jacket and hat, bright green and white. He was wearing new blue jeans and bright white running shoes with three stripes on them. He was stylin'.

He was also hungry. It had been 24 hours since he had eaten one-third of a submarine sandwich. His stomach was cramping. He exited at Hamburg because he figured there had to be a good burger joint in Hamburg. Instead, he saw a billboard for Boulanger's café three blocks away. The picture of giant platters of food made his mouth water. He would go there.

The parking lot was almost full, which was a good sign; the food must be good here. He backed into a parking spot directly opposite the driveway so he could leave fast if he had to.

The smell of coffee and hot food inside the big glass doors was intoxicating. Louis spotted a two-top table and grabbed it. A young waitress brought coffee and a menu and recited the day's specials. They all sounded good, but Louis had set his heart on a big American breakfast of steak and eggs and pancakes. He gave his order and was mildly surprised when a middle-aged woman who seemed to be the boss brought him a piece of hot apple pie with vanilla ice cream.

"We are very busy, so your breakfast may take a bit longer than usual. The pie is on the house while you wait. No charge. Enjoy."

She turned and walked away. Louis dug into the wonderful pie and ice cream. His stomach felt better already. A few minutes later the boss lady refilled his cup and assured him that his breakfast would be done soon. He was content to wait. And then he saw the huge platter of food coming at him. There was steak on one plate, eggs on another, and pancakes on another. A feast!

Louis was getting warm with his New York Jets jacket on, but he could not remove it because he had a Glock in a shoulder holster under his left arm. So he unbuttoned the jacket part way and let some air into his chest. Then, he began eating in earnest.

Sheila had been watching him. When he unbuttoned the jacket, she saw the big gun shift under his shoulder. She would never have noticed without Mac's warning. She thought about carrying a big tray of food over and dumping it on his head, but then what? No, she needed to do as Mac said and wait.

Just then, the glass doors swung open, and New York State Police Investigator Jonetta Pope walked through, waved to Sheila like an old friend, and went to chat with her at the cash register.

"He's the one in the green New York Jets jacket," Sheila said. "I saw his gun move under his left arm."

Jonetta turned to get a good look at him. She had memorized the photo of Louis Lopez. This was him, for sure.

"Shall I pull the fire alarm?" asked Sheila.

"Not yet," said Jonetta, "I am waiting for backup to cover the exits. I will let you know."

A five-year-old boy finished his breakfast and climbed down from the booth opposite Louis Lopez. He tugged at the sleeve of the Jets jacket.

"Hey, Mister, are you a football player? Are you a Jet? Can I have your autograph, Mister?"

Louis froze. He shook his head and kept eating.

"Mister, are you a football player?" the kid shrieked as he grabbed his left sleeve of the Jets jacket and pulled it hard. The butt of the Glock stuck out.

Louis Lopez shoved the kid, and he fell to the floor.

The little kid's father jumped out of his booth.

"You don't touch my boy!" he growled and moved toward Louis Lopez. Louis yanked his Glock from its holster and scooped up the boy like a shield.

Someone shouted, "He's got a gun!"

People screamed and ran for the door.

"Nobody move!" Louis shouted. "I'm going out of here! Anyone tries to stop me, I'll kill the kid and kill you all!"

"Daddy!" the kid screamed.

The Dad did the unthinkable: he rushed Louis, grabbed his son, and threw him across the table to a bystander.

Louis raised his Glock and fired.

'POW!'

The father staggered, twisted, and toppled over on the table. It was the opening for Jonetta, and she took it. She had her Colt Python .357 Magnum Revolver with a 3" barrel under her coat. She slipped it out and yelled:

"GET DOWN!"

Everyone ducked. Everyone, that is, except Louis Lopez. He spun around with his gun in an arc, searching for its target.

Jonetta aimed and fired.

'BOOM!

The bullet hit Louis Lopez in the heart. He tottered backwards, dropped the gun, and collapsed. He was dead before he hit the floor. Blood gushed from his chest. Jonetta kicked his gun away and picked it up. She held up her badge.

"I'M INVESTIGATOR JONETTA POPE OF THE NEW YORK STATE POLICE!" she shouted. "It's all over, folks. Please take your seats. There will be officers coming. We need your witness statements. Those close to the body may move, but nobody leave. Thank you!"

Jonetta said to Sheila: "Please call 911 and ask for a squad."

"I'm a Doctor!" yelled a woman who rushed to the fallen father. Two men got him on the floor, and she began assessing the damage. He was alive and conscious. The bullet appeared to have passed through his leg but missed the femoral artery. The doctor grabbed a hand-full of napkins and began a compress.

"Get me some towels, a big stack of towels, quick!" She ordered. She looked down at the man.

"Can you hear me, sir?"

"Yes," he said weakly.

"What is your name, sir?"

"Jon Stark."

"Mr. Stark, don't move, sir. You've got a bad wound, but no major artery was hit. You will be fine. In a few weeks, you'll be playing ball with your son. Just rest now and don't move."

"OK, thank you, Doctor."

Jonetta whipped out her phone and punched the number for Colonel Justice.

"Jonetta, give me a full report!"

"Colonel Justice, suspect Louis Lopez is dead. I shot him; no other option, Sir. He took a little boy hostage and shot his father. I had the shot and took it, Sir."

"I'm sure you did the right thing, Jonetta. Is your backup there?"

"No Sir, please tell them to hurry, lights and sirens. We have about a hundred witness statements to take."

"Will do, Jonetta. Well done. Well done."

Sheila came out with a large dark tablecloth and spread it over the body.

"That took guts, Officer Pope," she said. "Have I seen you in here before?"

"Yes," said Jonetta, "under better circumstances. Sheila, I could use a strong cup of coffee."

"Jonetta you can have the entire menu anytime you come in, on the house."

**

Monday October 9
Canandaigua, NY
12:00 Noon

Andrés had been trying to sleep all night while riding buses. He was tired and hungry, but excited. He was free! He had enough money to start over. And he soon would be with his best friend since the barrio, Ruiz Ortega. Ruiz had worked hard enough at the orchard that the owner asked him to stay full-time and work the vineyard.

The bus changed roads at Manchester, New York. It drove south to Canandaigua, where there was a short wait, and then a new bus went to Avon, Caledonia, and LeRoy. It would be two hours before the next bus left, so Andrés decided to stretch his legs and find some food.

There was a lake in this town, a big lake. He decided to walk down Main Street and see this big lake. There were shops and stores and tourists, lots of tourists. He bought a good sandwich and a cold bottle of Coke, walked all the way to the end of the long pier, and ate. He wanted to call Ruiz and tell him he was coming, but first he wanted to take a picture of himself on the beautiful pier with this big lake and the sailboats behind him.

Andrés sat on the concrete wall and waited for someone to come and take his picture. Two boys rode bikes around the circle at the end of the pier. He asked them:

"Would you take my picture?"

"Sure!" they said. "Sit by the water."

So Andrés turned around and sat on the concrete wall with the water behind him. The boy, who could not have been more than seven, took three pictures just to make sure. Then his friend said, "Come on, Bobby, let's go!"

So Bobby ran to give the camera back to Andrés, but he tripped, and the camera flew out of his hand. It sailed over the concrete wall into the deep lake with a "spa-loop!"

"Sorry!" Bobby said. He jumped on his bike and rode away.

Andrés looked over the wall. He could not see his phone. The water was deep and dark. It was gone. He could buy another phone. This throw-away kind was cheap. But he did not get his picture.

He shrugged his shoulders and trudged back towards the bus station. On the way there, he bought a new throw-away phone and had a grownup tourist take his picture in front of a Mexican restaurant.

All in all, it had been a good day.

**

Monday October 9
Newbury, NH
Mac Morrison's Steel Barn
2:30 p.m.

Mac was setting up folding tables in the clean garage bay of his new shop barn. He had taken the Ford F 450 stake bed truck to the rental store and rented three eight-foot-long tables and folding chairs. He bought plastic tableware and plates and even fresh-cut flowers to put in plastic vases.

Mac wanted to celebrate the Rodriguez family's freedom. They owed no money to any jobber. They were not implicated in any of the Locos gang's wrongdoings, and Paco was home and getting well.

Mac made a list of his invitees. Roger and Ursula Lemonier; Mickey Fisher and Jodie Moreno; Maria, Tomas, Paco, Ramon, Miguel, and Lupe Rodriguez; firemen Johnny and Doc; Morgan Hillman and Angelica Morelli; Jaqueline Beaulieu; Colonel Trammel Bradford and Sanford Daltry. He sent a batch text message inviting them to a come-as-you-are celebration Bar B Que.

These people survived their encounter with the deadly Los Locos gang, and he wanted to throw a party for them. Mac's phone buzzed. (*Colonel Samuel Justice calling.*)

"Hello, Colonel. Give me a full report."

"Mac, you had a good plan, but a five-year-old boy spoiled it. Long story short, Lopez took the boy hostage in the crowded café. His father lunged at Lopez, who shot him. Jonetta killed Lopez with one shot to the heart. She saved lives. He had threatened to kill many people if he were challenged. The boy's father is going to be all right."

"Wow! I'm sure she is a bit shook up. Is that her first kill?"

"As a Trooper, yes. She had military service, so possibly there."

"All good, no red tape for her?"

"All good. Very professional. She will be on desk duty while the post-shooting-protocols are followed, which is good to reset her emotions."

"I agree. Well, I hope that Rupert Bisbee's murder is now solved," said Mac.

"Is there any question in your mind, Mac?"

"There may be one more member of the Los Locos gang still out there, but if there is, he may not have been involved in Bisbee's murder. Bisbee's wife counted four gang members, and now, with Lopez dead, we have accounted for five, but two of them, the Diaz brothers, say they were not involved in Bisbee's murder. Are they lying? Who knows? So there is possibly one more, but we don't have a name. Anyway, I think that case is closed."

"Mac, someday I want you to explain how you delivered this killer to us on a plate."

"Colonel, I will."

"Thank you, Mac."

"Anytime, Sir. Always at your service."

Mac closed the call. He thought for a moment about calling Jonetta Pope. But then he had a better idea. He hit speed dial for Juan Johnson. Juan was the ex-Army-Captain-turned-body shop owner in Jamestown, New York. Juan had bought Marybeth's parents' wrecked car, saved it for two years, and found paint evidence that matched it to the car Joey Minetti used to kill them. Juan, a widower, had been introduced by Mac to BCI Investigator Jonetta Pope, who was perhaps fifteen years younger than he, and single. They had clicked, and Mac knew that they had been dating.

"Juan, this is Mac Morrison calling."

"Mac, I have you in my contacts man, no need for intros. What's happening?"

"Juan, have you heard from Jonetta today?"

"No, is there a reason I should have?"

"You two still close?"

"Yes. What has happened, Mac?"

"Not gonna sugar coat it. She killed a man today in a life-or-death shootout, Juan. He was a murderer with a three-state manhunt after him. I am the one who put her onto him and put her in that Hamburg café on the orders of her boss, Colonel Justice. She had to make a split-second decision to save dozens of lives, and she did the right thing. She had the shot, the only shot, and she took it. But as you know, if this is her first kill, she may be taking it hard. You need to call her. Drop whatever you are working on and be with her tonight, man. Don't let her be alone to think about this."

"Mac, you are like the Big Daddy to a growing family, you know that? You collect all these folk, and then you look after them."

"Huh. Well, I have no response to that, Juan."

"Of course you don't. Thanks for the call, Mac. I'll call Jonetta right now."

"Good deal, Juan. Stay in touch, man."

**

**Monday October 9
Newbury, NH
Mac Morrison's Steel Barn
5:00 p.m.**

Mac set up a cinder block fire pit three feet by four feet and built a roaring starter fire of pine fatwood before tossing on chunks of red oak, cherry, and maple with some smaller branches of cedar. All of the wood was slash from his tree farm. He laid down a sheet of perforated stainless steel over the concrete blocks and soon he was ready to grill.

The fire had an intoxicating aroma. Mickey Fisher cut 24 half-pound, ribeye-on-the-bone steaks and delivered them with three cases of American and Canadian beer, ten bottles of wine, and a huge bowl of iced, peeled, and cooked jumbo shrimp. Jodie baked two enormous sheet cakes.

The only question Mac had on his mind was: how many people would show up for a garage barbeque on *four hours' notice?*

The answer was: *all of them*!

By 6:00 p.m. there were 18 chatty people gathered around the fire pit with steaks grilling. Maria wrapped potatoes in aluminum foil and dropped them in the coals below the grill. The beer was flowing, the wine was sipped and there was a lot of laughter, which is exactly what was needed to wash away violent memories.

"So Mac," said Colonel Bradford, "how did you and Jackie find Louis Lopez in a western New York café?"

It was the first chance Mac had to really take a look at the man. Colonel Bradford was, as expected, in his early 50s, but stocky, rather than tall, perhaps 5'9", and built with a powerful frame that looked like a UNH linebacker with enough strength and speed for the NFL but not enough size. He rocked an old school flat top haircut under his flat brim hat, which he removed while sipping a cold Pilsener. The smile lines around the corners of his eyes said he liked to laugh even though he was in a very serious business.

"Some of it was luck," Mac said.

"After our scuffle with the Diaz Boyz, Jackie confiscated their truck, so the rest of the gang needed wheels to escape this region. You had a three-state BOLO looking for four Mexicans, so they couldn't take a bus, they couldn't realistically take an Uber, and they couldn't do a carjacking without attracting more attention to themselves.

"As you know, the two Martine brothers were riding stolen Vespa scooters when they stopped at Fisher's Store. Ramon recognized them, and they engaged us in a gun battle. After their arrest, Jackie ran the scooter VINs. As I suspected, they belonged to my friend Doc Lawson, who owns a cabin I built on Mascoma Lake. Because I maintain his security system, I have a key, so we went to the cabin to look for clues to Louis Lopez. It was obvious there had been a break-in, but no evidence was found.

"But a man named Sanford Daltry, who lives up the road from that cabin, had seen Lopez's picture in the paper and called New Hampshire State Police to report he might have sold a car to Lopez. When Jackie told me she was going to see him, I said I knew him, so I went along because he's had a stroke, but I knew he would talk to me.

"Sanford had sold Lopez an old Cadillac, but forgotten to give him his second set of keys. We asked for them. Because Sanford is forgetful, he uses AirTags™ as key fobs. So he used his iPhone™ to point out their location in his house. We asked him if he had put an AirTag on the keys he sold with the car. He had. So Jackie asked him to use his iPhone's app to look for that AirTag. He found it sitting in Boulanger's café, which ironically is my favorite breakfast restaurant when I'm in western New York.

"So, Colonel, I called your counterpart, Colonel Justice of the New York State Police, and did a conference call with BCI Investigator Jonetta Pope, who I also know from a previous murder case. Jonetta was the lead on the Lopez manhunt in New York. She is a plain-clothes BCI Investigator based out of Buffalo, and was on the road ten minutes from Boulanger's, so she took the call, and we planned a takedown outside the café.

"But a five-year-old spoiled the plan. Lopez took the kid hostage and was threatening to empty his Glock into the crowd unless he was allowed to escape. He shot the little boy's father, which gave Trooper Jonetta Pope a chance. She killed Lopez with one shot to the heart at close range inside a crowded café. Kill or be killed."

"Holy Mother of God," Colonel Bradford said. "Mackenzie Morrison, I swear, I just heard you connect an absolutely unconnected series of events and postulations that you somehow boogered together to allow State Police in two states to capture five criminals, potentially all killers, and you did it in two days, with no loss of civilian life! I just heard it, and I still cannot believe it!"

"Well, I lived through it, and I still can't believe it either," said Investigator Jackie Beaulieu. "Colonel, you need to make Mac your Chief of Detectives!"

"No, No!" said Mac, laughing as he took a slug of Labatt's Pilsener Blue Ale. "I'm happy with my life! Roger and I appreciate these forays into complex criminal cases so long as we don't get ensnared in the legal mumbo jumbo that follows them. I'll keep Jackie and you on my speed dial, Colonel, and hope for a call to help with a mystery now and then. That will be enough excitement."

'Row-Rowrf!' Buddy nudged Mac's knee and sat down.

"Yes, Buddy, I hear you. The steaks are done, and you and Emma want a pile of bones! C'mon folks, let's eat!"

**

Chapter Fourteen

Tuesday, October 10
Sunapee, NH
Eleanor's Café
6:00 a.m.

It was a cold, clear morning. Temps in the low 40s were a precursor of the true New Hampshire autumn.

Buddy and Emma liked the cold. They rode on the big front bench seat of Mac's 1971 green Chevy Impala to Eleanor's Café. They also liked Eleanor. She spoiled them with bits of bacon and a bowl of fresh water at the outdoor tables. The propane standing heaters were set up so the contractors could eat outside.

The 6:00 a.m. regulars were there talking about the shootings at Fisher's store and the capture of two Locos. Mac was telling of the shootout in Hamburg and the death of gang leader Louis Lopez.

"Well, Mac, that chapter is closed, and you survived again. Now let's get back to building!" said Roger Lemonier.

"Right, Rog. Drywall is next. And I see Mario is here."

Mario DuPont was the gold standard in drywall. His finishes were so smooth that one guy with a sanding stick could touch up a ten-room house in half a day. At one time, he and his wife had a 300-man union crew in Boston. That was then. After the pandemic, Mario sold his union business, bought a house in Newbury, New Hampshire and semi-retired. He and his wife were content to do the smaller non-union jobs that built his company. He even liked to pick up a trowel and sling some mud now and then.

Mario had leading man good looks, which probably helped him get his start. He had come down from Magog, Quebec, to southern New Hampshire in the early 80s, the boom years, with a satchel of tools and an earnest desire to succeed. He had done the same thing he was doing now, cruising the breakfast restaurants looking for builders. He would be there by 4 a.m. and on the job by 7. He was bright, honest, handsome, and hardworking.

And he had cousins in Quebec, lots of cousins. If he got a small job, he would hang and finish the drywall himself. If it was bigger, he would make a call, and the next day, some cousins would arrive ready to work. And they worked hard and fast, these French Canadian drywallers.

Mario's wife Denise had been a teenage beauty queen in Magog. She even did some television commercials. She had long black hair and black eyes and skin so pale she looked like a porcelain doll. Many men pursued her, but no man could take her breath away like Mario. So when he had built his business in southern New Hampshire, she married him, and they built a rambling ranch house with two huge barns on ten acres outside Derry. From there, Mario branched out into the Boston market, just 40 minutes away, and Denise ran the back office: books, invoicing, and personnel for the whole growing operation.

Approaching sixty, they were still a handsome couple. Mario typically dressed in a white formal shirt with a navy blue sweater-vest, black wool slacks, and dress loafers. Denise was partial to high-collar white silk blouses with an elegant necklace. Her clothes came from Montreal or Paris, France. She was a startling sight to first-time contractors who came into their barn office.

Today, Mario was looking for work. One of his builders was not ready, and he had a hole in his schedule.

"So Mac," said Mario, turning in his chair to face him. "I hear you're ready for drywall, eh?" Mario had been working in the U.S. for over forty years, but he still had that delightful French Canadian accent. Inside his offices, it was all they spoke. Denise was a big fan of the Montreal Canadians, but Mario and his son were Maple Leafs, first and always.

"Mario," said Mac, "you crafty old dog, I know you have your sources watching Roger's house."

"Infantini tells me de walls are insulated, so you are ready for drywall. I got a crew ready to go. 'Dere job was postponed. I can get in 'dere today. And I give you a good deal, you know me. Denise will make you a very good deal because you always pay quick. So, we start today?"

"HAHA!" Mac laughed. "Yes, today. I bet your guys are over there right now checking it out. Did they call you and say I'm ready?"

Mario grinned. "Marcel is 'dere now. We have de boards at de shop in Newport. You say go, we load up, deliver dis morning, be hanging by lunch time. *Ça va?*" (Does that work?)

"*Oui Mario*, *ça va.*" (Yes Mario, that works) Mac said. "You got the job. Where is Denise's office now, in Newport?"

"Yes, at de shop."

"Really? Mario, no offense, but you need a better office for her. That's OK for material storage, but come on, man, she is an elegant lady, and that place is just a heated storage locker."

"She don't complain, Mac, but you are right. And it will be cold in winter."

"Mario, you did the drywall at my new shop. What about one of my bays?"

"I thought you rented them."

"Roger took three big ones, I have two. There is one left. It's twenty by fifty, 1,000 square feet. One-third of it is finished office, and the other two-thirds have a high clearance overhead door and eighteen-foot ceilings for storing lifts of drywall. Your shop in Newport has eight-foot ceilings. You can't even park a big truck inside. Here, there are big office windows overlooking the beaver pond and only three miles to your house, Mario. All new and clean, Denise can decorate anyway she likes. Can't beat the location, and Maria cooks lunch for our crew. She would love to have Denise to talk to."

"Maria is a good cook, but she speaks Spanish, not French, Mac."

"She is going to learn if she hangs out with you guys."

"So, Mac, dis is good for Denise, but I think maybe we need a little more space so I could get out of Newport, have my big truck and material storage, a table for my guys to come and clock in. Can you help?"

Mac already knew the answer. Marybeth and Gabriella were in Barcelona Harbor. They were pulling him there. He had kept two shop bays for himself, one for his building business and one for his classic car restoration business. But he could see that he probably only needed one.

"Mario, how about I rent you two bays, side by side, with a connecting door. So that would be 36' x 50', 1,800 square feet, all high clear in one bay and office and high clear in the other. Fit them up to suit yourself."

"And you give me good deal?"

"HA! Of course, Mario, of course, so do we have a deal?"

"Yes. We start fitting up tomorrow. I got more guys to work den I need on

Roger's house so we come in, paint, set up shop lockers, OK?"

"I'll give you keys this morning. Meet you at Roger's house."

Norman Pelletier had been sitting with Mario, but now he looked at Mac. "Are you happy with Roger's roof, Mac?" Norman asked.

"It's perfect, as always, Norman. What are you working on next?"

"Nothing this week. Next week we're doing the library, it's a big job. Today, I'm doing estimates."

"Norman, I have to strip and re-shingle a 150-year-old house in New York. It's 300 feet from Lake Erie, where they get vicious wind and lake-effect snow. What shingle do you recommend?"

"Mac, I would use this one here," he said, opening his catalog. "Too bad it's New York, or I would come do it for you, Mac."

"Norman, could you send René to run my crew? I'll help, too."

"How big is the roof, Mac?"

"40 squares. It's two A roofs, both are 12 pitch, and a dormer, Norman."

"Yes, I can send René if it's this week."

"Let's do it, Norman. I can take the crew tomorrow and we start work Thursday."

"OK, Mac. René will bring the trailer with ladders and tools. I can order material from here, have it delivered by a local supplier there. They will put it on my account, and you can pay me later."

"Great Norman. René can stay at the house with me. It's a nice B & B. The owner is my good friend Marybeth. I'll text you the address. You can go to Google Earth to see it."

"Mac. What color is the house?"

"Cream yellow with black shutters."

"OK, dark charcoal shingle?"

"Perfect. It's 450 miles here to there. Can he leave tomorrow, Norman?"

"Sure, be there tomorrow night, Mac."

"Perfect, thanks, Norman."

**

Tuesday, October 10
Newbury, NH
Roger Lemonier's House - Mac's Job Site
7:00 a.m.

Mac made one last sweep through the house. Paco had added structure in the kitchen to attach the wall cabinets, so that was ready. He could not find any missing drywall nailers, but if there were, Mario's crew would add them.

Really, Mac thought, a week for drywall and a week for painters. They don't need me here for two weeks. Ursula had already picked the colors. She would be watching the painters like a hawk.

And that was good, because he was going back to Barcelona Harbor.

He wrapped the F-450 stake bed in its tarp and loaded the tool boxes. Tomas would drive it with the twins. Mac would drive the '57 Chevy Bel Air with Emma and Buddy. Now, he just needed to tell Marybeth he was coming with four guests.

Mac's phone buzzed. (*Investigator Jackie Beaulieu.*)

"Morning Jackie, what's up?"

"First of all, thank you for that lovely barbeque last night, Mac. It was just what we needed to put a cap on the Bisbee murder, and I thought we had."

"Something new come up?"

"My techs were looking through the Lopez burner phone we got from Jaime Charbonneau in Enfield. By the way, he prefers to be called Jamie. There was one number Lopez called twice to a different burner phone. That phone moved from Enfield to Lebanon, then traveled to Canandaigua, New York, where the *signal went dead an hour after Louis Lopez was killed*. Don't know if it is important, but I was wondering if we still have one more unknown gang member out there."

"But you have no name and no witness identification from Mrs. Bisbee. Without that the phone sounds like a dead end."

"It is, unless we connect it up. You are so good at that, Mac."

"Jackie, I am busy building a house and tomorrow I leave for New York."

"Well, there is one more thing. Our techs went through the pictures on the phone Jaime found in the trash, and there were photos of a pistol, a Ruger pocket gun. I'm wondering if this is a gun used by the missing gang member."

"If there is a missing gang member."

"Mac, you said so yourself. You wondered if there was a sixth guy."

"I know, and now you've hooked me again. What do you want me to do?"

"Jaime Charbonneau does not have a phone, so I can't call him and ask if he knew anything about the gun. Maybe Lopez took the pictures. Maybe the gun belongs to Charbonneau. Anyway, I am in Concord chasing this lead and was wondering if you could drive up and talk to Charbonneau. It's not far for you. You have a knack with people. I would appreciate your input, and so would Colonel Bradford."

"OK, I guess I can do that, Jackie. Text me his name and address. I'll do it this morning."

"Will do Mac. And thanks."

"Sure, Jackie."

**

Tuesday, October 10
En route to Enfield, NH
8:00 a.m.

Mac left Emma with Maria Rodriguez and took Buddy with him in the '71 Impala. He wanted to put some miles on it to find its flaws. Enfield was only 30 miles from Newbury, so if he broke down it was an easy tow home. The day had started chilly, but the sun was warming, and soon he had the windows down and Buddy's head was hanging out drinking in the fall smells.

He drove along the west side of Mascoma Lake. There were peek-a-boo views through the old Shaker Village before he turned right over the bridge at Shakoma Beach and entered the village center. He passed through it and followed phone directions to the address on Moose Mountain Road. A tall, thin man in faded overalls was sanding a rusty mailbox. He had a rattle can of silver spray paint at his feet.

Mac stopped the Impala. The man stopped sanding.

"Nice Chevy," he said. "What year?"

"71."

"My Grandad had a '70 Monte Carlo. Wish I still had it."

"Right," said Mac, stepping out and letting Buddy loose. "The dog is friendly."

"I like dogs. Come here, buddy. What's his name?"

"Buddy."

"Really? Hey, Buddy, can you shake?"

Buddy sat and gave him a giant white paw. Jaime Charbonneau had unknowingly passed the Buddy test.

"Are you Jamie Charbonneau?" Mac asked.

"Hey, yes, I am," Jaime replied. "It's actually Jaime, but I prefer Jamie, thanks."

"Someone tipped me off, Jamie."

"Oh?"

"State Police Investigator Jackie Beaulieu."

"Oh, yes, Jackie. She sent the SWAT team here yesterday, all in black. Scared the shit out of me. Almost made me take up drinking again. He pointed to the three unopened bottles of bourbon on his front porch. "I'm giving it up. Been a boozer all my life. Today, I'm a painter. What brings you here, Mister…?"

"Mac Morrison. Pleased to meet you, Jamie. Buddy says he's pleased to meet you too, don't you, Buddy?"

'Rowrf!'

"Jamie, that phone that you found belonged to a killer, Louis Lopez."

"Yeah, he's dead, read it in today's paper. I used to read the day-old paper from the trash can on the side of the grocery store. That's how I found the phone. But I'm starting fresh, no booze, so today I bought this morning's paper."

"Yes, he's dead, killed in a shootout. So you found the phone in the trash can. Is that where you got the gun?"

Jaime looked startled.

"The gun? You know about the gun?"

"Jamie, there were pictures of a Ruger pocket pistol on that phone. That is why Jackie asked me to come speak to you. Was that your gun? Did you take those pictures?"

"Well, I guess I should have mentioned it, but Ted wanted a gun for personal protection. He's my driver on the delivery app I use to buy booze. He meets some rough customers. Now he's making deliveries up north where those illegals have been coming in. Yes, I found it in the trash. I took pictures so I could sell it on the Net, but Ted came by just as I finished shooting it out back. He liked it, so I traded him for two bottles of bourbon. Am I in trouble?"

"No, you didn't know whose gun it was. Finders keepers from the trash, Jamie. But that gun could have belonged to Louis Lopez, and if it did, it might have been used in a crime, and that might tie it to a missing gang member. That's why I'm here. State Police would like to test fire that gun and see if the firing pin marks on the shell casings match any in the NIBIN."

"What's that, the N..."

"National Integrated Ballistics Information Network. So, Ted, your delivery guy has the gun?"

"Yes, he was gonna buy ammo down in Newbury. The clip was empty because I did some target practice out back."

"You did? What did you do with the shell casings, Jamie?"

"Oh, they're still lying on the ground. I was gonna clean them up after I paint this mailbox. I got a lot of cleanup work to do on this place now that I'm sober. Twenty years' worth of work."

"Jamie, let's go see those casings."

"Sure, c'mon Buddy!"

'Rowrf!'

They walked out back to a stump. There were some broken bottles on the ground and some more bottles sitting on a log.

"That little gun shoots straight, which was amazing 'cause I was just sobering up. Felt pretty good that I hit four. Haven't fired a gun in a long time."

Mac bent over and looked at the shell casings.

"Jamie, I'm going to take these with me, OK? I'll give them to Jackie for the State Police lab to examine and enter into the NIBIN. With these casings and the pictures, they don't actually need the gun just yet. Ted can keep it if the gun was not used to commit a crime. But he might want to talk to the State Police about what constitutes proper ownership and get a permit for concealed carry."

"Sure, I can see that, Mac."

Mac used a folded grocery list from his pocket to scoop up the casings. Whoever loaded them into the clip may have left fingerprints, and he did not want to disturb them.

"Jamie, do you have an envelope in the cabin?"

"Sure." Jamie got the envelope, and Mac dumped the shell casings in it.

Mac got the name and phone number of Ted Downing, the delivery driver, shook Jamie's hand, and invited him to stop in and have lunch the next time he was in Newbury. Then Mac and Buddy jumped in the Impala and headed back through town.

He stopped at the grocery store. He looked at the location of the trash can and the orientation of security cameras before he walked inside and bought a coffee. As he set it on the counter, he saw today's newspaper on the rack. He picked one up and scanned the front page story about Louis Lopez and the Martine brothers.

"Big news," said the cashier. "You know the cops said that guy's phone was found in our trash can. I saw his picture; can't say I ever saw him come in here. There was another guy, could have been Mexican, he came in here a few times and bought food. And then another one came in and bought sunglasses."

"Would they be on your store camera?" asked Mac.

"They might be, but the files are copied over after a certain time."

"Can you call it up?"

"Let me get the manager. She can."

A short, stocky woman came out of the back room, invited Mac to join her in her office, and they pulled up the security camera files.

"The camera files automatically refresh after 48 hours," she said.

"Let's go back to Sunday," said Mac. "That's when the phone and gun were found in the trash can."

"Gun?" she said, surprised.

"Yes, there was a gun too," said Mac.

"Oh, wow! Right in sleepy Enfield!"

She scrolled back as far as she could go. She found Luca Martine wearing a tan canvas coat and hunter's hat, trying on sunglasses, and paying for them with food and cigarettes. But that was as far back as the file went. Mac thanked her, took his coffee, and headed out to the car. He hit his contacts for Jackie Beaulieu, and she answered immediately.

"Yes, Mac?"

"Jackie, the pictures you recovered from the phone, did you get a pistol serial number?"

"Yes."

"Did you run it?"

"Yes, the gun was legally purchased in Texas, but the person sold it at a garage sale with no record of the buyer. Nothing in criminal history related to that serial number that we found. What did you find?"

"Jamie Charbonneau found the gun in the trash can at the same time he found the phone. He traded it to a friend for a couple bottles of booze, and the friend has the gun. But I have eleven spent shell casings that were untouched after Jamie used the gun for target practice in his backyard. I'll bring the casings back to Newbury, and you can have a Trooper pick them up at my house, OK?"

"Terrific. And we can retrieve the gun from Jamie's friend if we need it."

"Yes, he's a delivery driver. I've got his contact info."

"Great! Thanks, Mac! I promise I won't bug you again for at least a minute or two!"

"Make it two. Remember, I'll be in New York tomorrow for a week or so."

"OK, Mac."

**

Mac called Marybeth next.

"Hello, my love," she said, when are you coming to see me and Gabriella?"

"Is Gabby there already?"

"Just drove in this morning. She's tired after that 1800-mile drive, but excited about this new venture with her guy friend J.P."

"Well, it's going to be up to you to figure out how much he is her guy or her friend, M."

"Mac! Always the protective Daddy, aren't you!"

"Yes. M, did you hear about Jonetta Pope stopping that killer in Hamburg?"

"I did. It's been all over the news. So glad she wasn't hurt."

"I called Juan. He was going to make sure she is OK. M, are you booked up this week?"

"No, just Harry in the Cottage, Mac."

"Good, I'll be arriving tomorrow night with four more guys: Tomas Rodriguez, his 17-year-old twin cousins, and Rene, the foreman for my roofer up here. We are going to put a new roof on your house. I'll pay for it."

"No, you will not, Mackenzie Morrison! I'll pay for it. I thought you fixed it before you left."

"M, that was a patch job. You'll never make it through this winter without water damage. René is gonna run the crew. Will you cook for us, please?"

"Of course I will! How exciting! You've hardly been gone a minute, and you're coming back! And I'm so glad because I need you here now, Mac."

"Why, what's up?"

"I got a call from Morgan Hillman not a half hour ago. The judge granted his request for a disinterment of Jim's body, Mac. They are going to perform a new autopsy. It's going to be very emotional for me. I need you here."

"Of course, M. I'll stay as long as you need me, you know that. I'm surprised Morgan didn't call me."

"He did, but your line was busy."

"Oh, I was just on the phone with the State Police. They asked me to do some private eye work, without pay, of course."

"You just can't stay out of trouble, can you Mac?"

"I'll try while I'm with you. OK, gotta go 'cause I'm driving, but see you tomorrow night, probably about supper time."

"I'll wait supper until you guys get here. Harry can join us. We'll all eat on the porch with the dogs. Just like our big family. Love you, Sweetie. Drive safe."

"Love you, M. *A bientôt.*"

**

Part Two:
Return to Barcelona Harbor

Vineyards at Barcelona Harbor with the Escarpment in the background

Chapter Fifteen

Wednesday October 11
Captain Murphy B & B
Barcelona Harbor, New York
6:00 p.m.

Philip C. Laurien

When René rolled in with a dozen aluminum ladders on racks, his trailer rattled like an 1870 pots and pans salesman in a Conestoga wagon.

Gabby made introductions for J.P. before they sat down to a contractor's feast of fruit salad, meatloaf, mashed potatoes, green bean casserole with mushrooms, popovers baked in the bread oven, and peach pie.

After dinner, the workers retired to their rooms. They would start the roof early in the a.m. On the back porch, the lights were dimmed, and candles were lit. Gabriella, Marybeth, Mac, and J.P. stayed to talk.

"So, Jean-Paul," said Mac, "Gabby has told us you want to graft a hardier version of your Bordeaux grape onto rootstock here to develop a new American Bordeaux. Is that right?"

"Yes, Mister Morrison. There are two forces driving this venture. First, climate change has affected our vineyard in southern France. The grapes we grow now are less suited to a hotter, drier climate. Second, reduced French wine consumption means less demand. If we don't adapt, in ten years, we could go out of business. But American wine consumption is up. American tastes are becoming more sophisticated. New York is a huge wine market. California Bordeaux wines are grown in a climate similar to Bordeaux, France, but shipping wines from California or France to New York requires adding sulfite preservatives to the wine.

"For some people, adding sulfites can cause allergic reactions. And, it is not traditional wine making. It makes wine into a processed food, like American cheese.

"What my father and I want to do is grow organic New York Bordeaux grapes to make a fine fresh organic table wine with no sulfites. It will be marketed regionally and promoted in good restaurants. We hope that once people taste this wine, they will prefer it over all other Bordeaux wines.

"Did you know, Mr. Morrison, that 175 million bottles of wine were produced in New York State last year? To be part of that huge regional market, we could initially be profitable on ten acres, but in the long run, one hundred acres or more would be the goal. It takes eight to ten years to achieve organic certification, so we would ramp up organic wine over time, but we could market sulfite-free wine within 3-5 years."

"What do you think, Dad?" asked Gabriella. Mac could tell she wanted his approval.

"I think it's a worthwhile venture, and an interesting challenge. Marybeth and I are planning an elder village of four new cottages on one acre of her back four acres, but there will be three acres she could lease to J.P. for his experimental grafting."

Marybeth gave Mac a quizzical side-eye look.

"And I'm sure she would give you the same fair deal she gives the farmer who leases them now, with the understanding the vines are hers, and she retains possession whether the experiment succeeds or not. But all of those arrangements can be worked out with her attorney."

J.P. said nothing, because there was nothing to say.

"Of course," he said. "Well, I must be getting back to my apartment. Mrs. Murphy, thank you for dinner. My father and I look forward to working with you. Gabriella, would you walk me to my car?"

"Of course, Jean Paul. Goodnight Marybeth. Good night, Dad."

"Goodnight, Sweetheart," Marybeth said.

**

"You never stop looking out for your ladies, do you?" Marybeth said to Mac. "You basically just drew up a verbal contract and made Jean Paul agree to terms without my discussing it with him."

"Marybeth, you were about to give away the farm just to help Gabriella because you think she is in love with J.P, and you are a hopeless romantic. That would have been bad on all counts. This is J.P.'s business. If you listened carefully, he did not include any discussion about Gabby's role in it, so she is dreaming by projecting herself into it as his partner.

"Her first business opportunity is to buy a shipping container of his father's wine and market it. I support that. The creation of a new American Bordeaux grape and organic wine is commendable, and I hope it succeeds. But it could fail, just as their relationship could fail. So, let's keep the business separate from the love interest. And yes, I did just back him into a corner. And yes, Morgan and I will protect your interests, my dear."

"Well, *Monsieur Mac*, let's turn out the lights. But the party's not over. I have some other interests for you to attend to before we sleep."

"Then, my queen, let us retire to the castle keep."

**

Chapter Sixteen

Thursday October 12
Barcelona Harbor
Murphy B & B
5:45 a.m.

Mac woke to the grunt of a diesel engine. René was outside directing the unloading of a huge roll-off container. Mac lifted the window sash to watch. Buddy stood next to Mac with his paws on the sill.

'Rowrf!' he barked at the commotion.

"*C'est bon!*" René shouted as the big steel box slid down its tracks and sat on the front lawn.

"Miguel, Lupe, unload the ladders, then the planks. Take tool belts, hammers, and shingle shovels. Then we tell Mac to wake up and make us breakfast. We start first light."

"Marybeth," said Mac, "did you hear that?"

"I heard, and I'm getting up. I didn't know roofers worked in the dark."

"You've never worked with French Canadians. I'll go down and get the coffee going. There's gonna be a lot of noise overhead once they get those shovels going. I'll be on the ground tossing debris into the roll-off."

"OK, Mac, give me ten minutes, and I'll be in the kitchen. Gotta feed the crew!"

**

Thursday October 12
12:00 noon

The roof was stripped. Weather was clear. Temps that had begun in the 50s had risen to the 60s.

"Mac," said René between bites of an enormous grilled cheeseburger, "after lunch, we dry-in the roof, then we flash and shingle. Marybeth, if we have breakfast at 6:30 then we are on the roof at sunrise. Mac, I'll cut the slot for a ridge vent, but the attic still needs more ventilation."

"Yeah," said Mac, "We need two power vents for make-up air. I'll run up to the lumber company and get them."

Thursday October 12
2:00 p.m.

Mac was cutting in the power vents when his phone buzzed. (*Sarah Lieberman calling.*)

"Hello Sarah, what's up?" said Mac.

"Mac, are you in New Hampshire?"

"Actually, I'm in Barcelona Harbor putting a roof on the Murphy B & B."

"Oh! That's good. Could you meet me in Erie? Sol's in the hospital, Mac."

"The hospital? What happened?"

"I don't know. His foreman found him unconscious this morning. He was beaten."

"Beaten? What do you mean beaten?"

"Somebody beat him pretty badly, but he got in some licks, too. They told me his knuckles are scarred and bloody. His foreman found my card on his desk and called me. I just spoke to the hospital. He's out of intensive care and is stable."

Mac could feel his blood starting to boil. "Who would beat an 85-year-old man?"

"I don't know," said Sarah. "I'm going to drive down to Erie to see him. Can you come, Mac?"

"Of course I can, Sarah! Look, where are you now?"

"At our Jamestown office."

"OK, text me the address. Give me forty-five minutes, and I'll pick you up."

"Good, thanks, Mac."

Mac called over to René.

"René, I've got an emergency, I have to leave. Can you finish up with the boys?"

"Sure Mac. Anything I can do to help?"

"No, it's a personal situation. See you at supper."

Five minutes later, Mac was down in the kitchen. Marybeth was rolling out pizza dough.

"How's it going?" she asked.

"Good. The boys are hard workers, and René is directing them. I've gotta go. I'm leaving Buddy and Emma with you, OK, M?"

"Sure. Where are you going?"

"I've gotta pick up Sol Weinstein's lawyer in Jamestown. We're driving to Erie. Sol is in the hospital."

"Sol is in the hospital? What happened?"

"Sarah said someone beat him up pretty bad. His crew found him unconscious this morning."

"WHAT?" she shrieked. "Someone beat up Sol? Why? Who would harm that sweet old man, Mac?"

"I don't know, M, but I'm gonna find out."

"Should we expect you back for supper, Mac?"

"Let me find out what's going on. Then I can do something about it."

"Mac, give my love to Sol. I want him here in my elder village, you know that. He deserves a peaceful retirement, that poor man."

**

Thursday October 12
I-90, En Route to Memorial Hospital, Erie, PA
3:30 p.m.

"Sarah, any update on the CCBUTT letter?' asked Mac.

"I heard from their shyster lawyer named Simon Long. He's been on the edge of some ethics violations before but never had his license pulled."

"What did he say?"

"They offered Sol $2,000,000 for his five acres."

"Sarah, there are five buildings, a deep water dock, and at least a couple million dollars worth of equipment, plus the land. It's worth more."

"Mac, it's worth a lot more. I used the CCBUTT plan as the basis for a ballpark appraisal of what the five acres would be worth zoned for the lakefront park, marina, and the condos."

"And?"

"My appraiser said between four to five million dollars."

Mac whistled. "And did you respond to that verbal offer?"

"We did. Sol authorized me to negotiate, so once I got the value from the appraiser, I called Attorney Long and told him we wanted five million. He swallowed the phone from the sound of it. Then he said that was ridiculous, and that if we would not make a reasonable counteroffer, then he would have to consider their eminent domain options, which could drag out the process for years, and given Sol's advanced age, he could not promise that a deal could be reached while he was still alive."

"And what did you say to that?"

"I told him to go fuck himself."

"HA-HA!" said Mac. "Good for you, Sarah!"

"I told you, Mac, He's a sleaze bag. Ten minutes later, he called back to offer three million, final offer, take it or they would explore the eminent domain process. I told him he could fuck the eminent domain process too because he was not a legal public entity, and he should get out of this sleazy deal before he gets disbarred."

"I love you, Sarah. You're my kind of lawyer. My friend Marybeth Murphy is about to enter into a land lease with a lot of moving parts, including a foreign winery. Morgan Hillman represents her, but we would benefit from your expertise."

"I'd be glad to, Mac."

"Well, here we are. Let's go see how Sol is doing."

**

Erie, PA
General Hospital
4:00 p.m.

Sol Weinstein looked like he was sleeping when they entered his room. He turned his head.

"Nurse?" he said.

"It's Sarah Lieberman and Mac Morrison, Sol. We're here."

Sometimes, that's all a friend has to say.

A tear fell from Sol's closed right eye. Now Mac could see that he was not sleeping. Both his eyes were swollen shut. Sarah threw her arms around him and kissed his forehead gingerly.

"Oh Sol, what happened? Who did this to you?"

"Mackenzie," Sol croaked, "you are here?"

"Yes, Sol."

"Come here. Sit down. Take my hands, both of you. I vant to feel your power so it vill come into me. Dere. Dat is good. So, you vant to know vat happened? Two guys beat me for being a Jew. But I smell a rat. I tell you vat I know, den maybe my friend Mackenzie he can figure it out.

"So, last night after da scadap yard close, da phone rings. Vee closed, so I don't answer it. It rings and rings. Somebody calling over and over, but vee closed, so I don't answer."

"What time was that Sol?" said Mac.

"Maybe six o'clock. Vee close at five, so maybe at six da calls start. It keeps ringing so eventually I answer. A man says he has a load of copper scadap, can he bring in da morning. I say bring it, but make sure it's not stolen. Dat's a problem vit copper scadap. I tell dem I vill check before he unload it. If it's new copper I don't take it. He say it's not stolen, OK, I say bring it. Vee open at 8 o'clock. He says he vant to come early so he can deliver three loads by noon. He say he vant to come at seven a.m. So I say OK, bring it at seven."

"Sol, did you ask who he was?"

"No, but he vould not haff given me real name if he gonna beat me up."

"That's true. OK, continue, Sol."

"So at seven a.m., I unlock da gate and tell dem to drive on da scale. I go into my blue building to read da scale vit truck loaded. After dey unload vee read da scale again. So I go into da office und I look out da vindow. Dey getting out of da truck and it's not on da scale. I vonder, why dey not on da scale? Den dey come in my office vit dose blue masks, you know Covid masks, and I cannot see faces, just eyes. Dey vearing coats and gloves. I tink, vat is dis, a stickup? I tell dem, I don't have cash, it goes to night deposit and da safe is on a time lock, cannot be opened before eight o'clock."

"So what did they do then, Sol?"

"Den dey open dere coats and I see svastikas on dere shirts!"

"Nazi swastikas?" Sarah asked, horrified.

"Yah, Nazi svastikas! Da big vun, he laugh like a donkey and say it's time for me to leave dis place. He say I gotta get out of town, dey don't vant me here. He say dey don't vant my kind.

"I tell him get out. Get off my property and never come back. I keep a gun in a drawer but ven I try to grab it da smaller one block me. He say dey don't vant to hurt me, but be smart, take da deal und get out of da neighborhood and dere vill be no trouble. Just take da deal.

"Vat deal, I say? And da big one, he snort like a donkey again and he say: You know vat deal, you dumb Kike."

"I survive da Nazis. Dey experiment vit me as a baby, make me look like I do. Dey kill my father and mother. Nobody gonna come here, to my house, and call me a dumb Kike. I'm small and dis guy, da big one, laughing like a donkey, is standing in front of me. My head only come up to his waist. So I punch his balls, hard as I can. He yell und bend over. I butt him vit my head. I smash his teeth I tink, you see da tooth marks on my head."

Sure enough, there were tooth marks on his skull. Mac took out his cell phone and photographed Sols' injuries.

"Sarah," said Mac, "I want you to have the nurse take an impression of those tooth marks before we leave. OK, Sol, then what happened?"

"Den vile he bent over I pound his face vit both fists." Sol held up his scarred and swollen hands. "Da little tough one, he hit me from behind. Hit me in da kidney, make me spin around. I'm going down, but before I do, I hit him in da face vit my ring."

He held up his swollen hands. Mac could see a silver ring, like a graduation-style ring with a prominent Star of David that jutted up like a sculpture from the base.

"Den da little one, he hit me vit someting hard, and I go down. I try to get up, but da big vun hitting me in da face and on da head. I hear da gate bell ring, means some vun coming. I hope some vun save me, but I black out. I vake up here, in hospital. Martin brought me. I vass unconscious a long time. Maybe an hour."

"Sol," said Mac, "Martin is outside. I'm sure he would like to see you."

"Martin's a good man, been vit me many years. I vant to tank him."

Mac went out and came back with a sturdy-looking man in his fifties with a weather-beaten face from many years working outdoors. He trembled with anger as he looked at Sol lying in bed with his eyes closed.

"Sol," Martin said, "I'm so sorry. If only I had come to work ten minutes earlier. I drove through the gate, so the bell rang. They must have heard it, because they walked out of your office acting like nothing had happened, got in their truck and drove off, never looked at me, just drove away. Why

Sol, why would anyone do this to you? You have no enemies."

"Dey say get out, call me a dumb Kike. Dey vore Nazi shirts, so could be because I am a Jew, but could be some-ting else too. I smell a rat. My friend Mackenzie, I gonna ask him to find out."

"You don't have to ask Sol," said Mac, "I'm going to find out. And I will make them pay. Sarah, I'm going to get the doctor. Will you call the police? They can talk to Sol now. Martin, I will be stopping at the Bank's yard later. Will you be there so I can look things over?"

"Yes, sir, anything I can do to help."

**

Thursday October 12
Erie, PA
General Hospital
4:25 p.m.

The police interviewed Sol. After he repeated his story, Sarah asked if they would investigate the beating as a hate crime. They said they would like to see the security camera video to see if the swastikas Sol described were captured on camera. Martin, Sol's foreman, agreed to drive back to the Bank's Scrapyard and show them the video. The nurse shooed them all out of Sol's room so he could rest. He had a concussion, a swollen face, bruised hands, and a bruised kidney. They would not know if his vision was damaged until he could open his eyes.

The marks on his back and the damage to his kidney were the work of brass knuckles. Mac knew that. So the little tough shit had used the knuckles on Sol. He would pay for that.

Mac and Sarah walked out to the blue '57 Bel Air. Before they left the hospital parking lot, Mac called Marybeth and told her to feed the roofing crew. He would be delayed.

""Sarah," Mac said, "do you mind taking a short ride with me before I take you back to Jamestown?"

"No, of course not, Mac. Where are we going?"

"To find a laughing donkey."

**

Thursday October 12
Ashtabula, OH
B & W Boat Club & Wilkins Scrap Yard
5:15 p.m.

The gate was locked, so Mac rang the bell, as he had before. While he waited for a response he whipped out his cellphone and snapped some pictures of the scrap yard through the chain link fence, as he had done before.

This time, he could see a forklift moving pallets of large wooden crates with what looked like exhaust pipes sticking out of the top. The pallets were coming out of a tractor-trailer with California plates and another with New York plates. They were being loaded into a forty-foot steel shipping container set on a rail car flatbed. The rail cars were lined up to be pushed down to the dock.

Mac could see crushed stone being offloaded at the dock while a freighter lay anchored offshore in the channel.

A guard in a rent-a-cop uniform came out of his shack. He was mid-sixties, with a paunch. His shirt patch said 'Arthur'.

"Hey!" he yelled, "no pictures!"

"Sorry," said Mac, "Nice view of the water. Too bad the boats are grounded."

"Yeah, it's a problem, and getting worse every year. The current pushes silt around that jetty, and it all comes in here. We have to dredge all the time, which costs a fortune. Look at the members' boats. Can't even float them. Pretty soon, there won't be any members if we don't move outta here."

"Yeah, I can see that," said Mac. "You load the rail cars at your dock?"

"It's not our dock; it's private. We have to wait until they have an opening, that's why that freighter is anchored out, that and the dang wind. When we get a south wind like this, it pushes the water to the Canadian side. The harbor needs to be dredged. Sometimes those ships can't come in until the wind shifts and the water level rises."

"Huh," Mac said. "Interesting. Say, where's your partner today, Herman? I met him last time I came to see Mace."

"You a friend of Mace? Good guy. Pays bonuses for night deliveries."

"You do a lot of night deliveries?" asked Mac.

"Those wooden bins come from California. The way it works out, they usually come at night. I'm glad for the extra pay because I'm retired on a fixed income. This is a load we just got in."

He pointed to the crates.

"Good for him to pay you extra," said Mac. "Yeah, I met Mace last May. He bought a boat from a guy I know. The big guard knows the boat, *Mace's Mistress*."

"Yeah. You're talkin' about Slugger. His real name's Herman, but he ain't gone by that for a long time. He used to do a little pro boxing. That's how he got his name."

"Is that how his nose got busted?" Mac said.

"Mister, don't ever let him hear you say that, or he'll tear your head off. He's mean when he's angry, and today he's angry."

"So, it's not his shift today, huh? I thought he worked days."

"He does, but he called in sick today. Secretary said he sounded pissed off and terrible on the phone. Him and Stubby probably tied one on last night."

"Stubby?" said Mac.

"That's his drinking pal. Short little fucker, but tough as nails. They usually go up to Ricky's Road House in Erie. Been busted for too many bar fights in Ash-town. Them two like to mix it up with strangers, usually wind up outside in the parking lot. It's kinda like Slugger's old days in the ring. They're tough, those two."

"Guess Mace's boat is still with the cops, eh?" said Mac. "I don't see it."

"You know about that, eh?" said the guard. "Yeah, it could be a while before he gets it back. But whatever the cops are interested in happened before he bought it from that Minetti guy in New York. I hear he got killed."

"You heard right," said Mac. "Well, I guess Mace is not around. See ya, Arthur."

**

Sarah had been listening to the conversation from the car. She grinned as Mac got behind the big steering wheel and fired the throaty 383 V8 to life.

"You'd make a hell of a prosecuting attorney, Mac," she said. "You drew every drop of information out of him without him knowing you were doing it."

"Nope, I'd make a lousy prosecuting attorney, Sarah, because the way I prosecute bad guys is not something the law wants to know."

"What are you thinking, Mac?"

"The donkey laugh. Sol's description of the big guy's laugh was perfect. The regular daytime guard here is tall, kinda dopey looking, and has a busted nose from being slugged once too many times. Ergo, the nickname Slugger."

"You think he's the big guy that beat up Sol?"

"Could be. It's the donkey laugh that would give it away, and the fact he called in sick fits. He got punched in the balls, head-butted, and beat around the ears, so he was in no shape to show up for work. I'd like to get a look at him today, but first, I want to stop at the Banks yard and look at the security video. Then I'll take you home."

" You are the bloodhound on a scent, Mac. Joe Delmonico told me how you cracked a murder case that was two years old."

"Correction, I cracked five murder cases dating back forty years. But I couldn't prove two of them."

"Oh? Who were those two, Mac?"

"My parents."

**

5:30 p.m.
En Route to Banks Scrap Yard

Mac called Investigator Jonetta Pope as he drove. He advised her of the New York trucks he had seen being unloaded at the Wilkins Scrap Yard and asked if she had heard of a large catalytic converter fencing operation in northeast Ohio. She had not, but said if the trucks had New York plates and the converters were indeed stolen, then it would be a federal crime, so she would get the New York State Police to look into it. Mac also told her about the attack in Erie, Pennsylvania on Sol Weinstein, and how the stolen CATS in Ohio could be related. He gave her the Erie Police Department number if she wanted to check with them.

**

Thursday October 12
Erie, PA
Bank's Breakers and Scrap
6:15 p.m.

"Martin," said Mac, "thank you for staying. Let's see the video feed. Have the police seen it?"

"Yes, they got a copy from the crew. They are going to ask the local TV stations to play it. Maybe the public can identify these thugs."

The video was black and white and good quality. There were multiple feeds from eight cameras, four outside and four inside Sol's office with his classic cars. The feed began with the pickup truck arriving at 7:00 a.m. Sol was seen opening the gate and letting it in. It was a twenty-year-old Chevy pickup, totally nondescript, with no license plate on the front. The camera at the gate showed the truck pass by and then captured its rear, where, of course, the license plate had been smeared with mud to make it unreadable.

The next three cameras were located on poles by the car crusher, the shredder, and the magnetic separator. It showed two men entering the blue office building where the assault took place.

The four cameras inside Sol's blue building had views of his office, the desk, and two views of his classic cars. The videos showed multiple angles of Sol being surprised by the two men, one tall and one short. Both were wearing Covid face masks, hats, and gloves. There was no accompanying soundtrack. At one point, it appears an argument starts, then both men open their jackets, and large swastikas are clearly displayed on their chests. The tall one steps close to Sol, looks down at him, and says something. Sol responds, which was probably where he is telling them to leave.

Then the tall one says something again, and Sol punches his balls, hard. It was a good punch, Mac thought. The man doubles over. Sol head-butts him and punches his ears. The short man reaches into his pocket, slips on brass knuckles, and punches Sol in the kidney from behind. Sol spins around and hits the smaller man in the face, which knocks his ball cap off. The small man punches Sol in the stomach, and he drops to the floor. Then the big man rolls Sol over and starts beating his face with both fists.

Mac is so angry he has to force himself to keep watching. Tears are rolling down Sarah's cheeks.

Suddenly the men stopped, as if they heard a sound. Sol lies lifeless. The men are seen going out to their truck and driving off. It is now 7:15 a.m.

The video continues. Martin drives through the gate at 7:15 a.m. His truck is passed by the other truck as the two men leave. He parks and goes inside the blue building. He finds Sol lying on the floor next to his desk. He attends to Sol, picks up the phone and calls. There is a baseball cap on the floor under the desk. He picks it up and places it on the desk. The rescue squad arrives at 7:33 and takes Sol away in the ambulance. The video ends.

Mac sat at Sol's desk, looking at the computer screen frozen at the last image of the ambulance driving away. A baseball cap lies on the desk next to the computer. Mac looks at it, then scrolls back and watches the video feed again. As he pushes back the chair, he notices something on the floor. He bends over to see what it is. It was small and white, about the size of a Chiclet™. It had a slanted edge, not square on one side, and it was tapered on two sides. It was a piece of a front tooth.

Did Sol's one good tooth get knocked out? Mac wondered. But no, he remembered seeing it as Sol spoke to him at the hospital.

"Martin, look here," Mac said.

"Mac, you can call me Marty," he said.

"OK, Marty, look, it has to be the big guy's tooth. Remember when Sol head-butted him? And Sol had a tooth mark on top of his head. Marty, let's see if there is anything else that we missed the first time. And that means the police missed it too."

They watched the video several times over. Since it was in black and white, they could not make any judgment about the color of the clothes. The two men wore plain, dark color jackets and jeans. The short one had on a baseball cap turned backwards. When he was beating Sol, Mac could see an unfamiliar logo. It looked like a dog face with a straw hat. The big guy wore a black watch cap, the knit type that sailors wear. It had a square white tag visible where the cap had been rolled back up at the bottom, but Mac could not read it.

Mac looked at the baseball cap lying on Sol's desk. Then he looked at the video feed again. It looked like the same cap the short guy wore.

"Marty, is this your baseball cap?"

"No, it's Sol's. We both have caps like that. They give them out as a promotion at the spring Big Dogs game."

"What are the Big Dogs?"

"A Triple-A baseball team, Mac. It's the best entertainment value in summer. Dollar hot dogs, free hat night, cheap beer, and good ball. Sol and I go regularly."

"Marty, this short guy in the video is wearing a hat like this. Sol knocks it off when he punches him in the head. At the end of the video, I can see a hat lying on the floor. Is this that hat?"

"Whoa!" said Marty. "I thought this was Sol's hat, so I picked it up and put it on the desk. Wait a minute."

Marty walked into the room behind the office. He came back holding an identical hat.

"This is Sol's hat. It has his initials on the brim. So, that hat on the floor has to belong to the short guy, Mac."

"Sarah," said Mac, "call the Erie P.D. and ask for the detective assigned to this case. Tell them we found physical evidence. Ask them to come here now and collect it. We have not touched it."

"OK, Mac." She pulled out her cell phone and walked away to make the call.

Mac asked Martin if he could copy the video and e-mail it to them. He did.

"I'll be sleeping here until Sol comes back." Martin said. "There's a cot behind the kitchen. I know where Sol keeps his gun, and if those two come back, I won't hesitate to use it."

"Sol will appreciate that, Marty," Mac said. "But they won't be back. Rest assured, they are not going to get away with this."

"Mac," said Sarah, "Detective Jenny Thompson is on her way over here right now."

"Marty, I've got to take Sarah home, but you'll show the Detective the tooth and the hat, won't you?"

"Will do, Mac."

**

Thursday October 12
6:45 p.m.

Mac and Sarah drove a ways in silence before she spoke.

"Mac, did we just see a hate crime or an assault made to look like a hate crime?"

"Both, Sarah. The goons showed their swastikas to intimidate Sol. They made it sound like an anti-Semitic group from the neighborhood was trying to drive Sol out. But their real message was 'take the money and sell out.' The swastikas, calling Sol a dumb Kike, and the beating certainly made it a hate crime. But this is something bigger and more sinister, Sarah. This is the work of Mace Wilkins."

"How do you figure, Mac?"

"Sarah, I'm a builder. I do project financial analysis, site feasibility, and construction costs. I deal with planners on land use and zoning. Something about this does not make sense. My figure for the finished value of the condos and boat storage in the waterfront redevelopment plan is about $24 million. The land value of any building project is typically 20%, which would be $4.8 million. That jibes with the appraisal you had done.

"So, if this were a legitimate plan with the backing of the city, why wouldn't the city just offer Sol $4.8 million dollars? They would know they cannot condemn his land for the private redevelopment. They would have to make him a fair market offer. And they would not use a sleazy lawyer like Simon Long to convey such an offer. No, it would be a lengthy process. Meet with the landowner to see if he would be willing to sell. Discuss fair market values, do appraisals *then* make an offer *subject to funding being secured*.

"That funding would likely be made up of city capital improvements budgets, state or federal recreational grants, possible EPA grants to clean up an old industrial site, and part from the private sector.

"The advance planning for a project like that could be years in the making. So no, you don't just hire a mercenary planning consultant to draw up a plan that the developer client wants, and then send a phony eminent domain threat letter to a landowner with no advance notice. No way. This is a scam, Sarah."

"Mac," said Sarah, "the city attorney is going to have to deal with the assault on Sol as a hate crime, and that is the way he should see it. But we know the CCBUTT plan and letter was a cover for Barnes and Wilkins' ambitions, which gives Wilkins a motive to intimidate Sol Weinstein into selling. I'm going to give a copy of the CCBUTT letter to the city attorney and see if he can link Wilkins to the assault."

"Good, Sarah," said Mac, "and when that is done, I want you to do the following…"

Mac spent the next twenty minutes outlining his plan. He finished just as his blue Bel Air parked in front of the Delmonico firm's law office in

Jamestown.

Sarah said "Mac, I've been doing land use law for seven years. I know I'm young in the legal profession, but I have unraveled some very complicated deals. You have an interesting mind, my friend. Now get busy on your research while I get busy on mine."

"Will do, Sarah. Oh! One more thing. Do you have a good contact with the Pennsylvania State Police Bureau of Criminal Investigation?"

"No, why do you ask?"

"Might come in handy."

**

Thursday October 12
Barcelona Harbor
Murphy B & B
7:30 p.m.

"So, Sol is hurt," Marybeth said, "but the prognosis is good?"

They ate alone in the dining room. Five dogs watched them from the back porch. Candles were the only light, but it was not fully dark outside, with a pinkish glow of lake sunset streaming in the windows.

"Hopefully," said Mac. "His eyes looked bad, so swollen he could not see. Maybe by tomorrow, they'll know if his vision was damaged."

"I know you're in hunt mode 'Mr. Lone Ranger,' but isn't this a matter for the police?"

"Yep, and I'm going to let them investigate their way. Meanwhile, I'm pretty sure I know who one of the goons is. I can get the other one's name out of him with my own interrogation techniques."

"Mac, we have a good plan for our future. I can't do it if you are in jail."

"M, you know me well enough. I won't let that happen."

"Please be extra careful. What are you doing tonight? I can see how restless you are."

"I'm gonna get on your laptop and do some research. Not sure what I'm looking for, but it has to do with Sol's land, so I'll start with that and work my way out. All of life is cause and effect, action and reaction. So this beating is part of something related to the desire to control Sol's land. I have to think macro-economics, which I suck at. But I'll keep asking myself: if this, then what? I want to see where my curiosity leads. I could be up all night, M, so you retire when you need to. You've got a hungry crew who want to be fed at 6:30 tomorrow morning."

"I know. I've already got pancake mix made and a huge bowl of fresh fruit cocktail in the fridge. I'll be up by 5:30 and good to go by 6:00. Would you help me set the back porch table before you get started?"

"I will if you give me a smooch. I've got a lot of pent-up anger, and I need a little sweetness to bring me down. "

"I'll give you more than one, my love. Go turn on the computer. I'll bring the coffee to the back porch, so Buddy and Emma can lie at your feet."

"That would be perfect, M."

**

Mac's builder brain was starting with the basics. In real estate, it's always location, location, location. He began with the Erie planning department's website and long-range plans. Nothing there.

Next, he shifted to newspaper archives about the Erie waterfront redevelopment. He found an article with a captioned picture that interested him. It was the same group of local leaders in the picture from the CCBUTT website. The implication was these were members of a coalition to promote waterfront redevelopment. Mac read the caption. It was taken at a city council summer picnic on the waterfront. It was actually a fundraiser. Huh.

Bank's Breakers and Scrap Yard had a good website. Their information was concise and helpful. Next, he Googled Wilkins Scrap Yard in Ashtabula. Its website was limited, but he was able to make some comparisons.

It was a four-mile drive from I-90 to the Wilkins site and less than one mile from the Shoreway connector to Sol's site, so truck access was easier at Sol's.

Both scrap yards had rail and dock access. Sol had a private dock, but Wilkins had a rail siding to the neighboring bulk materials company's dock. He probably had to pay a fee to use it, Mac guessed. And, of course, their materials would have priority over his scrap metal, which was why the freighter was laying in the channel for their turn to load.

Erie had a deep draft harbor with federally funded maintenance that was "A" rated by the U.S. Army Corps of Engineers. Ashtabula was a busier freight port than Erie, but its condition was rated "D." Mac wondered what that meant.

Both harbors needed dredging to remain viable. He remembered seeing boats aground at the B & W Boat Club.

He called Martin at the Banks' yard.

"Martin? This is Mac Morrison. Any update on Sol?"

"Yes, Mac. They removed the ice packs from his eyes. He can see, so that is a blessing. His vision is blurry, but they think that is the concussion. He was hit hard at the base of the skull by a metal object that left a circular impression."

"That comes from brass knuckles, Martin, and I should know because I've had to disarm guys in the service who used them."

"What service, Mac?"

"Army. Desert Storm three years, then two in Afghanistan as paid security. How about you?"

"Rangers, 1st Platoon Company A, 1st Battalion, 75th Ranger Regiment, deployed to Saudi Arabia, Feb. 12, 1991 to April 15, 1991, in support of Operation Desert Storm. It was a short deployment, but we did some heavy work in the early days."

"So Marty, you are a bad dude!"

"I can handle myself, Mac. I'd like to get my hands on whoever did this to Sol!"

"Marty, if the opportunity arises, I'll invite you to the dance. Now, can I ask you some questions? It might help me figure out what was behind this beating."

"Go ahead, Mac."

"I've seen the Wilkins scrap yard from the road. They don't want anyone taking pictures. Why?"

"Wilkins is a shifty guy. Wouldn't surprise me if he's doing something shady with his scrap operation. That's total speculation, but he always has a lot of handy cash. We deposit ours daily, but he brags about how much cash he keeps on hand."

"OK, next question. Banks is a Breakers and Scrapyard. Wilkins calls himself a scrap yard. Is there a difference, Marty?"

"Yes, a big difference. We separate and refine our metals to get the highest price for them. Instead of crushing all vehicles, we subcontract with an auto junkyard to piece out the better ones that get trucked here. They bring their own crew to our shop in one of the big Quonset huts. We separate tires, wheels, alternators, radiator cores, radiator end caps, catalytic converters, copper wire, engines, transmissions, frames, you name it. Engines and trannies are trucked to a rebuilder in the Midwest. Tires go to a New York asphalt plant that shreds them and uses the rubber pellets in their hot mix. All of the other parts are cataloged and stored here until we have a big load. Depending on where prices are highest, we ship by rail or by freighter.

"Mac, because we have the shredder, which Wilkins does not have, we can fine shred the metal and mechanically and magnetically sort it so it brings a much higher price. It also compacts better, so we can get more tonnage in a railroad car or freighter compartment. Wilkins has a car crusher, and a dragline with an electromagnet, but he has no sorters or shredders. He ships crushed cars and bulk metal, which has a lot of air space in the load. Plus, he gets a much lower price per ton because his crushed cars have to be shredded and separated by his buyer.

"Our refined scrap can go direct to a smelter and be reprocessed into steel, aluminum, copper, titanium: all the metals. We are classified as a high-grade breakers and refined scrap yard. And we have a private dock on Lake Erie, with great Interstate and rail connections, Mac."

"So why did the guard at Wilkins' boat club tell me Wilkins expects more business if Sol sells out to a group to redevelop the waterfront?"

"What? I hadn't heard Sol was selling out, and he would tell me first."

"He's not. He got approached by a sleazy lawyer with a low-ball buyout number. Sarah Lieberman told him to go fuck himself. So, it looks like the beating was a warning, because they told him to be smart and take the deal."

"Those fuckers! Mac, that guard was crazy. This yard is more valuable than ever. The 'save the planet' geeks love us. We have a big sign that hangs over our shredder that says, '*Every ton of steel we recycle saves 2500 pounds of iron ore, 1400 pounds of coal, and 120 pounds of limestone.*' No, Mac, it makes no sense to think that this yard is going to cease operations. Even if Sol retires or sells out, it will transition to a new owner who will continue and expand this operation."

"OK, Marty, last question. You said you ship wherever prices are highest. Is there a big difference for refined, separated metals?"

"Not much Mac, but if the quantity is big, the difference can be a lot. Sometimes, we ship east, sometimes west, sometimes south. That is Sol's call. He gets a daily printout of our scrap and what market prices are regionally.

Do you want me to send you the link?"

"Yes, please, Marty."

"OK, glad to be of help."

"Marty, wait! One more thing. In the scrap world, who would benefit the most by acquiring the Banks Yard?"

"Mac, on the East Coast, there is really only one guy. His name is Angelo Murano. We do business with him, and his staff knows me. His Jersey operation is the biggest Breakers Yard and scrap metal dealer in the Northeast. I would guess he could buy out Sol for pocket change, but to my knowledge he's never approached us. And that's funny because he has a summer home thirty miles from here with a replica mahogany boat he cruises on Chautauqua Lake. I've seen it. It looks kind of like the one Henry Fonda crashed in that movie <u>On Golden Pond</u>.[6] Angelo is also big into classic cars from the 50s."

"Jeez," said Mac, "sounds like someone I'd like."

"Well, there's a classic boat shindig this weekend on Chautauqua Lake, Mac. Last confab of the season before all the owners put their wooden boats away for the winter. Angelo will be there. It's at noon Saturday at the Jamestown main basin marina."

"Martin, you are a wealth of information. Thank you for all you've done for Sol. You certainly saved his life."

"Mac, he saved mine, I'll tell you that story another time."

**

Thursday October 12
Barcelona Harbor
Murphy B & B
10:30 p.m.

Mac was whistling a Van Morrison tune when he walked into the kitchen. Marybeth was finishing up her next-day breakfast prep. She caught the tune and began singing from the first stanza.

Have I told you lately
That I love you?

---

6   On Golden Pond, film starring Hendry Fonda and Katherine Hepburn, Jane Fonda, released 1981, MGM, Universal Pictures

Have I told you
There's no one above you?
Fill my heart with gladness,
Take away my sadness,
Ease my troubles,
That's what you do.[7]

Mac slipped his arm around her waist, and they danced round and round. She sang, and he whistled symphonically, as only he could. Buddy, Emma, and the three labradoodles woke up and sat in a line watching them.

Buddy could see his Poppa was a happy man again.

'Rowrf!' He barked because he was a happy dog, and he was in a house of love. This was a good world Mac had introduced him to. So much better than the nasty man who chained him out without food or water and beat him with a steel rod until Mac took him away and beat the bad man. Life had been good since then, and it was getting better all the time.

When Mac finished the tune, Marybeth turned out the lights, and the whole troop of five dogs followed their humans to the castle keep, the top floor master suite. There would be peace in the house tonight.

**

---

[7] Have I Told you Lately That I Love You? ; music and lyrics by Van Morrison on his album Avalon Sunset, June 1989 by mercury Records

Chapter Seventeen

Friday October 13
Barcelona Harbor
Murphy B & B
6:30 a.m.

Buddy and Emma took Mac for his early walk to the pier. It was another crisp, clear morning, a perfect day for shingling the roof.

Over breakfast, Mac asked René if he thought the five of them could finish the roof today. Yes, it was possible.

"OK, guys," Mac said, "$200 bonus for each of you if we finish by sundown. We'll have a quick lunch at noon and be back on the roof at 12:45."

That got their attention.

Before they finished breakfast, the rattle of a diesel engine shattered the morning air. René excused himself and ran up the forty-foot ladder to direct the delivery of the shingles. Mac herded the crew out to the truck, and they all grabbed the compressor, air hoses, staple guns, and tool belts, then climbed up on the roof. Soon, the special starter strip was laid around the edges, and the 'pop-pop-pop-pop' of the staple guns could be heard.

"Four staples per shingle!" shouted René. It was organized bedlam, with Mac on the ridge unpacking the bundles and tossing shingles to the twins, one on each side of the roof. They placed them ahead of René and Tomas, who stapled as fast as they were laid in front of them.

Friday October 13
12:00 p.m.

They were more than half done by noon. After a high-protein lunch, René and Mac step-flashed the front dormers while the boys kept working their way up the back side of the house. By four o'clock, the roof was completely shingled except for the ridge vent. Mac cut the slot, and René had the boys lay it out and nail it while he capped it.

By five o'clock, the roof was done.

While the boys cleaned up the tools and René hung the ladders back on the trailer, Mac peeled off two, one hundred dollar bills and handed them to each of the crew. With that job complete, René, Tomas, and the twins would be returning to New Hampshire in the morning.

But Mac had work to do here.

**

Friday October 13
Murphy B & B
5:30 p.m.

Marybeth had a feast for the hungry crew: chef salad, thick ribeye steaks, mashed potatoes and gravy, caramelized carrots, and triple-layer chocolate cake with chocolate icing and vanilla ice cream. Everyone stuffed themselves, everyone except Mac. He ate lightly and only drank coffee.

"Mac," said Marybeth, "you worked like a horse today. Aren't you hungry tonight?"

"I might have to go out, and I need to be light on my feet."

"Uh-oh. I won't ask."

"Best not to."

Marybeth said, "I saw the Erie TV news, Mac. They showed a video clip of the two thugs that beat Sol. They asked the public if they could help identify them. The video got a good look at the two guys, but they had on masks and hats so you couldn't see their faces. They showed swastikas on their chests. This was a hate crime."

"That is what they wanted it to look like, but there's more to it than that, M."

**

Friday October 13
6:30 p.m.

Mac called Banks Scrap Yard. Martin answered.

"Marty, can I buy you a beer tonight?"

"Sure Mac. Where are we going?"

"I'll meet you at Ricky's Road House in an hour. Route 20, west. Do you know the place?"

"I know it. Pretty rough crowd on a Friday night, Mac."

"I'm hoping we might run into a couple apes who need to be taught a lesson."

"Ah! Now you're talking, Mac. See you in an hour."

**

Friday October 13
Erie, PA
U.S. Route 20
Ricky's Road House
7:30 p.m.

Ricky's Road House was located in a no-man's-land of farm fields and scattered small businesses on the western edge of Erie's city limits. It had been a gas station once upon a time before the interstate took away the through traffic. Someone had thoughtfully bricked up the windows so that no one could see in or out, which allowed the patrons' privacy from prying eyes to nurse their shot and a beer. The parking lot was a rough mixture of gravel, grass, and dirt. After a rain, it would assume the delightful consistency of rutted mud.

Ricky had considerately placed an old military-megaphone-style speaker outside the wooden shed entrance to give his patrons the flavor of twangy country music before they entered. This was undoubtedly appreciated by the neighbors, who happened to be a flock of wild turkeys nesting in the scrubby bushes lining the sparsely traveled two-lane road. All in all, it was the kind of place that one entered at one's own risk.

The parking lot held twenty mud-splattered pickup trucks parked willy-nilly in a hurry to get that first beer before the bar stools were taken. At a neighborhood hangout such as this, there would be the unspoken rule that *certain stools* belonged to *certain hard cases*, and no one would dare sit there.

Mac was counting on that.

The bartender had to be Ricky. He wore a faded sweatshirt that said, 'I'm Ricky!' which was pretty much a giveaway. Mac and Marty entered through the battered wood shed covering the side door, paused, and scanned the dimly lit bar. There was the click of billiard balls in the back where a couple guys were shooting pool. All the stools were occupied except for two at the very end of the bar. Mac did not see Slugger Herman German in the room. He and Marty walked over and took the last two swivel-post stools. Mac spun around one time and looked over the bar, then spun back to face Ricky.

Ricky was drying shot glasses and eyeing them. He turned around and looked at the big clock over the mirror behind the bar. Then he turned back and said:

"Gents, I think you'd be more comfortable at a table."

Mac and Marty ignored him. Ricky put down the shot glass, tossed his towel over his shoulder, and walked down the bar to stand in front of them.

"I'll take a Labatt's Blue in a bottle, Mac said.

"Make it two," Marty added.

"Sure," said Ricky. "I'll bring them to your table."

Mac looked around the bar and said, "I don't see us sitting at a table, Ricky. Right here at the bar will do fine."

"Gents," Ricky continued, "I don't think you understood my meaning. Those two stools belong to two of my regulars. Nobody sits there but them. Ever."

"Really?" said Mac. "Gee, it looks like we're sitting here now. If they come in, point them out to us, OK? We'll buy them a beer at their table."

"Gents, I don't want any trouble, but if you don't get off those stools before Slugger and Stubby come through that door, there's gonna be trouble, and you're gonna get your ass kicked."

"Really?" said Marty. "Who's gonna kick it?"

"Gents, I'm asking you nicely. Slugger and Stubby come through that door at 7:30 every Friday night. You can set your watch by it. You got about two seconds to move, or believe me, they are gonna move you right out to the parking lot."

Just then, the side door opened, and a tall man whom Mac recognized as Slugger and a short man who could be Stubby entered the bar. Both men had bruised faces. The big one was wearing a black watch cap.

And he was big. Standing by the doorway gave a better context to his size than Mac's first glimpse at the B & W Boat Club. Mac was guessing 6'6" and 260 pounds. His hands hung down almost to his knees. Mac's Cro-Magnon brain noted: Gorilla reach, stay out of it.

As soon as Slugger saw Mac and Marty on their stools, he scowled and stomped up to the bar.

"What the fuck, Ricky!" said Slugger. "You let these assholes take our stools?"

"I told them, Slugger," Ricky said. He turned to Mac and Marty. "Gents, I'm asking you nice, one last time. Take a table. Please. Next round is on the house."

Mac ignored him.

Slugger took two giant steps and stood behind Mac.

"OK, Mister, move. Those are our stools."

Mac and Marty didn't move. They were staring straight ahead, watching Slugger in the large mirror over the bar.

"Look, asshole," said Slugger, "he asked you nice, and I warned you; now get off them stools before I break your head open."

"Go fuck yourself, Tarzan," Mac said, watching Slugger's reflection in the mirror.

Mac saw the sucker punch coming. He ducked, spun the stool, and shot his fist into the big man's gut. He grunted as air whooshed out, and he staggered, but only for a moment. He was a pro fighter; he had taken a lot of punches, and he recovered quickly. He hit Mac with a looping left hook that rang his bell and knocked him off the stool. Mac bumped into Stubby, who hit him with another hard left to the head.

Mohammed Ali had a "little room" in his brain where he went to recover from a devastating punch. He would cover up, retreat, and go to his little room. Mac's head was spinning. He went into his little room, doubled over, and retreated, but the gorilla arms of Slugger were long, and they pounded his ribs. Mac needed time to recover.

"CRACK!" Marty's wooden nun chuks whacked Slugger's shin! He howled, but kept coming!

"CRACK!" Marty slung the nun chucks around on their chain and whacked him a second time!

Slugger stopped, staggered, and backtracked.

It was just enough time for Mac to reset his brain, come out of his little room, and attack. He lunged forward to get under Slugger's jab. His punch started at the shoulder, and he threw it with all his strength, driving his fist into Slugger's larynx! Then he spun around and whacked his temple in its soft spot above the ear with the point of a backwards elbow. That dropped the big man in a heap, gagging.

Stubby slipped on his brass knuckles, but Marty whipped his hand with the wooden baton. The crunch of bones crushed between wood and brass could be felt across the room.

"YOW!" Stubby yelled and grabbed his smashed hand. Marty delivered a slap to his ear that exploded the drum, then a kick to the gut that felled him on top of Slugger. Neither one moved.

"Ricky!" snarled Mac, "call Erie Police. Tell them two thugs that look like the guys wanted on TV tried to bust up your bar. You think they are the goons that beat up the old man at the Scrap Yard. Your patrons made a citizen's arrest."

"Glad to," said Ricky. "I never want those guys in here again!"

Mac lifted Slugger's body off the floor and sat him in a wooden chair. He was having trouble breathing. Marty lifted Stubby and did the same. They placed the two chairs back to back. Mac took the still-groggy Slugger's belt, cinched it tight around their two necks, and felt for a pulse. They were dazed but not out. Marty took Stubby's belt and cinched their hands to one leg of the chair.

"Would someone lend me another belt? Mac asked.

Half a dozen men stood up and whipped off their belts. Obviously, Slugger and Stubby had no friends in that bar. Marty cinched their other hands to the other chair leg. They sat trussed like pigs on a spit. Blood dripped from Stubby's ear. Slugger made a hacking noise, gasping for air.

Erie PD responded fast, perhaps faster than usual, because they might be nabbing the thugs who beat up Sol Weinstein. Sol was going to find out that he had a lot of friends in Erie that night.

Detective Jenny Thompson arrived as soon as the first black and white cruiser. She took a look at the two men bound up. Mac and Marty introduced themselves to her.

"Mr. Morrison," she said. "Did you do this?"

"Detective, Marty and I stopped in for a friendly beer. We were sitting on these two stools minding our own business when these two apes came in and picked a fight. The big one tried to sucker punch me. I guess Marty and me surprised them with our response. We didn't appreciate being disturbed."

"Hmm. I guess you didn't. Can anyone in the bar corroborate their story?" she shouted.

"That's how it happened, Detective!" said a chorus of men. "Those two, Slugger and Stubby, they came in and started cussing out these guys, who were minding their own business. Slugger's always pushing people around and starting fights. It's getting so we can't even come in for a friendly game of pool on a Friday night. It's time someone pushed back."

"Detective," said Mac, "see that camera over the bar? I'm sure Ricky will give you a copy of the video feed."

Mac moved over to Slugger and pulled up his lip to expose a broken tooth.

"Detective, I think you'll find that this man's broken tooth will match the piece of tooth we found at the scene of the brutal hate crime and beating at the Bank's Scrap Yard yesterday. And if you'll look carefully at this other man's eyebrow," said Mac as he pointed to Stubby's face, "you'll notice there is a very clear scar in the shape of a six pointed star. I think you'll find that scar matches perfectly with the Star of David ring worn by 85-year-old Sol Weinstein when he punched this man in self-defense. These are the two cowards who, while displaying swastikas on their chest, beat an 85-year-old man with brass knuckles, an old man who is barely four feet tall."

"Mr. Morrison," Detective Thompson said, "how is it that you just happened to go for a quiet beer in the same bar frequented by the same two thugs who appear to be the ones who beat Mr. Weinstein, and that you were able to subdue those same two thugs, one armed with brass knuckles, and make a clean citizen's arrest?"

"You know," Mac said, "I would call it good luck and serendipity."

"Huh!" said Detective Thompson. "I was warned about you. It seems you have some friends in high places."

"Really?" said Mac.

"Yes, I got a call from the Pennsylvania Bureau of Criminal Investigation, who got a call from Investigator Jonetta Pope of the New York State Police BCI, asking that we cooperate in the investigation of Mr. Weinstein's beating, and that this was going to be linked to an investigation into possible interstate shipment of stolen catalytic converters, which could be traced back to the Wilkins Scrap Yard. Do you know anything about that?"

"I seem to remember making a call to my friend Jonetta Pope, yes."

"Well, Investigator Pope told me you have some kind of golden halo as a super sleuth and that I should not question your methods but just accept your results. And that New York State's top cop Colonel Samuel Justice would be requesting the cooperation of his counterpart at the Pennsylvania State Police. Care to comment?"

"I guess I am fortunate to have some quality friends, Detective. Can Marty and I finish our beer while you take our statements? I am now releasing my prisoners into your custody."

**

**Friday October 13
Erie, PA
Ricky's Road House
9:00 p.m.**

After the police left with their prisoners, Mac was in a celebratory mood. He and Marty stayed for a second beer, and Mac bought a round for the bar. Then he got in his baby blue Bel Air, called up Bob Seger's *Roll Me Away* on his iPhone and connected it to his in-dash stereo. As the piano intro ramped up the melody, Mac was transported back in time. Looking into his life's rear view mirror, he was once again tormented by many events:

- Joey Minetti pushing his parents in front of the big truck in 1983, exploding their Ford into a fireball, ending his childhood at age ten, and beginning his fight through life;
- Leaving his childhood Chautauqua County vineyard and moving to the dark, cold New Hampshire woods;
- Being the new kid who talked funny and had to fight bullies;
- The kills that haunted him: in war and being a "helpful avenger";
- Divorce and loss of his lake house;
- His barn fire, loss of every possession, home and business;
- Joey Minetti spearing Jim Murphy with his big boat, smashing his head and killing him;
- Joey Minetti fiendishly pushing Marybeth's parents' off the precipice down to their death;

- Him snapping Joey Minetti's neck in a fit of rage.

A 'zap' crackled the air. Mac felt in front of his ear. The bulging blood clot was back. His head was pounding. He'd been warned of ischemic stroke. He reached for the little box in his pocket and chewed four, to be sure. The gritty orange aspirin dissolved under his tongue, and soon it began to work.

He turned up the stereo and let his mind leave the dark past and be carried away.

Seger whispered:
Took a look down a westbound road
Right away I made my choice
Headed out to my big two-wheeler
I was tired of my own voice
Took a bead on the northern plains
And just rolled that power on
And then he screamed![8]...
Roll, roll me away
Won't you roll me away tonight
I, too, am lost, I feel double-crossed (Mac envisions his parents burning to death)
And I'm sick of what's wrong and what's right
Roll, roll me away
I'm gonna roll me away tonight
Gotta keep rollin', gotta keep ridin'
Keep searchin' 'til I find what's right
And as the sunset faded I spoke to the faintest first starlight
And I said next time...
Next time....
We'll get it right!

Mac slammed the hammer down on the Bel Air. The clock style speedometer on his baby blue '57 Chevy rolled past 80, 90, 100 miles an hour as Mac and his Blue Bel Air rolled away back to Marybeth Murphy. Because, this time...in her...he had found what's right.

**

---

8   Roll Me Away, music and lyrics by Bob Seger, 1982 from the album The Distance, on Capitol Records

Friday October 13
Barcelona Harbor, New York
Murphy B & B
10:00 p.m.

The familiar sound of the Bel Air's tires crunching on pea stone perked Buddy's ears. He raced to the back porch door to greet Poppa Mac. The rusty spring 'gronked' as Mac pulled open the old wooden screen door. Marybeth heard it, turned from her kitchen stove, removed her apron and smoothed back her flowing chestnut hair. Her man was home!

Mac entered with a battered face and a tormented look in his eyes. He blinked and a tear rolled down his cheek. He stopped to give his Buddy-dog a hug and a kiss. Then he silently strode over to Marybeth, scooped her in his arms, carried her up three flights of stairs, ripped off her clothes and made passionate love to her.

Chapter Eighteen

Saturday October 14
Barcelona Harbor
Murphy B & B
6:00 a.m.

The sash was up three inches as cool air fluttered the lace curtains. Mac was alive another day. That was something he never took for granted.

He looked at Marybeth's angelic face, snuggled in the crook of his arm, which was tingly asleep. So too was his leg, because Buddy-dog was crushing it with his one hundred pounds. Buddy rolled over, stuck out his tongue, and offered Mac his belly for a rub. Mac obliged, and Buddy purred. The vibration shook the bed. Marybeth opened her eyes.

"Good morning, my love," she said as she kissed him. She gently traced the welts on his face with her fingers. "Rough night?"

"Mm," said Mac.

"Martin called me from the bar. He told me what happened. Good job, Mac. I hope those thugs go to prison."

"With all the press coverage, I'm sure they will. I didn't protect Sol, but he'll feel better knowing they got punished."

"You can't protect *everyone*, Mac. So now that you made that right, what are we doing today?"

"I'm going to make some phone calls, and then we'll take a drive with Buddy to meet Mr. Angelo Murano, the King of Scrap, but don't you dare call him that."

"Is he the same Murano who owns a big summer home on Bemus Point and is a prominent patron of local charities?"

"He could be."

"When are we taking this drive?"

"Leaving at 11:30. I hope to find him with the classic wooden boaters at the Jamestown docks."

"Oh! I have to dress for that! And I have to dress you for that, too, Mr.

Bruised Face. How are you feeling this morning?"

"Top o' the world, Sweetheart. Top o' the world."

"Good. Race you to the shower, and then we make breakfast for our crew before we give them a great send-off. They worked hard. Thank you for my new roof, Mac."

**

**Saturday October 14
7:30 a.m.**

A voice answered on the first ring.

"Chautauqua Chopper Service, may I help you?"

"My name is Mac Morrison in Barcelona Harbor. Can you fly to Ashtabula this morning, take a few aerial photos, and e-mail them to me?"

"Well, as it happens, I do have the morning open. Ashtabula? What are we photographing?"

"I want the name and registry number of a freighter that is lying at anchor off a materials dock at the port. I can text you the address and coordinates of the Wilkins Scrap Yard. I also want photos of the rail cars being loaded at the Wilkins yard and the freighter. Can you do that?"

"Ashtabula Harbor is 80 miles direct flight. Weather is clear, so we can cruise at about 120 miles an hour. If we leave in the next fifteen minutes, I could be there in 45 minutes. Let's say it takes ten minutes for pictures. We land at the nearest airport and e-mail you the photos to make sure we got what you wanted. If you need more pictures, we are still right there, and we can take them and then return. Your cost would be $2,000. Does that work for you, Mr. Morrison?"

"That's perfect. Call me Mac, please. To whom am I speaking?"

"My name is Patrick McGoohan, owner of Chautauqua Choppers."

"That is a famous name, Patrick."

"Yes, but no relation. My ancestors came over from Scotland in the 1850s."

"Well then, cousin Patrick," Mac said, "We might be related. My great-great-something grandfather settled on Chautauqua Lake in 1847 at what is now the village of Dewittville."

"Well, cousin Mac, I think we should meet for lunch sometime. So, let us get in the air. Do you have my email?"

"Yep, got it off your website. Sending the location coordinates now."

"We'll e-mail you an invoice, Mac. You can call and give me a credit card."

"Perfect, Patrick, thank you."

M**ac's next call was to Detective Jenny Thompson.

"Good morning, Mr. Morrison," she said. "How's that bruised face today?"

"Badge of honor. What's the status of your two prisoners?"

"You were right. Herman German, aka Slugger, has a broken tooth that matches the piece we recovered from the Banks Breakers Yard office. And the scar over Samuel, aka Stubby, Smith's eye is star shaped. Once the swelling leaves Sol Weinstein's hands, we'll be able to remove his ring and try to match it. But we also have the baseball cap they left at the scene. We are testing that for DNA. If it matches Smith, then we have him regardless."

"Arraignment set?"

"Possibly Monday. They are in the hospital. You guys did a number on them."

"All because we were sitting on their favorite barstools. Can you believe it?"

"Hmm, right, Mac. Anyway, tell me more about this interstate traffic in stolen catalytic converters."

"I'll know more in two hours. But for now, I can tell you I saw large wooden bins of catalytic converters being off-loaded from tractor trailers with California and New York plates. Those bins were awaiting loading onto a freighter lying offshore at the Ashtabula docks. I hired aerial surveillance to get photos of the bins and the freighter's name and registry. I think it's Chinese.

"I know that legitimate 'Breakers' like the Banks Yard do a careful check of the source of cat converters, and they also neatly trim off the exhaust pipes so that they can resell to legal recyclers to extract the precious metals.

"The bins I saw at Wilkins Scrap yard were a tangled mess of hacked-off CATs with long exhaust pipes still attached. Only thieves would do that, and only the black market would buy them in that condition. Anyway, that's not my case. Investigator Jonetta Pope is on it for New York BCI because some of these trucks are running out of New York into Pennsylvania and then Ohio. Ohio BCI, Penn State Police, and the California CHIPS will also be working this from their end."

"And you deduced this from a casual look through the fence at the B & W Boat Club?"

"Well, it had to simmer in my brain a bit, but yeah. After talking to Martin at the Banks Yard and learning how they separate scrap and sell it legally, I knew what I saw had to be an illegal operation."

"Jesus, Mary, and Joseph! Jonetta said you had a sleuth's golden halo. I'm beginning to see why."

"May I call you Jenny, Detective?"

"Of course."

"Jenny, would you go see Sol Weinstein today? I've got something important I have to do, but I want him to know that you captured the goons who beat him and that Marty and I punished them, and they are going to prison."

"I will. You take care, Mac."

**

Saturday October 14
Murphy B & B
9:00 a.m.

As soon as René, Tomas, and the twins left for New Hampshire, Marybeth and Mac washed the Bel Air and dressed up for a classic boat shindig. The day had warmed into Indian summer. The smell of burning leaves was in the air, the sky was deep Delft blue, and temps in the high 60s meant the top was down on the Chevy.

Buddy sat by the open window. Marybeth sat next to Mac on the big bench seat. She slipped her arm through his as they drove down the east side of Chautauqua Lake, stopping at the Morrison cemetery in Dewittville. As was now his custom, Mac brought flowers to place on his parent's grave and on the stone of his namesake, the original Mackenzie Morrison.

Old State Route 430 crossed under I-86 at Bemus Point, so they continued on the old road into Jamestown, curling around the east end of the lake and sneaking in the back door to the industrial section. They arrived at the main docks and found a hand-lettered sign that said, 'Classic Boats Meet at Chautauqua Harbor and Lucille Ball Memorial Park.'

Marybeth gave directions, and in a minute, they were parked by the shore with three dozen gorgeous wooden boats from the 1920s to the 1960s. Some were in the water, and some were on trailers.

Mac knew what Henry Fonda's boat in <u>On Golden Pond</u> looked like, so he was looking for a new replica, which meant it probably had a modern inboard engine. He knew he found it when he heard it. The sound of the engine was not that of a carbureted 1950's GM V-8. This was a smooth, even sound of a big Marine V8 with direct fuel injection, and it was docking in front of his Bel Air.

Marybeth let go of Mac's hand and went to the car to grab her digital camera. When she returned, a handsome man in his early 60s with wavy black hair and a touch of white at the temples was jumping off a gorgeous mahogany boat with a white cove. Mac stood there, eyeing it, while Marybeth took a picture.

"Is that your Larkspur Blue '57 Bel Air?" the handsome man asked Mac.

"Yes sir. You know your Chevys. I'm Mac Morrison. This is Marybeth Murphy and my dog Buddy. Buddy, can you shake?"

Buddy sat and offered his paw. The man passed the Buddy test.

"Pleased to meet you, I'm Angelo Murano. And this is my replica of a 1959 Century Resorter."

"She's a beauty," said Mac. "I see you went with the white-painted cove, reminiscent of the 1959 Corvette."

"Good eye, Mac. The Corvette is a small, fast Cruiser ship, so I thought it would be appropriate. I think I see some modifications on your Bel Air. Did you lower it?"

"I reinforced the frame to take more power and installed modern suspension and brakes. The coil-over shocks lowered it slightly."

"But you kept the stock wheel covers. I approve," said Angelo. "Interior?"

"All stock, but I used blue and white leather to match the interior and top. Makes it easier to clean up after my dog."

"Wonderful! Convertibles are for dogs!" Angelo said. "Can we look under the hood?"

"Of course," said Mac.

Angelo whistled. "So, Mac, is this a replacement engine?"

"Stroker 383 Chevy crate engine with fuel injection."

"Nice, very nice, Mac. I have a '55 and '56 Chevy in my collection but never found a '57 that I would like. This one can be driven, and I like that. Would you be offended if I asked if she were for sale?"

"Not at all. But she's a family heirloom. My uncle bought her new and gave her to me 34 years ago. I'll pass her to my daughter."

"Congratulations on keeping her pristine. And you did the work yourself?"

"Yes. How about your boat? Who built it?

"Dominic Strovino. He's a very talented replica boat builder on Seneca Lake. He's a 'paisan,' a friend.

"Beautiful workmanship, and I should know. I'm a home builder. This is like fine cabinet work that floats. So, Angelo, would you like to take my Bel Air for a drive?" Mac asked.

"Could I?"

"Of course. Buddy, Marybeth, let's go."

They all piled into the baby blue Bel Air. Angelo sat proudly behind the wheel. Mac was in the shotgun seat with Buddy and Marybeth in back. She pulled a blue silk scarf from the glove box and tied her hair back like Dinah Shore[9] in the old Chevy ads.

Angelo tooled through town out onto the open road.

"Punch it, Angelo," said Mac.

The V8 responded with its 450 horsepower, pinning Angelo back in the seat. He grinned and grinned. Mac looked back at Marybeth holding onto Buddy. Angelo made a loop along the west side of the lake. Marybeth suggested they stop at a Lakewood ice cream stand.

"Mac," said Angelo as they licked cones under a fiery red maple tree, "I love this car. Could you build me one like it? One with my own touches, but stock-looking and modern driving?"

"It's possible, Angelo. I would have to find you a good car to begin with. Then there is the question of budget. What would you expect to pay for a car built like mine? Remember, I did this over a period of 30 years with my own labor. A build like this will be expensive."

---

9 Dinah shore; American film actress, singer and TV personality. She was the official Chevrolet spokesperson in the 1950s-1960s.

"How much, Mac?"

"It could be over $100,000, depending on the quality of the car and what you wanted done."

"For a car like this, a bargain. What do you say, Mac? Will you do it?"

"Angelo, I have a lot on my plate right now. I am building two houses in New Hampshire, and I have four cabins to build for Marybeth next spring in Barcelona Harbor. So even if I said yes, and even if I could find you a good starter car, it would not be for a while. So let's say a conditional yes."

"Sounds good, Mac."

"Angelo," said Mac, "what is your business?"

"My business? Scrap metal. When I came to America forty years ago, I had an uncle in the trash business and another who was a barber. Italian barbers are the best, it's true. They both said, 'Come work with me.' I did not want to be a barber, so I said, 'I'll try the trash business.' I was a truck driver. It's a good way to learn the city, and New York is a big city. We had routes on Staten Island, Queens, and Hoboken. That's our home base, Hoboken.

"Recycling was getting started in the early 80s. Most people didn't want to do it. It was a money loser for us because the markets did not justify the collection and separation costs of the paper and glass. My uncle tried to get out of his contracts but I told him no, stick with it, politics are going to change. And by the 90s, they did. Paper and glass are tough markets, but metals are very good.

"When fuel prices go high, it's cheaper to recycle metal than mine new ore. Less pollution, too. You have to separate and sell clean components to make real money. Our operation is breakers, scrap and recycling. We break down vehicles and metal waste. We separate aluminum, steel, copper, and precious metals like those in catalytic converters. You can ship to the best market, but you gotta have rail or water for the cheapest shipping. And, you gotta store your valuable metals until the market is high, so you need space. Junk yards that just crush cars don't have that kind of space, especially in the big city. But we have room in Jersey."

"Angelo, maybe you know a friend of mine."

"Who is that Mac?"

"Sol Weinstein." Mac watched carefully for a facial tic or a flinch. There was none.

"Sol Weinstein? I don't think I know him. What does he do, Mac?"

"For the last fifty-two years, Sol has owned and operated Banks Breakers and Scrap in Erie, Pennsylvania."

"Banks Breakers," said Angelo, "of course I know Banks. I do business with Banks, but I don't think I ever met Mr. Weinstein. You say he has owned it for fifty-two years? He must be getting old."

"Yes. What about Mace Wilkins, and the Wilkins Scrap Yard in Ashtabula, Ohio. Do you know him?"

Angelo's face turned dark red, and his eyes bulged out.

"Is Mace Wilkins a friend of yours?" he growled with instant anger.

"No, Angelo. He's trying to screw Sol Weinstein, so that would make him my enemy."

"Mace Wilkins is a piss ant!" said Angelo. You know what we do to piss ants in Hoboken, Mac? We step on them!"

Mac and Buddy decided that Angelo Murano was OK, so Mac took a chance.

"Mace Wilkins is trying to acquire Sol Weinstein's land, which is not for sale. He made up a glossy plan with some consultants and pitched it to the city to redevelop the Erie waterfront. Wilkins is using the city's name and the threat of eminent domain to scam Sol. His real plan is to take Sol's land for a new marina and condo development. His attorney made Sol a low-ball offer to buy him out, but Sol refused, so Wilkins sent two thugs to muscle him.

"Wilkins' goons delivered a message to Sol: sell or else. They dressed in Nazi swastikas to scare him because he is a Polish Jew who was tortured by the Nazis as a child. His parents were killed at Auschwitz. The goons called him a dumb Kike, so he fought them. Sol is four feet six inches tall and 85 years old. A 6'6" professional boxer pounded his face while his partner hit him in the kidneys with brass knuckles. They nearly killed him. Sol survived that beating, but he is in the hospital."

"Sons of bitches!" Angelo thundered. "My grandfather guided the US Army 10th Mountain division through the passes of northern Italy in WWII. He was captured by the Germans and executed in a public square by the Nazis. After the war, my grandmother came to America, then my uncles came and then I came. These thugs that beat Sol Weinstein to steal his land were wearing Nazi swastikas! I would beat them with my bare hands!"

He was visibly trembling.

"Angelo," said Mac, "see these bruises on my face? Last night a friend and I tracked down those two thugs. We punished them. We beat the hell out of them. They are in the hospital and under arrest for their hate crime. They will be going to prison."

"Good, Mac," said Angelo. "Good for you!"

"Angelo, I wanted to learn how proper metal recycling is done, which is why I hoped to meet you today. I want to take down Mace Wilkins, put him out of business, and send him to prison with his thugs. I can do that if I can prove he's operating illegally. I think Wilkins is fencing a huge stash of stolen catalytic converters out of his scrap yard and shipping them to China. Look at these pictures of catalytic converters with the long pipes attached. You would not recycle them like that, would you?"

Mac gave Angelo his phone and let him scan through the aerial photos and the ground shots he took at the B & B Club.

"No, these are stolen, Mac, for sure. Son of a bitch! I heard rumors about an operation like this. I see the trucks in the photos from California and New York. They would not be unloading in Ohio, because the big cat recycling centers are in New York, Virginia and Ontario. You are onto something here, Mac."

"Angelo, I'm working with the New York State Police right now. I hope they will crack this case. I'm going to use these photos to help them."

"Good Mac. I will help if I can. But tell me, Does Sol Weinstein want to sell Banks Breakers and Scrap, the business and the land?"

"Angelo, I would have said no, because it's all he has, and he had no plans to do anything else. But now I think he might sell, to the right buyer. Would you be interested, Angelo?"

"Very interested. I would like to meet your friend Sol Weinstein and see his business. Could you arrange that, Mac?"

"I could. Tell you what, why don't we discuss this over dinner tonight? Marybeth is a great cook."

Marybeth said, "Angelo, is there a Mrs. Murano?"

"Yes, of course, a lovely lady. We have been married 40 years. She stayed in Jersey this weekend. She has friends here in the summer, but now they have all returned to New York."

"So, who cooks for you when you are alone, Angelo?"

"Oh, I cook something simple with a glass of wine. It's all I need."

"Angelo, you come to dinner at our house tonight. It will just be me and Mac, his daughter and Hubcap Harry, a friend who is staying in my cottage. Come have dinner with us Angelo; don't be alone tonight."

"Marybeth, you are a beautiful lady. Mac is lucky. I can see in your eyes how you feel about each other. OK, if you let me bring the wine, I will come. Should it be red or white?"

"Bring both," said Mac. "I'll text you the address and we'll see you at 7:00 p.m."

**

Saturday October 14
Leaving Jamestown in the Blue Bel Air
2:30 p.m.

While Marybeth drove the Bel Air, Mac made a phone call.

"Tim? Mac Morrison. Good, how are you? How's Anna? Good. Tim, did you go fishing today? You did. I need enough walleye to feed five tonight. You can? Great. Sure, we'll be home. Thanks, Tim."

**

Saturday October 14
Barcelona Harbor
Captain Murphy B &B, after dinner
8:30 p.m.

"Marybeth, I've never tasted better walleye." said Angelo. "How did you make it?"

"I wrap the fillets in aluminum foil, make a sauce out of fresh squeezed lemon and my secret seasonings, and bake until flaky on the stone base of a hundred-year-old wood fired brick oven."

"Do you want to open a restaurant, Marybeth?" said Angelo. "I'll back you."

"Nooo. I like to cook for friends and family. Besides, I'm closing the B & B and building cottages for long term elder residents, as Mac told you."

"Angelo," said Gabriella, "your Barbera red wine was superb."

"It's from my cousin's vineyard in Italy. I love this wine, but it is not available in the U.S., so my relatives send me a case now and then. I would love to grow my own grapes and make my own wine someday. But that's just a dream. Before I return to my empty lake house, I want to thank you all and remind Mac that I would be interested in purchasing the Banks Breakers Yard. That is, if Mr. Sol Weinstein is interested to sell to me. And, of course, subject to agreement on a fair price."

"Angelo, would you like to have a tour of the property and a look at their books?"

"I would."

"Meet me here Monday morning at 7:30 for breakfast."

**

Saturday October 14
Murphy B &B
9:00 p.m.

Mac studied the aerial photos from the chopper service. It was a Chinese registry ship if its home port of Guangzhou on its stern could be believed. There were bins on flatbed cars headed for the dock. The bins were the width of the shipping container: eight feet wide,. They were square, the same height as width. So, each bin was about 500 cubic feet.

Since the converters had been hacked off by thieves lying under cars, they cut wherever it was most accessible, so the bins were wastefully loaded. Mac assumed that each bin could contain 100 cats. There were five bins per shipping container, so 500 cats per container. With 40 containers, that worked out to 20,000 catalytic converters waiting to be loaded.

Mac was thinking about the 20,000 vehicle owners who were inconvenienced when they could not drive their cars, and the cost of replacement. As a car restorer, Mac knew the cost of exhaust systems. The internet said replacement CATS ranged in cost from $300-$2,500. It was fair to assume that, with labor and pipes, a stolen catalytic converter could cost $1,000 - $4,000 to replace.

So, there was $20 million in losses for insurance companies sitting on that dock. And worse, the precious metals were being shipped to China, which was not necessarily going to use them for peaceful purposes.

This was potentially a crime of international significance and way over

Mac's head.

Mac hit his speed dial for his longtime insurance agent in New Hampshire, Flavius Miller.

"Mac," said Flavius, "is everything OK?"

"Maybe not, Flavius. Are catalytic converter thefts a big loss to the insurance industry?"

"Huge, Mac. Billions huge. Why, what's up?"

"Suppose I told you I knew where a twenty million dollar load of stolen catalytic converters was and the guy who is running the operation and fencing them. Would there be some kind of insurance task force with a private investigator who would jump on such information and work with the correct law enforcement officials?"

"I'm sure there is. I could make one phone call and find out."

"Suppose I also told you that forty shipping containers holding those twenty million dollars worth of stolen cats were ready to be loaded onto a Chinese freighter lying in the harbor in Ashtabula, Ohio. Do you think that would light a fire under that private investigator to get in gear tonight and check this out?"

"You bet it would."

"OK, Flavius, I have a lot of circumstantial evidence but no proof, so what I'm going to do is send you an e-mail with two contacts in law enforcement working this case. There will be photos attached. Send the e-mail to your industry contact, and let's see if they can help law enforcement get a search warrant, raid that property, and put this fence in prison, OK?"

"OK!"

**

Mac assembled his assumptions with two dozen ground and aerial photos and batch emailed them to Flavius Miller, BCI Investigator Jonetta Pope, Colonel Samuel Justice, and Erie Detective Jenny Thompson. Colonel Justice would coordinate with the Ohio Highway Patrol and BCI.

Mac wanted to nail Mace Wilkins for the attack on Sol Weinstein in any way he could. Even though it was Saturday night, he knew Jenny Thompson would take his call.

She did.

"Mac Morrison, don't you ever quit? It's Saturday night, man!"

"Sorry if I'm interrupting a hot date."

"Hah! A cop is always on duty, you know that. I'm sitting here reading your e-mail and looking at pictures. Who paid for the aerials?"

"I did."

"You got a hard-on for Mace Wilkins, don't you?"

"He messed with my friend. You don't mess with my friends or family."

"Mr. Weinstein is not your responsibility now; he's the prosecutor's."

"He's still my obligation, all right, Jenny?"

"Morrison, you are a weird dude; anyone ever tell you that?"

"All the time. You told me Slugger and Stubby have not been arraigned, but I was wondering what they are going to be charged with."

"Hate crime, kidnapping, aggravated assault for starters."

"Attempted murder?"

"That would be a stretch since they left him alive, and they could have finished him off, Mac. But it's up to the city attorney to determine the charges."

"Their attack was interrupted by Martin's arrival, so maybe they had intended to finish him off. If they were charged with attempted murder, you could offer them a plea deal if they would flip whoever paid them to attack Sol. They didn't dream that up with their pea brains."

"I see your reasoning, but it's not my decision."

"Look, Slugger works for Mace Wilkins, and Wilkins has a motive, namely, he was trying to scam Sol Weinstein out of his land, but Sol would not take the bait. So, these guys were sent to intimidate him. Wilkins is behind this, I am sure, and I want to take him down.

"And I don't want that Chinese freighter to leave with that load. Do me a favor, Jenny. After you read my entire e-mail, call Jonetta Pope. Her contact info is attached to the e-mail. She will be coordinating with your Penn BCI and Ohio BCI. I think the Coast Guard, the IRS, Treasury, somebody higher up needs to get involved in this deal. It's way over my head. Besides, after last night, I need to go for a walk with my dogs, put an ice pack on my face, and let my lady coo in my ear."

"HA, HA! Good night, Morrison."

Chapter Nineteen

Sunday October 15
Barcelona Harbor
Murphy B & B
7:30 a.m.
Breakfast with Mac, Hubcap Harry, Marybeth and Gabriella

"Harry, how's the hip?" asked Mac as he poured New York maple syrup over a thick stack of blueberry pancakes.

"Better. You know, I'm getting pretty comfortable in that cottage. And I like eating Marybeth's cooking. If I want to stay on, can I? Will you do the deal?"

Marybeth chimed in. "I will, Harry, but what about your house in Conneaut?"

"The neighbor's kids want to buy it. They've been telling me for years that when I sell, they want to buy. I can have it appraised. If they're serious, I'll tell them this is the price, as is. My only concern is, what do I do with my beautiful parts cars and hubcaps?"

"Harry," said Mac, "Marybeth and I have been thinking about that. We can move your hubcaps into her big barn. You tell me how you want them organized, and I'll put up screws to hang them on the old wood walls. For your parts cars, maybe Gina Minetti has room in one of her warehouses as temporary storage. If not, we'll put them behind Marybeth's barn on blocks."

"Great," said Harry. "I'll call my neighbors. If they want it, I'll have the house appraised. It needs updates, but it's an acre commercial-zoned and has the big barn. It should bring at least $350,000. Their kids can afford it."

"Sounds good, Harry," said Mac. "Gabby, what are you doing today?"

"I put in my order for the shipping container of Bordeaux wine. I'm sending an e-mail to Angie asking for a certified check from the trust account. Once I get it, I'll pay half to Jean Paul. He'll give me a receipt and arrange for shipping from their vineyard in France. I'll pay the other half when the container arrives, and I can inspect the wines to make sure they are not spoiled. I'm excited to get marketing!"

"Good, I like that. Gabby, have you met the Ag professor who is grafting Jean Paul's grapes?"

"I have, Dad. He and his grad students, including Jean Paul, started with vines on the Ag lab campus last spring. Jean Paul's father will send as many additional grafts as we need to start on Marybeth's three acres."

"M," said Mac, we need to draw up a lease for Jean Paul that protects your rights before they start work on your vines. And you will have to terminate your lease with your farmer after this year's harvest. I'm going to suggest you have Sarah Lieberman sit with you, work out the draft, and then let Morgan review it. Does that sound good?"

"Sounds good, Mac. If you'll call her I can meet with her this week."

"Dad, there is one other thing."

"What's that, Gabby?"

"The professor at the Ag Extension suggests that we find a second, different geographic location for grafting. The first reason is the weather. If we have an early lake effect snow after the first grafting, there could be a high percentage of graft failure here in Chautauqua County. Or, too much rain could cause rust and plant failure."

"Second, if we could find a vineyard that is already certified organic, we could have organic status with the new Bordeaux variety as soon as the very first harvest. That would give us two wines to sample and market. They say central New York could work. It gets less snow, ten inches less rain, and two weeks more sun in the growing season. If we find such a vineyard, Jean Paul should enter into an agreement with that farmer now."

"Gabby," said Mac, "since Marybeth is already willing to lease her three acres to Jean Paul, does he have the ability to lease additional acreage? Does he have the money? Does he have the time to operate two separate locations? Central New York could be 2-3 hours away. An alternate site might make sense for the reasons you stated, but can he manage it and go to grad school, too?"

Gabby sat for a moment, silent. "I don't know Dad."

"Gabby," said Mac, "I'm glad you ordered the shipping container. Let's hope it arrives in good condition and the wines are of good quality. Then you and Gina can market them, and hopefully, you make a profit or at least get your money back. Do you see why I like that plan?"

She thought for a moment. "I'm trying to think like you, Dad. Give me a second. Oh! Because it's all up to me to succeed or fail, and I have limited my exposure to one year's worth of my trust fund. And I have time to do other things while I grow that business."

"Yes, Sweetheart," said Mac, "all of the above. You are the master of your own fate. You can't control how the wine will sell, but you can control your effort, and that is your best resource: you. Now, what is it about Jean Paul's experiment that worries your Dad, do you think?"

Marybeth elbowed Mac in the ribs, ever so gently, like a Mom protecting her daughter.

"I can't predict his effort, can I?" said Gabby.

"No, you can't. Furthermore, Sweetheart, you are still projecting yourself into his dream by saying 'we' when it should be 'he'."

"Gabriella, Honey," Marybeth said ever so gently, "your Dad worries that maybe your feelings about Jean Paul will cloud your judgement about his dream of creating this new grape, and then making wine, and then da, da, da, da, da. You see the two of you doing this together, but his words say he is doing it himself and using my land to do it. It's an imposition on me that he has attained by using you in the middle. I'm not saying you shouldn't have feelings for Jean Paul. He seems very nice, but we don't know him yet. And maybe you don't either. This is not après-ski, Sweetheart. This is life, and business is business."

Gabby was silent again and looked down at her hands. Then she stood up, walked around the table, and bear-hugged Marybeth. Tears fell from her eyes.

"Marybeth...you are the Mom I never had. I... love you."

Now tears fell from Marybeth's eyes. "Gabby, you are the daughter I never had, and I love you too. Now look, let's put our thinking caps on and plan, OK? I know your Dad well enough that the wheels are turning in his mind. After a second cup of coffee, he is going to have an idea like a lightning bolt struck him."

"Please, M, that was a bad analogy," said Mac. "One lightning bolt in my life was enough. It burned my New Hampshire home and 30 years of work."

Marybeth and Gabby both laughed and put their arms around each other. And that made Mac smile.

"OK, he said, I've got some calls to make. Talk more later."

**

Sunday October 15
8:15 a.m.

Mac pulled out his phone, but before he could dial, it buzzed. (*Investigator Jonetta Pope.*)

"Good morning, Jonetta."

"Mac Morrison, do you ever have a normal life? What the hell!"

"I presume you read my e-mail and saw the pictures about the catalytic converters and Mace Wilkins."

"I did, and Colonel Justice did, and he reached out to our liaison with the egg salad of some 400 federal agencies, and half a dozen have an interest in this case. Transportation, Homeland Security, Secret Service, Treasury - what a hornet's nest you stirred up! I had plans for today with Juan that got cancelled because of you, dang it!"

"Sorry. Hey, how about I make it up to you and Juan by having dinner with us soon? Marybeth will make something special for you."

"That, Mac, is a deal. Now, let me tell you what is happening. Interstate shipment of stolen goods is a federal offense. Precious metals in catalytic converters can be used in hi-tech and weaponry, and that, plus the fact that they may be shipped via the Great Lakes to China, gets Homeland Security and the Coast Guard involved. The possibility that these CATs are being fenced in such huge quantities makes it unlikely they are being paid for in cash, and certainly not by check, so some kind of cryptocurrency is suspected, which means no trail and no taxes collected, bringing in Treasury and Secret Service. The location is in Ohio, so Ohio Highway Patrol is involved, along with Penn State Police and New York State Police. A California truck is seen in your pictures unloading CATs, so CHIPS is involved, too. And the insurance industry appointed a private investigator to join the group since these are their losses.

"A Zoom meeting is being set up for this afternoon. We need you to attend. I would prefer it if you could join me at Troop A in Fredonia. You started this ball rolling, and you took pictures and hired the aerials, so there will be a question of who you are and your authenticity. You should answer those directly. And as if you hadn't already wrecked a dozen people's Sunday, because Erie PD is holding the two thugs you roughed up on various hate crime and assault charges, they tell me there is a good motive to link the assault on Weinstein back to Wilkins, so the Department of Justice will sit in on the meeting too."

"And I was gonna go fishing today, Jonetta."

"Not now, you're not. Can you meet me at one p.m. at Troop A?"

"I can. What do you see as the possible outcome of a meeting with the egg salad of feds?"

"If they see probable cause, they would obtain a search warrant for the Wilkins Scrap Yard and hit it ASAP. The Coast Guard has already been put on standby to monitor the Chinese freighter and prevent it from leaving if it gets loaded with those 40 bins."

"OK, see you at one p.m."

**

Sunday October 15
Murphy B & B
8:35 a.m.

To refresh his memory, Mac scrolled the pictures on his phone. They were rolling past his eye as he looked for his visit to B & W Boat Club, the one where he saw the trucks being unloaded. The pictures rolled too far backward and stopped at the picture that said *'Reasoner Orchards'*. Below the word *'Orchards'*, the next line read *'and Organic Vineyards.'* He looked at the date and time the photo was taken: Saturday, October 7.

"Huh!" said Mac out loud. He pulled out his cell phone and hit speed dial for *Matthew Reasoner*.

"Reasoner Orchards, Matt Reasoner speaking," answered the voice.

"Mr. Reasoner, this is Mac Morrison in Barcelona Harbor, New York. Perhaps you remember I met with you and Trooper Andy Gregor on October 7."

"Of course I remember you, Mr. Morrison. I read that Louis Lopez is dead, killed in Hamburg by the State Police. Were you involved in that?"

"I was, but not at the scene. And just so you know, Manuel and Raoul Diaz are in jail in New Hampshire awaiting trial on attempted murder charges. They almost killed Paco before my friend and I intervened. They are in hospital now. When they recover, they will be tried, convicted, and imprisoned. Paco has a concussion, but he'll be all right."

"Holy cow," said Reasoner, "I guess I'm lucky I showed them my Glock."

"Yes. But I'm actually calling you about something completely different. I want to talk to you about organic grapes and Northern Italian wine."

**

Sunday October 15
Fredonia, NY
New York State Police, Troop A
Zoom Virtual Meeting
1:00 p.m.

Mac expected nine people to join Jonetta's meeting, but there were eleven faces on the Zoom screen, including Assistant Attorneys General from New York and Ohio. All the faces looked bored, as if they wished they were doing anything but this on a lovely Sunday afternoon. Before Jonetta could begin the meeting, a twelfth face appeared with a placard that said 'Bradley Fellowes, Agent in Charge, FBI.' He wore a white shirt, dark tie, and dark suit.

"Oh great," Mac muttered, "the Friggin' Bureau of Incompetents."

Several of the faces on the screen burst out laughing.

Bradley Fellowes did not.

"Mac!" whispered Jonetta sideways, "that is a hot mic; we are live."

"Good!" Mac whispered back.

Jonetta opened the meeting by asking each participant to introduce themselves.

AIC Bradley Fellowes promptly interrupted her.

"My name is Bradley Fellowes, and I am the Agent in Charge of the Cleveland Office of the *Federal Bureau of Investigation*. His words were dripping with the arrogance of authority conferred, not earned.

"The Bureau will be the lead agency on this case. That is, if it is determined there *is a case* that warrants investigation. I understand that a large trove of allegedly stolen catalytic converters is now located on a dock in Ashtabula, Ohio, which is my jurisdiction. As AIC, I will lead the task force. The FBI will oversee all other federal agencies, determine the appropriate course of action, and delegate individual agency responsibilities. As representatives of your agencies, you will coordinate with your colleagues and report to your superiors. If there is a political aspect to the investigation, my office will contact the appropriate elected representatives to advise them so they are not caught off guard by any press releases concurrent with the investigation. If that is clear, we may proceed with introductions."

Mac leaned over to Jonetta Pope and whispered "Bet his fingernails are clean and his shoes are shined."

She shushed him, and they turned their attention back to the agents, each telling who and why they were involved. Investigator Pope introduced Mac as the last one. She asked him to explain what he had observed at the Wilkins Scrap Yard and give a little background on why he was at that yard to make his observations.

Mac briefly explained that Banks Breakers and Scrap Metal Yard in Erie properly recycles scrap metals, including catalytic converters. Banks had been owned since 1972 by his friend, 85-year-old Sol Weinstein, a Polish immigrant survivor of Nazi concentration camps. So when Mr. Weinstein received a letter that intimated the city of Erie would consider using eminent domain to purchase his property for redevelopment as a lakefront park with amenities, he asked Mac to help him understand it.

AIC Bradley Fellowes interrupted him at this point.

"Mister Morrison," he said, "are you an attorney?"

"No sir," said Mac.

"Then why would Mr. Weinstein consult you about a legal matter?"

"Because I am his friend."

"But you are not an attorney."

"I said I wasn't, didn't you hear me?"

There were some guffaws from the members of the Zoom meeting.

"Agent Fellowes," said Mac, "I build homes, so I deal with lawyers, cities, and government projects. I am well aware of the power of eminent domain and how it can be legally used for a public purpose, such as the extension of a road or the development of a public park. When I read this letter from the 'City County Basin Urban Transformation Triad,' or 'CCBUTT,' something about the wording wasn't right. It had arrived in an envelope with the city of Erie's return address, but the letter was not from the city. It was from CCBUTT.

"So I decided to find out who CCBUTT was.

"Doing internet research, I found a newspaper photo of the ad hoc representatives of CCBUTT, and it turns out that the 'Greater Area Sailing & Boating Affiliates Group' or 'GASBAG' had a representative on CCBUTT. That person was Mace Wilkins. I recognized his picture because he bought a boat from a guy who moored next to a friend of mine at Barcelona Harbor, New York. I knew Wilkins owned a scrap yard in Ohio, so it seemed odd that he was backing a harbor plan in Pennsylvania, but I accepted his role as the rep for GASBAG.

"At that point, I referred Mr. Weinstein to a very competent land use lawyer named Sarah Lieberman. Together, we determined that the waterfront plan was, in fact, an 'aspirational plan' put together by a consultant and paid for by Mace Wilkins and Billy Barnes, a production builder known locally as the Condo King.

"When we reviewed their aspirational plan, it was obvious that the majority of the Weinstein land would not be used as a park but rather as a private marina and high-rise lakeside condos. Those are not purposes for which eminent domain can be used, so we smelled a rat.

"Attorney Lieberman contacted the city and found they were not aware of the letter to Weinstein and had not made any official movement towards redevelopment of his land for public purposes.

"So this aspirational plan was obviously being driven by Wilkins and Barnes for their personal benefit. At this point, CCBUTT's sleazy lawyer made a verbal offer for Weinstein's land, which was rejected. The lawyer increased their offer and again threatened to take the land by eminent domain unless Weinstein would agree to sell. He again refused to sell.

"The next thing that happened was two goons dressed in Nazi swastikas with face masks arrived in a truck and tried to intimidate Weinstein to sell. He told them to get out. They insulted him and used a religious slur. He fought them. Mr. Weinstein is four and a half feet tall and 85 years old. A 6'6" professional boxer pounded him unconscious while a short thug punched his kidneys with brass knuckles. Fortunately, his foreman came to work early, forcing the goons to flee. His crew found him unconscious, lying in his own blood. The squad rushed him to hospital, and he survived.

"Based upon Mr. Weinstein's description of his attackers, I had reason to believe one of the goons was a guard at the B &W Boat Club, so I went to see for myself.

"B & W is adjacent to the Wilkins Scrap yard. Through the fence I could see these bins of scrap converters with pipes still attached. I took pictures, against the orders of the guard on duty. Then I asked Weinstein's foreman, Martin, to look at them. He was sure we were looking at stolen catalytic converters being loaded onto 40 shipping containers. So, I hired a helicopter to fly over the Wilkins yard and take aerial photos. We saw the Chinese freighter lying at anchor. The guard at B & W had told me the freighter was waiting its turn to dock, and it also needed the lake level to rise because the south winds had blown the water over to Canada."

Bradley Fellows strutted around in front of his laptop in Cleveland like a Peacock, rubbing his chin and scowling as Mac gave his brief summation.

"So, *Mister* Morrison," he sneered "am I to believe that you took it upon yourself to investigate this so-called fake waterfront redevelopment plan, and in doing so saw a photograph of Mr. Wilkins and decided to go to his boat club, and by so doing you casually observed and took pictures of these trucks unloading bins of what appeared to your untrained eye to be stolen catalytic converters, and that led to you contacting the New York State Police?"

"You can believe whatever you want," said Mac. "I did not want my friend Sol Weinstein to be scammed, so I decided to check into it. I did some research and drew some obvious conclusions. I went, I saw, and I reported."

"And you hired a helicopter to fly to Ohio from New York and take aerial photos?"

"I did."

"On whose authority?"

"On my own authority."

"Who paid for the helicopter and the aerials?"

"I did, of course."

"You did? You are not law enforcement, yet you spent how much of your own money to further investigate this Wilkins?"

"$2,000. You have a problem with me helping law enforcement, Bradley?"

"I am trying to understand if you have some underlying reason for this involvement. Weinstein is a competitor of Wilkins, is he not? I want to make sure that this expensive assembly of federal agents is not being entrapped into doing your dirty work to put this Wilkins Scrap Yard out of business on behalf of your friend Mr. Weinstein. The FBI will not be sullied by any such investigation, I can tell you that."

"Agent Fellows," said Mac, "forgive me, I am looking at a small picture of your face on this screen, and you look like a human being, but your words are coming from a horse's ass!"

Loud bursts of laughter came from all of the Zoom meeting members except AIC Bradley Fellowes.

"Agent Fellowes," Mac continued, "are you really as thick as that? Do you not understand that Mace Wilkins sent, correction, allegedly sent, the goons to assault Weinstein? Does the FBI and the Justice Department not have an obligation to investigate that as an egregious hate crime caught on film? Let's put aside the posturing here and get to the point. I had two experts on metal recycling examine the photos you have all seen and they both tell me that those bins are full of catalytic converters that have been hacked off by thieves, which is why the pipes are still attached to them, and which is why they have been brought, normally under cover of darkness, to an obscure scrap yard in Ashtabula to be fenced and exported. The value of insurance and consumer losses is estimated at $20 million.

"There is no reputable large scale catalytic converter recycling facility within 300 miles of that location and if these bins are loaded on that ship of Chinese registry, then they are not being sent to one of those recycling facilities, they are going out of country.

"And the reason I got involved, Agent Fellowes, is that I don't like people to fuck with me, my friends or my family. So, I saw something, and I said something. Now it's up to all of you, or at least some of you, to get off your asses and check it out, if I may be so vulgar. Time is short, the wind has changed, and the harbor level is rising. That freighter could begin loading at any time. Now, I apologize for being long-winded."

A stony silence impregnated the Zoom screen. Two federal agents could be seen covering their faces to conceal a laugh.

"Ahem!" said Colonel Samuel Justice. "I think it's fair for Mr. Morrison to show some frustration. He is trying to help all of us, and his good intentions are being questioned. I will say this in his defense. I have worked with Mr. Morrison on two previous cases and, although his methods seem unconventional, perhaps extraordinary, I have learned not to question his motives, just to accept his results."

"Yes, let's move on," said a Treasury Agent named Jobie.

"Well, I have heard enough to request a search warrant," said the Ohio Assistant AG.

The California Highway Patrol Lieutenant spoke up. "Catalytic converter theft is epidemic in California. Starting January 1, 2024, all new cars will have the VIN stamped on their CAT to deter theft. But with at least one tractor-trailer load of CATs from California, I would hope there would be at least one owner who had his VIN etched on his CAT. That is all we need to condemn the entire load as stolen. I need you to seize those CATs to inspect for etched VINs."

Now the Coast Guard Captain spoke. "The US Army Corps of Engineers is dredging Ashtabula Harbor at this time. I will make a phone call as soon as this meeting is over and ask them to immediately move their dredge to the Ashtabula materials dock and block any ships from using it. That should give the attorneys general time to obtain and serve their search warrant. Then the FBI can take the lead and organize the search of the materials found in those 40 shipping containers."

"That sounds like a plan," said Mac. "And I say this with all good intentions: Agent Fellowes, I know the FBI is good at what they do, and I know you will pursue this with all due haste, and we all appreciate your taking the lead. With that, I am leaving the meeting."

Mac got up and walked away from the table. He waved goodbye to Jonetta. She got up and moved out of view of her laptop camera so they both were no longer part of the Zoom meeting.

"Where are you going, Mac?"

"They don't need me now. Agent Fellowes needed a kick in the balls first, and then some positive reinforcement to save face. He got both, so now they'll get down to business. But they had better hurry, because once the wind shifts, and it has, the lake will rise, and that freighter will want to load.

"Meanwhile, Jonetta, it's a beautiful day; I have done enough crime fighting for the week, and the perch are biting. So, I am taking the family fishing this afternoon. Call me and tell me when you and Juan would like to come to dinner. But make it soon, because I have to get back to New Hampshire."

With that, he turned on his heel and left.

And, true to his word, Mac went and got Marybeth, Gabby, Buddy, and

Philip C. Laurien

Emma. Then they undertook the important family business of perch fishing on the Barcelona Harbor pier, laughing all afternoon, cleaning their catch, and grilling them with Hubcap Harry as the sun went down.

**

Chapter Twenty

Monday October 16
Murphy B & B
Barcelona Harbor
7:30 a.m.

"Angelo," said Mac, you have not lived until you have tasted Marybeth's Belgian waffles topped with confectionary sugar, a touch of cinnamon, glazed strawberries, and real organic New York maple syrup."

"Absolutely delicious," said Angelo. "But methinks you have something else on your mind, Mac."

"I do. I was thinking that my daughter Gabriella is looking to start a wine business. And you dream of making your own Barbera wine. We might have a way to marry the two visions."

"I would be interested to hear this idea."

"Enjoy your waffles, Angelo. Gabby will explain. Then we are going to Erie to inspect the Banks Scrap Yard with my new friend Martin."

**

Monday October 16
Erie PA
Banks Breakers and Scrap Metals
9:00 a.m.

Angelo cast an appraising eye over the Banks yard. Mac could tell he liked what he saw. The yard was as organized and neat as a scrap yard can be. Other than the shredder's iron and steel pile, which was loaded onto barges at their private dock by a giant dragline with electro-magnet, all other metals were separated and placed into open sheds. Smaller parts like catalytic converters were neatly trimmed and placed in bins that went into buildings. No mud. All of the working surfaces were concrete. The equipment all looked new or freshly painted. Inside the largest warehouse a team of six young men were breaking down vehicles into their components for recycling. The poorer quality vehicles or those with too much damage were crushed and shredded.

Sol's foreman, Martin, took them inside Sol's house, and that was a different story. It was clean and neat, but old and tired. Last, Martin took them inside Sol's blue steel 'special building.' Martin quickly looked around the immaculate office, kitchen, and Sol's sleeping room. He looked quickly because his eyes were riveted to the fifty, fabulous cars on racks. He walked silently down the aisle, nodding and murmuring about an uncle who had this one, a cousin who had that one. He was being transported back in time.

He stopped in front of the Tri-Five Chevys. There were six of them, two for each year, 55, 56 and 57. There was a copper 1957 Bel Air convertible with a white top. He stood and stared at it. He walked around it and looked underneath because it was on the top of the two-tier rack. Other than some minor surface rust on the chassis, the body was solid. And original.

All the cars were original and unrestored. Angelo wondered what the collection was worth, as-is. He had to believe it was worth at least a half million dollars. He turned and pointed to the copper Chevy.

"This is the car, Mackenzie. I want to buy this car. And then I want you to build it for me when you have the time."

"Well, Angelo, it doesn't hurt to ask."

**

Monday October 16
Ashtabula, OH
B & W Boat Club & Wilkins Scrap Metals
10:00 a.m.

Mace Wilkins was fuming. The lake level had risen three feet in the past 24 hours, and his shipping containers were ready to load. But the dock was blocked by a damned dredge that was not supposed to arrive until Wednesday! He had called the harbormaster and gotten the word that silt buildup had prevented ships from entering the harbor, so the Corps of Engineers ordered the dredge to move into position on Sunday afternoon. Now, a day later, they still had not begun dredging, and his freighter was going to leave if they could not get it loaded today.

Finally he called his sleazy lawyer Simon Long and told him to do something, and quick, which was why Attorney Long had gone to the Ashtabula County Courthouse first thing Monday morning to get a judge to order the dredge to move. After all, it could be moved back as soon as the freighter was loaded and gone. It seemed reasonable, and Simon Long was sure he had enough friends at the courthouse to grant him this order.

But when he got there, the presiding judge was already in session handling another case. So Simon Long slipped into the courtroom and quietly took a seat in the back to wait. But his ears perked up when he heard an Ohio Assistant Attorney General give oral arguments for a "no-knock" search warrant for the B & W Boat Club and Wilkins Scrap Metal yard. For a split second, Attorney Long felt he should jump up and intervene on behalf of the owner. But then he kept his cool and his seat and thought about this.

He was already in hot water over that damn letter he sent Sol Weinstein. He thought it had been cleverly worded to convey authority from the city without actually having the city's authority. But that was what had now got him called on the carpet, again. The City Attorney had filed a complaint, and the Bar Ethics Committee had been advised, again, of his shady actions.

And he was not authorized to intervene. He did not know why the State of Ohio was seeking a search warrant. No, it was better for him to slink back out of the courtroom and listen at the door. It only took a few minutes, and he heard the Judge rap his gavel and say the search warrant was "so ordered!"

Moving quickly, Simon Long took long strides to get out to the parking lot away from prying eyes and ears. He hit the speed dial on his cell phone and was immediately connected to Mace Wilkins.

"Did you get it, Simon? Did you get the judge to order the dredge moved?"

"Never got a chance. Listen, I just happened to be waiting my turn in the back of the courtroom when I heard an Ohio Assistant Attorney General request a no-knock search warrant for the B &W Boat Club and Wilkins Scrap Yard, Mace."

"WHAT!"

"I'm telling you, this was an order to be carried out by the Ohio State Highway Patrol in conjunction with the FBI and half a dozen other federal agencies. I did not get all their names. But it's a big fuckin' deal, Mace. Whatever they think you've got, you better get it and get the hell out of there because I guarantee they will be at your door within the hour!"

"I CAN'T BELIEVE THIS!" screamed Wilkins. "How the Hell! No, *who* the hell?"

There was no time to load the containers on the freighter now! But he did not want them found in his yard! An hour! What could he do?

As he looked out at the dock, the idea hit him. The materials yard had a tug railcar mover. They used it to move his cars into position. The materials yard let Slugger drive it, but he was in custody, so he couldn't use Slugger.

He ran down to the materials yard and found Max, the foreman. Max could drive it! He only needed to get the flatbed cars with the catalytic converters off the property and to the nearest siding! And he knew where there was one that had been abandoned!

"Max," he said, as coolly as he could fake, "look, the dredge is blocking the dock, and I got these cars ready to load, but now they tell me it could be days before the dock will be clear. The freighter just called and said they can't wait any longer. I need to clear my lot to get ready for my next incoming loads. Could you use your railcar tug to tow those cars a mile to the old coal yard siding? I'll pay you $1,000 to move them right now. I got trucks coming in a half hour. What do you say?"

"Cash, Mace?"

"Of course, cash. I can put it in your hand in two minutes. Will you do it? They are hooked up and ready to roll."

"OK, I'll do it. Let me tell the boss, and then I'll hook up the tug and get them out of here. Shouldn't take me more than 20 minutes. I'll come back after I drop them off. No one ever uses that siding anyway. They can sit there until you get another freighter to pick them up."

"Thanks, Max, thanks a million!"

"Cash, Mace!"

"Going to get it now! Meet you at the tug!"

**

Monday October 16
Ashtabula, OH
B & W Boat Club & Wilkins Scrap Metals
10:15 a.m.

Mace Wilkins cleaned out his safe of all the cash and personal papers, but there were too many business files to carry away. Many of them were records of fenced goods that he kept to monitor prices over time. He had never gotten used to doing spreadsheets anyway. The battered old wooden filing cabinets were stuffed full of papers that he did not want found by the police. The Boat Club was really just a big wooden shack with an outdoor bar and 20 docks. It was pretty pathetic, but it was a good front for the Wilkins Scrap Yard, which made his money. As the last of the train cars left the gate, Mac poured five gallons of marine gas on the file cabinets and all over the floor. Then he went outside and yelled:

"Closing up early today, Arthur! You can go home. I've got a bonus for you, so come get it."

Arthur came over, and Mace counted $500 into his hand.

"Thanks, Mace, but what is this for?"

"Arthur, the freighter is leaving without loading the containers because the dock is blocked. So we'll be closed for the rest of the week. I'll see you next Monday, OK?"

"OK, boss, thanks!"

Arthur almost ran, if he could run, to his old Buick and roared away. He would be heading for the nearest tavern.

Mace Wilkins took out a book of matches, lit them all, and tossed the book into the building. He walked away as a "ka-whump!" blew out the windows, and the building was ablaze.

Wilkins locked the gate, got in his Cadillac SUV, and drove away feeling pretty good about the whole deal. He needed to get out of Ohio. He knew just the place to go. He had an old hunting friend in New York who let him use his summer house near Dewittville. The key was over the door, and the larder was always stocked. It would be a great place to chill out, stay in touch with Simon, and watch the news. The contraband was off his property, and the fire would burn the evidence. Yes, he was gonna be OK, he thought.

**

**Monday October 16
Ashtabula, OH
10:25 a.m.**

The call went to Ashtabula Fire Station #2: B &W Boat Club was on fire!

Engines roared out of the brick building and raced to the scene. They found the gate locked and the wooden building fully engulfed. Using heavy-duty bolt cutters, they easily cut the lock on the chain link fence and gained entry. They set up a pumper truck and sucked water from Lake Erie to douse the flames. The building was too far gone to save, but they continued to soak it to prevent sparks igniting the materials office and shed on the adjacent lot.

**

**Monday October 16
Ashtabula, OH
B & W Boat Club & Wilkins Scrap Metals
10:35 a.m.**

Agent in Charge Bradley Fellowes and his entry team arrived with their search warrant only to see firemen fighting a blaze! The building they had hoped to search was burned, and the 40 shipping containers on rail cars were gone!

"Someone tipped him off," he muttered. Now, there was nothing to search. A tug rail car mover approached him and stopped at the gate.

"You lookin' for Mace Wilkins?" the driver asked.

"Yes," said Fellowes. "Who are you?"

"Max, I'm foreman at the materials yard."

"I'm FBI Agent Fellowes out of Cleveland office. We're here to serve a search warrant for forty shipping containers, but they're gone."

"I just hauled them over to the coal yard siding."

"Why did you do that, Max?"

"He paid me to, Wilkins did. Said he couldn't load the freighter, so it was gonna leave, and he had more trucks coming and needed the space, so I used the tug to tow them over there."

"Can we drive over there?"

"No, but I could run you over in the tug."

"Good, Max, let's go. Maybe by the time we get back, they'll have this fire under control. How did it start, Max?"

"He burned it down. Must've used gasoline because it exploded and blew out the windows."

They snaked along the waterfront to a thumb of land that had an old dock that looked like it had not been used for quite a while. The rails were rusty except for the siding with the 40 cars.

"Max, I have a court order to search those cars, but this location is not secure. I need my team to have access to their tools. Can you tow these cars back and lock them behind a secure fence?"

"Sure. Let me just hook up, and we can go."

By the time they returned to the materials yard, the Boat Club fire was mostly out. There was nothing left of the wooden building but soggy piles of smoldering black embers. Max drove the tug onto the materials yard and parked the front of the train on a siding, then moved the tug and spilt the train into four, 400' long sections on four parallel tracks. Once the law enforcement vehicles entered, he closed the gate and locked it.

Agent Fellowes might have been pompous during the Zoom meeting, but he was well-organized and focused on this task. There were 24 total agents assigned to enter and inventory the cars. They brought a trailer with folding tables to inspect each catalytic converter for identification markings and then replace them in the bin they came from. There were 20,000 CATs to inventory, but once they got a system going it went smoothly. Max used his top lift to raise a shipping container and place it on the ground. Then, an agent would use Max's forklift to extract a bin.

Agents laid the CATs on tables and inspected them. Each CAT could be inspected in less than a minute. Two agents could do 100 CATs per hour, or 800 in an eight-hour shift. That was good, but too slow. The trail for Wilkins was getting colder by the minute. It would take two days to inventory the mess. Agent Fellowes called for 25 more agents from the Erie and Cleveland FBI Bureau offices.

Brad Fellowes wanted to target the California CATs first because they had the greatest chance of being VIN-etched. He wondered which containers were from California. He hit speed dial for BCI Investigator Jonetta Pope.

"Hello, Agent Fellowes," she said.

"Investigator Pope…"

"It's faster to call me Jonetta, Bradley. What can I do for you?"

"Thank you, Jonetta; please call me Brad. I'm here at the Wilkins Scrap Yard. Wilkins moved the rail cars off-site, but I retrieved them and put them on a siding. He burned his boat club to the ground, so we are beginning to search the containers. I wanted to start with those from California, but no identification would tell me that. I remember that Mr. Morrison said he took pictures of tractor-trailers from New York and California unloading. I don't seem to have those on my phone. Could you check?"

"I'll do better than that; I'll call Mac and have him call you."

"Oh. We didn't get off to a very good start at our meeting. I know I can be a pompous ass, I always get that on my annual evaluation, but no one ever shamed me in front of colleagues like he did. I had it coming. Do you think he'll bury the hatchet and help me?"

"Of course he will. He complimented you on his way out of the meeting. That's just Mac's way of cutting the bullshit, Brad. Don't take it to heart. He'll help you."

"Good; give me his number, please, Jonetta."

**

Monday October 16
Barcelona Harbor, NY
Murphy B & B
10:45 a.m.

Mac and Gabby were researching Italian wines and climates when his phone rang. (*Ohio area code.*)

"Hello?" said Mac.

"Mr. Morrison, this is Bradley Fellowes from the Cleveland FBI office. First of all, I *was* being a horse's ass, and thank you for not rubbing my nose in it more than you did. I need your help."

"Brad, call me Mac. Anything I can do to nail Mace Wilkins, I will help you."

"Good, thanks, Mac. We had a surprise in Ashtabula. Someone must have tipped Wilkins that we were coming. He managed to move the 40 rail cars off-site and burned his Boat Club building. He's in the wind. I was able to retrieve the rail cars, so we are inventorying the contents. Can you identify which container was on the California truck you photographed?"

"Brad, let me check my pictures and call you right back, OK?"

"Good, thanks, Mac."

Mac went into Marybeth's hard drive to find the pictures he downloaded. He scrolled down until he found the truck trailer with the California license plate. Gabby took over and zoomed in, looking for markings on that shipping container. Then she asked the internet which marking would be unique and found the code:

The Container Number is a unique sequence of 4 letters and 7 numbers displayed on the top right part of the container door. The ISO (International Standards Organization) assigns the number to identify the unit internationally.

Gabby read off the ID on the container in the photo.

"BZTO8529017, Dad."

"Thanks, Gabby." He repeated it back to her and then called Agent Fellowes.

"Yes, Mac? That was fast."

"Brad, the ID is on the top right of the back door. The number is BZTO8529017."

"Thanks, Mac."

"Is Wilkins wanted for anything yet, Brad?"

"I'm sure the Fire Marshal would like to speak to him, but if he doesn't file an insurance claim, I guess he can burn his own building if he wants to. If we knew there was evidence inside that was destroyed we could charge him, but we don't know that. As far as receiving stolen property, let's wait and see if these CATs prove to be stolen. If they are, he'll probably argue he didn't know they were stolen, or he might say he suspected they were, and that is why he removed them from his property. Technically, they were not in his possession when we seized them."

"Hm," said Mac. "And Erie PD cannot connect him to the assault on Sol Weinstein."

"Not yet," said Agent Fellowes.

"Brad, if Weinstein's foreman hadn't arrived and startled those two thugs, maybe they were supposed to kill him. That is, if they couldn't scare him. If he were dead it would be easier for Wilkins to get his land. If German and Smith were charged with attempted murder, maybe one of them would flip."

"And Wilkins does have a motive to get Weinstein out of the way," said Agent Fellowes. "I think you're right, Mac. I am going to call the City Attorney and ask him to charge them with attempted murder. Meanwhile, I think we have enough to put out an APB Wilkins as a person of interest in the assault on Weinstein. That should give us a chance to pick him up while we inventory these CATs."

"Sounds like a plan, Brad. Keep me posted, please. Oh! You said someone tipped Wilkins that you were coming. Who knew about the hearing for the search warrant?"

"Just me, the Ohio Assistant Attorney General, the clerk of court, and the Judge. No one else."

"Well, I can't believe it would be the Judge," said Mac. "Was the hearing in chambers?"

"No, in open court, before the regular session."

"Were there others in the courtroom?"

"Not when we went in, just us, the stenographer, the Clerk, and the Judge."

"Hm. Another mystery. Wilkins had a friend at the courthouse."

**

**Monday October 16
Dewittville, NY
12:00 p.m.**

Mace Wilkins hadn't planned on any of this. He needed time to think. He thought old man Weinstein would take their $3 million dollar offer and sell, but he misjudged that. He thought Nazi swastikas would scare him, and he'd sell, but he misjudged that too. He didn't expect Slugger and Stubby to beat the hell out of the old man, maybe just rough him up. But he'd misjudged that, too. With those two in custody, he knew they would be charged, but would they give him up? That was worrying him most of all.

He'd never been hunted before, and if the cops were hunting him now, he wasn't sure what to do. His judgment sucked; he knew that. He had to disappear for a while, but first, he had to stash some money and make a call to his lawyer. He rented a storage locker in Mayville, one where you could access it 24 hours. He put the valise with the cash in there. It was close to $400,000. The catalytic converter fencing had been very profitable but risky, too. That was why he wanted to get out of the business, build a nice marina, sit back, collect rent, and go fishing. Billy Barnes would front all the capital. He figured the city would jump at the chance to buy an acre for a park on the lake, extending their greenbelt. It should have worked.

He'd left a couple million dollars worth of precious metals in those containers at the coal yard. Now, he could never recover them. They would be seized with that search warrant. If they hadn't already gotten them, they would soon. Jesus, the fucking FBI was after him! He considered giving himself up for the CATs, but what if Slugger turned him over to the cops on the Weinstein attack? Then he could be in for a long prison sentence. He needed to know if there was a warrant for his arrest, and the only way was to call Simon's private line. Then, he would ditch his cell phone.

"Simon?"

"Mace! Don't tell me where you are!"

"Simon, are the cops looking for me?"

"Yes, but only for the fire and the catalytic converters."

"What about Slugger German?"

"He's got a public defender. Word is he'll be arraigned on charges of religious hate crime with enhancements, meaning aggravated assault and kidnapping."

"He's screwed then."

"Mace, how much trouble are you in? Were you involved in the old man's beating? You need to tell me the truth, Mace because if I have to defend you, I need to know."

"I told them to scare him. The swastikas were my idea, but I didn't tell them to beat the hell out of him."

"Mace, if that old man dies, all three of you are in deep shit because that big dope German will turn on you to take a reduced charge. He'll say you ordered them and paid them."

"I can see that. What should I do, Simon?"

"Mace, do you have any cash?"

"Some."

"Look, can you get me $10,000 as a retainer? I'm probably going to work my ass off to defend you. I need to be legally retained."

"I thought you were."

"I drew up the LLC for CCBUTT, Mace, but that does not make me your personal attorney."

"Yeah, OK, look, I can't walk into your office if the cops are looking for me. What do you want me to do?"

"Put it at a drop location, and I'll come get it. I'll leave the retainer for you to sign. Mail it back to me. Then we wait to see what the FBI does. You could just be charged with receiving a shit load of stolen catalytic converters, in which case I would plead you no contest, saying you didn't know they were stolen. You could pay a fine and maybe get a suspended sentence and probation. You have no other criminal convictions, right?"

"Right"

"OK, where is the drop, Mace?"

"Do you know Mayville, New York?"

"Sure, I've been through it on my way to the Chautauqua summer series."

"OK, there is a gas station at the bottom of the hill on 394 by the lake, near the old train station. Behind the gas station is a steel storage shed. The roof has an overhang with a gap above the top of the wall. I'll put the envelope in the gap. I don't want it sitting there long. There's no camera on the back of that building. What time can you pick it up, Simon?"

"Give me two hours, say, 2:00 p.m."

"OK, so I'll leave it at 1:45, circle back later, and get the paperwork. Look, the way to do it is to go inside and ask them to pump your gas full service. It's an old-time station, and they will. Ask to use the restroom. It's outside at the back. While they gas your car, you can get the envelope. I'll do the same to drop it off, and then I'll go back tonight in a different car and get the paperwork. Got it?"

"Got it: 2:00 p.m. in Mayville, Mace."

**

Monday October 16
Mayville, NY
12:30 p.m.

Wilkins headed back to his storage locker to get cash. He stopped at a drug store, bought a padded envelope, and put the $10,000 in it. He was hungry. He knew where there was a good Mom and Pop diner with home-style food, but he was concerned his Cadillac Escalante with Ohio plates might be spotted. He parked on a side street behind a repair garage and walked two blocks to the diner. He wore sunglasses and a fisherman's pork pie hat over his eyes, sat in a corner booth, and faced out the window while ordering with the menu in front of his face.

Lunch was good, and the coffee was excellent so he ordered another to go. He was starting to calm down. His mind was thinking again, not just reacting. He knew he should probably ditch his cell phone, but where? It had to be a location without cameras, and it also had to be a location where it would not be found. As he drove down the hill toward Chautauqua Lake, the answer was right in front of him: the lake. He pulled into the old train station museum parking lot and scanned for cameras. They were on all sides of the building. So he drove next door into the empty Lakeside Park, walked out on the beach swimming dock, and dropped it casually into the water.

He drove across the road to the gas station and asked the attendant to fill the tank while he used the restroom. Then he strolled around the side, made sure there was no camera, and quickly pulled the envelope from his jacket and stuffed it in the shed roof rafters. He walked back to the Caddy, paid in cash, and headed around the east side of the lake for Dewittville.

His buddy Caleb Mitchell had an old farmhouse outside of the village. It was located on a bucolic tree-lined road with scattered farm fields and a horseback riding stable with a faded wooden sign that said *Bar B Ranch, Riding lessons, Rentals, and Trail Rides.*

The Mitchell house was a half mile past the Bar B, tucked into a small vale that backed up to a big wooded area, a perfect hideout. The cabin, as Caleb liked to call it, was private but close to town. There was good deer hunting in the big woods. In the barn out back, Caleb kept an old Ford pickup that ran great.

Wilkins got the key from its hidden location over the front door and entered the house from the side porch. He got the keys to the barn and opened it, then drove the Caddy inside. The keys were in the pickup, and it started immediately. He let it warm up, backed it out, and drove back into Mayville. It was now 2:15 p.m.

The envelope was gone under the shed roof, and another was left. He put it in his jacket and paid for the truck's gas in cash. He bought groceries, signed and mailed the pre-stamped letter with the attorney retainer, and dropped it in a blue USPS box. Then he returned to Caleb's cabin and turned on the TV. It was a modern type with streaming, so he carried it out to the side porch and watched an old movie while he heard the pleasant sound of horses trotting on the woods trails from the Bar B Ranch next door.

**

Philip C. Laurien

Monday October 16
Barcelona Harbor
Murphy B & B,
3:30 p.m.

Gabriella completed the conference call with Mac, Angelo Murano, and vineyard owner Matt Reasoner. They had a basic plan. There was little risk to any of them, but their combined efforts could launch a new organic American-grown Italian Barbera wine.

Gabby, Mac, and Marybeth were all sitting on the back porch with the dogs while Angelo poured each a glass of his cousin's Barbera wine.

"If we are successful," Angelo said, "soon we will be drinking our wine, grown in LeRoy, New York at the Reasoner vineyard, and bottle it under the Murano-Morrison label. A toast to our success, my friends."

Mac was looking at pictures and reading about Barbera grapes. At a glance, they could be mistaken for American Concord grapes, but unlike Concord, they make a dry, non-sparkling red wine.

"In my home in the Piemonte," said Angelo, "the Barbera grape is everywhere. It is the most common table wine, always satisfying after a day's hard work.

"A bottle of good California Barbera contains sulfites and costs $20-30. But we will sell ours for under $16 and market it regionally as a fresh wine. If you go to a bar with four friends and each has two mixed drinks, they will spend $40 - $50. But if you buy a good bottle of local Barbera and invite your friends home, you will spend only $16. So this is a wine for daily enjoyment. And my cousin's vineyard has a very special Barbera grape. Those will be the vines we import and the grafts we start at Reasoner's."

"I am so excited, Angelo," Gabby said. "Thank you for making this possible!"

"No, Gabriella, thank you for your vision and your enthusiasm. This will be a lot of hard work. Let us not kid ourselves. And most of it falls on you, dear. But you can do it. And we will help and guide you."

Mac's phone buzzed. He opened the old wooden screen door with a 'gronk' and walked outside to take the call from FBI Agent Brad Fellowes. Buddy followed behind.

"Brad, what's up?"

"Mac, I've got 50 FBI Agents inspecting the CATS. So far, we found a couple hundred with etched VINs that were reported stolen. Max, the foreman at the materials yard, told me Wilkins paid him to move the container cars off-site, so we can get him for possession of stolen CATs. We now have a federal warrant for Wilkins on charges of receiving, transporting, and selling stolen property. Your guess at insurance losses of $20 million looks like it could be pretty close."

"Brad, what will happen to that shipment now?"

"All of the stolen CATs with etched VINs will be evidence shared with law enforcement in the states they are traced to. The rest can be auctioned off as non-returnable assumed stolen property. A scrap dealer will be able to bid for them on line, provided they can assure the US EPA that the CATs will be properly recycled. Why do you ask?"

"I have friends in the legitimate scrap business. Good job, Brad. Congratulations."

"Thanks to you, Mac. Now we just have to catch Wilkins."

**

Monday October 16
Ashtabula, OH
Wilkins Scrap Yard
5:00 p.m.

FBI Agent Brad Fellowes put out an APB on Wilkins' Cadillac Escalante, then walked to the materials yard office and asked for Max. It was late, but he was still there.

"Max, do you know what places Wilkins frequents or people he hangs out with?"

"Billy Barnes is his pal. He's a condo developer in Erie. He used to keep a boat down here until the Boat Club silted up. The Corps won't dredge it because it's a private inlet, not part of the navigable harbor, and Wilkins wouldn't pay to keep it dredged, so Barnes moved his boat to Erie."

"OK, we'll check that. What about anyone else?"

"He liked to pal around with the Killer; that's his guard, Slugger German."

"Why do you call him Killer?"

"Slugger was a pro boxer. He liked to drink in all the local bars in

Ashtabula, Conneaut, Erie, the 'east coast,' as we like to call it. Anyway, with his temper, it didn't take much to set him off. He's missing that switch in your brain that says 'walk away.' Some guy in a bar had too many drinks, figured he could take him, and started mouthing off. Slugger said, 'OK buddy, right here, right now. You get one free punch.'

"That guy hit him hard. I was there, I saw it. But Slugger knew how to turn his head and take the blow. He staggered a step, then jabbed the guy three times and clobbered him with the haymaker. The guy went down and hit his head on the brass footrail. He died. The Boxing Commission pulled Slugger's ticket after that.

"Slugger had been good enough to go pro and make some money, but he was never gonna be champ. He was a ham and eggs club fighter. After the Commission yanked his license, he came back to Ash-town with his head low, looking for work. Mace gave him a job as yard guard."

"Why did Wilkins hang out with him?"

"Wilkins is a wimp. Hanging with Slugger made him feel like a big shot. Slugger had no friends other than Wilkins and Stubby. With the kind of operation Wilkins ran, there were a lot of tough characters that peddled stolen scrap. Wilkins knew that, so he'd lowball them. If they got rough, the Slugger would take care of business. I'll tell you one thing: I wouldn't want to be the guy who clobbered Slugger in that bar."

"Why is that?"

"He'll go looking for him, and if he doesn't kill him, it won't be for lack of trying."

"German is going to jail."

"Yeah, I heard."

"Look, Max. You must have Wilkins' cell number. He calls you to arrange docking, right?"

"Sure, I've got it." He pulled out his cell phone. "Here's the number."

Agent Fellowes entered it into his contacts. "I don't suppose he'd go to his house, but we'll look it up."

"No need, I have his home address. It's where we send his invoices."

"You don't invoice him here?"

"No, this building was just the Boat Club and a desk for the Yard. Here's the address."

"Thanks, Max. Is there anything else you can tell me about Wilkins?

Places he goes?"

"Well, he goes out on that boat of his, but the cops took it for that murder case in New York."

"Murder case?"

"Yeah, the previous owner of his boat was a killer. I guess the boat was evidence in a reopened murder case. Some New York Troopers seized it. It was a tall black lady Trooper. Very fit, looked like she could handle herself."

"Do you remember her name?"

"Uh, it was a short name, like smoke or hope ..."

"Pope? Investigator Jonetta Pope?"

"Pope! That's it. You know her?"

"I do. Thanks, Max."

**

**Monday October 16
Fredonia, NY
State Police Troop A Barracks
6:00 p.m.**

Jonetta Pope's cell phone buzzed. (*FBI Agent Fellowes.*)

"Investigator Pope," she said.

"Jonetta, this is Brad Fellowes, FBI."

"Brad, your team has been sending us a lot of VINs to check."

"Yes, thanks for your help. Jonetta, how is Mace Wilkins' boat involved in a murder?"

"It's regarding the death of State Trooper Jim Murphy two years ago. He was found floating near his small boat on Lake Erie. The cause of death was initially determined to be accidental drowning. New evidence suggests Wilkins' boat, which at the time of Trooper Murphy's death belonged to a guy named Joey Minetti, struck Murphy's boat and killed him to prevent his investigation into embezzlement by Minetti's wife. A judge just gave an order to disinter Trooper Murphy's body. A new autopsy will be performed to see if the official cause of death will be changed."

"But Wilkins wasn't involved in the murder?"

"No, Wilkins bought the boat when Minetti went on the lam. Minetti was wanted for two other murders, namely Jim Murphy's in-laws. He has since been posthumously found guilty."

"Posthumously?"

"Joey Minetti is dead. And there is little doubt he also committed two additional murders 40 years ago, but no way to prove it now."

"Who were those two?"

"Actually, they were Mac Morrison's parents."

"Holy shit!"

"Yeah, and Mac got revenge on Minetti. He broke his neck."

"Jeezus! Jonetta, Mac helped me like you said he would."

"He's a good guy, Brad, but not someone you want to tangle with. He killed Minetti with his bare hands. Ruled self-defense."

"Jonetta, we're putting out a BOLO for Wilkins' car and a general APB, so I'll stay in touch if we think he's headed your way."

"Sounds good, Brad. Good job on those CATs."

**

Monday October 16
Ashtabula, OH
6:30 p.m.

FBI Agents went to Wilkins' Ashtabula house but found it empty, so Agent Fellowes contacted Billy Barnes. He knew nothing of Wilkins' whereabouts and seemed genuinely surprised to hear about the B &W fire and stolen catalytic converters. He assured Agent Fellowes that Wilkins was just his fishing buddy. They had devised a plan to redevelop a piece of the Erie waterfront. But that was it; he was not a close friend. He knew Wilkins had a hunting buddy near Chautauqua Lake with a cabin he used.

Agent Fellowes thanked Barnes and rang off.

The murder bothered Brad Fellowes. Even though Wilkins was not involved, he bought his boat when Minetti was on the lam, so that took cash, and he was dealing with a serial killer. The Wilkins scrap yard was a pretty shabby operation for fencing stolen goods, so Wilkins probably dealt with a lot of shady characters. If Wilkins had ordered a hit on Weinstein, he needed to find this guy before he was in the wind.

He called Jonetta Pope back.

"Yes, Brad?"

"Jonetta, Mace Wilkins has a friend with a cabin near Chautauqua Lake. Is that your Troop area?"

"Yes, do you have an address?"

"No, but it's possible he's headed your way."

"OK Brad. I have a Trooper who lives in Mayville. We'll check the BOLO and be watching for his car. Mac Morrison stays in Barcelona Harbor when he's in town, not far from Chautauqua. I'll call him. The man gets lucky sometimes."

"OK, Jonetta, thanks; I'll keep you posted."

**

**Monday October 16
Barcelona Harbor, NY
Murphy B & B
7:00 p.m.**

Mac's phone buzzed as they were cleaning up the dinner dishes. (*Jonetta Pope calling*.)

"Hello, Jonetta."

"Mac, the containers from Wilkins' yard had CATs with etched VINs reported stolen, so Mace Wilkins is now wanted on a federal warrant. Brad Fellowes got a tip that Wilkins may be staying at a buddy's cabin near Chautauqua. We don't know the location or the buddy's name. I'm texting you Wilkins' vehicle info. It's a Cadillac Escalade with an Ohio plate. State Police Troop A and the County Sheriff will be looking for it. Since you are out and about, I figured another pair of eyes could help."

"Be glad to Jonetta. I'll call if I see anything."

**

**Monday October 16
Barcelona Harbor
Murphy B & B
7:30 p.m.**

"Marybeth, how about a trail ride tomorrow morning?"

"Sounds good, Mac. I'll call Betty and reserve the horses."

**

"Of course I'll have your horses ready!" Betty Wilson said. "What time, Marybeth?"

"How about 10:00 a.m.?"

"That's fine, I guess."

"Betty, is something wrong? You sound worried."

"No dear, not wrong, just ...something is odd."

"What is it?"

"It's the old farmhouse on the other side of my woods trail. I think someone is in there, but I didn't see a car when I drove by. Mr. Mitchell lets his friends use it, but it's too early for deer hunting, and weekenders usually are gone by Monday night. Tonight, I smell smoke from a wood fire, and that usually means it's coming from the Mitchell house because he just has a wood stove, no furnace. I'm not worried, Marybeth, just curious. Country folks look out for our neighbors, so I phoned the house, but no one answered. Since you're coming for a ride, maybe you can take a look. You'll see it from the woods trail."

"Betty, Mac loves a mystery, and he is fresh out of them. See you at 10."

**

Chapter Twenty One

Tuesday October 17
Barcelona Harbor
Murphy B & B
7:30 a.m.

Marybeth's phone rang.

"Captain Murphy B & B, may I help you? Yes, this is she. Who is calling? The Coroner's office?"

Mac motioned to put it on speaker.

"Mrs. Murphy, this is Dr. Thomas Wolfe, Erie County Coroner. The New York State Police have retained me to perform a new autopsy on your husband, James Murphy. The autopsy will be performed this morning at my office in Buffalo. I know this is an emotional call for you, but please be assured that I will treat Trooper Murphy with the utmost care and respect. We will only perform those tests needed to be sure of the cause of death. The Chautauqua County Coroner who performed the original autopsy will attend. I will call you with the results as soon as we have them."

Mac said, "This is Mackenzie Morrison, Dr. Wolfe, a close friend of Mrs. Murphy's. Has the body already been disinterred?"

"Yes sir, yesterday. The cement burial vault was intact, the casket was intact, and the body was in excellent condition. I have in my possession the analysis of all the new evidence presented to the coroner's jury to reopen this case. I will use my best judgement in interpreting the medical findings with the physical evidence presented by the State Police crime lab. The autopsy will begin as soon as I end this call. We should have preliminary results by early afternoon. May I call you later?"

"Yes, please," said Marybeth, visibly shaken. "Thank you, Dr. Wolfe. Goodbye."

Mac pushed the button to end the call.

"Oh, Mac, I feel like we should be there."

"No, M, there is nothing we can do, and by the time we got there, they would already be in progress. Marybeth, Jim is in good hands. Colonel Justice personally picked this Coroner. We are going for a trail ride in the crisp morning air, so let's clean up breakfast dishes and make sure Harry is all set."

"I told him Gabby will be making lunch for the two of them."

"Great. Let's do this, M. Let's make it a special day. We'll do our trail ride and then have lunch at Moly's Cafe. You've been talking about Francesca for months, but I've never been there."

"That would be great. Francesca taught me to cook and bake, Mac. It will take my mind off Jim."

**

Tuesday October 17
Barcelona Harbor
Murphy B & B
8:30 a.m.

Mac was in the barn giving the '57 Bel Air a quick spritz and polish. Buddy and Emma were wrestling in the corner. Buddy lay on the ground while Emma jumped over him, biting at his paws, ears, and face. Buddy would take just so much and then flip her off him and put his big jaws over her head and growl playfully. Emma would cry, Buddy would release her, and she would jump back on top of him and start chewing on him all over as if to say, "Let's do it again!"

His cell phone buzzed. (*Detective Jenny Thompson.*)

"Good morning Jenny, what's up?"

"Mac, just wanted to let you know that Herman German and Sammy Smith are being arraigned this morning. The City Attorney is charging them with attempted murder and aggravated assault in the commission of a hate crime on Sol Weinstein. They are also being charged with assault on you and Martin Thomas for the bar fight."

"Glad to hear it."

"Mac, German is asking for a plea deal on the Weinstein assault. He says he acted in self-defense because Weinstein hit him first. And the video does show that, which somewhat mitigates the aggravated assault charge. Unfortunately, the video has no sound, so we do not hear him using hate speech before that.

"This is the big one. As you suspected, being charged with attempted murder got German to flip Mace Wilkins. He claims Wilkins thought up the whole intimidation scheme, provided him and Smith with the Nazi swastika shirts, and dreamed up the scam for bringing a load of copper early. He paid them $1,000 each to carry out the scheme. German said Wilkins never told them to kill Weinstein, just scare him, maybe push him around, but not to hurt him.

"But when Weinstein told them to get off his property and reached for a gun in the desk, that's when Smith blocked him, and German called Weinstein a dumb Kike. That would be hate speech. In response, Weinstein punched him. German admits he did punch Weinstein in the head multiple times, but he did not intend to kill him.

"German's attorney says her client will plead guilty to using hate speech and assault on Weinstein in return for his testimony that Wilkins hired them, paid them, provided the Nazi shirts, and told them to tell Weinstein to take the deal, meaning the offer to buy his land on the lakefront. German says Wilkins' scrap yard business was doing poorly, so he was fencing stolen metal, especially catalytic converters. He was afraid the quantities that were coming in were getting so large that he would eventually get caught. The 40 shipping containers of CATs were supposed to be his last load.

"The Boat Club was also failing because of its harbor silting up. Constant dredging was costing more than the slip rentals brought in. Wilkins was hoping that Weinstein would take their offer, Barnes would finance the private land purchase, and they could get the city to buy the portion that would become a park next to the condos. Wilkins envisioned a future where he could go walleye fishing with Billy Barnes on his boat, *Maces Mistress*, collect marina rack and dock rentals, and basically be a lazy bum."

"Well, that is big news, Jenny. Will the city attorney take the plea deal?"

"He already agreed to it. German will testify, so they will lessen his charge and let him bond out. He owns a house and will use that as collateral."

"What about Stubby Smith?"

"He had nothing to bargain with because he was not present when Wilkins hired German. German brought him along for additional intimidation, but says he never expected Smith to smash Weinstein's kidney with brass knuckles. So, Smith is still being charged with aggravated assault and participating in a hate crime. He can't raise bail, so he'll go to jail pending trial. Mac, will you stick around for the trial on the bar fight?"

"I'd rather not. I've almost wrapped up my business here and need to return to New Hampshire. I have a crew building a house for a friend and they need my supervision. Don't you have video and plenty of eyewitnesses?"

"Yes, but you are the one who pressed charges against the two of them, so we want your direct testimony. You are on the court filings."

"Martin also signed the complaint, didn't he?"

"Yes,"

"Look, Jenny, with Martin's complaint, a dozen eyewitnesses, plus the bar video, you really don't need me. If I'm here, OK, but if I'm back in New Hampshire, I don't need to drive down for that trial. German's got a bigger problem with his assault on Sol Weinstein. I got my licks in on him. I'm good."

"You certainly did. The docs aren't sure if he'll ever talk normally again. Right now, he has a high-pitched squeak for a voice, Mac."

"Good, serves him right for picking on an old man."

"Pretty severe punishment. Who gets to tally up, Morrison?"

"For my family and friends, I do."

**

Barcelona Harbor
Murphy B &B
9:00 a.m.

The Bel Air was spit-polish-perfect, and the day was warming. By the time they saddled up for the trail ride, it would be in the 50s.

Mac's phone buzzed. (*Agent Brad Fellowes.*)

"Good morning, Brad."

"Mac, has Jenny Thompson called to fill you in on the new charges against Mace Wilkins?"

"She told me about German and Smith. What are the new charges on Wilkins?"

"Conspiracy to commit a hate crime, commissioning assailants to commit the hate crime, and accessory to their assault on Sol Weinstein. He could get serious prison time. The yard manager next to Wilkins Scrap told me Wilkins has terrible judgment. As he put it, if he is given two choices, he always picks the wrong one. My concern now is I don't know what he might do next. He's unpredictable, and if he's cornered, he could be dangerous. I also wanted to let you know that we tracked his cell phone, and its last ping location was Chautauqua Lake. That's near you, isn't it?"

"Not far. I'll keep my eyes open. Anything else"

"Yes, the yard manager Max also said German would come after you for humiliating him in the bar fight. I don't know if that's true, but be advised."

"Brad, I doubt he'd be dumb enough to do that with trials pending, but I appreciate the heads up."

"A word to the wise, Mac…"

**

Dewittville, NY
Bar B Ranch
10:00 a.m.

"Marybeth, would you like to ride Zorro today?" said Betty Wilson.

"Sure! Can I?"

"Of course, but remember he likes his head in the cold weather, so let him run."

Zorro was a black stallion that only the most experienced riders could handle, but Marybeth had been riding for 30 years. Betty knew she could ride any horse in the barn.

"Mac," said Betty, "I saddled Baby for you again today. Let Marybeth lead because Zorro will not follow Baby."

"OK, Betty," said Mac.

"And Marybeth, remember to look at Caleb Mitchell's house as you ride by. I still smell wood smoke, so I'd like to know if he's there."

"I will, Betty. C'mon, slowpoke, Zorro wants to run."

"I'm coming," said Mac as he stepped unsteadily into the stirrup and swung a leg over the western saddle. Baby swung her ass around and bumped Mac's leg against the stall.

"Now Mac," said Betty, "she knows you're a greenhorn. She's testing you. She wants you to straighten up and ride with confidence. Otherwise, she's gonna scrape you off on that first big maple tree. I see you still haven't bought boots. I don't like people riding in sneakers."

"Yes, Ma'am," said Mac, "duly noted." He clucked to Baby, and she took off on a trot with Zorro already breaking into a fast canter across the big corral. Buddy raced ahead of him, barking happily.

The corral emptied into a narrow meadow with dense woods on both sides. The trail wound up and down small hills. In some sections, the overhanging branches swept their faces. Marybeth set a safe pace through the first woods, but when they broke out into the big back pasture, she let Zorro go, and he was off!

Mac let Baby set her speed. Her gallop was nowhere near as fast as Zorro's. Mac was fine with that, because he was doing the chicken dance hanging over Baby's neck with one hand on the reins and one hand on the saddle horn. He knew he looked funny, but nobody was watching, and he was damned if he was going to fall off his head! Buddy barked as he ran, laughing at his Poppa's butt bouncing up and down.

The big meadow narrowed, and soon they were back into the deep woods heading towards "Caleb's Cabin," as Betty called it. Mac had smelled wood smoke all along the trail, but it was stronger now.

The woods trail meandered to the ranch fence line, where the horses walked slowly. Marybeth stopped Zorro, turned in her saddle, and gazed at the broad lawn, barn, and farmhouse next door. Wisps of smoke tailed out of the center chimney.

"Yep, someone's here for sure, Mac."

"I'll walk over and check it out," he said.

"No need," said Marybeth. She spurred her boots, and Zorro easily jumped the fence from a standstill. They took off at a trot towards the house.

"MARYBETH!" shouted Mac, "DON'T DO THAT! COME BACK! C'mon Buddy!" he said, scrambling between the rails as Buddy scooted underneath.

"Buddy, get Marybeth, come back!"

Buddy was a white blur as he overtook Zorro and turned the horse back towards Mac.

"Mac," she said, "why did you do that? I was just going to knock..."

"And maybe get your head blown off, Marybeth. We don't know who is in that house. There is a criminal loose in this area. Why is there no car out front? Why are the curtains drawn? Why didn't they answer the phone when Betty called them?"

"Oh. I see."

"M, the barn door has high windows, but you can see inside mounted on Zorro. Walk over casually and take a peek. I'll watch the house."

Mac pulled out his phone and called Betty Wilson.

"Betty, does Caleb have guns in that house?"

"Of course, he's a hunter, but he keeps them in a locked safe, Mac." Mac hung up the call.

Marybeth cantered back across the broad lawn. Mac and Buddy watched from the fence line as she looked in the window, turned, and cantered back to him.

"There are two cars in the barn," she said.

"Could you tell what they are?"

"One is a white Cadillac SUV with an Ohio plate. The other is some old pickup truck."

"Did you get the Ohio plate number?"

"Vanity plate reads 'Mace.'"

"That's all we need. Do not go back to that house, M."

Mac hit speed dial for Brad Fellowes.

"Yes, Mac?"

"Brad, I think we have Mace Wilkins located at an old farmhouse outside Dewittville. It's on Wright Road outside the village. I'll send you the coordinates. His Caddy is in the barn, and there is smoke coming from the chimney. The curtains are drawn, so I'm pretty sure he is in there. The cabin belongs to a hunter buddy. We know there are guns in the house."

"Mac, I'm on my way back to Cleveland now. Can you get Jonetta Pope to send a Trooper to check it out? We have an arrest warrant for Wilkins, so there is authority to pick him up. And can you stay in sight of the house to make sure he doesn't leave? I'll turn around and head your way, but it's going to take me an hour to get there."

"Can do. I'll send the coordinates and call Jonetta."

Mac dialed BCI Investigator Jonetta Pope.

"Hello, Mac, what's up?"

"Jonetta, I think we have Mace Wilkins holed up in a farmhouse near Dewittville, about two miles north of the lake on Wright Road. His car is in the barn, and smoke from the chimney indicates someone is home. No one answers the landline phone. Brad Fellowes is En route from Cleveland, but it will take him an hour to get here."

"I'm in Buffalo at the Murphy autopsy, Mac, but I'll call Troop A and dispatch the closest Trooper."

"Is Andy Gregor on patrol?"

"I think it's his day off, Mac."

"That could work. He lives less than five miles from here. I'll call him."

**

Mac dialed Trooper Andy Gregor.

"Hey, Mac, what are you doing today?"

"Sitting on a guy wanted on a federal warrant. Where are you, Andy?"

"At home, where are you, Mac?"

"Wright Road, two miles from the lake outside Dewittville. Jonetta wants you to respond ASAP if you can."

"I can, but I'm not in uniform and I don't have my cruiser, Mac."

"Bring your hat and badge and get over here quick, Andy. You know the Mitchell House north of the Bar B Ranch?"

"Sure."

"That's the place. I'm watching it from the Bar B north fence line. There's a woods trail through the trees. Pull in along the fence. We can wait for the uniforms to arrive. The FBI has a federal warrant out for this guy. It's Mace Wilkins, Andy, the guy who bought Joey Minetti's boat. Jonetta called for Troopers to respond, but you're closer."

"Sit tight, Mac; I'll be there in six minutes."

**

Dewittville, NY
Caleb Mitchell's Cabin next to the Bar B Ranch
10:00 a.m.

Mace Wilkins was getting antsy. He wondered what was happening with the CATs and the Boat Club fire. He used Caleb's landline phone to call Simon. He got his secretary, and she passed him on to Attorney Long.

"Mace! What are you doing?"

"Simon, anything happening?"

"The shit just hit the fan, Mace. The Erie City Attorney cut a plea deal with Slugger German. He's giving you up, Mace. Said you masterminded the hit on old man Weinstein. I just checked. FBI and Erie PD have federal and state warrants on you for conspiracy to commit a hate crime, commissioning agents to carry out a hate crime, and accessory to German's assault on old man Weinstein. This is not just stolen CATs now, Mace; these are big federal offenses. You need to surrender to me, and I'll surrender you to Detective Jenny Thompson. If you give yourself up, we'll work this out."

"Shit!" said Wilkins. "What's the penalty for all that, Simon?"

"I don't know, but maybe we can get reduced charges on the hate crime if you plead no contest on the accessory to the assault."

"Are we talking prison?"

"For a hate crime and aggravated assault, I would say yes. The Nazi shirts were a stupid idea, Mace, really stupid. What were you thinking?"

"I was thinking I'd scare the old fuck into selling, but like everything I touch, it turned to shit. I can't go to prison, Simon. A guy like me would be dog meat inside. I can't do that. I'd rather die. My life is fucked anyway. I'd rather die than go to prison."

Mace Wilkins hung up the phone. He was all done talking to attorneys. All Simon wanted was money. He got $10,000, and now he'd want more.

Wilkins called Caleb Mitchell.

"Caleb, this is Mace Wilkins."

"Hey, Mace. My cell says you're calling from my cabin. What's up?"

"I'm taking a break from work. Decided to come up and chill out, you don't mind, do you?"

"Heck no, Mace, make yourself at home."

"Caleb, it's too early for deer season, but I'd like to do some target shooting. Could I use your guns?"

"Sure Mace. They're in the gun safe. The combination is 36 left, 5 right, 22 left."

"OK, thanks, Caleb. I'll replace the ammo before I leave."

"No problem, Mace. Maybe I can borrow your boat some weekend."

"Anytime you want it. See ya, Caleb."

**

Mace Wilkins was a coward, and he knew it. He didn't know if he had the guts to stick the gun to his head and pull the trigger, but he was going to try. It would be better than prison. He'd rather someone else did it, but there was no one else. Who do you ask to blow your head off? That's too fucking crazy. They would put you in the Loony Bin for asking that. No, he'd have to do it himself.

He worked the combo and unlocked the safe. There was an impressive armory in there. Two shotguns, a Glock 21 pistol, and a Winchester SR Bolt Action deer rifle chambered for the 6.5 Creedmoor round. Hell of a deer gun, Mace thought, picking it up.

He heard the sound of hooves nearby. That was normal since the woods trail for the Bar B was just the other side of the fence, but these sounded closer. He walked to the window. A woman on a black horse was looking through the barn door window! And there was man and a dog at the fence line watching the house! What the hell!

Just then, an old 70s square-body Chevy pickup pulled into the yard along the fence line, 100 feet from the house. A man got out wearing a flat-brimmed hat like a Trooper with a badge clipped to his shirt, but he was not in a state trooper uniform. He got out and spoke to the man with the white dog. While they were talking, he handed the man a rifle that looked like the cut-down carbine in that old 50s western TV show.[10] He'd seen the reruns in black and white.

What the hell was going on? Who knew he was here? Who were those guys? Why did they have guns? Wilkins' head was spinning. He did not know what to do.

Two State Police SUVs pulled into his driveway and parked 60 feet from the house. What was happening?

And then he knew. He could get them to kill him! Yes! He ran to the gun locker, grabbed the deer rifle and a few cartridges, and opened the door to the side porch.

"Get back!" he shouted. "Get back, or I'll shoot!"

He held up the rifle to show it off. Then he realized he hadn't even loaded it. He fumbled with the cartridges, dropping two on the porch, finally getting one in the breach and closing the bolt.

---

10   Wanted: Dead or Alive: TV western show starring Steve McQueen as bounty hunter Josh Randall. The show aired on CBS network from 1958-61. Produced by Vincent Fennelly for Four Star Productions and CBS Productions. Randall's Mare's Leg gun was a cut down Winchester model 1892 carbine in 44-40 caliber.

"I mean it; get out of here, or I'll shoot!"

The two Troopers ducked behind their vehicles and pulled their service pistols, but the sun was in their eyes, and they were 60 feet away from Wilkins with no good angle to return fire.

"Don't shoot!" Mac yelled. "Everybody, don't shoot!"

Then Andy Gregor yelled: "I'm Trooper Andy Gregor, Mr. Wilkins! Nobody wants to harm you. We have a federal warrant for your arrest. You can put your rifle down and surrender. Nobody is going to shoot you."

"Marybeth!" Mac said. "Take Zorro, go! I'll meet you back at the Bar B. Go!"

Marybeth spurred Zorro. He jumped the fence back to the woods trail, and they galloped away from the fray.

"Hold your fire!" Mac shouted. "Everybody be cool!"

"I'll shoot!" yelled Wilkins. With a 'BOOM!' he shot a round over Mac's head into the trees.

The Troopers took aim.

"Hold your fire!" Mac yelled. "Mace Wilkins, this is Mac Morrison! Joey Minetti killed my parents! Don't be like him, Mace! You've got troubles, but you're not a killer! This warrant is nothing worth dying for!"

"I don't want to live!" Wilkins sobbed as he fumbled another cartridge into the breech and slammed the bolt shut. "I want to die! My life is fucked! I'm fucked! I can't do anything right! I'm not going to prison! I'd rather die! Shoot me! Somebody shoot me!"

"Andy," said Mac placing the .44 carbine on a fence post as a tripod, "when I say go, fire a couple shots into the wall to his left. If he turns that way, I'll shoot the gun out of his hands, and Buddy can go grab him."

"Mac, you think you can?"

"Andy, I did target practice with this rifle at your house. I know I can. It's only 100 feet. Are you ready?"

"Ready."

"Go!"

'POW! POW!' Andy fired two shots into the wall behind Wilkins. It startled him. He acted like he'd been shot. He stumbled backward into the wall, holding the rifle out with his right hand while he grabbed for the wall with his left. Mac fired one .44 round. It exploded with a 'BOOM!' The heavy bullet smashed Wilkin's wooden rifle stock, and he dropped it!

"Buddy! Packem!" Mac pointed to Wilkins.

'Rowrf!' Buddy raced off, covering 100 feet in three seconds. He leaped up on the porch, grabbed Wilkins' arm, and held on, yanking him away from the shattered gun.

"Hold your fire!" Andy Gregor shouted as he and Mac raced after Buddy. They grabbed Wilkins as Buddy held him down.

"Aus Buddy, Aus!" said Mac.

Buddy let go.

"Watch'em, Buddy!" The big dog stood over Wilkins' terrified body and growled low in his throat.

"I give up," Wilkins whimpered. "Don't kill me!"

Trooper Andy snapped handcuffs on Mace Wilkins as Mac stood him up.

"Good boy, Buddy, good boy! Sit."

"Wilkins," said Mac, "you wanted to die a minute ago. You wanted someone to kill you. Now you want to live. I would say that is a step in the right direction, wouldn't you, Andy?"

"I would. All right, Mr. Wilkins, I'm going to read your rights. These Troopers will take you to Fredonia and place you in a holding cell."

"Wilkins," said Mac, "I don't like what you did to Sol Weinstein, but I had no desire to kill you. And you know something? I think maybe you might get what you need. I'm going to speak to Investigator Pope and ask that you be evaluated for mental competency."

"C'mon, Buddy," said Mac, turning on his heel and walking away, "Let's see if Baby will let me ride her back to the barn."

'Rowrf!'

**

Bemus Point, NY
Moly's Café
Overlooking Chautauqua Lake
12:00 p.m.

"Mac," said Marybeth, "I was terrified that would end badly."

"M, in war, the first shot fired is a kill shot. It's not intended to miss. But Wilkins wanted suicide by cop. His first shot was way high from 100 feet. It was intended to miss. I think he was out of his mind. Maybe he has been out of his mind for a while. He had to be crazy to think that goofy plan he drew up with that fake letter his lawyer drafted would work, but I guess he figured Sol could be fooled because of his age.

"The big risk was the two Troopers who drove directly into his driveway. I hoped they would meet up with Andy first. That was bad tactics, and it could have started a war. I just wanted everyone to hold their fire because the FBI needs to question him about his fencing operation. They couldn't do that if he were dead."

"But you shot the gun out of his hands, Mac?"

"At 100 feet, that gunstock looked bigger than a bullseye. Andy fired two high shots to startle him. He staggered back with the rifle in one hand. As he fell against the wall, I took the shot. Anyway M, we are here at the café, we have the gorgeous sweep of the lake before us, the leaves are turning red, and we are at peace again."

"Mac Morrison!" said Marybeth, "Peace is defined differently with you than for the rest of the human race. This Lone Ranger thing never ends."

"Marybeth, that incident is over. Now let's think about a special lunch on our special day. I bet this little woman rushing over must be Francesca."

"Francesca!" said Marybeth, "You never age! You look wonderful!"

"Mary B, my dear, you lie, but I love you anyway. Who is this handsome man?"

"This is *my* handsome man, Fran. I want you to meet Mackenzie 'Mac' Morrison."

"So, is this the man who saved you from the killer Minetti?"

"This is the man, Fran."

"Can I kiss him, Mary B?"

"Of course you can, Fran."

Francesca held Mac's face in her two hands and kissed both his cheeks.

"In France, we kiss a lot. We kiss hello, we kiss goodbye, but I kiss this man because he saved my precious Mary B. She is like a daughter to me. Thank you, Mackenzie, thank you for me."

"You're welcome Francesca, and please, just call me Mac."

"Mary B always came here for a special lunch after her Bar B Ranch camp. Every summer, her parents brought her here. One summer, she asked if she could work with me. I saw this pretty young girl, so full of confidence and energy, of course I said yes. How many summers did you work here, Mary B?"

"Five summers, Fran. You taught me everything about cooking and baking. Five wonderful summers, Fran."

"But then you got married and taught school and opened a B & B. I don't see you enough. You came to Pascal's funeral a year ago, but I haven't seen you since."

"How are you, Fran?" said Marybeth.

"I'm good for an old lady, Mary B."

"Francesca, you're not old."

"I'm going to be 65. That's old when you work seven days a week."

"Fran, why do you work so much? The café is successful, why such long hours? Everyone needs time off."

"It's hard to get help now, Mary B, so my kids want to close Sunday and Monday and only serve supper on Saturday night like a formal dinner. It's time to let them take over. Maybe I can do something else. Did you know my son inherited our house when Pascal died? He's not pushing me out, but his family needs the space. It would be better if they lived behind the café with me, but then I would be underfoot. I guess I need to find a new place to live and something else to do with my life."

"Hmmm," said Marybeth as she looked at Mac. She tilted her head at Francesca, raised one eyebrow and then both eyebrows as if to say, "Well?"

He rolled his eyes, nodded, and stood up.

"Think I'll go look at the desserts," he said, walking away from the table.

"Fran," said Marybeth, "sit down. I want to talk to you about my idea."

**

Mayville, NY
Lakeside Park
Overlooking Chautauqua Lake
2:30 p.m.

Mac, Marybeth, and Buddy strolled along the lazy shore of the empty beach. The park was silent because kids were in school. The only sound was a gentle lapping of the water against the sandy shore. The water was crystal clear as far out as they could see. Mayville had a sewer system, so there were no algal blooms on this side of the lake. They sat on a park bench beneath a giant maple tree whose boughs drooped low to the grass covered in yellow, orange, and flame-red leaves.

"Mac," said Marybeth, "We can't live 400 miles apart."

"I'm working on that M. I'll finish Roger's house, get a few things buttoned up in the cabin and come back."

Marybeth's phone buzzed. *Erie County Coroner calling.* She pointed to the screen and showed it to Mac. He hit the speaker button.

"Mrs. Murphy?"

"Yes."

"This is Dr. Thomas Wolfe, Erie County Coroner. Is it all right to talk now?"

"Yes, it is. Please go ahead, Dr. Wolfe."

"I have completed the autopsy on your husband, Trooper James Murphy. I have ruled his death a homicide, Mrs. Murphy. It was not accidental drowning, as initially determined. In layman's terms, I can best describe it this way. First, the amount of water in his lungs was not the cause of death. The first of several incidents that resulted in his death was a very hard blow to the head, a head trauma that by itself could have killed him. He was struck in the temple by a hard object that knocked him unconscious. I assure you he felt nothing after that. Shall I go on?"

"Yes, I want to know it all."

"We know that he was found floating in the lake, kept in an upright position due to the large life vest strapped around his chest. His head was tipped over into the water. That is how he ingested a small amount of water. If he was not already dead, he could have suffocated in that position. But he also was struck on the top of the skull with a very violent blow from a V-shaped object. This was a moving object that made a black crease along the top of his skull as it passed over him.

"We know now, which the first coroner did not know at that time, that his 17-foot boat was struck by a black 34-foot fishing boat. The State Police crime lab has conclusively proved that. The bow cleat of the big black boat dented the side of your husband's boat, and then the taller hull of the black boat slammed the side of the smaller boat. That is when your husband's head was certainly struck by the larger boat, in all likelihood by the stainless steel rub rail on the top of the gunwale. At that time, he was undoubtedly pitched overboard and then run over by the black boat.

"Lake conditions were calm that day, so the assumption that he was pitched overboard by a rogue wave or the wake of a speeding boat seems preposterous in conjunction with the head injuries also present on the body.

"The black crease on his skull was caused by being run over by the V hull of the black boat. The gel coat on his skull matches the gel coat on the boat then owned by Joseph Minetti Jr. and now named *Mace's Mistress*. It also matches the gel coat residue from the impact of the black boat to the gunwale of his 17-foot boat. All of these facts were not known at the time of the first autopsy.

"The ultimate conclusion taken from the medical evidence and the physical crime lab evidence must be that this was a homicide, and that is how I have corrected his death certificate. May I say how sad I feel to tell you this news, but I can assure you that this is the correct cause of death, as you suspected. You are to be applauded for your courage to revisit the incident and your tenacity in seeing this injustice brought to light. My deepest condolences to you, Mrs. Murphy. I will have the final autopsy report typed and submitted to the Coroner's Jury, New York State Police Colonel Samuel Justice, Investigator Jonetta Pope of Troop A, and Erie County Sheriff Lowell Buckman. I apologize on behalf of the State of New York for the erroneous conclusions from the first autopsy. Still, without all of the ancillary physical evidence, it is understandable how such conclusions could have been reached. Thank you for your patience and understanding. Do you have any questions?"

"No, I think you explained it very well. Thank you very much for your good efforts, Dr. Wolfe. Goodbye."

Marybeth slipped her cell into her pocket, turned, buried her head in Mac's chest, and sobbed. He wrapped his arms around her and held her tight for a long minute.

"Mac, it's over. It's finally over. It was so awful, but we got the truth. Now, I want to ask you for a great favor, Mac."

"Of course, anything, Marybeth."

"I would like Jim to be buried in your Morrison family cemetery on the shore of Chautauqua Lake. I can go visit him when you go to visit your parents and he will be among friends. Will you do that for me, Mac?"

"Of course I will Marybeth, of course I will. I'm going to call Morgan and let him know the autopsy results. He will act as your attorney to contact the Erie County Coroner's office and arrange for Jim's body to be sent back to a funeral home of your choice. I will grant them permission to bury him at the location you chose in the cemetery. And then it will be done right."

**

On the phone with Attorney Morgan Hillman
3:30 p.m.

"So Morgan," said Mac, "what will you do now that the coroner declared Jim's death a homicide caused by Joey Minetti's boat?"

"I will work with the State Attorney. The case will be remanded back to the Coroner's Jury and then to the Grand Jury. With Tim Riley's deposition that Joey Minetti was out on his boat at the time of Murphy's death, plus Pops Rodgers' deposition that there was a long scrape on the side of Minetti's boat when he brought it into port shortly after that, and with the State Police evidence that proves Minetti's boat was the murder weapon, I will ask for a charge of first-degree murder against Joey Minetti posthumously, and then ask the court for a directed verdict of first-degree murder, just as I did with Marybeth's parents.

"There will be no defense put up by Minetti's heirs. There wasn't the previous time, so they won't this time either. Then, I will prepare a civil damage claim against the estate of Joey Minetti. This will be the second one, since I already have one pending for Marybeth's parents. The court may merge the two.

"But before I do any of that, I'm going to give the attorney for the Minetti estate, Joe Delmonico, a courtesy call to let him know what has happened and prepare him for my next filings."

"Why warn him, Morgan?"

"I'm not warning him, Mac. It's a courtesy call, and it could save us a lot of time and effort. He may offer us a one-time deal for all damages, because I doubt the Minetti estate is worth what I will demand. It's going to be in the neighborhood of $12 million for Jim and her parents' wrongful deaths. That would be for a combined loss of income and punitive damages. In view of that, they may see it as fruitless to litigate and make us an offer. That could be best for Marybeth. We'll see. Meanwhile, you can tell Marybeth I've drafted the land lease agreement."

"Morgan, I'd like to have it reviewed by Attorney Sarah Lieberman. You picked her to be Sol's lawyer, and I like her. She's the expert on New York land use law."

"I already gave it to her Mac. The lease is both of our work, and it's airtight."

**

Tuesday October 17
6:00 p.m.
Murphy B & B
Living Room

Present: Angelo Murano, Gabriella Morrison, Mac Morrison and Marybeth Murphy

"Thank you for allowing me to come back and talk to you," Angelo said. Things are happening very fast, and I needed to update you."

"Please go ahead, Angelo," Mac said.

"Mac, Marybeth, and Gabriella, meeting you started a whirlwind of events. I'm an entrepreneur. When I see an opportunity that speaks to my heart and my head, I jump on it. You have presented me with several opportunities. So we have a lot discuss."

"First, our Barbera wine project with Gabriella. I have verbally agreed to lease space on 200 of Mr. Reasoner's organic vines for grafting. And he will also plant an additional 200 Barbera cuttings to establish new rootstock vines. That will mean two new rows in his vineyard, taking up 1/6 of an acre. It's a modest land commitment. My cousin will send me the Barbera cuttings in spring. When mature, the 200 new vines should yield about 800 bottles of wine. "That's not enough to be a viable business, but it would be a very good first test to see which establishes itself quicker and is hardier, the grafts or rootstock plantings.

"Gabriella will be responsible for the project. She will help plant and graft the vines. Mr. Reasoner's staff will tend the vines, and Gabriella will visit regularly to see how they are doing. Reasoner will teach Gabriella how to make the wine in the fall. If we are lucky, we may have some grapes to make wine within five years. If we do, Reasoner gets 1/3. Gabriella and I get 2/3. Gabriella will market our wines as *Appellation Chautauqua, Murano-Morrison, Barbera Americana*."

Angelo said, "Does that sound like a plan? Is that a fair division?"

Mac looked at Gabriella. She nodded.

"So far, so good, Angelo," Mac said. "What's next?"

"I'm going to buy Banks Breakers and Scrap Yard. I met with Sol Weinstein and his lawyer Sarah, and we have agreed to terms. Attorney Lieberman had the land appraised for $5 million if it were used as described on Wilkins' fake land use plan. So, I offered him $5 million.

"But Sol doesn't want me to pay him five million because of taxes. He wants me to pay him $4 million for four acres. The entire scrap yard is included, except one lakefront acre around the old house. He will donate that one acre to the city of Erie for use only as a public park.

"Since he inherited the property 52 years ago, the value will be his basis, which is $500,000. So, he will have a capital gain of $3.5 million, and the 20% tax will be $700,000. The one-acre waterfront land donation should easily be valued at $1 million, offsetting his capital gain, and he will have a credit to carry over.

"Martin and the Banks staff will carry on. Martin gets a 10% ownership stake plus a salary increase. He will run the whole operation.

"OK," said Angelo, "here is where Sol wants your approval, Marybeth. He will move into one of your cottages once Mac builds it next year."

"We were hoping that, Angelo," said Marybeth. "Good for Sol; something to look forward to."

Angelo continued: "There is a 19-acre parcel of land adjacent to your property on the side, Marybeth. It has 17 acres of mature Concord grape vines plus a new 5,000 square foot shell building that looks like a barn but was built to be a winery."

"The Inglefinger property," said Marybeth.

"Correct. He is a hedge fund manager from New York City who bought the 19 acres of vines and built the shell of a building as a hobby. He has a summer house on Chautauqua, so his idea was to graft California grapes to make fine table wine and oversee the work while on vacation. He had no idea how complicated and time-consuming this would be. By the time he got the winery building built, he had discovered how much work and investment would be involved for a modest return, and he lost interest in the project. So he put it on the market, at a loss, for $319,000, but he has had no takers.

"Sol has a building filled with scrap copper he has been hoarding for 50 years. He estimates it contains five rail cars of copper. He will sell me the copper at the best price published nationally, which should be well over $300,000. He will take the cash from the copper sale and buy the Inglefinger property. His lawyer has already made a full-price offer subject to your approvals, Mac and Marybeth."

"Our approval?" Marybeth and Mac said together.

"Mac, Sol wants you to put in a foundation for his blue steel building next to the proposed winery on the 19 acres, which is a short walk from Marybeth's B & B. I will pay to move his blue steel building onto that site. Sol wants you to set up a complete auto restoration shop in the blue building."

"OK so far, Angelo," said Mac.

"OK, now comes the big idea and the big ask, Mac. Sol wants you to set up a 1950s classic car museum in the winery and move the fifty cars in his collection into it for display while they await restoration. He also wants you to establish a program to teach interested local high school students the skills to restore classic cars. He would like you to oversee it, be involved as much as you would like, and have time to do so.

"Sol will fund the program. He wants to be able to walk over from his cottage and watch the cars come back to life and be made beautiful. Remember, he has owned some of these cars for 60 years, so they are his family. The students who graduate from the program will hopefully go to work in the classic car restoration field, perhaps in his shop.

"Of course, he expects to pay you for your work, and you can pick one of his cars that you would like to restore for yourself. But the very first car to be restored will be..."

"The copper '57 Chevy," said Mac.

"Correct, "said Angelo. "I will pay for its restoration if you will do the work, Mac. And I will lend that car to the museum for Sol's use as long as he lives. I will drive it when I am here in town.

"Now Marybeth, Sol would like to lease you the 17 acres of vineyards for $1 per year and gift them to you upon his passing. They are to be used as vineyards while he is alive. I would hope that our wine making experiment succeeds and that those 17 acres would make a vineyard for Barbera grapes, and we could partner the winemaking.

"Attorney Sarah Lieberman has participated in all of these discussions, which obviously have happened very quickly, but time is of the essence with Sol's age and his injuries. He wanted to move fast, and so did I. So, this is my dream. Together, we can make it happen. Gabriella, Mac, and Marybeth, what do you say?"

"Wow!" said Gabriella.

"Wow!" said Marybeth.

"Wow!" said Mac.

No one said anything for a moment.

"This is a lot to take in, Angelo," said Mac. "And it is asking a big commitment of my time. I have a building business in New Hampshire, plus a building commitment to Marybeth for the spring, so I need to think about this. I like the overall deal, but we need to think about how this would affect our lives, Marybeth's, Gabby's, and mine. So, let us talk it over. I need to make a couple of phone calls, and then we'll let you know tomorrow, OK?"

**

Tuesday October 17
7:30 p.m.

Mac made the first call to Tim Riley. He answered right away.

"Hello, Mac, what's up?'

"Tim, are you fully retired now?"

"Do you mean do I have a job? I don't have a job, Mac. Why do you ask?"

"How would you feel about helping me and another friend teach high school students to restore classic cars? It would be part-time, as much as you wanted to participate, and it would pay you something. I can't promise how much at this time. And it would be here in Barcelona Harbor, just five minutes from your house and next to fishing on Lake Erie in Marybeth's boat, Tim."

"If I get to work with you, kids, and classic cars, I'm in, even if it's as a volunteer, Mac."

"Good Tim, I was hoping you would say that. I'll tell you more in the next few days. Right now, I am putting together a team. Thanks for joining us."

**Tuesday October 17
8:00 p.m.**

Juan Johnson answered the third ring.

"Hello, Mac. Are you in town?"

"I am Juan, and I was going to come see you tomorrow morning. Will you be at work?"

"Unless the world ends tonight. What's up, Mac?"

"Juan, I know you got your 20 in the Army. You're a little older than me, right?"

"I'm 56, Mac."

"Did you already start your pension?"

"No, my body shop pays me enough that I don't need it yet, and I get more if I wait. Why do you ask?"

"I want you to ponder two questions overnight: How much longer do you want to do what you are doing? And what would you like to do if you had your choice? I'll see you first thing tomorrow, Juan."

Chapter Twenty Two

Wednesday October 18
Johnson's Auto Body shop
Jamestown, NY
8:00 a.m.

Buddy jumped out of the baby blue Bel Air and ran to Juan Johnson. He whapped his leg with his tail, circled him, sat, and offered his paw.

"Juan," said Mac, "that is the biggest hello Buddy can give, and you just got it."

"Mac, you had me awake half the night. Get yourself a cup of coffee, and we'll talk."

Juan Johnson was a tall black man, a retired Army Captain widowed for two years, and now dating BCI Investigator Jonetta Pope. Mac had introduced them during his murder investigations last spring. He was impressive in a dignified, capable way. You just knew he could hold up his end of the bargain, whatever the bargain might be. And his deep "Barry White."[11] voice underlined his demeanor.

Juan pointed to a car on the rack.

"Mac, this VW Jetta is typical of what I work on: boring looks, dull performance, but adequate transportation. People lease them because they have cheap deals. They get rid of them at lease end, so they are cheap used cars for folks who can't afford better. Sort of a modern-day Model T.

"Many cars are like that now, especially the uni-body front-drive cars. Disposable. Without a frame, you're driving a tin can. In a front-end collision, there's often too much damage to make it worth fixing, so these cars usually get scrapped. This one here is light damage, and since it is two years old and leased, it has to get repaired before the guy turns it back in.

"This is the kind of car I get to work on today, but there's no joy in it. I would enjoy my work and make more money if I had more restoration work.

---

11   Barry White- Black American singer songwriter, and two time Grammy award winner with a sexy bass voice.

This Jetta kind of job, the insurance company knows how much they will pay and that's it. So it's a cut-throat job.

"Now, if someone brings me a car like your '57 Bel Air and they want a complete body restoration and paint job, then I'm working on a piece of art. I can charge my time and materials, make some money, and enjoy bringing an old classic back to life.

"What I'm saying is my job is not very fulfilling. When I got out of the service fourteen years ago, we still had a lot of old school cars with style and substance coming into the shop. Now, they all have plastic bumpers, plastic grilles, and sheet metal so thin you can dent it with your thumb.

"So now, Mac, now you go and disrupt my existence by asking me how much longer do I want to do what I'm doing? And then you want to know what I would like to be doing. I think I just told you, man, but I still have to pay the bills."

"Juan, I'm gonna make you a pitch that could improve your life. Let's walk over to my Bel Air and you hear me out."

**

Wednesday October 18
Erie, PA
Bricker's Bail Bonds
10:00 a.m.

George "Bull" Bricker accepted Herman German's house deed as collateral for his $50,000 bail and posted the bond for his release. Within an hour, Herman "Slugger" German was a free man wearing an ankle monitor that chafed his leg.

He went to the Clerk of Courts office and got the paperwork filed in the bar fight case. He read the names of the complainants, and their listed local addresses. Then he caught a half-hour Uber ride home to Ashtabula, Ohio, got his angle grinder and cut off the ankle monitor.

He showered, changed clothes, and packed a small bag of belongings. He went down to his basement, found a one-foot section of iron rebar, and slid it into his cargo pants side pocket. He removed the SIM card from his cell phone, smashed it with a hammer, and flushed the bits down the toilet. Last, he stuck his two-barrel derringer in the left pocket of his canvas jacket and put his Beretta 25A seven-round pocket pistol in the right pocket.

He got in his old Dodge pickup, drove to his bank and cleaned out his account. He tossed his cell phone in a gas station trash can, and drove to a bar for a steak sandwich and several beers. Then he headed for Barcelona Harbor.

**

Wednesday October 18
Samuels Funeral Home, Westfield, NY
11:00 a.m.

Ronald Samuels was a third-generation funeral director. He knew proper etiquette. He knew the decorum of the dead, but he had never reburied one of his "clients." Trooper James Murphy's body had been delivered back to him in the casket he had placed him in two years prior. The casket lining was stained, the exterior was scratched, and mud-splattered. It was a mess, and he would not allow such a travesty.

He removed the body, had his staff reline the casket, and installed a new satin pillow. The State Police had provided a new uniform for Trooper Murphy and he dressed him properly. The casket was going to be closed, but he would take pictures for the widow Murphy if she wanted to see them.

His staff cleaned the casket's exterior, touched up the scratch marks, sprayed a new coat of clear polyurethane over it, and polished the brass rails. When they were done, it looked as good as new.

Ronald made a phone call to a Mr. Mackenzie Morrison to request permission to open a new grave at his family cemetery in Dewittville. Permission was given. They would meet at the cemetery to select the grave location. The grave was to be hand-dug because of the age of the surrounding plots. The diggers would begin the following day. A protective canopy would be placed over the grave. There would be no advertisement of the burial. It would be friends and family only, on Friday. The weather forecast was still good. Indian summer continued with crisp mornings but mild afternoons.

It was the best time of year for a burial. The changing seasons signaled an end to the year, and people were more accepting of the loss. Spring was the worst time of the year, especially if the body had been stored over the winter until the ground thawed. It would be muddy. With life being renewed in nature, many people were devastated by the loss in spring. It was a reminder that death could catch you at any time when you weren't looking.

Ronald didn't think he was fatalistic, just practical. Death was the end of life, and we all had to meet it. Some took it better than others, but for Ronald it was all in a day's work.

But this burial was different, he had to admit: a second burial, and in a different grave. That was different, for sure. And the flowers! This Mr. Morrison, whoever he must be, certainly had bought out every florist within twenty miles. They were all busy making arrangements and hustling to get them to the cemetery by Friday morning. It seemed like there were going to be six van loads of flowers.

Ronald had been a funeral director for more than 30 years, but he had never done a burial in this Morrison private cemetery by the lake. The newest stone markers were for Shaun and Claudia Morrison way back in 1983. He noticed how clean and polished they were when he went to see the cemetery. Someone must still care, he thought. Good that people still care.

Ronald made sure the body was embalmed correctly after the coroner was done with it, then he dressed it in his uniform, and now all was ready for Friday. It was going to be a perfect day for a burial.

**

Wednesday October 18
Barcelona Harbor Pier
3:00 p.m.

The ten-year-old gray pickup had seen better days. It was a Dodge, and they all rusted, Slugger didn't know why. Especially in this part of the country with its wet snow and salted roads, you could tell a Dodge truck from 100 feet away because of the rust. What was the matter with Dodge that they never fixed that, he wondered? Fords and Chevys didn't rust nearly as bad, and neither did Toyotas.

But the old Dodge 5.7 liter V8 had 395 horsepower, and that was a great engine. Slugger appreciated that. The body might be rusty, but the engine was trusty; that's what he always said about his Dodge. He bought it after his last pro-fight. He made a good purse on that one and he paid cash for the truck, and paid off his house. He was 29 for that last fight. Then he lost his license. Truth be told, he had also lost a step, and his jab wasn't as good as it had been when he was 25.

But that was all water over the dam now. If he was convicted in court, he was going to go to prison, maybe for a long while. His voice was gone, and maybe it would never come back, the Docs told him. He squeaked like a mouse, a hell of a thing for a big man like him. And he wheezed. With his deviated septum, he already had trouble breathing, and now it was even harder. He wheezed to breathe through his mouth and squeaked when he spoke. If he squeaked in prison, some son of a bitch would surely make fun of him, and then he'd have to fight him and pound him into the ground. But there would be another tougher guy wanting to take him on. It would never end. And it was all because of Mace Wilkins and this guy Morrison who clocked him in the bar and filed the complaint.

That fuckin' Wilkins had gotten him into all this trouble, but he had gotten himself into it even worse. Slugger had made sure of that. He'd told the cops all about how Wilkins had hired him and Stubby, bought them those Nazi shirts, paid them to go rough up the old man. Looking back at it, he should have known better. It was a stupid idea, but he wanted the money, and so did Stubby.

If only the old man hadn't punched his balls! That was a rule in boxing, everyone knew that! He had to hit him back! Something just snapped in his head, and he couldn't stop.

No, he wasn't going to prison, because he wasn't going to court. He was going to get even with the Morrison guy and then disappear. And he knew just how to do it. He'd go to Cleveland, where one of Mace Wilkins' guys would sell him fake ID, give him a couple bucks for his truck and sell him some POS hooptie that ran good with fake papers to match his new ID. It would cost a few grand, but he had the cash in his stash. He would become that guy, hit the road and start over somewhere else far away. He could always get a job using his muscles. He'd heard that they were looking for loggers in Oregon. It would be a long drive, but he'd cleared out his bank account and had plenty of cash for a while.

Yes, he was gonna watch this guy Morrison in this big old house. He was gonna pick a time to beat hell out of him, make him squeak like a mouse, and then head out of town and start over far away. But the guy was tricky, and he could fight. Slugger had learned that, so he had his guns just in case.

The more he thought about it, he decided he should just kill him, and that way, he could never file another complaint.

So, Slugger slouched down in his old gray Dodge pickup and watched the Murphy B & B for a sign of the big man that had put him on the floor in Ricky's bar. That was a lucky punch, and that guy had set him up. Payback would be a bitch. He was looking forward to slamming that iron bar against *his* throat.

He had a thermos of hot coffee and a good submarine sandwich from Todd's Gas N Go. He could stay here all day and again tomorrow if he had to. He was going to pick the right moment and then strike.

**

Wednesday October 18
Barcelona Harbor
Murphy B & B
4:00 p.m.

Mac, Marybeth, Gabriella, and Buddy piled into the baby blue '57 Chevy Bel Air. The big 383 Stroker V8 and its 450 horsepower engine effortlessly sidled down the gravel driveway and out onto the nearly deserted Route 5 along Lake Erie. There were three dozen trucks in the Harbor Pier parking lot, all of them attached to boat trailers. All except one: a rusty gray Dodge pickup. The little camera in Mac's subconscious took a snapshot and tucked it away in his brain for future recall. Mac's frontal lobe was busy driving, but his warrior brain had registered a potential threat. It just had not notified him of it. Not yet.

The four of them were headed to Angelo Murano's big house at Bemus Point. Their collective answer was going to be yes, but a very qualified yes. Mac was too independent to be held to a schedule or to feel like an employee. He would help build and direct the restoration of Sol's cars, but it wasn't going to derail his life. So he had a counteroffer, and Marybeth and Gabby did, too.

It would be interesting.

Way back, too far back for him to notice, an old rusty Dodge pickup truck was following the Bel Air. Heck, you couldn't miss the baby blue '57 with those big tail fins and that white convertible top. Slugger could spot it a mile away. The gray Dodge, on the other hand, looked just like a hundred other farm trucks in Chautauqua County. All of them mud-splattered, and most of them rusty.

Angelo Murano's house could actually be called a mansion. Built in the 1920s in an overdone ornate stone and brick style, it was grand in every sense. Of course, it bordered the lake with an expansive view over green lawns, that was a given. But what took Mac's breath away was the intricate woodwork and fine craftsmanship inside the many huge rooms, all of which had been perfectly preserved.

It was not a summer cottage; it was more like an elegant mausoleum, too big for one man to rattle around in, as Angelo had described it. And he was right.

"Angelo," said Mac, "I won't ask what you paid, but I can tell you, to build this house today would easily cost $10 million dollars."

"Mac, it was a foolish purchase, done for my socialite wife. She loved it for about a year, but it's too big for the two of us, and our kids are too old for summers at Chautauqua. That's why I just listed it for $4 million. The agent already has several people interested. Anytime a property on the lake comes up, some sucker like me is always ready with the cash. I'm keeping the half-acre waterfront lot with the small guest cottage. I can live in that and be perfectly happy when I'm here."

"Well," said Mac, "let's talk about your proposals, Angelo."

"First, Gabriella is excited to do the Barbera wine with you and farmer Reasoner in LeRoy. She is willing to put the effort into it. But as her Dad, I have to intervene. Regardless of the outcome, she needs to be compensated for her time because that project may not make any money for five years. In the meantime, she could be spending thousands of hours planting, grafting, tending vines, making the wine, and marketing it.

"Angelo, you are investing some money to lease 1/6 of an acre from Reasoner. That is not costing you much. And you are paying for 200 grafts and 200 vines imported from your cousin in Italy. My guess is all of that will cost you less than ten thousand dollars. You are putting a little time into the project but will get 1/3 of the wine profit, if there is any."

"I'd say that's a fair estimate of her time and my costs," Angelo replied. "Mac, as her Dad, what are you telling me?"

"Gabriella needs a stipend, Angelo."

"I agree, Mac. How much do you suggest?"

"Fifty thousand the first year, to be adjusted annually as agreed by the two of you. That will barely cover her living expenses, even with free housing provided by Marybeth."

"That's fair," said Angelo. "I'll pay her $4,200 a month as an independent subcontractor who pays her own withholdings."

"Are you good with that, Gabby?" asked Mac.

She nodded.

"OK. Next is Sol's $1/year lease of 17 acres of vineyard to Marybeth for her continued use as a vineyard during Sol's life, and the donation of that land to her after his passing."

Marybeth said, "It's a very generous offer, and I accept, Angelo. Angelo, if your first year grafts do well at Reasoner's in LeRoy, I would be interested to do Barbera grafts on the 17 acres with you and Gabby. We would work out the profit sharing with you based on your actual involvement at that time. If Gabriella does all the work, she will get the majority of the profit. Do you agree?"

"That's fair," said Angelo.

"Now," said Mac, "Sol's museum is a challenge, but doable. First of all, I am elated that Sol wants to move his blue steel building from Erie to the winery building next door. I know the blue building can be disassembled, removed, and reassembled by a good rigging contractor in a matter of a few weeks. But can I get a good rigger before winter? I hope I can get a good local contractor to do a concrete slab before winter, but it's not just the slab; we also have to run underground utilities, I have to submit a site plan, and get permits.

"I already checked the zoning, and it's Rural. The auto restoration shop and car museum would be permitted. In fact, the Town would be happy to have a tourist attraction at the Harbor because now it's mostly all about the boat ramp, the pier, and fishing. And I'm happy to set up an auto restoration shop in the relocated blue steel building because mine burned last spring.

"But I must get inside that new Inglefinger winery building to see what it needs before we can move cars in. Does it have wiring? Are the walls finished? Is there heat? I don't know. It makes no sense to move Sol's cars in before the building is ready.

"OK," Mac continued, "the most complicated part is Sol's cars. There are 50 of them. All of them are original condition. Most of them do not run, but none of them are rusty, which is a huge plus. I do not believe Sol wants them all perfectly restored. I think he wants most of them renovated but kept original. But the paint, even if it is faded, can often be restored with modern chemicals and a lot of wet sanding and buffing. And those kinds of jobs are perfect for high school students to help with.

"Angelo, Marybeth and I are meeting with Dr. Small, the principal at Mayville High School. We would like you to join us. Dr. Small was the principal at Westfield when Marybeth attended 30 years ago, and she knows him well. We will see if he would be interested in setting up Sol's dream of a shop class to teach high school students how to restore classic cars. We are talking about all of the skills: mechanical, metal fab, body, and paint. If he is interested, we have to discuss getting it in their budget and funded."

"Mac," said Angelo, "If you will oversee the work, I will fund the restoration of the 1957 copper Chevy Bel Air convertible. Sol agrees. I want it to be a resto-mod just like yours, Mac. So you don't need to worry about getting a budget from the school. I am willing to fund additional cars with Sol."

"OK, Angelo," said Mac, "that's great. We'll keep it simple. This could be done on a car-by-car basis. The goal should be 2-3 cars per year. Some work will have to be subcontracted out. I am assembling a team of myself as project lead and mechanical specialist, Juan Johnson of Johnson Auto body in Jamestown as body and paint, and Tim Riley as an assistant. Tim is a retired BMV salvage vehicle inspector and a car guy. Does that sound like a plan, Angelo?"

"Yes, let's do it. That is another reason I am selling this big house: to liberate the $4 million dollars. A chunk of that will go towards the purchase of the Bank's Yard from Sol, and another chunk is going into accounts to fund the Barbera wine project, the '57 Chevy resto-mod, and the high school shop class for restoring classic cars."

"Angelo, I think this is the beginning of a beautiful relationship," said Mac.

"Me too," said Marybeth.

"I agree," said Gabriella,

'Rowrf,' said Buddy.

**

Philip C. Laurien

Wednesday October 18
Bemus Point, Chautauqua Lake
5:30 p.m.

Slugger German had parked his Dodge pickup in a restaurant lot by the old Stow ferry landing. But he could not see the driveway of the big house from there, so he walked to the corner of Main, bought a coffee, and sat at an outdoor table, watching.

He feared he might have missed them because they had been out of sight for so long. So he trotted back to his truck to move it to a parking lot in the downtown. He turned the corner and was heading south on Main Street when, there was the blue Bel Air, turning out right in front of him!

He slammed on his brakes and let it pass in the opposite direction. He flipped on his blinker and pulled into a side street, did a U-turn and crept back to the intersection and looked north. The Bel Air was far enough away that he could turn and follow it.

In the Bel Air, Marybeth and Gabby were chatting in the back seat. Buddy swiveled his head and growled when he saw the gray pickup truck behind him. Mac glanced in his rearview mirror. The Cro-Magnon part of his brain took another snapshot as the truck turned onto a side street. It stored the picture for future recall.

The Bel Air turned right on Center Street and left onto SR 430. They were heading north, probably going back to the Harbor, Slugger guessed. He eased onto SR 430, held back to stay out of sight, and the old Dodge resumed its cat-and-mouse game.

SR 430 was a better road for following because it narrowed as it went north, and the sides were tree-lined. With the autumn colors and leaves falling, Slugger felt sure there was too much beautiful scenery for the people in the Bel Air to be watching their rearview mirror. He felt confident he had not been spotted so far. But SR 430 was straight as an arrow, so he had to continually hold back.

They drove for several miles. Slugger was starting to get too confident. When he rounded a curve at the Dewittville Post Office, the blue Bel Air was out of sight! There was a double 'S' curve through there. Maybe he got too far ahead, Slugger wondered. Or perhaps he turned onto the side road. What to do?

He stomped on the gas, and his powerful engine leaped the truck ahead. He could still catch them if they were on this road. He rounded the second big curve and sped up even more. A half-mile went by too quickly, and no Bel Air. He was about to turn back when he hit a straightaway and - there it was, in the distance! He hustled ahead, eager to catch up.

Another mile passed, and then he saw the Bel Air's blinker light. It turned left and headed for Chautauqua Lake down a little residential road. He followed. He crossed a narrow power line right of way through the dense trees and found himself on a shoreline street that just served modest cottages.

The street was heavily wooded, but he could see the Bel Air at the dead end. He took a chance and pulled into a cottage driveway, hoping the place was empty. It was. He parked on the grass behind the cottage and walked down the narrow road to the end. He stood behind a tree, watching.

There was the big guy Morrison with two women and a white dog. They were talking to a thin man in a black suit. A black hearse was parked in the middle of the vacant lot where they were talking. Morrison walked down to the water's edge while the older of the two women pointed to a spot on the ground. The man in black took some stakes and tapped them into the ground. He shook the woman's hand. Morrison came back from the water's edge, and the group turned towards the Bel Air.

Slugger hustled to get out of sight. In a minute, the blue Bel Air drove past and back to Route 430. This time, Slugger did not follow. He knew where they were going. He wanted to see what the man in black was doing, the man with the hearse.

"Hi!" said Slugger in a slouchy sort of way, trying to conceal his true size as he walked onto the vacant lot. "Whatcha doin?"

"Oh, hello," said the man in the black suit, turning around to see who was speaking to him. "Just staking out a grave."

"A grave?" said Slugger.

"Yes, there's going to be a burial here Friday. My diggers are coming tomorrow. Do you live in the neighborhood?"

"Yeah, just down the street. Can't say I recall anyone ever bein' buried here."

"No, maybe not," said the man in black. "The last time was 1983. I've never had a burial here before. Kind of peaceful by the water."

"Sure is. What time is the burial?"

"Ten a.m., but it's just friends and family."

"Oh, I wasn't gonna come and look," said Slugger. "That would be impolite. I was just curious, is all. Good talkin' to you, mister."

Slugger turned on his heel and walked back to his truck. Friends and family. That would mean too many witnesses. He still needed a way to get Morrison alone. He would have to keep following him.

**

Chapter Twenty Three

Thursday October 19
Mayville High School
9:00 a.m.

"Dr. Small, thank you for taking the time to meet with us," said Marybeth. "I'd like to introduce you to my good friends Mackenzie Morrison and Angelo Murano."

"I believe I have read of some of Mr. Morrison's exploits here in Chautauqua County," said Dr. Small. Like his name, he was short in stature but with an elegant salt-and-pepper beard that pointed down to his vested suit. "Seems like a good man to have on your side when there's trouble. And Mr. Murano has donated generously to this school before, although I have never had the pleasure of meeting him personally. Very pleased to meet you both. What can I do for you folks?"

Marybeth said, "Dr. Small, it's not what you can do for us, it's what Mac and Angelo can do for your students is what we came to discuss."

"Really? I'm all ears, folks."

**

Thursday October 19
Mayville High School
10:00 a.m.

"OK," said Marybeth, "that went well, don't you guys think?"

"Really couldn't have asked for more," said Mac. "Dr. Small will make an announcement that student internships are available for six students next summer to learn how to restore classic cars. Students will be eligible for extra hours towards graduation if they are already enrolled in the auto shop classes. Students who pass two semesters of auto restoration class at Sol's shop can get paid for summer internships. That's perfect."

"Sol will be very pleased, Mac," said Angelo.

"Yeah, now all I have to do is finish two houses in New Hampshire, get a foundation and utilities installed here, move a building, set up a shop and a museum, and build two cottages before next summer! Holy crap!"

"Mac," said Marybeth, "you can do it. I know you can. You've got your four-man crew in New Hampshire. Bring them down here after you finish Roger's house. And you don't need to finish our cabin right away."

"Well, I know one thing I'm going to do. I'm going to hire the local Amish to frame the cottages. They'll prebuild the exterior walls in their shop and deliver them stacked flat on a truck with the trusses and metal roofing. They can put up one cottage frame per day, and my crew of five can finish each cottage in two weeks. That means if we can get slabs and underground utilities done in early April, I can have two cottages finished by early May for Pops and Sol. I'll get the winery building ready to move cars and get the blue building moved before Christmas. It's going to be fun!"

"And just think how much fun it will be for Harry, Sol, and Pops to walk next door and watch the auto restoration being done," said Marybeth. You just have to stay healthy, Mac!"

"Well, the best thing Dr. Small did was give me a list of reputable contractors who work for the schools. I'm going to make some calls. And I've got an appointment with a surveyor to go over the site plan for both the cottages and the blue steel building."

"What's for lunch, Marybeth?" said Angelo. "We're starving!"

"Moly's Café!"

**

Jamestown, NY
Perkins Surveyors and Engineers
1:30 p.m.

Jessica Perkins was both a licensed surveyor and civil engineer, and she was cute to boot, Mac thought. He looked at her diplomas on the wall and figured her to be mid-thirties, which meant she had ten years of experience.

She also had testimonial letters and awards on her "brag wall" from reputable firms like the D.O.T. If she could do work for the Thruway Authority, she was the right one for his project.

"So, Jessica," said Mac, "would you have time to do the Inglefinger site plan this fall?"

"Yes. We did the winery's boundary survey and grading plan, so I have a good base map and elevations. Since you are simply relocating a steel building onto that site, all we have to do is engineer the sanitary sewer. Storm drainage will go to the farm pond on site. The revised grading plan is basic and done in CAD, so it is not a problem. I can squeeze that work in early November. It will take me a week to do it."

"I need to get inside the winery barn. Have you been in it?"

"Yes. We did a post-construction interior floor plan because it had changed from the original. It's just one huge room with a commercial kitchen at one end. It had been planned to be divided into processing, storage, and tasting rooms, plus the office and sales room, but they never got that far. I have a key if you'd like to let yourself in. I heard from the realtor, so I know that Mr. Weinstein has made a generous deposit through his attorney. She signed a sales contract for him, so you have the right to enter as his agent."

"Great. I'll do that on my way home. It sits next to Marybeth's barn. It will be convenient to walk next door and check it out."

"OK, Mac, speaking of Marybeth's property, it needs a perimeter survey and topo for the cottage site plan. My survey crew is booked for the next month but we can do it by Thanksgiving. Does that work?"

"Yes. The cottages are a spring project, so we have all winter to get permits. But I hope the blue steel building can be moved before Christmas. I know you may get snow before then, but if I can get the plan engineered and the slab and underground utilities in, the rigger can move the building in snowy weather. Do you know a good contractor for those tasks?"

"Yes, John Higgins. I'll get you his contacts. He can do the site work, the underground utilities, and the slab. And he will pull your permits from the town once I get the site plan done. If you tell him I referred you, I think you can plan on breaking ground before Thanksgiving. It's been a slow restart to the construction business around here post-pandemic. A lot of projects got canceled because businesses went under. So, he'll be glad of a good job like this."

"Perfect. Jessica, I'm so glad I met you. I look forward to doing more business with you."

**

Philip C. Laurien

Jamestown, NY
Main Street
Outside Perkins Surveyors and Engineers
2:30 p.m.

The gray Dodge pickup was carefully concealed among a line of cars across from Perkins Survey, two blocks north of the Lucile Ball-Desi Arnez Museum. Everybody knew Lucille Ball, thought Slugger, but who knew her museum was in Jamestown, New York? Too bad he would probably never see it now, he thought. After he took care of Morrison he had to be gone, and quick. While he waited for Morrison to come out of the surveyor's office, he took the opportunity to steal a license plate off another gray Dodge pickup the same age as his and just as rusty. With four soft tires and backed into a stall against a gas station, it looked like it hadn't moved in a long time. Slugger tucked the plate under his front seat and continued to wait.

It was just Morrison who came out of the office. No one was with him this time. And he didn't see the big white dog either. Perfect. Now, if he could just get Morrison alone, he'd take care of business and get out of town. Too bad about the house; he'd lose that by skipping bail. But the bondsman wouldn't look hard to find him because the house was worth more than the bond, so the guy would make money through forfeiture. Owning a house was a pain in the ass anyway, thought Slugger. Property taxes, yard to mow, something always needing fixing. Naw, he was glad to be getting out of town while he still could. Most bars didn't want to serve him, the scrap yard would be closing with Wilkins in jail, and the boat club was a mud hole, so that was done, too.

He was going to enjoy a road trip to Oregon. After he took care of Morrison, he'd cross over into Ohio, buy his ID papers, swap cars, and head west. Working for Mace Wilkins had some benefits, and knowing his crooked network was one of them.

The baby blue Bel Air turned left on one-way West 6th Street. Slugger followed at a respectable distance. They passed a city park with colorful maple trees. Slugger was wondering if they had maple trees in Oregon. The Bel Air continued straight across the Chadakoin River Bridge and soon they were in the leafy outskirts of old Jamestown West. Once past toney Lakewood on SR 394, they were headed along the south side of Chautauqua Lake. The road would bend northwest as they approached Stow, Chautauqua, and Mayville. Slugger had driven around the lake many times deer hunting, so he knew these roads well. It was a shame he would never drive them again after today, but he was not going to court or prison. He had a job to do and then it was *Oregon here I come*!

**

Jamestown, NY
Leaving Perkins Surveyors and Engineers
2:30 p.m.

Mac noticed the old gray pickup because it was parked in a line of cars that were all facing Main Street, but it had backed in. Someone was sitting in it looking out the side view mirror. Mac's unevolved 40,000-year-old Cro-Magnon brain cells identified the oddity as not being like all the others and worthy of a second look. The second look identified it as an Ohio truck from its license plate.

Jamestown, New York, is on the Pennsylvania border, and from there, it's only 44 miles along Lake Erie to the Ohio border, so an Ohio plate was not unusual. But, an Ohio truck backed into its stall in downtown Jamestown on a Wednesday afternoon with its driver watching him in its sideview mirror *was* unusual. He would keep an eye on it to see if it moved with him.

And it did.

Mac turned left on West 6th Street. The gray Dodge turned with him but held back a distance. They passed a city park with colorful maple trees. The Bel Air continued straight toward the bridge.

His phone buzzed as he crossed over the Chadakoin River. It was linked to his radio, and the screen read *Detective Jenny Thompson* calling.

"Hello Jenny, what's up?"

"Mac, just wanted to let you know, Slugger Herman German bonded out of jail this morning. His cell mate said all he talked about, I should say squeaked about, was getting even with you. I heard it through the jail grapevine and decided to take a uniform officer and visit his house in Ashtabula. He wasn't there, his truck wasn't there, and his ankle monitor was cut off and in pieces. So, he's violated his bail bond and is in the wind. I'm looking for him."

"What kind of truck does he drive, Jenny?"

"It's a 2013 Dodge 1500 pickup, gray in color. Why do you ask?"

"He's three blocks behind me. He's been tailing me all day and is closing in."

"Mac, you know the guy is dangerous. I don't know if he's armed, so be careful."

"I always am, Jenny. Thanks for the warning."

**

Mac's next call was to Roger Lemonier in New Hampshire.

"Rog, how goes it?"

"Mac, this crew is incredible. I've never seen such fast workers and such good carpentry. Painters are done, trim is done, doors are installed, and tomorrow, they start the hardwood flooring. They said that will take ten days, and then flooring will be done. Finish electric is done, and the kitchen will be done before Thanksgiving, Mac!"

"Good, glad to hear it. Look, I'm about to have a spot of trouble here. Nothing I can't handle, but just in case, you check with Marybeth in an hour. If she needs you she will need Morgan too, so be ready to fly down here tonight if you don't hear an 'all-clear' from me."

"Mac, what's happening?"

"I got a guy after me. He's on my tail right now. I'm sending him to prison, and he ain't happy. He's jumped bail and skipping prosecution, but not until he deals with me. Don't know if he's armed, but I'll take precautions. Just be ready, man, OK?"

"OK, Mac, I'll wait to hear from you and notify Morgan."

**

4:00 p.m.

Mac called Trooper Andy Gregor. But there was no answer.

He called former Trooper Tim Riley. He answered.

"Mac, are we good with the restoration plan?"

"We're good, Tim. Now listen, Tim. I need a favor, a big one."

The serious tone in Mac's voice rang the Trooper bell in Tim's brain.

"Anything, you name it, Mac."

"I'm just crossing over I-90 at Westfield, going north on 394 and I've got trouble following me, a big guy with a score to settle. Don't know if he's armed but have to guess he is. He's got a serious beef with me. I'm sending him to prison for a long stretch, and he just jumped bail. I need you to go to the Murphy B & B and protect Marybeth and my daughter Gabriella, Tim. Right now."

"Mac, where are you going to be?"

"I'm decoying this guy to the new winery building next to Marybeth's barn. Its access is off 394. Do you know it?"

"Sure, but Mac, don't you want…"

"Just protect Marybeth and Gabby, Tim! Thanks, gotta go."

Next, he called Marybeth.

"Hello, love," she said, "when are you coming home?"

"Marybeth, listen carefully. Do as I ask, and do it now!"

"Mac, what's happening?"

"M, let Buddy out the back door and say 'FIND MAC!' Got it?"

"Got it, but what…"

"Tim Riley is coming to protect you and Gabby. Lock the doors, load your Ruger, and keep it handy. Send Buddy now, M! Love you!"

"MAC…!"

**

The winery driveway was on his right. He turned the Bel Air, goosed it all the way to the door and slewed to a stop, blew the horn three times for Buddy to hear, and got out. He took the key from his pocket and unlocked the door.

The entryway was a giant old wine cask, eight feet around, cut flush to the slab at the bottom. Clever, like walking into a round wooden cave. A glass door at its end led into one huge room. He stepped through it. He was looking at the opposite wall; it was all mirrors. And behind him was another wall of mirrors, floor to ceiling. It gave the illusion of grandeur, like the Hall of Mirrors at the Palace of Versailles. He was looking back at himself. It was also disconnecting, like a fun house at the circus because you were here, but you were also over there. Your brain had to ask, "Where are you?" because there were two of you.

'Rowrf, Rowrf, Rowrf!'

Buddy came charging into the cask, Mac opened the glass door, and

Buddy ran in and whapped his leg with his bushy tail.

"Good boy, Buddy."

Mac scanned the room. He had perhaps 30 seconds before Slugger arrived. There was some leftover construction material in a pile by the opposite wall. He spotted a four-foot piece of black iron gas pipe. He grabbed that. There was a small oak table. Mac set his iPhone on the table, propped it against a board, and hit record.

He motioned Buddy to the right side of the cask entry and behind it. Anyone entering could not see him directly, but they could see his reflection in the mirror on the opposite wall. There were two white dogs.

"Sit, Buddy." Buddy sat. "ALERT!" His ears went up.

Mac walked around to the other side of the cask and stood out of the direct line of sight of anyone entering the cask. Again, there were two of him. Which was real?

He heard the crunch of gravel as a heavy vehicle approached. Slugger was right-handed, so he placed Buddy to the right of the cask entry. He was on the left, which was good because he batted left-handed. A door slammed. He heard the outer cask door creak open and heavy feet shuffle on the dusty concrete. He looked in the mirror on the opposite wall and saw Slugger German through the glass inner door. He had a length of iron bar in his right hand. He saw Slugger's eyes as they looked through the door, saw his own reflection, and then saw Mac, both of him. He twitched his head back and forth as his brain tried to determine which was the real Mac. He pulled open the glass door and stepped inside tentatively.

"Hello, Slugger," said Mac, stepping away from the cask. He was beside and behind Slugger. Slugger raised his right arm to swing the pipe at Mac's throat.

"PACK'EM!" yelled Mac.

Buddy leaped through the air and clomped down on Slugger's right forearm. The big man howled in pain and tried to shake off the 100-pound dog, but Buddy held on. Slugger swung his arm around and slammed Buddy against the cask wall, but Buddy held on! Mac swung his four-foot black iron pipe with all his might at Sluggers' ankles.

"CRACK!"

"OOOOOWWWWWW!" Slugger howled and dropped to his knees. Mac dropped the pipe, stepped in, and punched his neck with a hard right, then connected with a left hook to his eye. Slugger slumped to the floor.

"AUS!" Mac commanded. Buddy let go of the arm.

"WATCH'EM!" Mac said, picking up his pipe again and wielding it over his head.

Buddy watched on full alert. As Mac moved in to frisk him, Slugger rolled over, grabbed the little .22 caliber Beretta from his right pocket, and pointed at Mac.

Buddy launched at the gun as Slugger pulled the trigger!

"POP, POP, POP, POP, POP, POP, POP! Click! Click!"

Bullets sprayed off the ceiling and walls! Mirrors shattered, and glass crashed to the terrazzo floor, but none hit Mac. Buddy tore the empty gun from Slugger's bloody hand!

"WATCH'EM!" Mac ordered.

Buddy stood growling over the big man lying on the floor.

Slugger was on his left side, his arm beneath him.

"SHOW ME YOUR HANDS!" yelled Mac, still holding the black iron pipe.

"OK, OK, I'm done!" squeaked Slugger, wheezing like an old accordion with a tear in its bellows. He raised his right hand up in surrender, but his left hand whipped out the two-shot Derringer from his jacket pocket. He pointed the gun at Buddy.

"Call the dog, or I kill him!" Slugger rasped.

"SIT, BUDDY! ALERT!" ordered Mac. Buddy sat and growled low in his belly.

"You set me up twice, you son of a bitch," Slugger squeaked. "Listen to my fuckin' voice. You did that to me!"

"You got no good options, Slugger," said Mac. "If you shoot the dog, I kill you with this iron pipe. If you shoot me, the dog will tear your throat out. Drop the gun and go back to jail. Maybe you'll get out of prison in time to be an old man."

"I ain't going to prison. And I can shoot both of you before you can move, so kiss your ass goodbye, 'cause you are gonna die."

"BOOM!"

The unmistakable sound of a Smith and Wesson .44 Magnum shattered the glass door. The bullet hit Slugger in his right shoulder, spinning him around on the floor.

"PACK'EM!" Mac shouted.

Buddy leaped forward, grabbed Slugger's right arm, and dragged him!

With his free left hand, Slugger put the derringer to his head and pulled the trigger.

"BAM!"

Slugger's head jerked, and he slumped to the floor.

"AUS!" Mac yelled. Buddy backed away.

Silence.

"YOU OK MAC?" It was the booming voice of Tim Riley.

"WE'RE OK, TIM! Come in!"

Tim walked through the cask, pulled open the shattered glass door, looked down at Slugger, and felt his neck.

"He's dead, Mac. Big boy, like you said. Tricky bastard. Two guns. Took all three of us to get him down. Troop A sent two guys. They should be here anytime."

The whoop of sirens could be heard in the distance.

"MAC!"

Marybeth ran though the doorway. She paused to absorb what she was seeing, then rushed to give him a hug.

"I'm OK, Marybeth," said Mac, "thanks to Tim and Buddy."

"I sent Tim to help you, Mac."

"I'm glad you did, Sweetheart. It's all over. Slugger German killed himself rather than go to prison."

Mac pointed to his phone.

"I recorded this on my phone, guys, so no worries. It was self-defense, no question. I'm gonna send this video to Jonetta Pope, since I've got a feeling she will be leading the after-investigation. I'm also going to send a copy to Colonel Justice, FBI agent Brad Fellowes, and Erie Detective Jenny Thompson. That closes this case."

"Good deal, Mac," said Tim. "I think the Troopers are here to take our statements."

**

Barcelona Harbor
Inglefinger Winery Building
5:00 p.m.

Mac called Roger and gave him the "all-clear." Forensic techs covered Slugger German's body as they began collecting evidence. While Tim was giving his statement, Mac strolled around, looking at the inside of this marvelous space.

It was a fabulously-finished shell. The walls were smooth drywall painted cream white but covered with eight-foot-tall mirrors spaced one foot apart. There were insulated overhead garage doors at both ends of the building to accommodate heavy machinery or automobiles. There were operational bathrooms and a functional kitchen. Soft LED lighting filtered down from big oak trusses. There was a vaulted pine ceiling. Two rows of six massive oak posts spaced twenty feet apart held up center beams that supported the king trusses holding up the roof of the 60' x 140' barn. South-facing skylights flooded the room with sunshine.

It could be more than just a car museum. It should be more, Mac thought.

Mac's phone buzzed. *(Colonel Samuel Justice calling.)*

"Yes, Sir, Colonel, did you get my video?"

"I certainly did, Mac. You are OK, I take it."

"Yep, thanks to Tim Riley. If he had not showed up, I might be dead."

"I saw that. Tim has certainly redeemed himself. Look, Mac, I heard from Jonetta Pope about Trooper James Murphy's burial tomorrow. There are a lot of Troopers who would like to come and pay last respects. Would Marybeth appreciate it?"

"She would, Sir. Let's make it a surprise. She thinks it's just going to be half a dozen close friends. She has no living family."

"Mac, there will be one hundred Troopers and color guard if you give the word."

"You got it. Let me text you the coordinates. It's a private cemetery at the end of a narrow lakeside lane, but bring'em all, and park anywhere you can. 10:00 a.m. tomorrow. And thank you, Sir."

**

Barcelona Harbor
Inglefinger Winery Building
5:30 p.m.

After Mac had finished his statement to the police, he called Jessica Perkins.

"Jessica, I would like to host an informal lunch at the Inglefinger winery building tomorrow. It will be after Trooper James Murphy's official reburial. Can you get permission from the realtor for me? I'll have it catered, and we'll clean up. Sol is definitely buying the property, no questions, so this will be a premature possession."

"I'm sure I can get it. Go ahead and plan it, Mac."

**

5:45 p.m.

Next, Mac called Francesca Molyneaux.

"Francesca, this is Mac Morrison. State Trooper Jim Murphy is being reburied tomorrow at 10:00 a.m. in Dewittville. There will be 100 State Troopers there to pay their last respects. I want to honor them by hosting an early informal lunch inside a new winery building next to Marybeth's barn. You know it? Good. Can you cater for 100 on such short notice? You can? Yes, there is a big kitchen. Yes, I'm at the building now. Do you want to come see the layout?"

**

6:15 p.m.

Francesca clucked her tongue as she entered the oak cask and saw the hall of Mirrors.

"Such a gorgeous room," she said. "Yes, we can serve in here. Let me look at the kitchen. Oh, it's a commercial kitchen! I am going to bring our big wood fired outdoor grill on a trailer. We'll grill steaks and baked potatoes. I will need to get started about 8:00 a.m. I can make soup overnight and bake rolls and cakes, too. This will be fun, and even better because it's for Mary B. Mac, I'll order the tables and chairs and all that stuff. Leave it to me, Mac, this will be fabulous!"

"Great, Francesca, but let's try to keep it a secret. I will be driving Marybeth to the cemetery about 9:15."

"Perfect, Mac. Thank you for doing this. She will be so happy to have the Troopers pay Jim his final respects. It makes me cry thinking about it."

**

Next, Mac sent a batch text message to everyone on his phone contacts who knew Marybeth. Then, he called contractor John Higgins and made plans to meet Saturday morning at the site. Lastly, he called his favorite car transport company and got a date to move Sol's 50 cars to the winery building in late November.

**

Chapter Twenty Four

Friday October 20
Morrison Private Cemetery
SR 430 between Hartfield Bay and Dewittville, NY
9:30 a.m.

Troopers are always on time. They have to be. And so it was that dozens and dozens of State Police vehicles were already lining the road as Mac and Marybeth, Gabriella and Buddy turned off the main highway onto the narrow lane past modest cottages on their way to Morrison Cemetery.

"I wonder what's going on?" Marybeth said. "I hope there isn't going to be any trouble today."

"There won't be any trouble today," Mac said. "Warm and sunny, not a cloud in the sky. It's a perfect fall day."

"But why all these police cars, Mac? Are they here for Jim?"

Mac turned the baby blue Bel Air into the opening through the trees. The cemetery lay before them, with the lake spread out behind. There was the black hearse and Ronald Samuels in his black suit. Dozens of State Troopers in their dress uniforms were making a perfect line for them to drive up to the grave site. Behind the blue Bel Air came Pops Rodgers, Hubcap Harry, and Sol Weinstein in Pops' truck.

Marybeth's mouth dropped open. "Mac, all of them came for Jim?"

"Yes, Sweetheart, to pay final respects to Trooper James Murphy and his widow."

"Oh, look!" said Marybeth. "There's Jonetta Pope and Juan Johnson; Roger and Ursula Lemonier, Angelica Morelli and Morgan Hillman; Andy and Sandy Gregor; Betty Wilson; Tim and Anna Riley; Todd, and the Shavelys. Oh, Mac, did you know all these people were coming? Did you ask them?"

"Yes. You have a lot of people who love you, Marybeth. Let's say hello to someone you haven't yet met. I believe this is Colonel Samuel Justice, Field Superintendent of the New York State Police."

Colonel Justice was a tall, big-framed black man with square shoulders and an iron face punctuated by a chiseled jaw. There was a softness in his eyes that belied the tough persona. He had gray fringes of close cropped hair under his flat brimmed hat. If Hollywood casting had called for an actor to play the part they would have sent Samuel Justice.

"You are correct, Mac. Pleased to finally meet you face to face. Thank you for your service to the people of New York in recent months. Mrs. Murphy, on behalf of all of the 5,000 sworn Troopers of the New York State Police, may I extend our most sincere condolences for the loss of your husband, Trooper James Murphy. He is being given a burial with honors today, most deserving of his life and work. And now, I think Director Samuels is calling us to take our places."

Morrison Cemetery
10:00 a.m.

Precisely on schedule, over one hundred Troopers lined up on both sides of an aisle that extended from the shimmering lake edge past the graves of Shaun and Claudia Morrison, to the canopy over the casket of James Murphy. Marybeth and Mac stood next to the casket. Buddy-dog sat proudly next to them with Gabriella holding his leash.

Marybeth turned to the assembly and spoke with a clear voice that was shaky with emotion.

"Thank you all for coming here for Jim's final resting place by beautiful Chautauqua Lake. It takes my breath away to see friends I know and new friends I have never met. Jim would be so proud to see all of you. He was born to be a Trooper; it was his first love. Troop A and fishing: that was Jim. He loved helping people and being a State Trooper. He was a good husband and a good man.

"I never believed that his death was accidental. For the past two years, I believed he was murdered. It was related to an investigation he was just beginning. But there was no proof of that until Mac Morrison burst into my life last May. But we have it now. We know he was murdered, maybe not in the line of duty, but because he was doing his duty as a BCI Investigator. I want to thank my friend Mac Morrison and the New York State Police for bringing justice to Jim's death. I want to specifically thank BCI Investigator

Jonetta Pope and Trooper Andy Gregor. And lastly, I want to thank all of you for showing so much respect by being here today. Thank you all very much."

Mac nodded to Ronald Samuels. The Trooper pallbearers lowered the casket slowly into the grave. A tall Trooper with perfect posture played taps, silhouetted against the morning sun over Chautauqua Lake. The air exploded with the firing of twelve rifles in a salute of three shots.

And then, silence. Marybeth took an armload of flowers from one of the dozens of flower stands surrounding the grave, dropped them on the casket, and wept. No one spoke or moved for a full minute until she turned and reached for Mac's hand. Buddy stood and announced that the ceremony had ended.

'Rowrf, Rowrf, Rowrf!'

Mac spoke loudly.

"Marybeth and I would like you all to join us for an early steak lunch at Barcelona Harbor. It is being held at the future home of the Sol Weinstein Classic Car Museum on State Route 394 just before old Route 5. If you drive into the lake you missed it. (*Laughter*).

"If you will please follow my blue '57 Chevy, we will make a slow procession back through Mayville, then north on State Route 394, up and over the escarpment, down through Westfield, crossing over the I-90 Thruway and into Barcelona Harbor. There will be a Trooper to welcome you. There is plenty of parking on the grass, and there will be food and drink for all."

"Mac," said Marybeth, "are you putting on a lunch in Sol's winery building?"

"I most certainly am. Francesca is doing steaks, baked potatoes, soup, and cake. It will be the first of many festive affairs in that building. I saw the way you were looking at it yesterday. You could see that there is enough space for the car museum and a wine store in the not-too-distant future. And I have another idea for a corner of that building. What do you think about Francesca starting a café next summer?"

"Mac! You read my mind!"

"I did?"

"Seriously, Mac, I was just talking to Francesca about opening a small café in my B & B on weekends because Moly's is closing! I think the big building with the car museum and a wine store is a much better idea!"

"Well, Sweetheart, let's see what Sol thinks about it. If he likes the idea, then let's talk to Francesca."

**

11:30 a.m.

Colonel Samuel Justice took Mac aside from the sizzle of steaks and cold beer.

"Mac," he said, "congratulations for stopping Herman German. He had all the markings of a sociopath. Once they get their first kill, many times it lights the fuse and they just keep going for the thrill of it.

"It's obvious you like chasing bad guys, Mac, and you're damn good at it. You think in ways that we don't train Troopers to think. And the fact that you solved all three Murphy deaths as cold cases, which no one was even looking at, proves you can peel back the pages of time on old crimes. For that very reason, I'm serious about wanting to retain you as a consultant on special cases. Can I count on you to help us?"

"You know, Colonel, I think I would enjoy that. Just don't tell Marybeth, at least not today. She needs some peace and quiet for a good long minute. But, if I were a consultant with the ability to work with Jonetta Pope and other top BCI Investigators, yes, I would be very interested. You may personally call me anytime. The only thing I would ask is that I be able to stay as close to my home here as possible."

"That's good, we can certainly do that. So Mac, when you are ready, I have a special case for you. It is a cold case that I worked as a young BCI Investigator 25 years ago, and it has never been solved. I call it *The Mayville Murders*, but local people would remember it as the Jenny Hartsall case. It has bothered me my entire career, and I want to see it solved. I think you are the one to crack it."

"Colonel, I am already interested. Tell you what, why don't you send me the case file, everything you have, and let me start thinking about it. I'll be busy building projects, but that is a good time to ruminate over the facts of the case and let my subconscious begin to parse out missing pieces."

"Will do, Mac. Thank you, and keep track of your time because I can compensate you for this."

Morgan Hillman and Angie walked over and introduced themselves to Colonel Justice. Morgan asked if he could speak with Mac privately. They stepped away to a corner of the cavernous building.

"What's up, Morgan?"

"Mac, today is not the day for me to broach the subject to Marybeth, but we have a settlement offer from the Minetti estate. And just so you know, the judge already indicated that, based on the coroner's conclusions, he will consider a directed verdict of first-degree murder."

"Attorney Joe Delmonico would like to see if Marybeth is willing to accept a settlement out of court for Jim's and her parents' deaths. The Minetti estate will have to be liquidated, and they know that, but they would like to cull a few properties that keep the children employed and allow Rosemary to retire on her library pension. Gina Minetti's wine business, warehouse, and store were all deeded to her by Joe Senior, so she is insulated from any claim made by the Murphy suit for damages."

"I think Marybeth would be willing to consider a reasonable offer, Morgan. I don't think she wants to strip the Minetti heirs of everything they have. So, do you have an offer in hand?"

"A verbal offer, Mac, but there is a complicating factor. The estate of Joseph Minetti Senior passed to Joe Minetti Jr. after Joe Senior's death, but since Joe Jr. predeceased him intestate, the estate would generally be divided among his wife Rosemary, son Gino and adopted daughter Gina. Such division would typically go through the Probate Court.

"Attorney Delmonico represents the Minetti heirs and the estates of Joe Senior and Junior. He has had their net worth evaluated by a CPA. This paper lists their assets."

He handed a copy to Mac.

"Mac, the estate, if liquidated, might yield $7.9 million dollars. Remember, if we sued, I would be demanding $12 million dollars. We cannot get more than they've got, to put it bluntly."

Minetti Assets:

Vineyard (200 acres of grapes plus 20 acres of wet woods):	$3,000,000
Three barns (fair condition):	$500,000

Farm machinery (good condition):	$1,000,000
	$4,500,000
Two residences (fair condition, not subdivided):	$400,000
Cash and investment portfolio (value today):	$2,000,000
Gino Minetti's auto parts building (steel) + one acre:	$300,000
Rosemary Minetti's warehouse (steel) + 1 acre:	$300,000
Perfect Auto Restoration building (steel) + 1 acre:	$400,000
Approximately 40 salvage cars (from 1950-1970):	$ 0
	$3,400,000

"What is the verbal offer, Morgan?"

"One million cash now, and one million a year from now, plus proceeds from the sale of the farm, with two years to sell or auction it. They would sell the auto shop and Rosemary's warehouse separately. They would like to keep one residence. Gino would like to lease back his shop and one acre around it. Total potential settlement value might be 7.4 million dollars, but it could take two years to collect it, and if the properties do not bring that much, then the amount would be whatever they sell for.

"It's far short of $12 million, but they don't have $12 million, Mac. A settlement with cash is good, but I think we can do better on a counteroffer. Would you be willing to discuss this with Marybeth tonight and ask her what she would like to do? Angie, the Lemoniers and I are leaving tomorrow at noon by my charter flight. I would like to know if she comes to any decision by then.

"And Mac, make sure Marybeth understands that any settlement she might get in a wrongful death suit is *tax-free*.

"Also, I know you had to surprise Marybeth to keep our attending the burial a secret. Was she OK with that us staying at the B & B?"

"Of course! She was so pleased that you all came! It meant a great deal to her and to me, Morgan."

"Good. We'll talk more at dinner, I'm sure."

**

Barcelona Harbor
Inglefinger Winery Building, lunch ending, and people leaving
12:30 p.m.

"Sol," said Mac, " how are you feeling?"

"Better, Mackenzie. So glad to get out of da hospital. Da big guy is dead, I heard."

"He's dead Sol. Did you sell your copper to Angelo?"

Sol smiled and showed his one remaining tooth.

"Yah, today." He pulled a check from his pocket. It was from Murano Metals Inc. to Sol Weinstein for $320,100.

"You did better than you thought, Sol."

"Dere vas vun hundred ten tousand pounds good mixed copper. He gave me $2.91 a pound. Mackenzie, dis check pays for dis beautiful buildink and da seventeen acres of vineyard around it."

"What do you think of your car museum, Sol?"

"I'm like a kink in his castle, Mackenzie. Dis is going to be mine. Soon as title iss done and deed made, Sarah says I own it. Den vee start to move da cars."

"Sol, I already contacted my movers. If you have cars that run, they can drive them onto the hauler and bring eight cars per load. The ones that don't run, we'll bring on ramp trucks one at a time."

"Ven can you move da blue buildink, Mackenzie?"

"I hope to do it in early December, Sol. I'm having plans drawn now. Once we get permits I have a contractor who will pour the foundation and install the underground utilities."

"I vill be happy here, Mackenzie. Peace and qviet, next to my cars in dis nice buildink. Say, vat about dis lunch! Such good food! And da little voman, Frannie she call herself, she cut my steak in little pieces so I can eat vit my one tooth. Nice lady! Cute too."

"Sol, are you flirting with Francesca?"

"Vy not? At my age, all I can do is flirt!"

"Sol," said Mac, "what would you think about a wine tasting room for my daughter's business and a café with Francesca's cooking inside your museum?"

"Here? In my museum? She vould do dat?"

"Would you like that, Sol?"

"I could valk over here from my little cottage ven you build it, and come see my cars, flirt vit Frannie, and eat like a kink? Vat's not to like? Let's do it Mackenzie, my friend!"

"All right Sol, let's go tell Frannie and Marybeth!"

**

4:00 p.m.

The day had started sunny and warm, but the Great Lakes are weather-makers, and a cold front blew in after the caterer cleaned up. Marybeth and Mac were having coffee on her back porch with the windows closed to drown out the noise from the rain pounding the metal roof overhead. Mac built a small fire in the wood stove. Four Labradoodles lay surrounding Marybeth on one sofa, and Buddy laid across Mac's lap on the opposite sofa as the fatwood crackled.

"Mac," said Marybeth, "that was a wonderful surprise having all the Troopers here for Jim's burial. He would have been so proud. And Colonel Justice has to be a very busy man. I was flattered that he came too."

"Jim deserved it, M. Now that everyone has melted away, I need to talk to you about a different subject. Are you ready?"

"I guess."

"Morgan notified Minetti's attorney that he would be filing for civil and punitive damages against their estate for Jim's death. The court would merge that claim with the damage request he already filed for your parents' death. Total demand would be 12 million dollars, half compensatory and half punitive. Morgan wants you to know that a wrongful death settlement is *non-taxable*[12]. So, whatever money you agree to accept, you keep tax-free.

"But Marybeth, a CPA estimates the Minetti total estate is only worth 7.9 million dollars. Two million dollars in cash. The rest is real estate and farm equipment. Liquidation of the real estate and farm requires subdivision of the house lots and warehouses. That also requires the sale of seven individual properties to get maximum prices. That could take a long time. Gina is not liable for any damages. Her property stands alone, safe."

---

12   Internal Revenue Service (IRS) Rule 1.104-1

"I never wanted anything from Gina, Mac."

"I know you didn't, M."

"The two residences are in fair condition. There are three good steel warehouses. The farmland is all in Concord grapes.

"All right, now we get down to it. Today, Morgan received a verbal settlement offer from the Minettis via their attorney. These are their assets."

Mac passed Marybeth the paper with the breakdown of the Minetti estate values. He gave her five minutes to digest it. When she put it on the coffee table, he spoke.

"They are offering you one million cash now, one million a year from now, plus the proceeds from the sale of their real estate. They would have two years to sell the farm, or it would go to auction. They would sell Joe's auto shop and Rosemary's warehouse separately. They would like to keep one residence, and Gino would like to lease back his shop and one acre around it. Total potential settlement value might be 7.4 million dollars, but it could take two years to collect it, and if the properties do not bring that much, then the amount would be whatever they sell for."

"Mac, wait, I don't know what to do. This is so sudden. We just buried Jim today."

"M, you don't have to decide now. However, rather than litigate for more money, which they don't have, I suggest a counteroffer."

"Okay, what do you suggest, Mac?"

"You take the $2 million cash now. Remember, it is tax-free, M. You give them 18 months to sell the farm, but you keep any equipment you want.

"They can keep *both* residences, and Gino can keep his salvage auto parts building and one acre, but he must pay to have it subdivided. His business would not be subject to any claim from you.

"You will take Rosemary's steel food warehouse. It can be used as farm storage and winemaking space here behind the winery. I will move it at your expense and place a lien on their property, so they must reimburse you when they sell the land under it.

"You will also take Joe's auto restoration shop, his equipment, tools and any of this salvage cars Sol wants for parts. I will move the building at your expense and place a lien on their property, so they must reimburse you when they sell the land under it.

"In summary, Marybeth, you would get $2 million cash now, tax-free. You should get an additional $4 million or more tax-free from the farm within 18 months. You get two good steel shell buildings worth at least $200,000. And you get all the tools and equipment needed to set up Sol's auto restoration workshop and to farm your 20-acre vineyard."

"I think I like that deal, Mac," said Marybeth. "I like that I get the cash now so we wouldn't have to finance the elder village or the café and wine store in Sol's museum. We would have plenty of cash to take us well into the future, and hopefully, our wine-making experiment will start making money in 3-5 years, so we are sustainable. And the sale of the Minetti farm would be icing on the cake. We should be set for life with our other businesses. Yes, I like that deal.

"The Minettis would still have two houses to live in, and Gino and Gina keep their buildings and businesses. That's good. We don't want to hurt them. Rosemary gets punished by losing her food warehouse. She will probably retire from the library, take her 40-year pension, and live with Gino. Sol gets his car museum but has no worries about its care or taxes. Yes, Mac. I like that deal. Will they take it?"

"Marybeth," said Mac, "they should jump at this deal. I will find Morgan. We can discuss this in the dining room in twenty minutes."

"OK, Mac. That will give me time to help Frannie with dinner prep. She is making us one of her special suppers."

**

4:30 p.m.

"Morgan, what do you think of Mac's counteroffer?" said Marybeth.

"I like it, Marybeth. Angie will type it up and e-mail it to Attorney Delmonico. I'll text him to let him know it's coming."

"I spoke to Sol," said Mac. "He will purchase the 19 acres with the winery building immediately. Angelo and I will move his blue steel building once I get the slab and utilities installed. That should be by Christmas. The winery building will become the *Sol Weinstein Classic Car Museum*. The blue steel building will be the second showroom. He needs that much floor space to get his cars off the racks and onto the ground for display. He also likes the

Philip C. Laurien

idea of the Minetti auto shop being moved next to the museum to become the museum's auto restoration shop.

"Sol and Francesca discussed the idea of a small café at one end of the museum, next to Gabriella's wine store and sampling station. They like the idea. Francesca could be ready to open the café in the spring since the kitchen is already there."

Morgan said "Marybeth, "to do those projects you need to own the 19-acre property now. Sol is agreeable to gift the land and building to you now, so long as you follow through on his plan for the museum. He gets a life estate in one of your cottages.

"You would have to pay 20% capital gains tax on the $319,000 value of the 19-acre property, but you would have the $2 million Minetti cash settlement upfront, so you can pay the $64,000 tax from that and still have plenty of cash to set up your new elder village, the café and wine business. And you can still count on whatever the Minetti real estate sales would yield within 18 months."

"OK," said Marybeth, "then I guess we have a plan!"

**

Friday October 20
Murphy B& B
Back porch dining area
7:00 p.m.

Present: Marybeth Murphy; Mac Morrison; Gabriella Morrison; Hubcap Harry; Sol Weinstein; Pops Rodgers; Francesca Molyneaux; Morgan Hillman and Angelica Morelli; Angelo Murano; Jean-Paul Bernard; Matthew Reasoner; Roger and Ursula Lemonier; Juan Johnson and Jonetta Pope; Tim and Anna Riley

Marybeth raised her wine glass:

"Friends, thank you for coming here tonight. This is now the extended Murphy and Morrison family, isn't it? Some of us are linked by blood, some by affection, and some will soon be linked by new ventures in the next year. To make sure you all know just how much fun this is going to be, Mac and I are going to review the ambitious list of changes that will be happening here.

"Most of you know that my husband Jim was killed two years ago by Joe Minetti. Thanks to the incredible efforts of Mac Morrison, who stormed into my life as a stranger last May, Minetti has now been posthumously found guilty of the murder of my husband Jim and my parents.

"Rather than litigate for damages, my Attorney Morgan Hillman has worked out a deal with the Minetti estate for compensation. It will not bring Jim back, but it means that I will be able to close the Captain Murphy B & B to concentrate on new projects.

"The first project will be to get the *Sol Weinstein Classic Car Museum* into the winery building next door. Sol's cars will be moved from his business in Erie into the winery building for storage over the winter. His steel office building will be moved from Erie to be placed next to the winery. It will become the second showroom for the museum.

"Half of the winery will be used for the museum. There will also be a wine store and café in the other half. Within a few years, we hope our small 20-acre vineyard will make wine to sell. Our wine partners include J.P. Bernard, Matthew Reasoner, and Angelo Murano. Francesca Molyneaux and I will open Francesca's Café in a corner of the winery before May 5.

"Mac Morrison is building me four new elder cottages in the spring. They can be rented by over-55 guests on an annual basis. Once the first two cottages are finished, Sol Weinstein and Pops Rodgers will move in. Hubcap Harry will stay on in the current cottage. They will be my first long-term tenants in the Captain Murphy Elder Village.

"Then we will turn our attention to disassembling and relocating the steel building that was Minetti's Auto Restoration Shop from Ripley to the museum site. It will become the museum's auto restoration shop. After that, we will also move the Minetti food warehouse to the winery site for farm storage and winemaking.

"In spring, Jean-Paul Bernard will be grafting his Bordeaux-Puttelange stock onto my vines on the three acres behind my barn. Angelo and Gabriella will be grafting Italian Barbera stock on the 17-acre Inglefinger vineyard next door.

"Gabby will also be grafting Angelo's Barbera grapes on vines at Reasoner's organic vineyard in Leroy. Matthew's staff will do most of the work, but they will teach Gabby, and she will assist in all phases of the process, including harvesting and winemaking. She has to learn how to do it all.

"And last, Mac's team of auto restorers, Juan Johnson and Tim Riley, will get busy working on Sol's classic cars in the fall. We will display them in unrestored condition to begin the museum while Mac's team teaches the restoration process to high school students.

"All right," said Marybeth, "Angelo is serving us his wonderful robust red Barbera wine, so Francesca made Ribollita, a Tuscan vegetable soup for our first course. We will have Frannie's French-style lasagna with Bolognese sauce, and Mac will grill us skewers of steak and walleye. Desert will be my caramel-cinnamon apple pie, made from Reasoner's fresh-picked organic apples with lattice crust served a la mode under vanilla ice cream with Irish coffee. Enjoy, my friends."

**

9:00 p.m.

Hubcap Harry, Sol, Pops, and Roger were playing euchre at the dining table. Francesca and Marybeth were in the kitchen. Mac, Angelo, Gabriella, Morgan, Angelica, and Matthew Reasoner were sitting on the back porch making notes.

Matt Reasoner said, "Gabby, I'd like you and Angelo to come to my vineyard tomorrow to see the vines you will be grafting and meet my workers."

Angelo said, "Since my cousin has never visited me, I will have him come over from Italy and help with the grafting next spring."

"I am so excited to get started!" said Gabby. "There is so much to learn!"

"We are counting on that youthful enthusiasm, Gabriella," said Matt. "You will be the key to success in planning, supervising, harvesting, and marketing the wine. It will take time, but be patient, and this could be a great new venture for us."

Mac said, "Since I'm meeting with my excavation contractor tomorrow morning, how about we meet mid-afternoon at Reasoner's?"

"Sounds good."

"Matthew," said Morgan, "do you want a legal partnership agreement?"

"Well, it's not a big project to start, but we probably should," said

Reasoner.

"When I get back to New Hampshire, I will draft something for all of you to review," said Morgan.

**

Friday October 20
Barcelona Harbor, NY
Harbor Pier
10:00 p.m.

Mac, Marybeth, and five dogs walked down onto the harbor beach. A cool west wind whipped up the waves. For the first time in days, there were whitecaps in the moonlight. Mac whistled a jaunty ragtime tune, but Marybeth could not quite identify it.

"So this is where it all started with us, Mac. Last May, you opened a mysterious 40-year-old wax-sealed envelope from your deceased Uncle Abe, containing two different police reports describing the fatal car accident that killed your parents in 1983. Something about those reports did not jibe with your crime-solving brain, so your Lone Ranger persona kicked in. You took a road trip here with Buddy to make inquiries and visit their graves, but got stopped on the Thruway for a loose trunk lid by Trooper Andy Gregor. You wound up having lunch with him at the Barcelona pier with sandwiches from Todd's and discovered you were both Bar B campers from way back. Andy sent you to me for a place to stay."

"Sounds like a Hollywood movie, doesn't it M?"

"It does, but no movie could envision all of the adventures you have woven into my life, Mac. It is becoming an addictive adrenaline high."

"Well, we have an ambitious next nine months ahead, Marybeth. Roger's house is almost done because of my great young Mexican crew. Once I get back to New Hampshire I'll see what is left to do and get it finished."

"Good, then you come back to me and the rest of our gang. We are all counting on you, Mac, so don't you go looking for trouble. What is that tune you are whistling? Sounds familiar. Keep going another bar or two. Let me see if I can get it."

Mac whistled with perfect pitch, note-for-note, and soon Marybeth was humming it. Then she began to sing the old jazz tune in her sultry Dusty

Springfield[13] voice:
I don't stay out late, no place to go
I'm home about eight, just me and my radio
Ain't misbehavin'[14]
I'm savin' my love for you

**

---

13   Dusty Springfield (1939-1999): British singer, songwriter and producer, born Mary Isobel Catherine Bernadette O'Brien in London England. Her voice was a smoky mezzo-soprano.
14   Ain't Misbehavin': 1929 jazz song by Fats Waller, lyrics by Andy Razaf

Chapter Twenty Five

Saturday October 21
SR 394, Barcelona Harbor, NY
Inglefinger Winery Building (Future Weinstein Classic Car Museum)
9:30 a.m.

John Higgins arrived early. Mac liked that. He drove a well-used ten-year-old Ford F-350 dually. It had faded paint and was mud splattered from yesterday's rain shower, but no rust. In western New York, that meant he had taken care of it. Mac liked that, too.

Mac, Sol Weinstein, and John Higgins stood back from the winery and surveyed the landscape. The land was level in the valley by the lake, so very little earth would be moved to set the building pads. Higgins had done the site work for the winery barn, so he knew the location and size of the underground utilities.

"Mac," he said, "since you will be bringing three steel buildings to this site and adding cottages behind them on Marybeth's back acreage, I suggest we run all the utilities for both projects off Route 394. We can run one main trunk line for the sewer to serve both sites and branch off to the cottages after it passes the winery compound.

"The parking area is gravel. You might want to pave a small portion, but gravel is better for the rest because it reduces runoff, which is an issue this close to the lake. Jessie will do the calculations on stormwater treatment. If the farm pond is large enough, we can send all the water to it. If not, then I would suggest we create a wetland retention basin.

"The wetland can be an asset if you install the correct plants to attract beautiful wildlife. It could be a nice spot for an outdoor picnic area, maybe an open pavilion. There is nothing like that within ten miles of here. With all the fishermen at the lake, it would give them a place to have fish fries. Just a thought."

"That's a good thought, John, "said Mac. "Sol, where would you like to see your blue building placed?"

Sol pointed to the left of the winery.

"I tink dere, Mackenzie. Because you haff da big door in the 'vinery at da end, und vee haff da big door in da blue buildink. So, dat's good to move cars from one showroom to da udder. Maybe leave space betveen da buildinks for eqvipment to move around."

"Good, I like that. How about putting the auto restoration shop in front of and to the side, making a court yard of the three buildings. Can you picture that Sol?"

"Yah. I like dat, vit good concrete pavement in da courtyard und some nice trees and flowers."

"It will be easy to branch off water and sewer to those buildings," said Higgins. What about the other steel building?"

"That will go on the opposite end of the winery," said Mac. It will be farm storage, but it will still need water and sewer for making wine."

"OK, we'll take a trunk line off the main to that end. Let's leave at least 40 feet between them," said Higgins.

"Good, sounds like a plan," said Mac. You can meet with Jessie and let her know how we laid it out. Sol, do you want to go inside and walk around your new building while John and I lay out the cottages with Marybeth?"

"Sure, sure, I just go in, sit down, und dream about my cars in dere."

**

Saturday October 21
Barcelona Harbor, NY
Behind the Murphy B & B, site of the Future Elder Village
10:00 a.m.

"Mac," said Marybeth, I want this to look like a college quadrangle, with the head of it being the existing cottage and two cottages on each side, open to the vineyard on the end. I think 80 feet from front porch to front porch is the right distance so they can see each other and walk across to visit, but they are far enough apart to feel privacy. So the quadrangle should be 80' x 120'."

"That's a 2 x 3 ratio," said Mac. "M, did you know King Philip's 1565 Spanish Law of the Indies decreed public squares should be laid out with a 2 x 3 dimension?"

"I did not, but it does not surprise me that you would know such an arcane fact, Mac. 80' x 120' just feels right."

"I agree," said Mac. "John, the cottages will be shotgun style, with a narrow end facing front toward the quad's open space. There will be a loop driveway that runs around the back. I drew a rough sketch for Jessie Perkins to make a site plan."

"Marybeth," said John, "how would you feel about a small retention pond in the center of the quad? Plant it with wetland plants and let the red-wing blackbirds nest in it. You'll have frogs, and deer will come to take water."

"I'd like that, John. Something for my tenants to look at. And nothing is more calming than the sounds of nature."

"Mac," said Higgins, "you mentioned you had a friend with a big new excavator and a D3 dozer. I have a small excavator, a backhoe, a big D9 dozer, and a skid steer Bobcat. If your friend wanted to join me and bring his crew for two weeks, I think we could get all the underground done, graded, and have the slabs ready to be poured. Jessie Perkins' survey crew can set all the elevations for us and shoot the grades."

"Let's plan on that, John. Roger's got the best excavator operator you've ever seen, guaranteed."

"Good. OK, Mac, I think I've seen enough. I'll talk to the town and the state about any issues they may have on SR 394 and let you know what I learn."

**

Saturday October 21
LeRoy, New York
Reasoner's Organic Orchard and Vineyard
2:30 p.m.

"Angelo, Mac, Gabriella, and Buddy-dog, welcome to my organic vineyard," said Matthew Reasoner. "This is a fourth-generation orchard, but we began growing wine grapes here twenty years ago. We make a white Riesling that is popular in our wine bar and picnic pavilion. The grapes originally came from vines in Luxembourg near Mondorf-Les-Bains."

"Oh!" said Gabriella, "I just visited Mondorf! My friend Jean-Paul's father is growing a Bordeaux variety in Puttelange, France."

"Well," said Matt, "their winters are warmer than ours, and their summers are cooler than ours, but the Riesling grapes are hardy and do well here. We grafted them initially onto our organic vines. They survived and thrived. So we now have planted cuttings and grow our vines from roots.

"That is what we will try with your Barbera grafts, Angelo. We will first graft them to our hardy rootstock. This climate is similar to that of the Northwestern Piedmont region of Italy. I'm optimistic they will do well here, but make sure you ask your cousin to describe the orientation of the vines when he takes his graft. Might not be important, but I like to have every opportunity to succeed."

Two young Latinos and an older man drove up on a green John Deere Gator. Matthew waved them down and they climbed out. They took off their hats as a show of respect to Gabriella.

"Angelo, Mac, and Gabriella, I'd like you to meet Henry, my foreman, Ruiz, and his friend Andrés. Henry will supervise your project, but Ruiz will do much of the actual tending of the vines and will teach you how to graft. He will also teach Andrés, who joined us recently. He came down from New Hampshire."

Mac's head swiveled around to take a look at Andrés. Andrés looked down at the ground under Mac's steady gaze. He was perhaps 5'7" with a smooth shaved face and short black hair with a curl that hung down on his forehead.

"By the way, Mac," said Matt Reasoner, "how are the Rodriguez boys working out for you?"

Andrés looked up at the mention of the Rodriguez brothers. His dark eyes looked worried, but not guilty, to Mac.

"They are terrific workers, Matt. It seems like they can do anything. Good carpenters, and Ramon is the best heavy equipment operator I've ever seen."

"I would like to have them here full time, Mac, but I knew they would take a job for someone like you. I can't pay farm workers what you pay carpenters and equipment operators, but I do provide good housing and steady pay. That way, I keep a core group here and hire seasonal labor as needed."

Mac kept his eyes on Andrés. He was looking at the ground, not making eye contact.

"Ruiz," said Mac, "did you work with the Rodriguez brothers last May?"

"Yes, I was here then," said Ruiz.

"How about you, Andrés?" asked Mac.

Andrés looked up at him and said quietly, "No sir, I was not here then."

"Do you boys like dogs?" Mac asked.

"Of course," said Ruiz quickly. "What is his name?"

"Buddy. Would you like to shake with him?"

"Can we?"

"Of course," said Mac. "Buddy, can you shake?"

While standing, Buddy lifted his right paw and shook Ruiz's hand.

"How about you, Andrés?" said Mac. "Would you like to shake with Buddy?"

Andrés hesitated and then reached out his hand.

Buddy sat, which Mac knew could mean "alert." He watched as Buddy sniffed the air and the hand. He slowly raised his paw and shook Andrés' hand.

"OK," said Matt Reasoner, "let's go look at the vines, and then I'm going to have Henry give Angelo and Gabriella the full tour of the winemaking process. The harvest is complete, so now we are pressing grapes."

**

Matt Reasoner was pouring wine into three tasting glasses.

"Mac, do you like white wine?"

"I do, Matt."

"See what you think of our Reasoner Riesling."

Mac took a sip and swished it around in his mouth.

"Very smooth," said Mac.

"Good. Now try this next Riesling."

Mac sipped it and tilted his head. "Maybe a bit more fruity, but very similar."

"The second one is from the home vineyard near Wellenstein on the Moselle River in Luxembourg," said Matt. "They have been growing grapes there for 1,000 years. This particular wine is $90 for a case of 6, or $15 per .75 liter bottle, plus shipping. It is rated 93 out of 100 and contains sulfites. All right now, Mac, try this third one."

Mac took a sip and nodded. "Also very smooth, not as fruity as the first two. All similar, but all slightly different."

"That third one is a New York Finger Lakes Riesling, Mac. It is rated 91 out of 100. It sells for $14 for a .75 liter bottle."

"What is your Reasoner Riesling rated, and how much does it sell for, Matt?" said Mac.

"It is rated 94 and sells for $16 for an entire one-liter bottle. It is organic, with no sulfites."

"I see," said Mac. "How many glasses of wine in a .75 liter bottle, Matt?"

"Five."

"And how many are in a one-liter bottle?"

"Seven. I can see you doing the math, Mac. It's about sixty cents per glass cheaper to buy a liter bottle of our organic wine with no sulfites. So, for social gatherings, there is no contest. Our local wine wins every time on taste and value. And because we only sell one-liter bottles, which we recycle, we have far less waste and a one-third less bottle cost than vintners who sell smaller .75-liter bottles."

"Matthew," said Mac, "how long will it take to get your first batch of Angelo's Barbera wine?"

"Three to five years. But we will know the first year if the grafts are successful."

"Do you think Marybeth's 20 acres of existing vines can be a viable Barbera vineyard if the grafting is successful?"

"Mac, 20 acres could eventually produce up to 200,000 bottles of wine. If you can sell it regionally for $16 per bottle, that is $3 million gross and potentially $600,000 to $1.5 million profit. But it's not an easy business. Weather, pests, blight, market resistance, labor availability, bad harvest, all of them take a toll. Being conservative, a 20-acre vineyard with an established popular wine should yield between $500,000 and one million dollars a year in profit.

"So, let's see how the grafting goes. If they take, we'll use the grafted vines to produce dormant cuttings. In five years, you could have a mixture of grafted and rootstock wine grapes. You have to be patient. That is the key, Mac, and lucky too."

"Matt," said Mac, "you are a fountain of knowledge. I hope you will continue to teach Gabby, because I think this is her future. Now that you have given me all this good information, I'd like to make a quick phone call, and then perhaps I can give you some information too. Meanwhile, how about you do a tasting for Gabby and Angelo?"

**

Mac pulled up his phone and hit speed dial for Paco Rodriguez. He sounded chipper.

"Mister Mac! I'm glad to hear from you! How are you doing?"

"I'm doing fine, Paco; the real question is, how are *you* doing?"

"Oh, I'm fine, Mister Mac. I've been back to work all week. My headaches are gone. I'm good."

"Good, Paco. Do you remember Mr. Reasoner's orchard in LeRoy, New York?"

"Of course, Mister Mac."

"Did you work with a young man named Ruiz?"

"Ruiz Ortega? Yes, we worked with him."

"Is he a good guy, Paco?"

"Very good, Mister Mac. Honest and hardworking. He likes Mister Reasoner. He hopes to become a foreman someday. He is living there full-time. He is happy there."

"Did you know another young man there named Andrés, Paco?"

"At Reasoner's farm? No, there was no Andrés at Reasoner's farm, Mister Mac. I know Andrés Santiago, but he did not work at Mr. Reasoner's farm."

"How did you know Andrés Santiago, Paco?"

"He was the driver for Louis Lopez, Mister Mac. He drove their van that transported farm workers. He was the one I was supposed to meet."

"What do you mean, Paco?"

"Oh! You don't know! I finally remembered what I was supposed to do the day after the big fight when Raoul hit my head and knocked me out. I remembered, but I figured it does not matter anymore with Los Locos either dead or in jail."

"What were you supposed to do, Paco?"

"I was supposed to drive my truck to Enfield and meet Andrés at a gas station, then drive to Lebanon and rent a U-Haul truck. Andrés would pay for it in cash. If they needed a credit card as security, I would use my card. Then, I would drive the U-Haul back to Shakoma Beach with Andrés following in my truck. Louis Lopez would meet us there and pay me $300.

"Louis said if I would do him this one favor, he would forgive the money he did not get for the week we didn't work in Vermont and for any work we did for you. But I was in the hospital, so I never went to meet Andrés, Mister Mac. I don't know what happened to him."

"Paco, what do you know about Andrés?"

"He was a good driver. And he could pass for American with his light skin and clean-shaven face. With the right clothes, he could pass for sure. That is why Louis liked him. He looked like he belonged here, less chance of being stopped or questioned by police."

"But he was a driver for the Locos, and they were bad dudes, Paco."

"They did not start out that way, Mister Mac, but yes, they were. Andrés was their driver, so if they were doing bad things, he would have known, but he would have just been the driver. Andrés was raised Catholic, and in Mexico, that means something extra. He knew right from wrong, but he had a mother, brothers, and sisters to feed back home, that is why he worked for Louis Lopez. I don't believe he would have killed anyone or hurt anyone. He was just their driver, Mister Mac."

"OK, Paco, thanks for telling me."

"Mister Mac, we need you here now. We are almost finished with all the work you gave us on Roger's house. When are you coming home?"

"Tomorrow night, Paco."

**

"OK, Matthew," said Mac, "let's go outside and talk."

They walked out into the crisp fall air with Delft-blue skies and bright sunshine. With no cloud cover, frost was likely overnight.

"Matthew, what do you think of your new hire, Andrés?"

"Well, he is a good worker. He's trying to make a good impression. Ruiz has known him since childhood. He speaks well of him, although he says there was a time Andrés worked for a jobber, I think maybe the jobber I fired, he did not say. If that were true, I would be well advised to keep an eye on him. He is very religious. He had some cash when he arrived here, so he bought a used electric bike, which he rides to the Catholic Church in Leroy for confession and communion."

"What is his last name?"

"Santiago. Why do you ask about Andrés, Mac?"

"Matthew, do you believe in second chances in life?"

"If a person is a good person and is sincere, yes, I do."

"Well," said Mac, "let me tell you a story."

**

There were many reasons that Mac did not pick up his phone and call Colonel Justice and Colonel Bradford.

First of all, he could not be certain Andrés was the driver for Louis Lopez when he killed Rupert Bisbee in Ascutney. Maybe he was not with them at that time. The police had no description or picture of the four gang members at the Ascutney farm. There was no evidence against the fourth member, and the other three were either dead or in jail.

Second, Andrés passed the Buddy test. Not with flying colors, no, because Buddy sat, sniffed, and cocked his head before he shook his hand. But he shook it, and he did not growl. It was a half-alert, then a belated OK. That's how Mac interpreted Buddy's reading of Andrés.

Third, Andrés was going to confession. That was a good sign.

Fourth, Andrés had good reason to work for Lopez: his family needed money. It was hard to criticize that.

Still, under normal circumstances, Mac would have made the call, let the police pick up and question this Andrés. If they had no evidence against him he would be let go.

But it seemed like Andrés Santiago was trying to go straight. Mac believed in second chances, so he advised Matthew Reasoner that Andrés could have been with Louis Lopez when the farmer was killed, but he would have probably just been driving. Maybe he was deserving of a chance to prove himself.

Matthew Reasoner understood. He patted his Glock in the hidden shoulder holster while he waved to Mac, Gabby, and Buddy dog in the baby blue 57 Chevy Bel Air.

As Mac drove away from the Reasoner farm, he knew the real reason he was not calling Colonel Justice. He promised Marybeth he would not go looking for trouble. Marybeth needed a lot of work from him between now and next May 5th. It was interesting how that date seemed to keep coming up. She wanted him to get the café running by May 5. Get the museum open by May 5. Get two cottages done by May 5. It was a lot.

He couldn't play Lone Ranger and get the work done.

**

Saturday October 21
Barcelona Harbor, NY
Murphy B & B
5:30 p.m.

The old screen door's rusty spring "gronked" its displeasure for having been disturbed a millionth time, then it 'whapped' the door on Mac's fanny as he scooted through after Buddy.

Just then, Mac's phone buzzed. (*Incoming e-mail.*)

Mac paused inside the back porch to read it. It was from Colonel Samuel Justice, and it was brief:

"Thanks for looking into this Mac. I'll provide all the support you need."

A JPEG file was attached. Mac clicked to open it. It was titled *"Murder Book, Jenny Hartsall and the Mayville Murders."*

Mac was instantly transfixed. He began reading, but only got to the date and place of the event before Marybeth called out from the kitchen to break his next Lone Ranger spell.

"Mac, did you have a good afternoon at Reasoner's?"

"Very good," he said. "We learned a lot. This 20-acre winery could be a good long-term deal for you and Gabby, but it will take 3-5 years before you will see any cash return. But you will have your $2 million settlement soon, so you have plenty of seed money, and then some. And when the Minetti real estate sells, you should be set for life. If the grapes like the climate in Barcelona Harbor, Gabby will make the wine thing go; I am confident of that. In the meantime, she can help you develop and run the elder village and market her shipping container of French wine."

"Mac," said Marybeth, "the best thing is we are doing these ventures as a family. I am happy when we are all here together. With Gabby helping me, Francesca starting her café, and you restoring Sol's cars, it will be one big family."

Mac told her of his suspicion that Andrés could have been the fourth Locos gang member.

"You believe in second chances, don't you, Marybeth?"

"Of course, Mac! Look at us! And our five rescue dogs! And Tim Riley! And Sol and Hubcap Harry and Pops! We all deserve a second chance at life, that is, if you have a good heart."

"Glad you agree, because I gave Andrés a big second chance, and he is going to be working with my daughter, so he better straighten up. Matt Reasoner will keep an eye on him."

"OK, so that's settled, what's next Mac?"

"M, I have to leave in the morning for New Hampshire."

"So soon, Mac? I was hoping you'd stay longer."

"You always say that, Sweetie. I've got to finish Roger's house, but with my crew, it will go fast. They have me a month ahead of schedule. So, as soon as we get permits for Sol's blue building, I will return with my whole crew. We'll get it moved and then start moving cars into the museum. I want both of those done by Christmas."

"Wonderful! Will we be spending Christmas here, my love, or in our snug new cabin?"

"I think we may do both. Morgan and Angie are having a New Year's wedding, so we'll be here for Christmas and then drive up to New Hampshire for New Year's. Can Francesca cook for Hubcap Harry while we are gone?"

"I'm sure she can. It will help her transition out of Moly's Café. Her kids are sort of pushing her aside after all these years. But she is ready for a change anyway. This will be good, and she can stay in the first-floor suite."

"So Marybeth, just one more thing."

"Yes, my love?"

"You heaped my plate with so much work that I have little time to sleep the next seven months. I know what's got to be done by May 5th: the Blue building moved, 50 cars moved, the café and museum up and running, and two cottages built and ready for Sol and Pops."

"Marybeth, is there something you haven't told me about May 5th?"

"Yes, there is, Mackenzie Morrison. If the doctor counted right, on May 5th, *you* get a second chance, my love... to be a Poppa. That's right, Mac... I'm pregnant."

**

Appendix
Cast of Characters
Principal characters in **bold**

Mackenzie "Mac" Morrison: builder, car restorer, and improbably capable investigator of lost causes; a one man wrecking crew seeking vigilante justice.

Buddy: Mac Morrison's rescue dog, an Alaskan Malamute-German Shepherd mix

Marybeth Murphy: widow owner of the Captain Murphy B & B, Barcelona Harbor, New York

Roger Lemonier and wife Ursula: Mac Morrison's best friend, comrade in arms

Morgan Hillman: renowned criminal attorney, friend of Mac Morrison

Angelica Milana Morelli: confidential secretary and fiancé to Attorney Morgan Hillman

Gabriella Morrison: Mac Morrison's daughter

Paco, Ramon and Thomas Rodriguez and Maria, their mother: Mac's three Mexican workers

Miguel and Lupe Rodriguez: twin cousins to Paco, Ramon and Thomas; apprentice carpenters working for Mac Morrison

Andy Gregor: New York State Trooper

Betty Wilson: owner of the former Bar B Ranch Camp

Jean Paul Bernard- Gabriella's friend and emissary to expand family French wine business to America

Rosemary Minetti: Librarian, wife of Joey Minetti.

Joseph "Joey" Minetti: now deceased, automotive genius, killer.

Joseph Minetti Senior: now deceased, patriarch, owner of the Minetti Vineyard

Gino Minetti: Joey and Rosemary's son

Gina Minetti: Joey and Rosemary's adopted daughter

Tim and Anna Riley: retired New York State Trooper and wife

Hubcap Harry: owner of Vintage GM Parts and Hubcaps

Pops: aka Roy Rodgers, owner of the *Miss Bertie*, and friend of Mac and Marybeth

Todd: owner of the Gas n Go station in Barcelona Harbor

Juan Johnson: owner of Johnson's Auto Body and Collision

Colonel Trammel Bradford: Field Superintendent, New Hampshire State Police

Colonel Samuel Justice: Field Superintendent, New York State Police

Jonetta Pope: New York BCI Investigator

Sol Weinstein: owner of Bank's Breakers and Scrap

Martin Thomas: Sol Weinstein's foreman at the Banks Breakers and Scrap yard

Mace Wilkins: scrap yard owner, Ashtabula, Ohio

Sarah Lieberman: Attorney for Sol Weinstein

Manual 'Manny' Diaz: jobber and employee of Louis Lopez

Raoul 'Roofy' Diaz: jobber and employee of Louis Lopez

Louis 'Loco' Lopez: leader of the Los Locos

Los Locos: gang consisting of Louis Lopez, Santo and Luca Martine

Andrés Santiago: driver for Los Locos

Ruiz Ortega: friend of Andrés Santiago

Jodie Moreno and Mickey Fisher: Owners of Fisher's General Store

Matthew Reasoner: Farmer and owner of Reasoner's Orchard and Winery in LeRoy, New York

Herman 'Slugger' German: B & W Boat Club guard, former pro boxer

Sammy 'Stubby' Smith: Slugger's sidekick

Detective Jenny Thompson: Erie Police Department

Francesca Molyneaux: French Café owner in Bemus Point

Angelo Murano: NJ scrap metal dealer

Jaqueline Beaulieu: Investigator, New Hampshire State Police

Jaime Charbonneau - Enfield town drunk

Ted Downing - Booze delivery driver

Eleanor: German-American Café owner, Sunapee, NH

Thomas Wolfe - Erie County Coroner

Bradley Fellowes - Agent In charge, FBI

Sanford Daltry - owner of Lake Mascoma Boat Rentalz

Rupert Bisbee - Farmer murdered in Ascutney, Vermont

Jessica Perkins - Surveyor, Jamestown, NY

John Higgins - Excavation contractor, Westfield, NY

Mario Dupont - Mac's drywall contractor

Flavius Miller - Mac Morrison's Insurance agent

Norman Pelletier - Mac's roofer, his foreman René

Rocco Infantini- Mac's insulation contractor

Remy Montague - Mac's electrician

Simon Long - sleazy lawyer for Mace Wilkins

Jim Murphy (deceased): Marybeth Murphy's former husband

Linda and Belinda Shavely - identical twin teens, Marybeth's next door neighbors

Sandy Gregor - wife of Andy, and best friends with Marybeth Murphy

Ronald Samuels - Funeral Director

Sheriff Lowell Buckman - Chautauqua County Sheriff

Abe Solomon (deceased) -WWII Bomber pilot, Mac's uncle and mentor

Madelaine Solomon (deceased) Abe's wife

Shaun Morrison and his wife Claudia - (deceased) Mac Morrison's parents

Doc - Sunapee, NH Fireman #1

John - Sunapee, NH Fireman #2

Jordan Solomon - Abe and Madelaine Solomon's son

Author Profile

Philip Laurien

Phil was born in Buffalo, New York, and spent his childhood there.

Although schooled as a community planner, he has also been a lifeguard, lumberjack, tour guide, town manager, acting police chief, car restorer, developer, builder, real estate consultant, land use lecturer and Innkeeper. The interesting people he has known in twelve countries and half the United States now inform the characters in his stories.

In 2007, while passing through Barcelona Harbor, New York he was reminded of his summers at a nearby riding camp on the shores of Chautauqua Lake, and the seed for a murder mystery was planted.

Return to Barcelona Harbor is the second in the Mac Morrison Mystery series. It is the sequel to Barcelona Harbor Murders. The RTBH story picks up where BHM left off, with Mac and Buddy-dog and the delightful widow Marybeth Murphy in Barcelona Harbor, on Lake Erie.

He currently resides in Ohio with his three-legged rescue dog, Sadie-Rose.

Phil and Sadie, Ripley, NY, (Lake Erie)
Photo by Whitney Laurien, May 4, 2024,

Made in the USA
Columbia, SC
18 May 2025